Fall of the Sands

BOOK THREE

R. M. MULLER

WILLOW HOUSE Publishing

For more information, or to book an event, contact:

authorrosemariemuller@gmail.com

www.authorrosemariemuller.com

Book design by R M Muller

Cover design by Christian Bentulan

ISBN - eBook: 978-0-6455759-4-1

ISBN - Paperback: 978-0-6455759-5-8

First Edition: March 2024

For anyone who has ever needed a second chance ...
And to the wonderful souls who granted them.

TRADING
POST
GUA
OU
ETONIA
PRISON
HUT
CATORI'S
PARENT'S
VILLAGE
FOREST

3: HEALERS SHELTER
4: HARM'S HOUSE
5: ARLO'S HOUSE
6: MASON'S HOUSE
7: HANGING POLE
NUNDEEN
DESERT
DONTERRA
SLENBIR
NDI
GUARDIAN OUTPOST
FARNO
GUARDIAN OUTPOST
TABARA
MAREYA
INDORI
NG AND ERFALL
LA'S AGE
W

THROUGH DARKNESS AND LIGHT, MY HEART IS
STILL YOURS.
OUR WORLD, LINED WITH CRUELTY, I WILL
CHANGE FOR YOU.

Fall
of the
Sands

CHAPTER 1
HARM

Timber explodes to splinters on impact against the stone hearth seconds after the chair leaves my hands. All around me, screams. My voice, my pain. I can't stop it. The fire that rips through my veins erodes a hole in my chest with every breath.

She's gone.

She left.

With Mason.

Staggering around our small home, I land hard against the dresser, spin around, and rip the blankets from the bed.

Our bed.

Guttural sobs replace the roaring coming from my chest. Every breath is fire, and my body tenses with every move. I stumble to the hearth and toss the blankets into the fire, smoke billowing around the folds of cloth and fur. My trembling hands press against the stone mantel, and the heat burns my palms. The sensations barely register; my hands feel numb.

"Harm." Callian pulls at my arm.

I can't move. He lingers for a moment, then disappears behind me. Catori is speaking, so softly, then she's gone. I replay Imani's face, the look on it as Callian dragged me from the tower. Her somber eyes that only just caught mine as I was hauled away by Callian and Catori. A last longing look at me before she betrayed me entirely. Mason stood next to her, an arm around her waist, that disgusting smug look on his face.

Another memory, another bolt of lightning right through my chest. I step to my left, where the dining table with the remaining chair and the entry table stand untouched. I snatch up the chair—Imani's chair—and hurtle it at the stone above the hearth. The roaring starts up again. Spinning around, I see Callian hovering in the doorway. Pain wrecks his face, his arms hang by his side, and his chest heaves, mouth moving. I can't hear him. Stinging starts in my hands; they are raw and blistered. The tremble in my hands turns to shaking.

Callian moves, and Hanola appears behind him. I turn back to the back wall of our home. Balling my hands into fists, I slam them into the wall over and over.

Imani.

No... *Imani!*

Mason's face flickers through my mind once more, and heat rises from my core to my neck. I turn with a growl and rip the small table from the floor, my hands burning against the wooden surface, and I hurl it against the stone. The splintering timber is silenced by the force of my own wails.

"Harmen." A small voice penetrates the thundering in my veins and the screaming that rattles my head, claiming the quieter space in between beats. I turn slightly to face the door.

Hanola steps into our home.

"Grandmother..." Callian warns.

She pays him no attention. Her eyes, fixed on mine, do not waver. "Callian," she says firmly, waving him off. His gaze flicks between me and his frail grandmother, then he sighs as he walks out the door, devastation clear on his face. I stand before Hanola, arms dangling, chest heaving, shaking like a brittle desert leaf after a sandstorm. The aching in my chest is the only feeling I have left as she looks me over before her gaze tracks the destruction in the room.

"Harm," she whispers, holding out a thin hand.

I sink to my knees, and my head drops to my chest. "She's gone," I choke out between sobs, gasping for breath.

I can't breathe.

Hanola's small feet and walking stick land in my blurry vision, and she settles herself on the floor in front of me. Taking my shaking hands in hers, she starts a rhythmic melody, rocking back and forth. I splutter through ragged breaths and sobs. The pain in my chest radiates through every inch of my body. *Imani.* My Imani... gone. I begin rocking as Hanola does, closing my eyes.

Two soft hands rest on my face, cool against my hot, wet cheeks. Her melody stops. "Harmen, look at me," she whispers.

I breathe through more sobs, reining them in, my chest burning like a desert bonfire.

"Harmen, open your eyes." Her thumbs wipe away the constant stream of tears. I suck in a deep breath, waiting a handful of heartbeats, then look at her. Kindness and concern stare back at me. Her chin trembles, but she forces a smile.

"I can't breathe, Hanola."

She pulls one hand from my cheek and places it over my heart. The gentle touch swells my chest again, and I suck in another breath to keep from losing myself even more.

"Imani didn't leave you, Harm. I sent her," she whispers.

My heart races underneath her palm. I stare deep into her eyes, searching for her meaning. Hands crawl through my hair, and I grasp them to stop the movement.

"You what?"

"I sent Imani, and Mason, to the tower." Her words are firmer now.

"You sent all of us there, Hanola—only Imani and Mason didn't come back. Mason had planned this all along, to spy on the rebels and take Imani with him."

Her face remains unchanged. "Mason is indeed a spy, but not for Fletcher—for *me*." She waits for a reaction, but I remain still. "And so is Imani."

Hanola sent her there to spy on Fletcher and Arthur? Heat rises in my face, and my hands release the scruff of hair, balling into fists at my side. "You sent her in as a *spy*?!"

She nods.

"If they find out she's a spy, they'll kill her, Hanola!"

"They will kill Mason too, if they are caught." Her hands return to her lap. "I could not tell you before the tower mission. It was too dangerous, and you might have tried to talk her out of it."

"Of course I would! This is insanity!"

She remains calm, her eyes serious now. "Harm, we need the information in that tower, and Mason and Imani have connections to the Guardians that we can use. Imani can do this. She has survival skills that none of you have."

"You mean like being a thief," I hiss.

"That is one of her talents, among others," she confirms. "You have to know that she did not want to go. It took a lot to convince her that this was the only way. She said she would not leave you, and it took a great toll on her, doing this. In the weeks leading up to the tower expedition, she struggled."

My mind files through the moments when Imani seemed too

quiet, or upset for reasons I didn't understand. I had seen it, not knowing what it was. "What about Mason? Are they just going to let him walk back in there?"

"As far as Fletcher knows, Mason has been here working to gather intel for the Guardians against us. It was a seamless transition for him. They have been expecting him."

"And Imani, how does she get in without suspicion? What's her role?"

Hanola's gaze hits the floor for the first time, and I scan her face, counting each passing breath.

Finally, her gaze lifts to mine. "She went in as Mason's Blended. His wife."

My stomach churns, and the breath leaves my lungs. Hanola watches me closely. Heat rises through my veins, and I stagger to my feet, hands sunk into my hair again.

"Mason made a deal with Fletcher months back," Hanola says, "around the time you were captured. If he brought you in, Fletcher would grant him permission to be Blended with Imani."

I spin and stare at her. The moment Mason met Imani in the desert comes flooding back to me. His predatory grin at her. His repeated visits to our campsite, while never turning us in. Hanola's small and frail body, sitting on the floor of our home, tempers my anger, but only just.

"No, Imani is not a possession to be bartered away!" I growl.

"It was just a pretense to get them both into that tower. As far as Fletcher is concerned, both sides of the bargain he struck with Mason have been carried out."

"Why? Surely, we could have just found this information *after* we took the tower by force?"

"Maybe, but we cannot change the dial without the information I have sent Imani to retrieve. We now know you cannot change the dial without it."

She's right; I couldn't even read it. Nothing happened at all when I touched it. I look around our broken home, which now reflects the mangled pieces of my heart.

"Harm, please know that if I'd had another way of getting that information, I would have used it. As it was, them staying was the backup plan if they couldn't get in and out in the same time as the rest of you."

"By the time we made it back down the stairs, they were on the bridge, in front of Fletcher. They must have been caught."

"It seems that way, from everything Catori has told me." She sighs, as if the past day has taken its toll on her as much as it has me. "If it helps, Mason swore to make sure Imani comes back to you."

I pace the floor in front of Hanola. "It doesn't," I snap.

"You cannot tell anyone of what is happening in that tower, or what Imani and Mason are there to do. If others get word of it, it will get back to the tower. The village people work in the tower. Mason's and Imani's lives depend on their true positions being kept secret. You must not breathe a word of it to anyone—not even Callian or Catori. Truly, Harm, Imani's life depends on it."

I halt. "What am I supposed to tell the others, then?"

"Nothing. Try not to get involved in those conversations. It will be hard to listen to the things people say about them. For now, as far as everyone else knows, you are devastated—and rightly so."

"I am, Hanola. I'm devastated! Imani isn't here, and now she's in danger—danger *you* put her in!"

"I understand your pain, Harm. I truly do. But you will get through this—you both will. You two are one of the strongest unions I have witnessed in all my lifetime. This is just another mountain you will conquer, together." She presses up from her sitting position to stand. Her balance wavers against her stick momentarily, but I make no move to assist her. She gives me one last long look, then leaves our home, closing the door behind her.

The click of the latch rips through the silence enveloping me. Everything is shrouded by the smoke from our burned blankets. All around me are the splintered pieces of our home, littering the floor in an array of brokenness.

I pad over to our bed, sitting on the edge and shoving my head in my hands. One final scream of anger, hurt, and helplessness rips out of me. I lie on the bare bunk, staring at nothing, until darkness finds me.

Across the table, Catori moves the food on her plate back and forth. Her once-elegant face is scrunched up with hurt. I set my plate down on the opposite side of the table, and she glances up at the noise. Her stare is laced with fire, but she says nothing to me before rising. She snatches up her own plate, tosses it on the kitchen workers' bench, and stalks toward the training fields. I realize right then that I'm not the only one who feels betrayed. Catori and Mason were close—and from the look on her face, she cares more for him than she lets on. I return to my plate, eating small mouthfuls of my breakfast. My stomach is still in knots, but I can't train or work on an empty stomach, so I persist.

Around me, eyes and whispers hone in. I hear Imani's name, and Mason's—the cruel whispers of a betrayed people. I fix my focus to my food, loading my fork so I can finish quickly. I chug down a cup of water and return my plate to the kitchen workers' bench, nodding my thanks, but today there is no smile back.

I amble home. The front door gives way under my palm, and I take in the chaotic mess of last night's devastation. Every piece of furniture Imani and I own has been destroyed, save for the dresser and our bunk. No blankets, no chairs. I pad over to the dresser and open the top drawer. Inside, Imani's things are neatly stored, folded and arranged into sections. I lift out one of her head scarves, the soft, flimsy fabric slipping through my calloused hands, catching. I bury my face in the burnt-orange cloth, and her scent floods in. My breath gets caught in my chest. I try to suck in air, but tears come first. For a moment, I stand holding her scarf, wallowing, letting the ache plunder through my chest.

Heavens, I miss her.

And heaven help Mason if anything happens to her.

I fold the scarf neatly and return it to her organized drawer before closing it. Turning around, I navigate my way through the broken wood, picking up the pieces as I go. I toss them in a pile beside the hearth.

A quiet knock on my door draws my attention from the cleanup. Callian stands across the threshold, face sympathetic, hands full of new blankets and two pillows. "Hanola sent these over for you."

"Thanks."

He sets them down on the bed before turning to survey the mess I made. "Harm, I'm sorry. If we had known, we wouldn't have let them go. Catori would have dragged Mason all the way back and flogged him to a pulp for it."

I train my face to stay neutral, looking him in the eyes, wishing I could tell him something. Anything. "There was nothing you could have done."

It's the truth. Hanola sent them. She makes the decisions, not us.

"You need a hand to clean up this wreck?" he offers, and I force a small smile and nod. We work in silence until the table is turned back on its feet, the broken pieces are all neatly piled up, and the floor is swept clean.

"Come on, let's go run off some steam," he quips, slapping me on the back.

I gather my weapons, and we leave the house, tearing into the forest, running hard to the west. By the time we stop in the first clearing, my head is clearer, and some of my anger and pain has ebbed, but the agony of missing Imani finds me again the moment I slow down.

CHAPTER 2
IMANI

The eyes of my father stare back at me in disbelief. Nothing I haven't seen before. But this time I need him to believe me, or everything is lost.

Mason sits beside me, close enough to make my body instantly repel his presence. We have been in the interrogation room all night —first Mason, then me, then both of us together. So far, our story has been watertight. No leaks.

"I believe this is yours," Fletcher says, dropping my Blending pendant into my lap. Satisfied for now, he walks out of the room and closes the door behind him. I stare at it, willing my face to stay frozen.

Early dawn light slips over the windowsill of the stone room in Arthur's tower. Mason has nodded off in his chair as we wait for Fletcher and Arthur to come back. An hour passes. Hunger pains grab at my stomach, and I lay my head back, gazing at the ceiling of the small room. Just a precaution, Fletcher told us. We are free to go to our chambers once the initial talks are done and they have assessed where our loyalties lie.

The door creaks open, and Nirri appears, her brows pulled

down as she takes in the both of us. "Arthur told me you were here. I didn't quite believe it." Her eyes burn into mine.

"Well, believe it, we're here," I snap.

Mason stirs beside me, lifting his tired eyes to meet Nirri's. She frowns at him and walks over to where he sits. "I suppose we have you to thank for this?" she hisses, eyes flicking between Mason and me.

"Think whatever you want. Your opinion of me doesn't matter," he says with a calm voice.

She shakes her head at him before stalking back to the door. "Follow me. You're to stay in the tower for a while." She gestures for us to follow, and we do.

Stretching my tired body, I fall in behind Nirri, and Mason follows a step behind. We wind our way up the tower, past the bridge level, past the old armory, past the Guardian quarters. On the next level, we pass the dining hall and the library before we reach the bedroom chambers. Mason throws me an anxious look as Nirri stops at the third door on the right, large and lined with iron. Her long key scrapes in the lock mechanism, and the door groans open. She holds it open for us, and I step inside. Her scathing look sends a twinge of pain through my chest, and Mason sucks in a breath behind me.

"The room is soundproof, if you want privacy," she mutters, lip curling in disgust before she unceremoniously closes the door.

Mason and I stare at the massive canopy bed dominating the most spacious room I have ever been in. Three high windows are embedded in the outside wall, letting in a flood of sunlight. Long, heavy drapes hang beside each in an exquisite dark-green shimmering fabric, trailing to the floor beneath. A small writing desk sits to the left of the door. And in the right-hand corner, a white bathtub with clawed feet sits surrounded by a sheer white screen, accompanied by a small table piled with rolled-up towels and a bar of soap.

I let out a breath in awe. Mason scans the room before turning back to me. He stands silently, staring at me. There is no malice in his eyes—not like the last time we were in a room together. But he shifts around, brows pulled down.

"What's wrong?" I ask.

"I won't hurt you, Imani, you have my word."

"I know." I walk around the room, taking in the elegant furnishings.

"How do you know?" A hint of amusement lines his voice.

"Because if you lay a hand on me, Rayner, that'll be the last thing you do."

He huffs out a small laugh and rubs his face. I trace the smooth surface of one of the cushions with a finger.

"Harm would kill me, anyway." His voice is strained. "He made me that promise before he let me out of the cells in the forest. So, you're safe, at least from me."

My fingers freeze on the cushion.

Harm.

Heavens above.

I drag my hands down the cushion, letting them fall to my sides. A breeze floats past, ruffling the drapes of the canopy bed. A lump rises in my throat as fire burns through my center, my eyes stinging. I pad over to the windows, shutting them soundly. After the last latch swivels closed, I turn back to the bed. The burning in my eyes turns into a flood of tears. Heaving sobs through ragged breaths, I wrap my arms around my chest.

Harm.

Pure pain was the last thing I saw registering on his face as Callian and Catori hauled him away from that doorframe. What have I done? My breaths come shallow and fast. I choke through my cries and fall to the floor next to the bed. Tangling my hands in the bedcovers, I pull on them, like the aching strings of my heart that threatens to explode. My hands shake, sending a quake through the covers. Heat prickles through my neck and face. Sobs keen from my chest and echo through the bedroom.

"Imani..." Mason whispers, laying a hand on my back.

"Don't you *touch* me!" Heat and fury flood through my entire body.

He backs off, eyes wide, and sits on the bed beside me, watching, like if he takes his eyes off me, I will somehow stop breathing from the agony of what we have done. I run my hand over my hair wrap and remove it, the mass of dark waves cascading onto my shoulders, and all I can think about is Harm's warm hands running through it. How could I do this to him?! Sobbing uncontrollably, I struggle to pull air into my lungs, my hands tingling with oncoming numbness, and stars flood my vision. I slam my eyes shut, laying my hot cheek on the cold stone. Tears slide down my temples, pooling beneath my face on the floor.

Mason settles in beside me, crouching on the floor between me and the window-lined wall. I power through more sobs. His hand touches my shoulder. Instantly, my chest bursts with ragged heartbeats, the prickle of fear working its way through my limbs. A strangled scream rips from my chest. He scrambles to his feet seconds before I lunge up toward him, my hand pinning him to the wall between two windows, his Adam's apple straining under my grip. "Don't you dare *touch* me!"

Wide-eyed, he stares back at me, then his gaze softens. My hand slides off his throat as I sink back to my knees. Keening echoes through our bedchamber, followed by Mason's footsteps, then the door softly closing. Breathing becomes heaving, and stars invade my vision. Hands cramped around my tunic, I lie on the floor, staring at nothing.

What have I done?!

Smothered in blankets, warm and cocooned, I wake in the bed. My hair is unwrapped, shoes off, and I am tucked in like a babe, safe, warm, and cared for. My eyes ache from crying for hours, and I rub them, running my hands over my face. Sunlight pours in through our eastern-facing windows. Morning. I sit up, taking in the room around me. Soft, rhythmic breaths are the only sound. Over by the writing desk, Mason is asleep on the floor, with only a pillow and blanket. He must have carried me to bed last night.

The agony of yesterday floods back in. Harm... The pain ripping through his face the last time I saw him, before Mason and I wound up in the tower. My breath catches, and I lay my hands over my chest, closing my eyes, steadying my breath. I can do this.

We can do this.

We have to.

I peel back the warm blankets and swing my legs over the edge of the bed. My feet make no sound on the cool stone floor, and I stand and pad over to where Mason lies asleep. I stand over him for a heartbeat before bending down. There is a red mark on his throat where I lunged at him and held him to the wall.

"Mason?" I whisper.

His eyes open, and he looks up at me. No hate or anger, just sadness. "Imani," he says cautiously.

I sink to the floor, hugging my knees to my chest. "I'm sorry about last night." I search the floor beside me. "I knew this would be hard, but..." I try to finish, but a lump in my throat stops words from forming.

He sits up and turns toward me. "It's okay." He hesitates. "He will forgive you, Imani. I've known Harm his whole life. He will forgive you; he won't even have a choice. It's just who he is."

I close my eyes and rise to my feet, offering a hand to Mason. He throws back a feigned look of shock.

"Come on, we have work to do. The sooner we can get this done, the sooner we can go home," I say quietly.

He nods, taking my hand, and I pull him to his feet.

"You do want to go home to the forest, don't you?" I ask.

Mason looks back at me, and it's only now that I realize he is wearing his Guardian uniform. For a second, I still.

"Of course I do. It's the only home I have left now." He reaches for his belt and boots. My head wrap, knife belt, and rucksack sit on the end of the bed. I comb out my long hair with my fingers and wrap it up with the blue scarf.

Mason is staring at me, lost in thought.

I slip on my belt. "What?"

He clears his throat. "Nothing, just running through the plan in my head."

"We should probably do that together. What did Hanola have planned for you?"

"The same as for you, I suppose: get the parchments, then get out."

"And they're in that basement room?"

"Yes, everything we need should be in there. Look, Imani, if it comes down to it and things go wrong, take what we came for. I can buy you time." He gestures to his uniform.

"Then what happens to you?"

"Nothing. I'll just say you were using me this entire time and then fled back to the forest." His face is straining to stay neutral, and I stare at him, not believing him at all.

"Fine, but that's the last resort. We stick to the original plan, and we leave together."

He nods with a tight smile.

"For now, I'm hungry. Let's go to breakfast."

"Sure thing, Mrs. Rayner." Mason smirks. I throw him a look that would bring down the devil. He chuckles and laces up his boots. I head to the door, his heavy footsteps following close behind. I hesitate with one hand on the doorknob.

"We can do this, Imani," he whispers.

"I know, I just hate it."

"It's just pretend. Both of our hearts lie elsewhere, but this pretense will keep us alive."

His heart lies elsewhere...? I turn and give him a wide-eyed stare. Catori. I should have known. If I hadn't been so caught up in my own loss, maybe I would have seen his.

"Well, let's stay very alive, then, Mr. Rayner." I swing the door open.

Breakfast in the tower is attended by Arthur, Emmie, Nirri, Fletcher, and his two highest-ranking officers. That would have been Mason, if he hadn't come over the wall looking for me. My breath hitches as Emmie holds out a hand to invite us to sit with her and Nirri. A sideways glance from Nirri tells me all I need to know, and I let Mason sit next to her, taking the seat next to Emmie.

"So, tell me, how is it that you two have come together, traveling both sides of the wall, and now here? That must have been somewhat of an adventure for you," Arthur says.

Judging by the blank look on Emmie's face, this conversation is for her; Arthur knows all too well that we are here as Fletcher's returned spies.

"Long story, actually, but I was on assignment..." Mason nods to Fletcher. "... when I met Imani."

The truth, if not the whole truth. I smile in agreement.

Fletcher stares through me, and for a moment, I'm not sure he buys the Mason-winning-my-heart-over scenario.

"You're both from the desert side, then?" Emmie asks.

"Yes," I say, as a plate loaded with food is placed in front of me.

"Well, it must be a nice change to be here." Emmie smiles, giving Nirri a final look before starting on her food. If she has figured something out, she is not letting on.

Mason and I finish our plates quickly before heading to the meeting room for our first briefing of the day. Two Guardians stand outside Arthur's meeting room, flanking the doorway. We are the first to arrive, so we wander around on the off chance that we might see something useful. Mason ambles over to the war table, not daring to touch any of the papers, but lingers long enough to discern whether there are any items of interest. I scan the bookshelves, running a finger along the spines of the volumes, even though most I can barely read. Then footsteps come fast and sharp, and I move closer to Mason and return my gaze to nowhere in particular.

Fletcher enters the meeting room alone and strides up to Mason and me with a callous expression. He looks us both over before holding out a hand. "Weapons. No weapons are allowed in the meeting room."

As he waits, I undo my belt and hand over the set of fighting knives, leaving the one tucked in my boot where it is. Mason watches as Fletcher places them in the hallway outside, his gaze flicking back to me while Fletcher's back is turned.

"This won't take long. You'll just be getting a new assignment and an update, then you'll be left to make your preparations for another journey," Fletcher says. I open my mouth to ask where to, but he raises his hand, brows lowering. "You are about to find out. Patience."

"Right, I see everyone is ready," Arthur says from the doorway.

"Let's get on with it, then." He walks over to the war table, gesturing for us to follow before sliding out a large map. It depicts the forest side of the wall.

"Now that you have successfully infiltrated both rebel camps, and the desert dwellers are running low on anything useful for tax provisions, I think it's time we set up Guardian outposts in the forest. Since you two have a rough idea of your way around and the people that inhabit the forest side, you will scout out the positions I have marked on this map, and report back in one week, letting me know if the positions are suitable."

My blood freezes in my veins, and I don't dare to look at Mason. Guardians on the forest side of the wall. They have been left untouched for decades. This would prevent any chance of the forest dwellers staging an uprising, especially now.

"What type of aspects are we considering?" Mason asks.

My heartbeat thunders in my head.

"Distance to villages, any potential threats from the existing people or animals, suitable terrain, and resources to build and maintain the outposts," Arthur says.

Mason looks from the maps to the Chancellor. "Not a problem, sir."

I force myself to breathe in and out, hoping the shock is not showing on my face.

"You understand you are a traitor to these people now, so staying inconspicuous is essential. Also, should they capture you, nothing we discuss leaves this room. Otherwise, it will be considered treason. Is that clear?" Arthur finishes and heads to his seat.

"We will be careful, sir, and be back within the week," Mason says.

I stare at him, incredulous. How is he so calm?

"Dismissed." Arthur waves us off.

Fletcher follows us to the door as we gather our weapons from the hallway.

"Rayner," Fletcher calls from behind.

We stop in our tracks and turn back together.

"I will be watching you—both of you. If you fail to report back in seven days after leaving, I will haul you back in for treason, and you will *both* hang," Fletcher snarls and steps past us, looking back over his shoulder. "You leave in three days."

Mason gives me a long, serious look before he turns. I follow him down the hall, and we stalk back to our room with orders that make my stomach churn. But if we don't follow them, it's a death sentence for Mason and me.

CHAPTER 3
MASON

Hours of planning in the library and arguing with Imani have given me a headache that would kill a desert beast. I pinch the bridge of my nose and rub my temples, sagging into the chair in our room, exhausted. Imani storms in after me, slamming the door. How Travesci lives with her moods, I'll never know. She and Catori are like night and day.

"Imani, calm down before you blow a vessel."

"Shut it, Mason! Outposts in the forest? That is absolutely not happening!" She tosses her belt on the bed.

"Of course not. But we have to play our part, and keep our heads."

"I know that. It doesn't mean I have to like it." Deflating almost instantly, she sits on the bed and starts unwrapping her hair.

A knock rattles from the hall, and we both look to the door. I push up from my seat and trudge over to it. Outside, a servant stands holding towels and a cake of soap.

"I have been sent to draw you both a bath," she says politely.

I nod and pull back the door. The woman steps into our room, stopping abruptly as her gaze falls on Imani.

"Oh," she whispers, her shocked gaze flicking between Imani and me.

"Is there a problem?" Imani asks, standing. But the moment her gaze lands on the servant, she stills, her mouth agape.

"No, not at all, my apologies." The woman dips her head and continues to the bath. I shoot Imani a confused look. The tap turns on, and running water drowns out all noise. I pad over to the bed, sitting next to Imani. Her gaze swings between me and the servant woman as she fidgets with the bedding.

I rub my temples, hoping to ease the pounding ache between them. "You can bathe first. I need some air."

Imani just nods and starts undoing her braid. The woman clears her throat, excusing herself and shutting the door.

"What was that all about?" I ask.

"She's the blacksmith's wife from home. I've known her since I first came to the forest, and she knows who I'm Blended to. I guess she was horrified, just like Nirri, that I'm here with you." Her voice is not harsh, only sad.

"For what it's worth, nobody will be giving you those looks once we get back and they learn what we've done to help the rebels." I lift my hand to touch hers but pull it back.

"I hope you're right, but when this is all over, the only person I want to believe me is Harm," she whispers.

My cue to leave. "Enjoy your bath," I say, shutting the door behind me.

I know my way around the tower, taking the first flight of stairs straight to the top. Fading sunlight struggles with its grip on the day. I lie on the stone, my arms under my head, eyes closed. The breeze drifts around my body, tugging at my clothes as the heat of the day ebbs, giving way to the cooler rolling winds. My head lightens, the pain easing with every breath.

"Do you need to be up here?" an elegant voice snarls.

Nirri.

I remain as I am, drawing another lungful. "Yes and no."

A small grunt comes from behind me. "This is *my* space. Find somewhere else to go," Nirri hisses.

I sit up and turn toward her. She is sitting on the stone, legs crossed, reading.

"It bothers you that much that I'm up here?"

"Everything about you bothers me, Mason."

"Okay, then." I study her face. She looks angry, and I can guess why: Harm. "I'll find somewhere else to unwind." I push up to my feet.

She looks up at me, her face twisted into a scowl. "Why don't you unwind in your room, with your betrothed?"

"Maybe I will."

"Pig," she whispers.

My gut sinks. After growing up with insults thrown at me daily, one little word from Nirri shouldn't hurt. But it does. I descend the stairs, and every shocked face and every wounded word tossed my way since Imani and I came here replays like the pages of a book being flipped. People care about Travesci, and a small part of my heart twinges, praying that one day, someone will care that much about me, that friendship will be part of my life again... the way Imani once was.

At the risk of looking suspicious knocking on my own door, I open it without knocking, praying that Imani is out of the bath already. To my surprise, she is clean, dressed in Nirri's clothes, and perched on the windowsill, staring at the fading horizon. She doesn't hear me come in, so I shut the door loudly. She looks at me for a moment before returning her gaze to the sky.

"Mind if I take a bath?" I say, reaching Imani at the window.

She swings her legs off the sill and jumps down to the floor. "Knock yourself out," she says, taking a step to walk past me. Her face is wet with tears, her voice shaky.

I raise a hand to stop her, but not touch her. "Imani…"

"Forget it, Mason, you wouldn't understand." She walks out the door, shutting it softly.

I stand in the empty room for a moment, taking in deep breaths. "… You'd be surprised."

I unbutton the grey shirt and peel it from my torso, tossing it onto the chair next to the bath. Slipping off my boots, I unbuckle my pants and let them fall. After the thick socks leave my weary feet, I slide into the bath. Blessedly, it's still warm, and I let out a groan that would wake the dead as my body unwinds and the pain in my head almost disappears. A fragrant cake of soap sits on the edge of the bath, and I scrub my aching muscles until every part of me is clean. Running a hand through my sandy and now scruffy hair, I wet it down before lathering the soap in my hands and rubbing it over my head and face. Stubble, longer than I usually like it, is abrasive under my fingers. To the left of the bath sits a mirror and blade. With careful sweeps, I remove the stubble until a softer, younger face fills the mirror.

Nirri's words return to my mind as I sit in the warm bath, my reflection staring back at me. Something in my stomach plummets, and I shove the mirror and blade back onto the side, sinking under the water, exhaling the assault from my mind.

The water above me trembles—footsteps. Imani is back. Heat rises to my neck and face, and I shoot up from under the water, sucking in a deep breath. She is leaning against the bedpost, arms crossed over her chest, her face serious.

"Finish up. We've been invited to dinner with Arthur." She stares at me, not moving.

"I need to get out of the bath for that."

She grunts a laugh and lies on the bed, closing her eyes. Her hands rest under her head, and her legs are crossed, like she is contemplating the world. I grab the towel next to the bath and step out. Wrapping the towel around my waist, I walk over to the bed, water dripping to the floor.

Imani's eyes open. "I think they would prefer you to be dressed for this dinner." She closes them again.

"Imani."

She cracks an eye open. "What?"

"I understand more than you know." I turn back to the chair where my uniform hangs, then slip behind the changing screen and pull on my pants and shirt before padding back out. Imani is standing just outside the screen, arms crossed, gaze pinning me down.

"Then you know how much we need to get this done and get home. We go down to that basement room tonight. No more wasting time." She turns on her heel and paces.

I run a hand through my wet hair to settle it and shove my feet into my boots. Sitting on the chair, I lace them up before standing to put on my belt. Imani watches me the whole time.

"What are you thinking?" I ask, wanting to know her plans.

She hesitates. "Just... You remind me of my father. I mean, when I was little, I used to watch him getting ready for work, putting his uniform on, lacing up his boots." Her face is neutral. I guess we all forgot she grew up a Guardian's daughter.

"Sorry for the bad memories."

"They weren't bad. He was different then." She walks out the door and waits for me in the hall.

We reach the dining hall just in time for the first course. I pull out a seat for Imani, having seen Harm do it for her a million times, and I take the seat next to hers. Nirri and Emmie are seated across the long wooden table from us, and Fletcher and Arthur sit at the head and tail of the table. Candles line the center of the enormous feast, the food piled up on platters carefully placed.

"Let's eat," Emmie says politely.

My white porcelain plate fills quickly with random items as Imani piles them on. Since she has already bitten into hers, I pick up some bread and follow her lead. It is divine. Flavor swirls around my mouth with every bite, and my plate is empty in no time. Emmie talks to Imani politely, asking about what we thought of the forest and its people, and Imani answers carefully. Nirri says nothing as her grandmother entertains her guests.

When everyone is finished with their food, Arthur suggests that the men retire to the library for a drink, and Fletcher gestures for me to follow. Imani gives me a smile before I leave.

"So, how long did it take to woo that one?" Arthur says, sinking into a leather chair, gesturing for Fletcher and me to sit opposite in the two remaining chairs.

"Imani?" I glance at Fletcher, acutely aware that I am speaking about his daughter. My father beat me for lesser offenses than less-than-savory talk, and I hesitate for a moment. "The normal amount of time, I suppose." I accept a glass half full of an amber liquid that makes my head spin just from sniffing it.

"So, she wasn't too caught up in Travesci after all, then?" Fletcher asks dryly.

Ah—this is another information-gathering exercise. "Not as much as he thought, I guess." I keep my face slightly amused.

"They certainly looked to be very much together at the gallows," Fletcher says, his voice taunting.

"She was pretty upset about it, but she got over him soon enough." I return my gaze to Arthur.

"Yes, well, women... Fickle little things they are. Probably knew when she was onto a good thing." He gestures with his glass toward my uniform and smiles, downing his drink. Fletcher huffs out a laugh and sips his own. My skin prickles with fear and anger at them insinuating that Imani would use me or Harm. But I force a grin and take one burning gulp of the amber liquid, instantly regretting it. I swallow down a cough and swirl the contents in the glass, as if that will lessen the burn.

Fletcher stares at me from my right. Every part of my body is screaming to get out of here before he backs me into a corner. I am going to have to use my wits and lie my way out of this. Not that it would be the first time.

"Were you aware that your deal with Fletcher was permanent?" Arthur says, watching me from over his glass.

"I assumed all Blended matches were."

Fletcher laughs.

I look at him directly. "Is there something you're not telling me?"

"No, son, there's not. Just be careful. Imani has always done what she wants." He finishes off his glass and stands, excusing himself.

I stand to take my leave as well, but Arthur points to my seat, and I sit. The blood in my veins accelerates with every second that ticks past, and he doesn't speak.

"You are to be promoted, I hear," Arthur says.

"Yes, second-in-command under Fletcher, sir."

Arthur looks to the doorway, then back at me. "Well, it just so happens that Fletcher is not in charge. I am." Half a smile pulls up on his conniving face.

Trying to sound deflated, I say, "So, no promotion, then?"

"Oh, no, you will get a promotion. If you return from your next assignment with everything I've asked for, I will promote you, but to officer of the fourth rank. You would be Fletcher's equal, not his underling."

I hold my breath and stare at the old man, watching for some clue that this is a trick. "But his men are loyal to him, not to me," I say.

"That's true, but remember, I make the rules. So, I will assign you your own legion to command. You have grit, determination, and the ability to get the job done, and then some. I admire that. Most men do the bare minimum, but you do more. I like that in my leaders." He places his glass on the side table, standing. I stand and throw back the liquid, swallowing with a grimace and a slight shake of my head. He laughs and gestures toward the door.

"Enjoy the rest of your night, son. We'll see you at breakfast."

I enter the hall, and he closes the door behind me. I stalk my way back to our bedroom.

Imani is perched on the windowsill again, and I grab a pillow and blanket from the bed, creating a makeshift pallet on the floor, knowing I won't sleep much tonight anyway. My mind whirls over the events of the past few months.

"What did Arthur want?" Imani asks.

"Nothing much," I lie.

She raises an eyebrow before returning her gaze to the stars.

I sit and undo the laces of my boots. "When do you want to go downstairs?"

"Later, when they're all asleep and there are minimal guards." Her gaze is fixed on the sky.

"Fine. Wake me when you're ready." I pull off my belt, lie on the floor, and close my eyes, letting out a breath, considering Arthur's words.

Soft footsteps stop beside my head. I open my eyes to see Imani standing over me. She plonks to the floor and sits with her legs crossed, facing me, hands in her lap. "Do you want the bed this time?"

"No, you take it," I say and close my eyes, but she remains next to me. Finally, I ask, "Tell me what you're looking at in the sky?"

She stares at me for a moment and sighs. "Stars."

"Get some rest," I say. "I'll wake you when its midnight."

Pushing to her feet, she pads over to the bed and lies facing the window. I lie back on my pillow and wait for the hours to pass until midnight.

Just after the moon reaches her apex, I stand over Imani. Her face bears a smile, her breathing steady. Her dreams must be pleasant. Harm is probably there. I reach out and touch her shoulder. "Imani."

She bolts upright, heat warming her cheeks.

I try and fail to hide the amusement on my face. "It's past midnight. Let's go."

She springs from the bed, following me out the door. The soft click of it closing behind us is the only sound. We wind our way down the dim hall, then down the stairs to the ground level. So far, no Guardians. We round the last corner.

I halt instantly, and Imani freezes beside me. Two Guardians lean against the wall up ahead. I turn to Imani, trying to make out her expression in the darkness. Concern warps her face. We turn to leave as one. Footsteps echo toward us from the way we came. Any second now, they will be here.

I grab her shoulders, pushing her against the wall. She gives way under my hands, her soft skin only separated from me by the thin shirt she wears. Wide eyes stare back at me, and I nudge up against her, my cheek touching hers. She sucks in a sharp breath. Her hands hit my chest, balled into fists. My body covers hers, smaller than mine; finer, more elegant, softer. Her scent hits me, and I swallow the lump in my throat, hoping it will ease the ache in my chest as my memory dances around the scent of Catori, her figure under my hands. I close my eyes. The steps halt, mere feet from where we are pressed against the stone wall.

"Don't," Imani whispers, voice trembling as she breathes into my ear.

"Quiet." The word is so soft, I worry that she won't hear me and will start making a ruckus about me touching her or being so close.

A second set of footsteps stops next to the first.

"You two should retire to your room if it's privacy you're looking for," the Guardian says.

I peel myself away from Imani, tracking my gaze from her red, seething face to the deadpan expression of the bored Guardian beside us.

"Sorry, won't happen again," I say, pulling Imani off the wall by the hand. The dim light mostly hides her face. I hold my breath and her hand every step back to the corner. The instant we round the bend, she rips her hand from mine. I follow her as she stalks back to our room. I shove my hands in my pockets, trailing a step behind. My breathing slows slightly by the time I shut our door behind us.

I turn to apologize to Imani—and her hand hits my cheek. Fire lances across the side of my face. Eyes wild, she steps into my space. "Don't you *ever* lay another finger on me." Her chest rises and falls in quick cycles, her chin trembling, and her hands balled into fists at her sides. After a handful of heartbeats, she lets out a whimper and stalks over to the window. Climbing onto the ledge, she wraps her arms around her knees and hangs her head. Sobs follow shortly after, and I stand fixed to the spot, cheek ablaze, watching as she falls apart.

CHAPTER 4
HARM

"Time to get up, Harm." Callian prods me, standing over my bed, a wide grin on his square face. He is dressed in full fighting clothes and armed to the teeth.

I sit up and rub my face. "You going somewhere, Callian?"

"*We* are going to the wall. Hanola needs us to collect a woman and her son. Enid sent them, according to yesterday's messenger."

I swing my legs over the bed and run a hand through my crushed bedhead. "Just give me a minute to look like you." I wave at the multiple weapons strapped to his body. "Then we can grab some breakfast."

Callian smiles and lets himself out. I pad over to the dresser and pour water into our basin, washing my face and sliding my wet fingers through my hair to tame it. I pull my boots on and fasten my belt around my waist. Tightening the buckle, I look up, and Callian is waiting patiently outside. I sheathe my knives and sword. Properly dressed, I walk out the door and fall into step next to him on our way to breakfast.

"Were you up late?" Callian asks, worry plain on his face.

"Just couldn't sleep." Not a lie. Last night was the same as the night before—the same as every night since Imani left—tossing and turning, worrying about her, praying that she is safe and comes back not a day later than necessary.

"Well, maybe a trip into the trees is exactly what you need to take your mind off her," he says, but his eyes burn with the fire of his words.

I swallow my retort. "Maybe." The ache in my chest tightens slightly.

"I'm starved," Callian says, plopping onto the bench next to Catori, grabbing a plate and loading it up. I slide in beside him, taking a plate, but I don't feel that hungry. Callian gives me a look of encouragement, and I put some fruit and bread on my plate.

"You need to eat, Harm. Otherwise, you'll be useless against a bear, if we run into one." He shoves a chunk of bread into his mouth. I grab some cold meat and a spoonful of last night's greens. Alternating between the foods on my plate, I finish before Callian.

"Do you know much about the people you're going to collect?" Catori asks.

"Nope, just that Enid sent them," Callian says between chews, his plate almost clean. Throwing back a mug of water, I stand. The tables are full, with hardly any spare seats. A few villagers divert their gaze as they notice me looking around. At the table beside us, a woman whispers. Catching most of her words, I can make out that she is talking about Imani. Her words are harsh. I turn to meet her stare, hoping she will quit her gossip. She leans away from the other woman and returns to her food, cheeks flushed. Loosing a breath, I release my clenched teeth. Callian comes to stand beside me.

"Bunch of old windbags," he mutters, eyes full of empathy and worry. He slaps me on the back. "Come on, let's get out of here."

I nod and follow. "You would think they'd have better things to talk about," I hiss, a few steps behind Callian.

He chuckles. "They will. All you have to do is wait for the wind to change."

"I have to grab my rucksack. Meet you at Hanola's?"

"Yep, see you in a minute."

I break into a jog, putting distance between myself and the gossipers. Pushing through my front door, I halt. Our home feels empty. My heart feels empty. They are one and the same. I snatch up my rucksack and sleeping mat from the hooks behind the door and close it. Only two houses before Hanola's, I hear three men talking, not bothering to pause their conversation as I walk past.

"I heard she was always with that Guardian, poor fool," one man says, tossing me a pitying look.

"You can't trust anyone from over the wall. I've said this all along," another pipes up.

"Who knows what kind of damage she can do now, knowing all about us and the desert dwellers? And that Guardian warming her bed... They're a good pair. Better that they're not here, if you ask me," the third man says.

I force my breath in and out, curling and uncurling my fists as I keep my pace past the three men. Heat rises through my neck. If I slow down, my fist is going to connect with one of their faces.

Callian stands beside Hanola's door, waiting for me.

"Get me out of here, Callian."

His eyes drift to the three men two houses down. "Right. Let's go."

We run for the trees, Callian behind me, striding hard to keep up.

Shimmering light filters through the canopy above us. Spindles of bright rays dance on the forest floor, adding to the beauty of the space around us that teems with life. Back to a jog, we follow the path to the wall, like we have so many times before. Our steps and rhythm are one as we float through the forest without speaking. Hours later, we arrive at our first clearing. Callian wanders into the forest to gather wood, and I wind between the trees, hunting for berries, sweet bark, and grubs to supplement our food from home. Within half an hour, we have a substantial fire and the makings of a filling supper.

Callian watches me from the other side of the fire. I pretend not to notice, staring into the flickering amber flames.

"Why do you think she did it?" Callian asks.

I blink, holding my breath, buying time to come up with a lie that I can swallow. Callian is still, chewing on his sweet bark, waiting for my answer. I can't think of an explanation—not one he will believe, knowing both of us so well.

"I have no idea, Callian," I breathe, picking up a small stick from the kindling pile and tossing it into the fire. But I know exactly why she did it: to help me. Imani is always selfless when it comes to me—to us all. But I can't tell him the truth, and a knot twists its way through my stomach. I hate lying to him. I don't meet his gaze.

"I mean, it doesn't make sense to me. You two were insepara-ble," he says. "She never so much as looked at another person, even while she was here without you. Something feels off."

"Maybe, but she left, didn't she? So, I guess the Imani we thought we knew is not the one who is in that tower now." Not entirely a lie, since her current situation and her staying alive relies on her playing the role of Mason's newly besotted betrothed. Ugh... Even the thought makes me nauseous. My breath quickens, and my heart skips a beat.

I change the subject. "Hanola didn't tell you anything more about the people we're collecting from over the wall?"

Callian shakes his head, mouth full of food. I pluck my canteen out from my rucksack and throw back a mouthful of water, followed by another. Tossing the last of the kindling into the fire, I roll out my sleeping mat.

"Guess we'll find out more when we get there, then."

A small break in the trees above us is dotted with stars, their flickering light piercing the darkness. The small cluster that makes up the Cassiopeia constellation is just visible on the opening's border. I follow them as they track their way across the night sky. My chest tightens. Is Imani watching them now too? I hope so. That way, we are still connected, the silver thread that holds us together still tugging both ways, keeping our two hearts as one, a perfect reflection of the heart-shaped nebula tucked away amongst the constellation, hidden for now to keep her safe.

I lie on my sleeping mat, breathing through the ache in my chest. The small group of stars finally edges past the gap, disappearing. A tear runs from the corner of my eye. I miss her. Her fire. Her elegant face. Her soft touch. That feeling of happiness when she is beside me. The bond we have that holds us up—just like my parents had.

Moments later, Callian is snoring. I roll onto my side and close my eyes, sucking in a long breath.

Flittering life in the canopy above drifts into my consciousness. I pry one eye open. Callian is snuffing out the fire with moss and a dribble of his canteen. I sit up, running my hands through my hair.

"Morning," he offers.

"Ready to run?" I ask.

"Harm, about last night... I'm sorry if I upset you. We don't have to talk about it if you don't want to."

I force a smile. "Thanks, I'd rather not."

At least now I won't have to lie to him. We gather up our ruck-sacks, tying the sleeping mats to the top of them. I shove my arms through mine, and Callian follows my lead.

"We should reach the wall by lunch, if we don't slouch," he says, then flies out of the clearing, looking back with a grin plas-tered over his face.

A challenge.

Accepted.

I take off after him.

Five hours and two breaks later, we reach the last clearing before the wall. Callian slows to a walk, and I steady beside him. I drop onto a fallen tree just short of the edge of the forest. "We're early, I think."

Callian walks in circles in the clearing in front of me, muttering to himself. "This is where we met Imani."

"I thought we weren't talking about it."

"Sorry, I know. It's just that it tears me up seeing you like this. What she did to you, to all of us..." Callian stammers, his face is twisted in pain. He is hurting too. Pain laces his eyes, his fists balled up, and still he stalks in circles.

"It hasn't been easy for any of us." I grip my sides, trying to lessen the stitch blooming under my ribs.

He stops and stares at me. "I hate this. For you. For us. For Catori. I thought Imani was our friend," he whispers.

"I know." That's all I can say. I put an arm around Callian. "We should keep moving, make it to the wall before they do."

"Sure."

I drop my arm, and we walk the rest of the few miles in silence. I don't know what to say to him—to any of them. I just want this to be over. I want Imani to be safe. I want her to come home.

The wall looks the same as the last time we were here. The large stone door to the inner passage is still shut tight. I wander through the trees, waiting for the door to slide open.

Minutes pass, then an hour. Finally, the stone groans open. Three people stand on its threshold. I freeze and hold my breath. A beat later, I jog over to the old woman, whose loving eyes are lit up with tears and chuckles.

Enid.

Her arms wrap around me in a tight hold before I have a chance to say anything. She lets a few sobs loose before stepping back, hands on my shoulders, inspecting every inch of me.

"Hello, Grandmother," I whisper, choking on my words.

"Hello, my dear boy." She pulls me into her embrace again, and this time, the sobs pour out of her. We stay huddled together for minutes, until Callian offers a polite exchange with the other woman standing by her child.

I draw back from Enid, gaze turning to the woman, and my throat thickens. I breathe through it. "Petria."

She stands next to Callian, and I alternate my gaze between the two of them cautiously.

"Harmen." She smiles and steps over, hugging me.

"Hey, Harmen!" Miles runs in for a hug, throwing his arms around my waist.

"I wondered how long it would be before I got to see my new son-in-law." Petria smiles.

Callian's face drains of color, his gaze fixed on my face.

"Jonah is well?" I ask, trying to sound casual as the recognition dawns on Callian's tortured face.

"Yes, fighting fit, my brother, and wishing he was here too. But he has rebel business to attend to."

"Do you get to hunt in the forest, Harmen?" Miles asks, his eyes scanning the trees for any movement.

"You can call me Harm, and yes, sometimes."

Callian has regained his composure, his faced drawn into a neutral expression. I guess it is safe to introduce them.

"Callian, this is Imani's mother, Petria." I try to sound as matter-of-fact as possible.

"Hi," he says to her, glancing back at me.

"Harm, I can't stay. I need to get back. I have a lot to do, and Jonah will be waiting for me," Enid says, grasping my hands. Hers shake slightly as she reaches up to kiss my forehead. "It is so good to see you, my boy. Say hello to your Imani for me and Jonah. I know he misses her deeply." She forces a smile before turning back to the stone door. We wait until the door slides shut behind her.

I ruffle Miles's hair, and he pulls a face.

"We should move," I say. "Standing around here too long only makes you bear food."

"You've seen a real bear?" he asks.

"Yep. Let's hope we don't see any on this trip."

His eyes widen slightly.

"I'll lead," Callian grunts and walks off, leaving us to follow.

"You two follow, and I'll be your rear runner."

Petria frowns. "Goodness, Harm, I don't think Miles and I can run all that way!"

"We can walk. It just takes longer."

She smiles and heads off, following Callian.

Miles walks for a solid hour before his reddened face and breathlessness get the better of him. He stops, and I whistle a call to Callian, who is still stalking his way through the forest. A moment later, he stops and turns to face us. His face is twisted into lines of annoyance, and he fidgets with his fighting knives, swinging them back and forth impatiently.

"We might need a break," I say.

"We're not stopping," he snaps.

I school the rising anger out of my face, staring at him. "Fine. Miles, would you like a piggyback ride?"

Miles jumps on the spot. "Yes, please!"

I kneel on the grass, and he jumps on my back. His bony frame weighs next to nothing. His small hands clasp together around my neck, and I readjust him with one arm. "Let's keep going."

Callian moves out instantly.

"Did I say something wrong?" Petria asks quietly.

"No, it's fine. He's angry at me, that's all."

We walk until the sun has almost sunk below the horizon, to the next clearing. I set Miles down in the open space. Petria wanders around the perimeter, looking at the trees, touching the bark and leaves of small shrubs. They are so foreign to her.

"I'll get the firewood," I say to Callian.

"Nope, I'll do it." He stalks past the tree line. Still angry, then.

"Miles, come with me," I say. "I'll show you how to find food in the forest."

He walks beside me as we break through the dense ferns and shrubs. "Do you always have to find your own food out here?" he asks.

"Sometimes, and sometimes we bring our own, but the fresh stuff is nicer." I bend back a large fern frond to expose a bush covered in red berries. "These are sweet. Take a handful."

He plucks a dozen from the bush. I pull out my shirt and fold it up, showing him how to create a makeshift pocket to carry the food in. He folds his shirt up from the hem and drops his berries in.

"A bit further in, we'll find some bark that you can eat. It's very filling."

We soon reach the right tree, and I pull down a small slab for him, dropping it into his shirt. Pulling off a bigger slab for the rest of us, I throw it over my shoulder and bend down to the log that lies beneath the undergrowth. The wriggling pale grubs scurry as I scoop up a handful and drop them into Miles's shirt. He looks at me with a horrified expression.

"They taste better than they look... slightly."

I chuckle as he looks at the wriggling grubs in his shirt, then back at me. "Okay," he murmurs.

"Come on, that'll do. We have bread, cheese, and dried meat in our rucksacks." I wind my way back through the trees to the clearing. Miles follows, his soft footsteps almost inaudible.

"You can dump them on that big green leaf," I instruct him. "That's our plate to share."

He does as instructed. The fire is roaring, and Callian sits staring into it, ignoring Petria, who digs through her rucksack. I sit on the grass near the fire and pull out the food we brought, adding half to the large leaf in front of us.

"How's my daughter, Harm?" Petria asks innocently.

Callian's heated gaze shoots up to me.

"Fine. Away at the moment," I say, praying that Callian will keep his thoughts to himself.

"She isn't in the village with you?"

"No," I breathe. *Please don't ask anything else.*

"Oh, okay." She goes back to her rucksack. "I'll see her when she comes home, then."

"Yes" is all I can say.

Callian breathes out a grunt, shaking his head, and fetches a handful of food from the leaf. We eat in silence, periodically scanning for bears or other predators that wander the forest at night.

"You can lie back and watch the stars if you like," I offer to Miles after he finishes eating. His sleeping mat is rolled out in between Petria's and mine. He lies back, his hands under his head, and grins at me.

"What?"

"Imani is so lucky to have you and the forest people. Living here must be so great."

My heart skips a beat.

Callian rolls over, putting his back to us.

"Yeah, I guess." I lie down beside him on my mat, hands under my head. I gaze up at the stars, torn between wanting to tell Callian everything and keeping Imani safe. It's no contest. I don't say another word to him.

Sleep finds me eventually.

Another day of piggybacks and walking. Another night of foraging and Callian ignoring me before we make it to the village.

Hanola stands at her door, ushering in Callian, the scowl he has carried on his face firmly in place. He thunders past her into her home.

"Wait just a moment, please, I will need to talk to you both when I am done with my grandson," she says, turning on her walking stick and disappearing through her door.

"This is home," I explain to our new guests. "Meals are had in the village center; we will go past it to get to your home. Water tanks are behind the kitchen, and urns are in your home already. Me and Imani's home is on the western border, last house. The training fields are to the east of the village, and if we aren't home, we're usually there, or here at Hanola's."

Miles looks around with wide eyes, taking in the unfamiliar dress and the unique houses of the forest villages. He turns back to me. "When can I see Imani?"

And then it hits me: the two have never actually met. Imani has never spoken of a little brother. Does she know?

"I'm not sure. Soon, I hope." I turn back to Hanola's as Callian walks out. He doesn't look at me, pacing his way through the village center.

"Come in," Hanola says, waving us in.

I lead the way, and Petria and Miles follow. I pad over to the cushions on the floor and drop onto one. With a polite smile at Hanola, Petria does the same. Miles sits on the cushion for a moment, then fidgets with the tassels on its corners.

"Enid has sent you to us in case your husband's actions became a threat to you and your son?" Hanola asks, confirming what Enid had told her via messenger, I assume.

I look to Petria. Her face is tight, her eyes sad. "Yes, a precaution. Thank you for offering us a place in your village."

Hanola bows her head in thanks.

"What's happening with Fletcher?" I ask, my gaze swinging between Hanola and Petria.

Hanola remains silent. Petria lets out a breath, looking to Miles.

"Mandy, can you take the young lad out to the training area to watch the warriors?" Hanola asks.

Mandy swoops in with a wide smile and holds out a hand to Miles.

"It's okay, I'll meet you there," Petria says, smiling at her son.

He jumps up from his cushion, taking Mandy's hand, and they leave Hanola's home.

"Something has changed in him," Petria says. "He's becoming more desperate. He's not the man I once knew..." She draws a breath. "... and loved."

Hanola lays a hand on Petria's. "Enid's message said she was concerned that he would harm you or your son to draw out Imani or Harm."

"We believe that may happen. Things are bad on our side of the wall. I'm not sure if the people can wait much longer." Her eyes fall to me now.

"You are safe here, and I can help you set up your home," I offer. "I can take care of Miles during the day, when I'm not training, if you need space and time to settle in."

Petria's eyes well with tears. "When is Imani returning from her task? I would love to see her. I'm not sure if she'll be happy I'm here though."

Hanola's eyes find mine. "We are not certain, but soon. However, her current assignment is sensitive, and I have asked Harm—and now I ask you—to not speak of her whereabouts, or the fact that she is expected back." Hanola adjusts her cushion. "If you don't mind, Harm will show you to your home shortly, but I need a quick word before he goes."

Petria schools her wide eyes and stunned face. She thanks Hanola again and leaves to wait outside.

"I haven't breathed a word of it to her," I say before Hanola can ask.

"I know. It will be more difficult for you now that Imani's mother is here. I have asked Callian not to tell the others who she is, or who she is related to. It is easier that way. You can go, Harm." She squeezes my hands, as she always does.

I rise and walk to the door.

"Harm," she says.

I pause.

"You are like a brother to Callian. And this has been hard on him too, but he will come around."

"I hope so." I smile, nod and walk out the door into the mists of a rainstorm.

CHAPTER 5
IMANI

Nirri won't look at me. Leaning against the tower's turreted half wall, head tilted to the blue sky above, she is watching the agile birds that dive and glide over the canopy—the canopy that Harm is under, and my home is sheltered by. I step closer, reaching the center of the tower. Scattered around the outdoor space are Nirri's books and cushions and her small table. Flowers in a white vase, half dead from the unrelenting sunlight in this exposed, elevated spot, mark the little outpost as her own.

"Nirri," I say, stepping closer again.

"I have nothing to say to you, Imani."

"I just want to talk to you. I need your help."

"Something your Guardian can't help you with?" As she turns to face me, anger twists her face, her eyes filled with fire—the same fire that consumes mine at times.

"Yes," I breathe.

"There is nothing you could ask that I would agree to," she snaps. "Not after what you've done to the people who love you most." She steps closer to me. Her hands curl into fists, and she folds her arms across her chest abruptly.

"Please, if not for me, then for Harm. Just hear me out, please."

She shakes her head, storming to the door to descend the stairs. I move swiftly and block her exit. She growls, freezing mere inches from me, her blonde curls bouncing around her shoulders.

"Get out of my way, Imani, before I call for my guard."

"No. Not until you hear what I need to tell you."

She stands motionless now, staring me down. After a handful of heartbeats, she huffs out a sigh. "Okay, so talk. And this had better be good."

"Thank you. I know you're upset about Harm, but things are not what they seem. I need your help, so I can leave for the forest. I only have one night left before we go—"

"If you think I'm going to assist you in your plan of sending Guardians into the forest, against my grandmother's wishes, then you are sorely mistaken." Her words are quiet but fierce.

"Not that plan. Another one," I say, so quietly I am not sure she hears me.

But her eyes widen, and she shifts on one foot. She got it. Good.

"I have to gather some resources before our trip. Perhaps you could help me?"

"First, you tell me how you ended up here with that filthy Guardian, and what's going on. Then, maybe, I'll help you." She walks back over to the cushions by the tower wall.

I hesitate. The feel of Mason pressed against me lingers. I swallow and ignore the knot twisting in my stomach. What if she tells Arthur—or she tells Emmie, and Emmie tells Arthur? Sucking in a breath, I follow her to the cushions, sitting on one next to her. She waits, her eyes still carrying that fire, but now it's lined with hope—at least a sliver of it, anyway.

"Mason and I have not come here on some victorious return to the regime. We are going home to the forest. We only came to retrieve a bunch of old parchments. The sooner we can get to the storage room and find them, the sooner I can go home, to Harm."

Recognition slowly alights in her eyes, and she drops her hands into her lap. "Okay, but I can't get you down there, Imani. The Guardians follow me everywhere but this tower, and even if I could, it's locked."

"Alright, well, how about this: Mason and I can get in, but should things go wrong, can you take the parchments to Hanola?" I know full well that that simple act would make Nirri a traitor if she were caught.

She looks over the short turreted wall opposite us, then back at me. "So, you and Harm... You're okay, then?"

"I hope so." Fighting the wobble in my chin, I let out a long breath. The tightness in my chest I have felt for days constricts a little more, and the splintering ache has my eyes burning with unshed tears.

Nirri watches my face crumple as silver lines my eyes. She grasps my hands. "You'll be fine, and yes, if you fail, I will find a way to get those parchments to Hanola." She looks to the skies, and then back to me. "But if you fail, Imani, you will be tried for treason. You'll be executed."

I nod. That statement alone sends tears cascading down my cheeks. If I am executed, I will never see Harm again. Ragged breaths spill from my chest, and Nirri folds me in her arms.

"That is not going to happen. You will see him again, Imani. I promise you that." Her hands run over my unbound hair.

"Thank you, Nirri," I whisper.

Breaking from our embrace, she nods. She stands, then offers me her hand. I take it and pull up to my feet. Composing myself, I wipe the wetness from my face. "We should train up here." I take in the large round rooftop.

With a wicked grin, Nirri pulls her fighting knives from her hips in one fluid movement. "Yes, we should." Taking a stance mere feet from me, she raises her weapons.

I need a distraction, and to move my body. The whine of my broadsword echoes over the top of the tower, and we begin our dance of steel and wills. A smile spreads over my face.

The room is empty when I return. A written note sits on the bed, in Mason's handwriting.

Imani,
Come straight to the dining hall when you get back.
Please.

                                                        Mason.

I try to make out the letters and shape of the line of text, but nothing familiar springs to mind. I crumple it up and toss it into the corner, then flop onto the bed, boots and all. I close my eyes, flipping through my favorite memories of Harm. A moment passes —his square face, the brown eyes that see me so well, his hair messed up, framing his gorgeous face. I imagine touching his cheek and jaw.

The door slams. My eyes fly open. Mason stands in front of it. I didn't hear it open.

"Where have you been?" he asks.

"With Nirri." I close my eyes again.

"I needed you to come to the meeting room. I left you a note."

I stare at him. The note on the bed. Dammit.

He sinks into the chair and unties his laces.

"I didn't see a note." Hopefully, he won't see it crumpled in the corner.

His hands work at removing his boots, and he looks up at me. His light-blue eyes scan me automatically, looking for an injury. I sit up, hair falling over my shoulders. He notices.

"I'm going to bathe before supper," he says, hinting for me to leave.

I lie back down on the bed. He lets out a grunt before disappearing behind the changing screen. Minutes later, towel around his waist, he moves to the edge of the bath. "How do we summon that maid to fill the tub?"

"No idea. Maybe I can find her for you." I swing my legs over the bed and make for the door.

"Imani, we still have to keep up this pretense, especially at mealtimes, or everything is going to be shot to hell." His mouth is pulled into a tight line, brows lowered.

"Yep, got it." I pull the door open and head for Nirri's rooms.

A young Guardian stands next to Nirri's door. His uniform is white, like that of the Guardians Emmie brought to the supper in the forest. His dark hair, like mine, frames his round face set with green eyes that flash a greeting as I pause before Nirri's room. He offers me a small smile and nods. The door is ajar, and I knock softly before she calls me in.

She is sitting at her desk, writing in a small journal about the same size as Harm's mother's journal. She finishes and shoves the book and pencil into a desk drawer. "Everything alright?" she asks.

"How do we get the maid to fill the bath?"

She lets out a small laugh. "I'll tell Elijah. He can organize that for you."

"It's not for me, it's for Mason."

Nirri raises an eyebrow, but doesn't hesitate. She calls for the Guardian outside her room, telling him what is needed. He nods and is down the hallway heading toward the kitchens a heartbeat later.

"I was just heading to the library," she says. "Would you like to come? There are resources you can use to plan your outpost trip." She tilts her head with a grin.

"Sure." I fall into step with her, knowing she means my return home.

One flight of stairs and one long hallway later, we arrive at large wooden double doors.

"Not many people use this library anymore. It's usually just me, accompanied by Elijah, of course." She drags a finger along the spines of the books.

I step inside, taking in the size of the room. It could take up half of this whole level, easily. Every wall is covered in shelves with hosts of books. Nothing like this exists in the desert; they would never allow such a grand place there. In the center of the expansive space, three long lounges are organized like a border around a low, polished wooden table. Books are scattered on top of it, some open. The breeze through the two large windows plays endlessly with the pages, flipping them back and forth.

Nirri picks up a book from the low table. "I come here often. Being an only child gets lonely and boring. Elijah is the only company I have most days." She opens it to a page marked by a scrap of paper and plops onto the lounge behind her. "Help yourself. The current maps and anthologies of the forest sector are over there." She points to the eastern wall, closest to the open windows.

I smile back, but she has already retreated into her book. The thick carpets adorning the wooden floors scrunch under my footsteps. I follow the shelves around until I reach the eastern window.

Laying a finger on one spine, I try to make out the embossed golden words, failing. I pull out the first book, cracking it open to see what it hides. All words. Nothing I understand. I shove it back in place. Running a finger along a few more spines, I pull out an aging brown leather book and flip it open.

Maps. Excellent.

Grey sketching marks the pages. These maps are of the forest. And they are current; all the villages seem to be marked. Each turn reveals the names and locations and approximate population of every village under Hanola's care.

"Can I take some of these books back to my room?"

"Mm-hmm," she answers, lost in her story.

I start making a pile of every book that looks useful. A few have half-drawn maps. Some look unfamiliar, with more words than images, but I add them to the pile. A little while later, I have a stack of books that I can take back. Mason can use these to plan our trip, at least, so he can present our fake plan to the Chancellor the evening before we make a run for it. I pick up the stack. It's heavy, and I sway a little to get moving. Grunting, I readjust the books to get a better hold.

Nirri looks up from her book. "Elijah can carry those for you. He would have tracked me down by now. Elijah?" she calls.

The dark-haired young man steps into the library, kindness lighting his eyes.

"Give Imani a hand with the books, please." She smiles at him and returns to her book.

"Of course, Miss Nirri," he says, taking the books from my hands. He offers me a smile and nods toward the door. I lead the way back to our room. Resting a hand on the knob, I pray that Mason is done with the bath as I hold the door open for Elijah.

He steps inside and halts beside the chair. "Where would you like these?"

I point to the small desk by the wall, and he walks over, depositing them.

"Thank you."

"No thanks needed," he tells me and leaves with a smile. It is the first time I have felt any kinship with or admiration for a Guardian.

A chuckle from the bed turns me on my heel. Mason lies there, fully dressed for supper, hands under his head. He sits up, lowering his boots to the floor and patting the bed beside him. I stay where I am. He breathes out through his nose, pinching his fingers around the bridge of it. A small parcel sits by his side. Curious, I move closer.

"I know, we have a pretense to keep. I get it, okay?" I huff, making for the dresser by the bath. I pull my hair up into a knot. With one hand, I pull the top drawer open, plucking out the blue scarf Harm gave me. I weave it around my dark, wavy hair and tie it off under the soft bundle at the back. With a quick glance in the mirror, my eyes meet Mason's. He sits staring at me for a moment before rising to his feet.

I turn, and he is merely feet from me. His face is paler than usual, arms hanging at his sides. "You don't like me. I understand that. And frankly, I deserve it. But can I tell you something?"

I nod, holding his gaze, eyes slightly squinting, the mistrust that lingers pulling my mouth tight. "If you must."

He gestures to the bed. Stiffening slightly, I follow him and sit on the spot he patted earlier. He sits beside me, turning toward me. I sit facing the wall, hands in my lap, waiting for the words to come.

"For a long time—most of my childhood—I wanted what Harm had. I envied his family, the loving parents and sister he adored that loved him back just as fiercely. I hated him for that. And I hated myself." He sucks in a breath, hands shaking, and smooths over the bedclothes. "He was a constant reminder of what

I didn't have, a constant reminder there was a better existence—better than the lousy one my parents gave my sister and me, if you remember any of that."

"I remember, Mason." I twist the hem of my tunic between my fingers, recalling the memories of when we first met. I was twelve. He had helped me that first day when I arrived in Amondo, dying of thirst and hunger. The friendship we had had before he betrayed me was a loss I carried for so long. Seeing him again years later, it was like the day it happened all over again. So, I shut Mason out, determined to not let him in ever again. My heart races in my chest with the memory. "So, did you keep me in that cage to spite Harm, or because my father told you to?"

He drops his gaze to his hands before meeting mine. "Neither. I needed you to want to stay in that cage, Imani. It was the only way I could keep you safe. And..." He rubs a hand over his face and sighs. "I knew the thought of betraying Harm's affections would be enough to keep you there."

"Oh." The word is so small compared to the monumental understanding that comes with it. I stare at him, mouth agape, processing. He was *helping* me—just like the first day we met back in Amondo, when I wandered in from the blistering sands. In fact, I can't think of a single time Mason has *ever* actively done wrong by me. Not really. Going against his sister back in Amondo would have seen him flogged at his father's hand. Mason's methods may be a little left of center, but they are always effective. Sure, he has carried out his Guardian orders, but when it has been up to his free will, he has let me be. He let Harm and I go multiple times. Every horrible thought I have ever had about him churns in my gut. His parents made him the way he is. I recognized this even at the age of twelve. It is a wonder that he is this stable and thoughtful after the childhood he had. The memories of his father beating on him in the goat pen on so many occasions sink into my chest.

His way of keeping me in that cage was harsh, but he knew it was the one thing that would hold me there. I know now that he had no intention of ever touching me.

"I said I wanted to help, not that I was a saint." His words replay in my mind, and I realize he meant his methods, not his intentions.

My heart cracks a little. His words pull me from my epiphany.

"I figured there was only one way I could change my circumstances," he says, almost in a whisper. "Become a Guardian. So, finally, I did. And it was better than daily beatings from my father —only just. But the higher I went through the ranks, the worse my assignments became. It only took me twelve months. At some point—I don't know exactly when it was—I stopped caring. Most boys taken at selection give up during the training. It gets bad, so they just check out. But that never broke me. The mind control helped, I guess. It was afterward, when I was second-in-command to Fletcher, that I stopped caring. If it wasn't happening to me, I didn't care. Then Harm came that day, to tell me my family was gone." He grips the bed with white fists, breathing ragged breaths.

I sit staring at him, not moving, the ache in my chest turning to fire.

"Marla, my parents—they were gone. I had nothing left. And the most ridiculous part is that I never considered them to be something I would care about losing. I wanted to get as far away from them as possible. It wasn't long afterward when my half-lived reality just crumbled. I couldn't see a way out—not one where I was free and loved, like Harm is. I hated him again for a while. Then I just wanted it to end. Hanola saw that, and she got me through it. Then Catori was with me every day after. I'm not that person, you see—the one who locked you up. The person who traded freedom from cruel parents for the pain of others—your freedom. Not anymore. Never again, Imani."

His hands tremble, still clutching the bedclothes, his chest heaving. I draw in a breath, eyes burning with tears fixed on his. The stream of tears that runs down his cheeks sends a pang through me.

Mason stares at me, and I stare back. Elijah's kind face passes through my mind. A Guardian, unbroken—one of the lucky ones. I slide closer to Mason, and he looks at me, eyes searching. I let out a long breath and wrap both arms around him. His starched uniform, smooth under my hands on his back, trembles. Suddenly, he is letting out years' worth of hurt, sobs racking his body.

After a few moments, he inhales roughly, and I release him, sitting back on the bed. My gaze stays on his torn face. He wipes away his tears and looks down at the bed. "Sorry."

"It's not your fault," I breathe. All of this hurt and pain, caused by one man—the Chancellor. The next opportunity I get, he is dead. The heat rises in my chest, coursing through my neck up to my face. Every lash of pain he has caused another person will be taken out of his soul, as slowly as I can manage it. My hands in my lap, gripping my pants, are shaking.

"I'll make sure you go home, Mason. We both will. And we'll build the life we deserved from the start. Catori and you, you can build the life you want. When our job with the Chancellor and this regime is done, we go home, and we build a life, for the people we love."

Mason stares at me, his composure slowly returning. "You never give up, Imani. That's one of the things we all love about you," he whispers.

"You have to fight for the people you love, Mason, and never stop. That's what makes the difference." The words tremble their way out.

He lifts a hand from the bed, palm held open. An offering.

I slap my hand in his and squeeze it tight.

A small smile flickers across his face. "Then we fight. For Catori, for Harm, and for the people we love."

I nod. *Now* we are on the same page.

The flicker of something familiar spurs to life in my chest: friendship. The friendship with Mason I thought I'd lost. It almost takes my breath away.

He plucks the small parcel from the bed and lays it in my lap. I meet his gaze, and he smiles. "I thought maybe we could pick up where we left off back in Amondo—if you want to, that is?"

I open the packet. The aroma of cheese makes my mouth water. He brought me cheese, just like he used to when we were fourteen. "Mason, you brought me cheese!"

He grins. "What are friends for?"

He is practically beaming and I can't help but smile back.

CHAPTER 6
HARM

Curls of smoke drift past the one eye I have cracked open. Hanola sits on her cushion, hands holding mine as chants pulse from her lips. We have been here for almost an hour, and my stomach growls, reminding me that I'm missing lunch. Her eyes fly open, as if my wandering thoughts have interrupted hers.

"Harm, it is not going to work if you don't concentrate." She gives my hands a jiggle.

I breathe out, long and slow, and close my eyes again. Her chanting resumes. She told me to think of Imani and nothing else. I slowly pull my way through every happy memory I have of her. The day we met, lying in the sands under the stars with her, curled up together in an abandoned hut, the day she found me near the wall, the first time we kissed, our Blending ceremony, the first night we were Blended... The ache tightens in my chest with that memory of her body wrapped in mine.

A shudder travels through my body. Smoke curls into my senses, and every inhale makes me lighter.

Old books, filled with maps and small sections of text, lie on the floor around me—no, around Imani. Mason is sitting with his knees up on a canopy bed, reading one of the tattered leather-bound books. Their bedroom. Mason leans down and writes a note on a piece of paper.

"What did you find?" Imani asks.

"Just some locations, and a description of an underground water source in the forest," Mason replies. He looks up and smiles at Imani.

I tense, my breathing ragged. Heat rises in my neck, and I tighten my hands around Hanola's. A small yelp. I open my eyes and stare at the kind face looking back at me.

"What did you see, Harm?"

"Both of them."

"Are they alright?"

"They're fine, going through some old books. Mason was taking notes." I pull my hands from Hanola's.

"What did you see that upset you?"

"Just..." I hesitate; maybe I was misreading things. "The way he looked at me—I mean, at Imani. The way he looked at her."

"Friendships are often forged under circumstances like this. I wouldn't worry about where either of their loyalties lie, my boy." She smiles, shifting on her cushion.

"Thank you for letting me see her."

I make to rise, but her hands land on mine again. "I want you to do something for me."

"What do you need?"

"Not for me; an old lady like me doesn't want for much. For Imani. I want you to build her something. When your hands are busy, your mind is clear."

She waves toward the door. I am excused.

I nod and make my way to it, pausing over the threshold. I turn back to Hanola. "I am grateful for everything you have done for me, and for Imani."

She nods and smiles at me.

I walk through the village, the mist of the coming rain hanging around me. What can I make for Imani that would kill another week? Something she can use. The image of the grand bed sitting in the center of their room flashes through my mind, followed by a knot twisting in my gut. Well, that settles it: I will build her a bed. Build *us* a bed.

I weave through the crowd at the tables to find Catori and Callian already stuffing food into their mouths. This time I sit near Catori. She studies my face before swigging from her mug of water.

"Mason is okay."

Her eyes widen, but her face turns to stone.

"Hanola helped me see Imani. He was there too. I just needed to know they're alright."

"I don't care." She slams her mug down and bolts up, stalking off before I can say another word.

"Why do you still care about those traitors, Harm?" Callian says, his eyes burning into mine.

I swallow the lump in my throat. "I just wanted to know she's okay. It doesn't mean I'll ever forgive her, or ever want to see her again." The words burn my tongue. I rub my chest just above my heart, trying to dislodge the constant ache.

"Just forget about them. We have more important things to focus on now. Hanola is sending you and me to the other six villages, to take numbers and tally inventory before the siege."

"When do we leave?"

"First thing tomorrow morning," he says, rising. "Until then, you can try to beat me in the sparring ring." A lopsided grin takes over his face.

"You're on, brother." I shovel food onto my plate.

"See you in ten." He jogs off to the training area.

I eat my food absently, replaying the scene I just saw through Imani. She felt okay, if there is such a thing as feeling someone through a vision. Hanola assured me that everything I saw, felt, and heard was Imani's current reality. There was no hate or distrust of Mason—nothing like what she felt before she left. Only a mutual understanding, and a need to get their task done. I didn't see any text about or images of the dial on the pages she saw. They must be somewhere else.

Moments later, staring at my empty plate, I blow out a breath and gather the dishes. I return them to the kitchen, thanking the women, even if they refuse to accept my gratitude. I wander through the houses toward the training area. Miles is playing outside his new home, on the grass between the front door and the training area.

"Hey buddy, what are you playing?"

"Harm!" he squeals and flies toward me, slamming into me for a hug, his arms wrapping around my waist. I scruff up his hair, and he jumps back. "Just kicking around this ball one of the other kids gave me," he says, kicking it toward me. I kick it back, and we volley it back and forth. He laughs as I slide across the grass to reach his wide kick with my foot, sending it back over his head.

"Harm!" Callian calls from the sparring ring, annoyance lacing his tone.

"I have to start building a special project," I tell Miles. "You want to help me later?"

"Sure!" He grabs his ball and waves, running back inside.

I jog to the sparring ring and pick out a sword from the weapons stand. Callian's focus is still fixed on Petria's house.

"You ready for a beating, my friend?" I say, taking up my stance across from him in the ring.

"Ready when you are, brother." Something less than friendly glimmers behind his eyes.

The clashing ring of his sword on mine echoes through the trees, winding its way through the forest. I shove him off and lunge. Offense is better than defense: Miya's first sparring lesson to me. That feels like years ago now.

We go three rounds before Callian calls it. Neither of us will be besting the other today.

"You okay?" I ask.

"Fine."

He is not fine. Something is bothering him, and he doesn't want to tell me.

"That's a lie, Callian."

He spins to look at me. I stand my ground and shove my shoulders back.

"My parents live in the next village over. I was excited for you to meet them. But with you so preoccupied with Imani and her family..." He waves his hand at me, then toward Petria's house. "I can't stomach this."

"I'm not going to disown them just because Imani left us."

"She didn't just leave *us*, Harm. She left *you*. She betrayed you, in the worst way possible!" he shouts. "And with *him*! With *Mason*, of all people. Every day, I see the pain you carry, because of her. Why aren't you fighting this?"

My fists clench by my sides, and I hold my breath, fighting the urge to tell him everything, to defend Imani. "What good would that do? She isn't here to fight with, or to fight for," I say, more quietly than I meant to, raising my chin.

"Forget it. I'll see you at supper." He throws his weapons on the table and runs into the forest, not stopping. I watch until I lose him in the trees, then pack up the weapons. Callian's scream rips through the canopy, startled birds flinging themselves skyward. I run my hands through my hair and wander toward home. What Callian thinks Imani is doing to me is hurting him. My pain is his. Maybe he thinks I've lost it, not being more upset about this.

Maybe he's right.

Dappled sunlight streams through the sparse gaps in the canopy overhead, illuminating the ground with shadow and glimmers alike. I lead the way to the first clearing to the north, with Callian only a few steps behind me. He hasn't said a word to me since we left. I don't know what to say to him. I've never had a brother before. Arlo was the closest thing I had to a brother, and we were just kids; we never went through anything like this.

A rustle to my left. I stop, raising a fist, the only signal to Callian that we are stopping. His footsteps halt. There is movement further in the trees, the smaller shrubs jostled by whatever is trying to conceal itself.

"Wolves," Callian says—his first word to me in hours.

"Keep moving?"

"Yep."

I walk on, but rest both hands on my fighting knives, just in case. Straining to hear any further sound from the wolves, I step quietly.

An hour later, we reach the clearing, and I sink to the ground. Pulling my rucksack around, I rummage through it for some food. I unwrap a bundle and rip a chunk of bread from the cluster of curated pieces the kitchen women supplied.

"I'm sorry about yesterday. I didn't mean to add to your pain, Harm," Callian says, his voice wobbling on my name.

"I know." I look up from my food.

Callian stares at me, his face wrecked by lines of worry. "I hate that she did this to you," he whispers.

I don't answer, letting out a shaky sigh. I chug half of my canteen before tossing everything back in my rucksack. Every part of me burns to tell him, to save him from worry and pain. *My brother, who feels too much.* I throw him a crooked smile and rise to my feet. *Or maybe he feels just the right amount.*

"Lucky I have you, then, Callian, to help me keep my sanity." I dangle a hand in front of him. His hand grips mine, and I pull him to his feet.

He stares at me for a moment. "Women. More trouble than they're worth," he jokes, but the amusement doesn't reach his eyes.

I let him take the lead this time, not knowing my way to the next village to the north. No more rustling from the undergrowth haunts us as we walk. Callian chatters away about weapons and Catori's plans for the villages after the dial is changed. I listen contentedly, happy to have his company again.

The smiling face of Callian's father greets me. His green eyes beam as his large hand slaps my back. His face is the spitting image of his son's, only it carries more years. His mother, who resembles her daughter, except with blue eyes, pulls me into a hug, fierce and warm, like her son.

"Harm, this is my mother." Callian chuckles.

"Anya," she says with a wide smile that matches her son's.

"And my father." Callian nods toward the man who stands beside him.

"Call me Enzo, son." He extends a hand, and I shake it. The second his hand leaves mine, we are being ushered into his family home.

After a warm meal that fills my stomach, we slump into two lounge chairs by the hearth, letting the fire penetrate our tired and damp bodies all the way to the bone. Callian sits with his head back and eyes shut. His parents made the chairs from wood, leather, and a soft filling that threatens to pull me under completely. I study the family room of his parents' home. Wooden toys and trinkets that Callian made as a boy line one of the shelves of their lone bookcase. A mat of hide that suspiciously resembles a black bear covers the center of the room.

"You two boys must be exhausted," Anya says.

Callian's eyes open, and he extends a hand over his shoulder, which his mother grasps between hers. "Sure am," he says. She lets go of his hand, and he swings forward, rising from his chair.

"Callian, you can show Harm to Catori's old room. I'm sure he'll be comfortable there." She smiles and bids us good night. Enzo nods to us, then trails after his wife to the small room opposite the hearth. Callian drops a hand to help me up, and I push myself out of the lounge chair, my weary bones reminding me that they are done for the day with every aching step. I follow Callian to Catori's room. It is small like the others, with only a bunk and a small table. A large window is positioned over the bunk, the shutters swinging slightly in the forest breeze.

"Night," I say and pad over to the bunk. Callian smiles and retreats down the hall.

The smell of bread baking wakes me. Rubbing my eyes, I wait for Amaya's curls in my face, her small fists thumping playfully on my chest. But only the thatched ceiling stares back at me. After a heartbeat, I remember where I am. The bread... I thought I was home with my family. I swallow the lump in my throat and wipe a tear away as I sit up and shove my hands through my hair. The stubble on my face is longer than I usually let it grow. Sliding my boots on, I stand and wander past the family room back to the kitchen.

Callian sits at the table with his father, their faces drawn with concern. I sink onto the bench seat next to Callian.

"Morning," I say to all.

"Morning, Harm. Hungry?" Anya asks, placing a bowl of porridge in front of me and handing me a spoon.

"Thank you." I dig into the warm, sweet porridge, rubbing my prickly jaw between mouthfuls.

"There's a wash basin and a blade in the washroom if you need it," she says, sitting down opposite me with a smile. "It is so nice to finally meet you. Callian has told us so much about you."

"Catori was always off doing things with her friends," Enzo adds. "He used to beg us for a brother, for years. Now, he finally has one." He chuckles, grinning at me. He chugs down his drink and returns to the map that lies between him and his son.

"Father, must you tell Harm all my greatest secrets?" Callian says, smiling widely.

"At least your prayers were answered eventually, son." Enzo grips his shoulder, loosing a brief smile in my direction.

I finish my bowl and take it to the sink. The hot water burns my hands as I wash it and set it on the drying rack.

Back at the table, Callian has his book out, taking down numbers of rebel forest warriors for this village. I slide in beside Enzo, opposite Callian, and study the map. It's like the one Imani had in front of her in the vision.

Callian shuts the book. "Let's go and count some inventory." He rises, and his father follows. I stand, stretching before moving out the front door behind them.

The weapons hut is almost as big as Hanola's home. The double wooden doors are guarded by two armed forest men. They nod, letting us in. Callian pulls a rope in the center of the room, and a sunroof slides back, filling the space with light. The walls are lined with spears and bows. Arrows lie in bundles along the shelves, and in the center of the room, hundreds of fighting knives and daggers glint under the streaming rays of sunlight. It takes two hours to account for every piece in the hut, Callian counting while I scribe.

"We need to keep going. The next village is only a day away. We'll have to make the next clearing before sundown," Callian says.

We wander through the village, so like Hanola's, and back to Callian's home. Within a few moments, we have gathered our rucksacks and weapons, with food parcels tucked into our packs and tight hugs from both of Callian's parents.

"Give Catori our love when you get home," Anya says.

Callian nods, waving as he smiles, walking northeast.

"Want to run?" he asks, a grin still on his face.

"You're on!" I tear off into the forest before he can speak. A chuckle echoes behind me, and we run northeast, not stopping until we break through the tree line into the clearing, the stars only just visible in the twilight sky.

CHAPTER 7
MASON

"We're running out of time."

Imani paces beside the bed. "I know that."

"We go tonight."

She stops and stares at me. "Fine."

But she is anything but fine with it. My gut twists too, but we have little choice.

"I asked Nirri to get the parchments and those maps to Hanola if we fail," she says.

"You did what?"

"She cares about the forest people just as much as we do. She's our ally, our friend." She steps toward me.

"And you trust her to do this?" I shove my hands in my pockets to hide my fists.

"Yes, I trust her."

"You realize if we fail, and she has to do this, that means you and I are dead, and she will be a traitor to her own family."

Shaking her head at me, she takes up her pacing again. "We're both aware of what's at stake here, Mason."

"So, that's like plan C, then?" I chuckle.

Imani flips me a foul gesture and stalks over to the cupboard. Flinging the doors open, she rummages through the spare clothes before snatching a rucksack from its hook, stuffing her belongings into it. Then she walks over to the dresser and scoops out her hair wraps, placing them all in the bag, except the blue one, which she leaves on the bed. Sliding her weapons into place around her body, she turns to face me. "Aren't you going to pack?"

"I don't have anything to take." I sit in the chair to put my boots on. "Besides, if we get caught, it will look too suspicious if we have a rucksack packed and ready to go before it's time."

"You're right." Her hand stills on her packed bag. She doesn't move for a moment, then pulls her hair back and wraps it in the blue scarf, which brings out her blue eyes. She tosses the bag under the bed.

"How on earth did you accumulate possessions in this place?"

"Nirri lent me some things and gave me a few to take home." She rearranges her hair. Turning to face me, she looks my uniform over. "You can't go home in that."

"I don't think I have a choice." I pack the books up on the table. "Unless you think naked would be more suitable?"

She tosses a boot at me, but huffs out a laugh. "The sooner you get back to Catori, the better," she says, pulling on her remaining boot.

"I couldn't agree more." I toss her other boot back. She catches it with one hand and slips it on, shaking her head.

A knock on our door has us both freezing on the spot. I walk over and pull the door open a fraction. Elijah stands there, a smile on his face.

"Elijah, what can I do for you?"

"I've come to collect the books you borrowed from the library. Miss Nirri's request."

I open the door wider to let him in. The heavy stack wobbles, and I prop them up in a neat tower before handing them over to Nirri's Guardian.

"Thank you, Elijah," Imani says, smiling. She genuinely likes him. If only Elijah knew what a win that is for him; Imani despises all Guardians on principle. Elijah nods with a friendly smile back and leaves the room. I close the door behind him.

"Ready for supper?" I ask.

"Uh-huh," she grunts back, kicking the rucksack further under the bed.

"Our last night as a Blended couple, Imani. Let's make it count." I give her a wink. She rolls her eyes at me, punching me hard in the arm as she walks past, heading for the door.

The dinner table is quiet. Even Nirri and Emmie have little to say to Imani. Fletcher isn't here, but Arthur heads his end of the table. He swirls his drink, watching the four of us, his wife included.

"So, Rayner, you're off to the forest tomorrow. Are you ready?" Arthur asks.

"Yes, I will present our plan to you at our meeting tomorrow morning before we head off."

"Excellent. The sooner we can get our forces into that chaotic mess they call a civilization, the better. Not to mention that the desert dwellers have been lacking of late. Due to their numbers dwindling, I assume." A smirk grows over his face.

Imani's hand freezes midway to her mouth. I clear my throat, praying he hasn't noticed her reaction. But his eyes burning into Imani tell me he did.

"Still a little sympathetic to your desert friends, Imani?" he coaxes, menacingly casual.

I rest my hand on her arm between us, where Arthur can't see. She doesn't flinch. Instead, she shoves the spoon into her mouth and swallows. She faces Arthur, taking another spoonful of broth. Her gaze holds his. "The desert people are none of my concern, Chancellor. Not if they impede progress."

"A smart sentiment. I hope you hold to it in the coming days." He throws the remaining contents of his glass down his throat, plonks it onto the wooden table, and looks to Nirri. "My granddaughter will no doubt miss you," he says with a strained smile.

Nirri meets Imani's gaze.

"And I will miss her. She has been great company throughout my stay here. I am very grateful for the time we have spent together this past week," Imani says. She means it. Her eyes crinkle with her smile, her chin wobbling slightly.

"Do you have an answer for me in regards to you being promoted to commander, Rayner?" Arthur says.

Now *my* hand stops midway, clutching my spoon. I place it back into the bowl. Imani has stiffened beside me.

"Yes, I have, sir." I turn slightly to give Arthur my full attention, hoping my body will block Imani, so he doesn't see her reaction.

"And?" he prods.

My heart races in my chest. "I accept."

I know full well that to turn down an offer directly from the Chancellor would at best raise suspicion, or at worst see me thrown in the cells.

"Excellent! Your training will commence when you *both* return from the forest." He drops his silverware onto his plate and rises from the table with a stony look at Emmie. She shifts slightly in her seat, but her face shows no sign of submission. "Well, I've had enough for tonight. I will see you all in the morning."

"I'm done too." Imani stands, jostling the table. "Sorry, Emmie. Night, Nirri." She stalks off into the hallway. I stare at the now empty spot beside me.

"So, a promotion. Commander. That's big, Mason," Nirri says sweetly.

I look over the table at her, and her face is anything but sweet. Her curled lips show her teeth, and the fire lacing her eyes could bring down this entire stone tower.

"Yep," I say, rising. "Night, Emmie, Nirri." I stride after Imani, knowing full well I will never catch her.

The door to our room is open. I walk in, expecting another slap to the face, for not telling Imani, and for agreeing to the promotion, even though I have absolutely no intention of taking it.

It doesn't come. Imani sits in the windowsill again. I close the door. She doesn't look at me, so I pad over to the window.

"You know I have no intention whatsoever of taking that promotion."

Her eyes scan the stars. "I know."

"But you're still angry at me?"

She turns to face me. "No. I realized around five steps down the hallway that you were never going to take it. You just need Arthur to think you will."

"So, we're still friends?" A nervous laugh follows the words.

"We are still friends. But why didn't you tell me about this? How close were you to becoming commander before all this?"

"Infiltrating the rebels was my last assignment before your father was to promote me."

"You're not tempted at all?" Her voice is soft.

"No, I'm not. Things change. *I've* changed. I just hope by coming here, with you..." I hesitate, running a hand behind my neck. "... I haven't shot everything I care about to pieces."

"If you mean Catori, and the others, they'll get over it," Imani says firmly, turning back to the stars outside our window.

I watch her for a moment. "What are you looking at every damn night?"

"I told you. Stars."

"No, not just stars. What is it you stare at?"

She rolls her eyes. "Harm was teaching me about the constellations, okay?"

"Of course he was." Harm is always doing something good for someone.

Imani jumps off the ledge. "You know, you don't have to be jealous of Harm anymore."

I scoff at her.

She grabs my shoulder, stepping closer to me. I look at her hand on my shoulder, then back to her face.

"I guess sometimes, old habits slip through." I hold her gaze.

Her eyes narrow, and one side of her mouth curves up. "I'm sure that Mason, just the way he is, is more than enough for Catori. You have plenty to offer. I see it. At least, I do now. The others will too; just give them time. Remember, we fight for the people we love." She drops her hand back to her side.

I swallow the lump in my throat. "It's almost time."

"I'm ready to go home." She glances around the room one last time.

"So am I." Grabbing my daggers from the desk, I slip them into my boots. Imani readjusts her fighting knives, sheathing her broadsword with a slow whine. I bundle up the information and maps we copied from the books for Hanola and hand them to her. Imani shoves the rolled-up paper down the back of her shirt, tucked in behind her sword.

We have one more stop before we run: the basement. Harm needs those parchments.

"Ready?" she breathes.

"Let's go home." I extend my hand, palm up. She slaps her hand in mine, and we slide through our door and into the dim hallway.

The door to the lower basement storage room is locked, again. No Guardians. Just as before, Imani slides her sword through the arch of the metal lock, and we push down together. The clink of the metal splintering apart echoes down the hall.

Please don't hear us.

We stand motionless for a moment, expecting to see grey uniforms spilling around the corner.

Nothing.

Imani pushes the door open, and we slip inside. I lean against it, closing it with a dull thud. With light, quick steps, we scurry around the room, hunting for information on the dial. I search through every blueprint and scrap of paper on the large table in the center of the room. Imani disappears down one of the many aisles, turning over items and rummaging through boxes, her soft curses telling me she hasn't found anything yet.

I step into the same aisle, checking the row of shelves opposite her. She is flicking through large, tattered leather-bound books. Her fingers turn the pages slowly. Something, maybe? I step up behind her, looking over her shoulder.

It is a narrative, a story. She hasn't noticed me behind her, her face scrunched up in concentration. With an annoyed flip of the page, she traces a finger under the first word, then curses.

She can't read.

As if she heard my thoughts, she spins around to see me standing right behind her.

"You can't read?"

"Harm was teaching me that too." Her cheeks flush, and she throws the book back on the shelf.

"There's nothing here." Stalking through the aisle, she yanks open the drawers of some rusted file cabinets, one after the other, not quietly. She flicks through the contents in a flurry, her back to me. I return to my search through the shelf behind me. Trinkets, old maps we have already seen, more storybooks, metal objects with long covered, corded ropes—everything but what I am looking for.

"Mason," Imani breathes.

I jog over to where she stands. We stand shoulder to shoulder as she holds up a yellowed document. The dial. The symbols. She turns it over. A legend, with the meaning and translations of the symbols.

This is it. This is what Hanola wanted. This is what Harm needs to change the dial.

"Quick, roll it up and put it with the maps. Let's go home."

Her hands shake, and I fold them in mine, giving her an encouraging nod. She sucks in a breath before rolling up the papers. I hunt around in the drawer for anything else related to the dial, but there is nothing.

Imani follows me to the door, tucking the paper in behind her sword, out of sight. I stop, checking for any sounds on the other side of the door. It's quiet. We slip through the door and into the hallway, winding our way up the stairs to ground level.

"I slipped Nirri a note at supper, telling her we're leaving tonight," Imani whispers.

"Good."

"Nirri is a good person. I'll miss her."

"I know." I halt before the next turn. We reach the ground level hallway, turning toward the door to the outside. One more turn, and we are free. "You'll see her again, I'm sure."

We round the corner—and my breath catches. Imani grabs my hand and stiffens beside me.

Three Guardians block the servants' entrance.

And Fletcher.

"Going somewhere, Mr. and Mrs. Rayner?"

CHAPTER 8
IMANI

Releasing a long, slow breath, I draw my fighting knives. Fletcher chuckles, watching Mason retrieve the knives from his boots.

"Step aside," I growl.

My father's gaze narrows under the firelight in the passageway. "Not likely."

I take a step toward him. He only lifts his chin and pushes his shoulders back.

Fine. You want a fight, old man? Let's fight. Every pattern and strategy Miya and Catori taught me files through my mind. One against four. Not great odds, but I am armed with blades; they only carry their canes.

Mason steps up beside me. Two against four—even better.

Please let him have learned enough to actually be useful.

Two of the officers step into our space, canes out, malicious smirks on their faces, eyes vacant. They lunge as one, canes raised. In unison, Mason and I meet their weapons with crossed blades, sidestepping before swiping our blades into their sides. Blood glitters red along my knife. The wounded Guardian hisses and grabs his side, but lunges again. Mason is on the offense, keeping his opponent occupied with a slow dance of metal and cane. The Guardian slashes his cane at my head again, and I deflect with one knife, thrusting the other into his chest. He staggers toward me.

"Enough, move!" Fletcher rumbles, pushing his officer aside.

"No," Mason breathes, his focus wavering from the Guardian in front of him as Fletcher steps into my space. I stand square, blades ready at my sides.

In an instant, both Guardians grab Mason, pinning him to the wall.

Dammit, Mason!

Fletcher turns on his heel, his gaze still on mine as he flogs Mason across the face with his cane. A grunt leaves Mason, and he strains against the hands holding him back.

"Stop it," I hiss.

Fletcher sinks his fist into Mason's gut. Another swing of his cane. *Crack!* Ribs give way under the force of the long wooden weapon. Mason stares Fletcher down, barely grimacing through the pain. The commander drops his cane and slams a fist into Mason's face. Blood gushes from his nose, and his head bobs. He shakes his head, looking up at Fletcher. I stand frozen, unable to move. Breath catches in my throat. This is what he does to his finest officers: beats them within an inch of their life. But as if he has had plenty of practice with this dance before, Mason spits blood onto the stone floor and lifts his chin at Fletcher.

Fletcher swings again. His fist hits Mason's face with a crack, and his head lolls on his shoulders, eyes half-closed.

"Hold him," he grunts to his officers. Then he turns back to me. I remain still, unflinching as he saunters over, his fists still curled. I bend my knees slightly.

Mason's battered face is just visible over the commander's shoulder, and his eyes flicker, then widen as Fletcher picks up his cane and swings toward my left. I block, staying upright, but only just. He's a lot stronger than the Guardian before him. He steps toward me again. I lunge, scraping his chest with a blade before the cane connects with the side of my face. Splintering fire rips through my head, and I falter back half a step. I shove my knives back into their sheaths and rip the sword from my back.

I need range. "You're really going to do this?"

"I knew you weren't really Blended with Rayner. Guardians don't have wives, especially not the high-ranking ones."

"What happened to you, then? Last I checked, you were still Blended to my mother."

"You know damn well what happened." He lunges again. This time, my sword connects with his cane, snapping it in half.

"That's right: you signed up for a second time, even after Mother begged you not to!"

"I did it..." The sharp end of his broken cane thrusts toward my throat. "... for my family. To protect them," he says, as if it's another daughter and another wife he is talking about.

He growls, spearing the broken cane toward my chest. I deflect it with my sword, and it bounces across the stone floor. He charges at me. My swing is too slow, and his arm pushes against my throat as he slams me into the stone wall. One hand at my throat, I try to pry him off.

I can't breathe.

He rips Harm's pendant from my chest, shoving it in his pocket.

No, no! Please, no!

"The only person we need protection from is *you*!"

His eyes glaze over, as if my words have inflicted damage well beyond the capacity of any weapon.

Dammit. He is lost to the mind control now.

I try to stab him, but the sword is too long. I drop it and

fumble for my fighting knife. Stars begin to creep into my vision. Tossing the knife in my hand to reposition it, I slam it into his shoulder up to the hilt. He roars and stumbles backward. I double over, gasping for air.

A boot connects with my stomach, and the wind leaves my lungs again as I slump against the wall. I push up with both hands, and Fletcher steps up to me, looming over me. Holding my side, pressing on the cramps that rip through my breathless torso, I slide my feet under me and push up. Leaning against the wall for leverage, I pause.

His face is twisted with rage. His hands curl and uncurl as the blood from his shoulder soaks its way down his sleeve. He rips out the knife and tosses it down the passageway. I watch it clatter along the stone. He raises a boot and slams it into the leg I have outstretched, holding me up. The crack echoes through the windowless space. Pain courses along my leg, fueling the scream that spills from my lips. I look down, and it is bent backward. My hands tremble against the wall. Nausea charges up my throat with every shaking movement I make to ease myself back down the wall.

Fletcher steps over me again. He bends down and picks up my sword, turning it over in his hands. He raises it over me, centering it over my chest.

"No, Fletcher!" Mason rasps. "Commander, sir! Stop, please, you don't want to do this!"

Fletcher snarls at him, turning only briefly to lay eyes on his half-limp traitorous officer.

"Imani," Mason breathes, catching my gaze. The hands holding him against the wall press down harder as he tries to struggle free. "Get up!"

I push up from the stone floor, but the pain holds me down, ripping the breath from my lungs with each hellish movement.

"Get up, Imani," he begs, "fight back!"

Hot tears course down my cheeks. "I can't."

"Get up, for Harm. Please, just get up!" he growls, pain twisting his face.

"I knew you were still with Travesci, you lying, traitorous bitch!" Fletcher snarls. The sword jolts as he grips it in both hands, ready for impact. I keep my gaze on Mason for a moment before turning it up to Fletcher. My father—the man who adored me as a child. A pang of something I buried a long time ago lances its way through my heart. My mother's face meets me as I close my eyes, readying for the downswing of that long blade in his white grip.

He is really going to kill me.

I send out long breaths with every memory and thought that spirals out. Everything I have done—for Harm, for every helpless soul my father has harmed—I would do all over again. I let out a pained laugh through ragged breaths. Opening my eyes, I look my father in the eye, holding his raging stare. His face turns to stone. Letting out a low moan, I try to stand.

Get up.

Get up!

Fire rips through my leg, and a whimper escapes my mouth. I push against the wall, and my good leg trembles as I slide my back up the stone, until the eyes of my father are level with mine. Vacant —they are utterly vacant.

My heart aches in my chest. "Go on, do it!"

He pulls the sword back, swinging it forward with both hands, feet twisting on the floor. I lean away from the blade's advance.

A shadow appears to the side, hovering between the points of light that have penetrated my vision. I drag my gaze back to Fletcher's face. The long blade plunges toward me.

Crack!

Fletcher topples to the floor beside me.

My sword clatters harmlessly to the stone, the sharp tip only narrowly missing my good leg. The shadow steps in front of me. I strain my eyes to focus.

Nirri.

She is holding the remnants of an old urn. Elijah stands beside her. The Guardians holding Mason sputter protests. Nirri merely raises her hand, her face wrapped in distaste. "Stand down."

They let Mason slump to the floor, but stand guard over him and Fletcher.

With Nirri on one side and Elijah on the other, they haul my half-useless body off the stone wall. "Come on, you have to get out of here."

Agony tears through my leg, bone grating on bone. I suck in deep breaths, gripping Nirri's hand until my knuckles turn white. She doesn't even wince. I adjust my weight onto my good leg.

"Can you make it to the door?" she asks.

"Mason," I choke.

"I can't carry you both, Imani." Sorrow laces her eyes.

"No, I won't leave him here!" I try to stand on my own, but pain grips me again, and bile rises to my mouth.

"If you stay, you *both* die."

I stare at Mason. His half-closed eyes meet mine.

"Go, Imani. Go home," he rasps, blood dribbling from the corner of his mouth.

Nirri tugs me along, Elijah holding me up. Hanging my head back, I struggle to maintain eye contact, sobs escaping with every step taking me further away from him.

I promised him.

"No, I can't leave him here!"

"Go, Imani," Mason growls.

No, it's not fair!

Please, no!

Mason forces a smile and nods at me. I try to put on a smile for him, but breathing through sobs, I can't. He is mouthing "go." One of the Guardians throws a kick to his ribs, and a heavy grunt leaves his lips. I keep my eyes on him until Elijah forces Nirri and me out the door.

"No! Nirri, no, *please!*"

"You, stay here," Nirri says to Elijah.

"No, Miss Nirri, let me help you." His eyes scan her face, but she shakes her head.

"No, Elijah, you will be tried as a traitor if you help me."

He flinches.

"I'll be back in a second. Hold her up," Nirri commands, ducking back inside.

Elijah takes a step back, and I wobble on my feet. Footsteps patter down the passageway. Moments later, she reappears, sheathing her knives. She slides under my arm, supporting my broken leg.

"I disposed of the two lower-ranking officers. No witnesses. Go back inside. Tell Grandmother I ran away, and that I wouldn't let you follow me. She'll understand."

He steps closer to her, and she leans over, hugging him with one arm.

"If you wish, Miss Nirri." Standing taller, he offers her a kind smile. That smile diminishes as his focus moves to me before he walks back inside and shuts the door. The metal bolt slides closed with a clunk.

"Let's get out of here," Nirri whispers.

Mason. Dammit. I promised him.

I promised him we would both go home.

My heart breaks.

The pain in my leg is cascading through my entire body. Every step, every stumble further into the forest is torture. The ringing in my ears is the only sensation that breaks through the blinding pain. Nirri's body, holding mine up under one arm, has not faltered. We make our way through the dense undergrowth. By now, they will have found Fletcher and Mason, along with the two officers whose throats Nirri went back to slit. As far as Fletcher knows, *I* slit their throats and somehow escaped, leaving Mason behind. And as far as they know, Nirri ran away, tired of being locked in the tower. How long it will take them to put two and two together as more than just coincidence, I don't know.

Nirri slows in the first clearing.

"I need to sit for a while," I say.

"I know, so do I." She lowers me to a large log flanking the clearing. Every muscle around my shattered leg tenses with the movement. Releasing my shoulder, she plonks onto the ground next to the log. Her breathing is heavy, and she lays her head back on the bark, breathing through her exhaustion.

"Thank you, Nirri."

She lifts a hand, and I take it, squeezing it firmly before letting out a long breath.

"My life has been utterly boring until you five were a part of it," she says. "I should be thanking *you*, for saving me from a life of boredom and misery." She huffs out a laugh.

I choke out a pained laugh in response. "I guess you're one of us now. Traitorous filth all the way." I hope she is on board with what saving me means for her now, once they figure out what really happened.

She looks up at me, her kind face wrapped in a smile that warms my heart. She turns back to the clearing ahead of us, unclipping her canteen and drawing a long mouthful. "I guess so. But it does feel good to be free, finally. Here." She hands it up to me.

I take a long draw too before handing it back. "Let's keep moving. The sooner we can get back, the sooner you can get rid of me."

Nirri stands, and I lean forward, pressing on the log to rise. *Ahhh... Dammit.* I hold my breath and try again, and this time she slips under my bad side. We keep moving. If we can reach the last clearing before dawn, we will be out of range of the Guardians... until they start infiltrating the forest villages, at least. But that is tomorrow's problem.

An excruciating sixteen hours later, Nirri busies herself with kindling, and I instruct her on starting a small fire to keep us warm and deter any lurking predators that might find us an easy meal. She has a small fire rippling with heat before long and wanders off into the bushes to find the berries I described. I shift my good leg under myself, trying to sit closer to the fire.

The rustling of shrubs brings her back with an armful of bark and berries.

"Wow, how many people are you feeding?" I chuckle.

She dumps the food next to me and plonks to the grassy ground. The night is starting to take a toll on her; she looks tired, eyes heavy, her cheeks streaked with moisture.

"Hey, are you okay?"

"Sure. The events of today are just catching up with me." She forces a smile and grabs a piece of sweet bark.

The pit of my stomach curls up. "Your entire existence changed today... because of me. I'm sorry, Nirri."

She sniffles. "I've wanted this life for so long, but I wasn't expecting to be sorry for what I would lose. *Who* I would lose."

"Your grandmother?"

"... Yeah," she says after a beat, eyes fixed on the fire. "My grandmother will miss me."

"But that's not who you meant, is it?"

She turns to me and shakes her head.

"Elijah?"

She nods.

"He'll be alright," I assure her.

"I hope so, Imani."

"You told him not to come with us though."

She picks at the berries in her hand. "I don't want him to throw his life away because he feels obligated to me. That's not fair."

"Does he feel the same way you do?"

"I don't know. He's never said anything. But he has been my guard for almost three years. I can't imagine my life without him." She shoves her head in her hands and groans.

"We'll figure something out." I wrap an arm around her. Cooler air creeps its way through the trees, and we move closer to the fire. Before the moon has risen to its apex, Nirri is curled up asleep beside me. Heavy with fatigue, I rearrange myself to sleep next to her. The throbbing in my broken leg torments me until sleep drags me under.

A figure hovers above me. I strain my eyes in the dim light under the canopy. Our fire has long since gone out, and the smoldering embers seethe beside me. A low growl cuts through our clearing, followed by another. The shadow above me hovers, the glint of my fighting knives swaying in their hands. I slam my eyes shut, and the smoke curling around us stings. I open my eyes, waiting for them to focus.

Nirri is crouched over my stretched-out limbs, knives in her hands, breathing hard.

Wolves. Six of them. All snarling at the girl crouched over my bloody leg.

"Nirri," I breathe.

She doesn't look back.

One wolf steps closer, dropping his head low, teeth bared. Nirri shifts on her feet, raising the fighting knives higher. I grapple for a weapon—a stick, a rock, anything. I push up with both hands, scanning the ground furiously for something that can help us. Behind me comes another low growl. So close... Shivers whip up my spine, followed by a prickle of fear that sends my gut plummeting.

We are in trouble.

I slide my legs out from under Nirri and turn onto my good knee. Searing pain rips through my broken leg, fire lancing through my lungs with every breath as I wobble my way to my feet. Nirri's sword—no, my sword—is on the other side of the fire. Nirri must have carried it on her back. I look away from the wolf advancing on us to the blade. It's too far away. Even if I were not injured, I would never be able to retrieve it in time to strike first.

Nirri rises to stand, aware that I am standing behind her. I can't hold myself up much longer; my good leg is shaking with the weight of my body, and the pain sends points of light through my vision. I breathe through the nausea as I try to move, but the jagged bone scrapes together, and I fail to hold in my whimper.

The wolf launches toward Nirri.

"Nirri, no!"

She slams her knife into its neck just as its ferocious jagged teeth sink into her arm. Nirri screams and staggers backward. I stumble toward her, but dizziness pulls me to the ground.

"Nirri!"

An agonizing scream comes as another wolf dives onto her.

Two others stalk toward where I lie crumpled on the ground, and two more launch at my friend.

"Nirri! *Nirri!* No!" I try to scramble toward her, but the blinding pain locks up every muscle. "Get off her! *Nirri!*"

She is fighting the wolves. I drag myself closer, picking up one of her knives that scattered on the ground when she fell. I throw it into the side of the second wolf. A horrendous shriek rips from its muzzle, and it staggers sideways, retreating.

Another flies onto her, taking its place.

No, no, stop!

"Nirri!" I scream, long and terrified, utterly helpless.

CHAPTER 9
HARM

The last village is stocked much the same as the others we have visited: more weapons than men and women to hold them. The tallies in my book are good, but not great, against the numbers of the Guardians. Hopefully, Enid and Jonah are having more luck on the desert side. The people are willing, but there are just not that many. The villages here are smaller than Hanola's, and most of the people are either too old or too young to fight.

"Ready to go home?" I ask Callian.

"More than ready. Makeshift bunks and all this traveling is making me homesick and hungry."

"Agreed. Home sounds like a great place right now."

"Let's take a different way home this time. I can show you some more of the forest."

The pit of my stomach sinks a little further, remembering Imani will not be there when I return. Our home will still feel empty, cold. The unease that has been plaguing me since the day we came home from the tower will still gnaw at me relentlessly, the way it does now, the distractions of traveling not nearly enough to make me forget she is not here.

Callian takes off at a run, making way toward the first clearing on our way home. I follow, slipping into our steady rhythm, a comfort I have come to rely on over the last few days.

The day is warm, even for the forest. Humidity hangs around us like a wet blanket that never dries. Sweat pours from my entire body; the smothering air around us doesn't bother to carry a breeze. Hours pass before we reach the clearing, hot, sweaty, and hungry. I slow and walk in circles, trying to cool off. I drop my rucksack and remove my weapons, ridding my sides and back of the sticky, hot surfaces. I have never been to this clearing before, nor have I ever returned from this direction.

Callian rips off his shirt and throws a grin my way, bending down to tug off his boots.

"What are you doing?"

"How about a swim?"

"A swim? Where?"

"Just a few hundred yards from here is a rock pool. One of the perks of being a forest dweller."

I can't swim, but I can still cool down in the water. "You're on!" I rip my shirt off and pull my boots from my aching feet.

He charges through the trees, letting out a call and a whoop. I thunder through the brush behind him. The splash hits before I even see the water. The rock pool is a large oval swimming hole, lined with ferns and dark stone. Ripples near the center span out over Callian's submerged body, shimmering in the clear water. The bottom of the pool is covered in a smattering of rocks and something green. Small silver fish swim around Callian curiously, darting out of his way as he circles around under the silvery surface of the water. Putting his legs under him, he shoots upward, breaking the calm film. He shakes his head, and water sprinkles from his ragged blond hair. With a grin permanently etched on his face, his blue eyes light up. "Come on, Harm!"

I pad into the water. He shoves a hand across the top, and it sprays up at me. Callian stands with the water up to his armpits, slightly bobbing. I dive under and wave my arms back and forth like he did. The clear water teems with life: fish, some small wriggling thing, and the stems of a plant whose round green leaves float like platforms above me, each sporting a white flower that adorns the rock pool like a jewel.

I shove my feet into the mud beneath as I reach Callian and lunge up out of the water. Drawing in a deep breath, I throw myself at him, arms outstretched. I hit his chest and push him under. He grabs my arms and flips me over underwater. I lie sinking for a moment—and for a heartbeat, I imagine the dark hair of Imani billowing in the currents around me.

I choke on the water and jerk upward. Callian's eyes widen, and he moves back, grabbing my shoulders. He rips me out of the water, holding me up. I gasp for breath.

"Harm, I'm sorry, I forgot." He slaps me on the back. I choke out a mouthful of water and put a hand on his shoulder. I suck in a fiery breath, hanging my head.

"I'm sorry, brother, I completely forgot." The pleading in his voice twangs in my chest.

"It's fine, it wasn't you," I rasp and start for the edge. Callian follows. I slump onto the rocks at the lip of the pool.

"What happened?" he asks.

"It was the same sensation as when I was thrown in the well."

"By Fletcher?"

I hesitate, picking up a stick and drawing circles in the mud. "By Mason."

Callian draws back, his head tilted, mouth a thin line and brows lowered. "*Mason* threw you in that well? And you gave him a second chance? Then he locked Imani up, and you *still* gave him a second chance." It's as if he is cataloguing all the ways I should hate Mason.

"Yes," I breathe. What else can I say? I won't lie to Callian—not anymore. Not about that.

"Why?" he asks, picking up a handful of rocks and tossing them into the water one by one. His gaze tracks each growing ripple.

"You don't think people deserve a second chance?"

He pulls his gaze from the water to meet mine. "I guess. But that's a pretty big second chance, Harm."

"Hanola sees something in him that we don't. At least, that's what I'm guessing, since it was her idea that he gets a second chance."

Callian's brows shoot up. "Huh... my grandmother. She's always ruled that way: kindness first, people first. It doesn't surprise me that it was her idea. But with Imani and Mason gone, swapped over to the Guardians' side, it makes me think that maybe she saw something that wasn't there, in both of them." He flings another rock into the water.

I hold my composure, saying nothing. Lying to my brother, *again*. Damn, I hate this. Fiddling with the stick, I have no idea what to say. What I want to do is tell Callian everything, to trust him with Imani's life. I know I could—but Hanola made me swear to reveal this to no one, and she knows her people better than I do.

"I guess we all get it wrong at some point," I say, pushing up from the ground and walking back through the forest. Picking up kindling as I go, I reach the edge of the clearing with an armful of wood for our fire and dump it in the center on the grass.

Callian breaks through the brush ten minutes later, hands full of berries, sweet bark, and fruits. I strike a flint to light the fire I have built, waiting for it to catch, gifting it small puffs of breath to help it along. The flame finally flickers to life as the bark and kindling catch. I sit back, put my boots back on, and stretch my legs out to dry off my pants. With a few hours left until the sun sets, I pull out a small journal and start sketching the bed I will build for Imani. I draw the long lines of the frame, with a new page for each view of the bed's design. The headboard I sketch with the markings of the Cassiopeia constellation. Harmony stars, five of them, arranged in the image of the queen on constellations whose center contains the heart-shaped nebula. It is an ever-burning heart that is hidden behind a facade of stars that others see, the queen. The never-bending strength that fights for her family. Nature imitating life: the queen of stars is in nature, and in life, it's Imani. Both strong, both fighters. Both have my heart and every part of my being.

The scratch of my pencil across the page consumes me. I hurry to capture every detail of the bed that I have been envisioning since Hanola suggested I put my hands to work to spare my mind. I have to admit, it helps. I flip back through the handful of pages, checking that I have included every joint and detail.

"What are you working on?" Callian interrupts my reverie.

"Just thinking about building again."

"Is that a bed? Or parts of one..." He rests a finger on the page closest to him.

I clear my throat as heat flushes my face. No one has ever seen my sketches before. It is a reminder of my life before being laid bare, with all my mistakes for Callian to see.

"Hopefully, it will be, if I don't get some part of it wrong. It's been a while since I built anything."

"I can help you, if you like. I've always wanted to have a trade —other than being the muscle, that is." He shoves a handful of berries into his mouth.

"Sure, if you want. Miles might help too. At least, I offered to teach him what I know."

Callian nods, his gaze tracking to the fire. I slide the journal into the pocket of my pants and gaze at the flames that have him mesmerized.

Screams rip through my slumber. I jolt up off the grass.

Silence. Was it just a night bird?

Another scream. The familiar tone sends lightning through my veins.

Imani!

I throw my shirt on and crash through the forest undergrowth toward the screaming. Another one, louder... I am getting closer.

A second later, thundering footsteps halt beside me.

Callian.

"You heard it too," I rasp through the fiery breath cycling through my lungs.

"They can't be far."

We thunder through the bushes and ferns, hurdling logs and weaving through the trees, every scream propelling us faster.

"Nirri!" she screams.

Imani *and* Nirri? What the hell is happening?!

Callian breaks through the tree line seconds behind me. Eight wolves are on them, three mauling Nirri, who fights underneath them. Imani is sprawled on the ground, struggling to stand. Callian hurtles into the three on Nirri, running a dagger through each one he flings off of her. They hit the ground and do not rise. The rest scatter into the forest.

I drop down beside Imani. Her face is white, her eyes gleaming with pain. She is dazed. Vomit covers the grass beside her. Her left leg is bent at an awkward angle, and her entire body shakes violently. Eyes wide and terrified, she stares at Nirri's limp body under Callian's searching hands.

"Nirri," she chokes.

I pull her into my chest. Callian is running a hand over Nirri. Blood stains the grass around her, coating his hands. His blue eyes meet mine, and he shakes his head. He scoops Nirri up and stands. Her blonde hair falls over his arm, her head lolling with every step Callian takes.

"She has lost too much blood," he says grimly. "I have to get her to Hanola and the healer."

"Go. I'll bring Imani."

Imani... Her eyes vacantly trail after Nirri. Callian breaks into a run, faster than he has run in weeks, holding Nirri close. Sobs choke from Imani as they disappear amidst the trees.

I close my eyes, head on hers, still holding her tight. With deep breaths, I take in her scent, not daring to open them, in case I wake up and this is all just a dream. Her hand grabs mine, and I settle onto my heels. She stares at me, her chest heaving through rough breaths.

"Harm?" She touches my face, and my heart almost shatters into a thousand pieces.

"I'm here," I breathe, resting my hand over hers.

Her eyes flutter, and she whimpers a soft moan, going limp in my arms. I feel her chest for the rise and fall of breath. She has passed out—probably from the pain from her leg. I scoop her up, readjusting her weight in my arms so that her head rests on my shoulder.

I run, plowing through the forest, the journal in my pocket slapping my leg, through the trees, through the endless hours of the night. The burning in my arms and the fire that rips through my chest with every labored breath reminds me that she is real.

She is home.

CHAPTER 10

IMANI

Warmth covers my side, a weight draped across my chest. Pine-scented currents waft around me. I open my eyes and see the thatched roof above me, two more bunks sit either side of me. The weight is an arm hanging over my chest. A hand—*his* hand. A breath catches in my throat, and I exhale through the swell in my chest.

No pain.

My leg is braced and bandaged. A blanket covers most of my body, underneath the arm that rests on me. Breath hits my neck in a shallow, steady rhythm. I turn my head to the left, my face almost touching his. The defined lines of his face take away the last of my ragged breaths.

Harm.

Stubble covers his face, and his hair is a little longer than the last time I saw him. Oh, heavens, the last time I saw him...

I lift my right arm and press my hand against his chest. His warmth fills my palm. I close my eyes, breathing him in, remembering every moment I wished for this while we were apart. Then the heaviness of sleep finds me again. Wrapped in Harm's warmth, I let go.

Voices filter through my half-closed eyes, familiar. People who live in my village. The healer. Callian. I lie still, waiting for Harm's voice, waiting to hear him speak, his low tones. It doesn't come. The bunk under me is cold; he is gone.

I open my eyes and push upright in the bunk. My clothes have been removed; a cotton tunic now covers my upper body. Pants, loose and comfortable, cover my legs, the left ripped up to my hip, exposing the brace and bandages. Heavy breathing cycles in the bunk beside me.

Nirri.

Her chest rises after each fall, her body dressed in cotton garments like mine, but with many more bandages. Her petite features are pale and drawn. Callian is sitting beside her, his hands wrapped around hers.

"Callian," I rasp.

He looks up, glaring at me, eyes narrowed, mouth a thin line. My stomach drops as my breath stalls out.

He hates me.

I suck in a breath, gripping the blankets, and force a smile. He looks away.

A robe hangs over the foot of the bunk. I can't stay here, with him hating me. The look on his face tears at a piece of my heart.

The healer pads over to my bunk, holding a small vial of something white. "You're awake. How is the pain?"

"Gone. I can't feel any pain at the moment."

A smile blooms on her face. "Good. We gave you some pretty

strong herbs for the pain, and to keep you out for a day, to let the leg set." Her eyes drift down the bunk.

"Can I get up? I need to get out of here."

"That's up to you. I can help you up." She picks up the robe, placing it over my shoulders. I shove my arms through and wrap the middle around with the tie. She stands beside me. "Just swing your legs over the bed, using your hands, and then lean forward. I'll help you push up off the bunk."

I swing the good leg over and tug the bad over, gently at first. With no pain, I pull my left leg over the edge and move forward. I brace my arms on the bunk, and she grabs me under my left arm. With my good leg, I push up. It trembles with the weight, but the healer's strong grip holds me steady. I stand taller and wait for my balance to settle. A wash of dizziness hits me, my stomach flipping, and I falter backward slightly.

A steady hand meets my back. "Easy."

"Thank you."

"I'll get you a stick to aid your walking. Then you can move about as much as you can tolerate," she says, cautiously letting me go and walking over to a bench. She reaches under it, feeling for a stick, and pulls out two, assessing their length before choosing the shorter one and returning.

"Here. This will be your faithful companion until your leg is healed, which will take several weeks." She gives me a look of warning.

"Thank you again." I check that my robe is tied up properly. "Do you know where Harm went?"

"I believe he's helping the new lady on the edge of the village, near the training grounds."

New lady? I smile and start my wobbly departure. A mumble comes from behind me, and I stop, gripping the stick to steady myself. Slowly turning back, I see that Nirri's eyes are open. Callian stares at me, stone-faced.

"Imani," she whimpers frantically, trying to sit up.

"She's okay. Here, see?" Callian says, his tender words settling her panic.

Nirri's focus finds me. I limp over to her bunk, stopping a few feet from Callian.

"He... he broke your leg. I heard it snap," she rasps. "And the wolves... There were so many, and you..." Sobs heave from her chest.

Callian grabs her hands, moving closer to her. "You're safe, Nirri. You're in the village," he says.

Her eyes fly open, and she tries to push up off the bed. Callian lays a hand on her shoulder, but she struggles against him.

"No," she says.

He helps her sit up.

"Mason... No," she breathes, gripping her tunic, her eyes flicking between Callian and me.

"It's okay, Nirri," Callian whispers, wrapping an arm around her shoulders.

"No, no, you don't understand. Mason... They'll kill him!" Her body trembles under Callian's arm. He runs a worried gaze over her.

I force myself forward two steps. "How long does he have?" I breathe.

She stares at her blankets, tears streaming down her face.

"Nirri, how long?" I snap.

"Don't, Imani," Callian growls.

"How long, Nirri?!"

Her eyes drag up to mine, her face twisted with fear. "Three days," she whispers.

"Dammit." Spinning as fast as the stick allows, I limp with hurried steps out of the healer's shelter and toward Hanola's.

Every painstakingly slow step feels like an eternity, another moment that we lose. The village people stop their tasks, staring at me openly. Nobody speaks to me. I didn't expect them to. I reach Hanola's door and swing it open. No time for pleasantries.

Hanola sits on her cushion across from Catori. Their eyes are closed. Smoke billows around them. Channeling.

"Hanola."

Her eyes crack open, widening as she runs a gaze over me. Catori's face is stone, her eyes scanning me, but not with the concern and kindness her grandmother holds.

"We're in the middle of something, Imani," Catori says flatly.

I turn to Hanola, and her eyes search mine.

"Mason—they're going to execute him! He has only three days! This was not part of the plan. You have to do something!"

Catori looks between her grandmother and me. "What? What plan?"

"Help me up, Catori," Hanola urges, her face tightened with concern.

"Grandmother, what is going on? What plan?" Catori repeats, helping her to her feet.

Hanola pads over on her stick, much like mine. "You are right: this was not part of the plan. And I promised him he would come home to us," she says, grabbing the hand that holds my stick.

Catori closes her eyes, shaking her head. "*You* sent them? Both?"

"Yes, I sent them to retrieve the parchments and information we need to win this war. They were both supposed to return home."

Catori opens her eyes, her gaze burning into her grandmother's, and shakes her head. "But Mason didn't come home—and now he has three days to live?"

"Those three days would have started from the time he was caught, child. He may already be lost," she whispers.

Catori's eyes widen. "This is not happening," she growls, low and feral.

"Child, there is nothing we can do. If he did not escape with Imani, there is little chance that he will now."

Catori slams the door open on her way out. I hobble after her as fast as I can. She is headed for her home. I push myself to catch up. Rounding the last house before hers, I slam into Callian's chest.

"Sorry." I wobble a sidestep past him.

He stands still, watching me. "How could you do that to Harm?"

"Callian..." I plead.

Taking a step forward, he grabs my arm. "How could you do that to *us*?" He steps closer, the hurt in his eyes raising a lump in my throat.

"Not now, okay? You can hate me later. Right now, I need to get to Catori." I rip my arm from his grip and hobble to her door. Metal clanks; she is strapping on her weapons. Lots of them.

"Catori, what are you going to do?"

"I'm going to get him back. I am responsible for him. He is coming home." She snaps her weapons belt tight.

"Where are you going?" Callian says from behind me.

She meets his stare with a look that could put down her worst enemy. "The tower. To get Mason."

Callian tenses, crossing his arms over his chest and blocking her door. "You are not! Not for that lying, good-for-nothing mongrel!"

"You can either let me go by myself, or you can come with me. I could use the muscle. And I am not arguing about this, Callian."

He stares at her for a heartbeat.

"I'll be one minute." He runs off toward his own home.

"How are you going to get him out of that tower?" I ask. "There are Guardians everywhere. You could very well end up dead yourself." I hobble up to my friend, the huntress and the warrior. Leader.

"I'm not afraid of dying, Imani. And I will not leave one of our people to die because of a poor choice on my grandmother's part." The words mince their way out. It is the first time I have ever heard her speak poorly of Hanola.

Without another word, she walks past me and out the door. Moments later, Callian steps in beside her as she strides her way north, toward the tower. Just before reaching the training area, they break into a run, faster than I have ever seen the siblings go before.

A child's voice echoes from the open front door of the last home near the training area, the place where the healer said Harm had gone to help a new family settle in. A ball flies out the front door toward me. I stop it with my stick, teetering briefly as I return the stick to the ground. A boy around five runs toward me, face lit up, bright blue eyes, a grin from ear to ear, like this is the best game in the world.

"Miles," Harm calls from inside.

"Hello," Miles says, looking up at me, ball now in his hands.

"Hey, you're Miles?"

He wipes his face with a dirty hand. His dark hair is coated in dust of some sort, his clothes worn but not ragged yet. "Yep. Who are you?"

"My name is Imani."

His eyes widen instantly, his mouth gaping open.

Harm steps up behind him. "Hey, you're up." His eyes are lit up with a warm smile.

"Yep. I'm allowed to hobble around the place."

Miles touches my stick, looking at my leg.

"Miles!" a voice calls.

The tone sinks in. I tilt my head slightly, trying to follow the voice.

"Miles, time to clean up for supper," she calls again.

My breath stops, my eyes tracking to the door. Harm watches me.

A new family. I watch the doorframe, holding my breath. Then my mother walks over the threshold, looking for Miles. Her eyes find Harm, then meet mine. She freezes.

Mother.

She drops the rag in her hands to the ground. A hand raises to her mouth, and she closes her eyes briefly. Harm is watching me, and every breath comes heavy and fast. I hobble past him, reaching my mother in a handful of heartbeats.

"Imani," she breathes, resting a hand on my cheek.

My gut twists into a million sharp knots. I don't know what to say to her; I haven't seen her for almost six years. I stand there, staring at her, not speaking.

Her hand drops from my face. "I've been waiting for you," she whispers.

Miles cuddles into her skirt, hugging his ball with one arm. I look down at the little boy who shares most of my features—my mother's and Fletcher's.

"Is this my Mani, Momma?"

She looks down at him, smiling. "Imani, this is Miles, your little brother."

"What?! How?"

"I was pregnant when you left. I hadn't told anyone yet. And by the time he was born, I didn't know where you were, only that Jonah sometimes saw you. I'm sorry I didn't tell you sooner." Her gaze moves to Harm.

He knew.

Somehow, he knew long before I did. Heat rises in my face, and the hand holding my stick turns white. "Why are you here?"

Her face slackens, brows lowering. "Enid sent us. She was afraid of what may happen with the commander." She hesitates on the last word. Her husband. My father. The man who almost killed me only a day ago.

Her arm shifts around Miles. Enid was right to worry. There is nothing left of my father, just a vacant homicidal maniac blind with mind control. No one is safe—not his daughter, not even his wife and son.

Harm has been helping them, helping my mother and brother. Of course he has. Kindness is involuntary for him.

I turn, facing Harm. He holds out a hand. I walk past it.

"Imani..." he pleads.

"Don't, Travesci!" I hobble as fast as I can toward the grassy training area.

CHAPTER II
MASON

Heavy chains rub my already broken skin. The rusted metal stings every inch around my wrists and ankles.

One day left. One day until they haul me out to execution... by hanging.

Death doesn't bother me as much as leaving before getting to see Catori again. Just one touch. To hold her—really hold her. To show her what she means to me, to this damaged heart of mine. To wake up beside her. I imagine every feature of hers—her vibrant green eyes, her swagger, her unrelenting strength, her smile that always tugs up on one side first. Bittersweet thoughts to occupy my mind while I hang here, helpless, whittling away my last hours.

The few Guardians that stand outside my cell don't speak to me. Their faces carry only resentment and hatred. I'm a traitor, a rebel, a dead man.

Metal clinking echoes past my cell, and the door to our containment area opens. Fletcher walks in, flanked by two officers, one of whom has taken my place, judging by the silver epaulets on his shoulders.

They stop at my cell door, taking in every bruise and cut they have inflicted over the last twenty-four hours.

"Come back for another round?" I growl.

"Is that a request?" Fletcher huffs out a laugh. A smirk follows; he is going to enjoy this. And I'm guessing it's going to hurt.

"Open the door," he barks to the new officer with the silver epaulets. Keys jangle, metal creaks, and the door swings open. Fletcher steps up to me, his pace slow, as if he is savoring every second of my torment.

"Do your worst," I breathe, closing my eyes.

Knuckles hit my face, and fire burns through my jaw. I dangle in the chains for a moment before opening my eyes, spitting blood onto the floor. Fletcher's fist slams into my stomach. Air gushes from my chest, and I hang by my wrists, gasping for breath. Another blow under my chin, and my head whips backward, nausea rising in my throat. As I cough through bile, my throat threatens to close up. I lower my head to look him in the eye.

A smirk creeps over his face. "I hope all that rebel filth was worth it, Rayner, since you've given up everything for them." He paces back and forth in front of me, shaking out his reddened hands.

I would do it all again just for one day with Catori—a day of freedom in the forest villages, amongst the happy, kind souls who sheltered me, even knowing who I was, the things I have done.

"One day," I start, spitting bile and blood onto the floor at his feet, "you might find out." I force a hard smile.

He stares at me, stepping into my space. His breath hits my face. I know this move; I have used it to intimidate people I deemed lesser than me. I did it to Harm.

"I doubt that, boy," he says, throwing a fist into the center of my nose. Blood gushes to the floor, adding to the stains from yesterday. The floor is slimy, and my footing slips. I bark from the pain when my wrists catch my entire weight.

Fletcher's boot sinks into my stomach, into my ribs. *Crack!* Fire runs along my side, wrapping around my torso, lighting up my back. Another—*crack!* Screams leave my mouth. But my mind wanders as the blows come, one after another. I find her face, blonde hair whipping around it, towering trees lining the sky above her.

Catori.

Crack!

Darkness.

I wasted an entire night on sleep. The guards from last night stir at the slim wooden desk by the containment door, their shift almost over. Pulling his boots off the desk, one of the guards runs a hand through his sandy hair before stretching. Rubbing his eyes, he yawns and unlocks the door for the next shift. He wanders down the narrow passage separating the cells on either side, not bothering to glance at me as he walks past. No other prisoners are down here. At least that spares me from dealing with their waste and wailing for my remaining hours.

I adjust my feet under me, careful not to slip on the slimy floor. Pushing up with my legs, I straighten to almost my full height. The cracked ribs in my side shift, and pain sparks in my torso. I suck in a breath, pulling my shoulders back. My last hours will be spent with dignity, not cowering like a fool.

The guard passes by on his way back, looking sideways at me standing shackled and staring him down through swollen eyes. Blood is caked on my shirt, streaked down my neck and chest. He turns his gaze back to the floor, quickening his pace, like prey trying not to be noticed by its predator.

Three knocks on the door, and he makes for it. The next shift is here. He opens the door, holding it back. Three officers come in, heavy, short chains in the first officer's hands. Hobble chains.

They have come for me.

I'm out of hours. Now, I can start counting breaths.

I swallow the lump chased up by the pit of fear in my stomach. I will go out proud. A last pitiful look from the night shift guard, and he slips out the door. The three officers mutter over a paper to be signed. Two make their way over to the cell moments later. They reach for my chains without a word, flipping the clasps off like they are made of nothing. One holds me by the arm as the other places manacles around my wrists and ankles, joining them together with the heavy hobble chains. I find a stone in the opposite wall and keep my focus on it, running through all the things I cherish in my mind to keep me from begging for my life. That is what my scattered thoughts are urging me to do.

I will not beg. I will die with dignity, knowing I served a purpose, helping Catori, Harm, and Imani create a better world.

A tug on the chain between my wrists tells me we are moving. The sting from the manacles barely registers. My peripheral vision blurs as we walk down the hall and into the passageway. The door shuts behind us. Past an alcove in the hallway, I see a vision of Catori. Her eyes burn into mine, hands resting on her hips, inches from her blades. She fades, and I shake my head, turning back to the hall in front of me. My heart pounds in my chest, breaths coming all too shallow now.

The shadows in the hallway lighten, and we reach the last door before the outside training yard—the last door I will ever walk through.

"Wait," the Guardian to my left says, searching his pockets. "I left the paper on the desk."

The other Guardian curses. "We can't leave this one with just one guard. We'll all have to go back for it. Fletcher will have us strung up too, if we mess this up," he snarls.

We turn, and the hands gripping my arms shove me forward as we walk back to the cells. A few more breaths to add to my count.

We reach the door, and it's ajar. The Guardians glance past me at each other. One holds me as the other steps inside the containment room. When he reaches the desk, the paper is nowhere to be seen.

"Looking for something?" a soft voice drawls from behind us.

My breath stops.

Catori!

She wasn't just a vision.

Instantly, the Guardian spins me around, his grip tightening, sending shooting pains up my arms. Catori stands mere feet from us, the paper they are looking for impaled on her blade.

"No," I breathe. She shouldn't have come! She will die trying to save my worthless soul.

Twin swords poke over her shoulders. Four daggers are strapped to her chest. Two fighting knives rest on each hip. The dagger in her hand would have been tucked into her boot. Her lithe shape doesn't waver as the second Guardian steps up beside me, grabbing my other arm. The features of her face are drawn tight, eyes lit with fire. Her hand rests on her hip as she looks me up and down. A brief flash of horror crosses her face before she schools it away.

No one else is in the hall. She stands alone, against an entire tower full of Guardians. Fear grows in my core, spiraling through my body limb by limb. My heart flips against my aching ribs.

"You're too late. This traitor hangs," the Guardian on my right spits.

"That's what you think," Catori purrs. She rips the paper from her dagger. Resting the blade between her teeth, she slowly rips the paper in half. We all watch as it floats to the floor in pieces.

"You think one arrogant forest girl is going to be able to stop two Guardians?" the officer gripping my left arm says.

Catori steps closer, fury twisting her face. "One forest girl could beat you useless bullies anytime." Her words are calm, despite the fire in her eyes.

"You don't stand a chance," he spits, shuffling closer to her.

"I wouldn't be so cocky if I were you," a male voice says—and Callian steps out from behind the corner of the hall. The whine of his twin blades bounces through the narrow hallway. Catori rips two blades from her hips, thrusting them into the throats of the officers holding me. Instantly, they both slump backward, releasing my arms to grope at their necks. Catori pulls the blade from the officer to my left and slits his throat in one fluid move. He crumples to the floor, his last wet, raspy gurgle spilling bright red blood over the stone. The eyes of the officer to my right widen as he pulls back in terror. Seconds later, he is lying on the floor, vacant eyes staring at his comrade.

"Why did I bother coming along again?" Callian chuckles.

Catori stands in front of me, eyes searching. She raises a hand, reaching for my face, but drops it before she touches my skin. Ripping a sword from her back, she jams the blade into the links of the chain binding my hands. The rusted metal against the honed blade all but falls apart. I spread my hands apart, and the chains dangle from the manacles on my wrists. She crouches and slides the blade through the links between my ankles. Another clank, and I am no longer bound.

"Let's go home," she says, sliding her sword into its sheath behind her back.

Callian falls in behind us as we make a run for the ground level exit on the forest side. We have seen too much of this tower and its hallways already.

At the last corner before the exit, we skitter to a halt. Five Guardians stand watch, as if they were waiting for a rescue attempt. All hold the standard-issue canes, but to my horror, they all carry twin daggers.

Catori stops. Callian files in beside her.

She gives me one last look before launching herself at all five. Her fighting knives fly at the men stalking around her, slicing and bleeding each one of them. Once they are sufficiently afraid of her, she slowly pulls her twin swords from her back with a metallic whine, raising fear in the Guardians' eyes. One launches at her, both daggers raised. Her swords reach him before he has a chance to even make a scratch, one blade sinking into his stomach, the other slicing through his throat as he drops to his knees. Another attacks from behind, and she rips the blade from the officer's stomach, thrusting it behind herself, impaling him. He drops. She lets go of the hilt and spins around to retrieve her sword, shoving her second blade through his chest. Three remain, terrified. One officer's daggers drop to the floor from his trembling hands, and a dark stain blooms over his pants.

"None of you are leaving here alive," she growls.

The three men exchange looks. Two lunge for her. Catori's long blades cross above her, and when she brings them down, blood spills from both men's throats. Clutching their necks, they sink to the floor.

The last man, not much older than us, is whimpering now. She steps over to him.

"Please, at least make it quick," he begs.

"As you wish." Her hand moves to her hip before slashing across his bobbing, trembling throat. He crashes to the floor. She stands over him for a moment.

"Catori," Callian urges, "we need to leave."

"I know. Can you run?" Her eyes settle on my banged-up frame.

"I'll manage."

Yelling hurtles toward us. We are still nowhere near the door.

"We can't have any witnesses," she says, stalking toward the yelling.

Oh no... Callian's eyes widen. He rips both swords from his back. Catori turns back, her eyes running over me again. Pain tightens her face, her eyes full of anger and hurt. She sucks in a breath, ripping her blades from her back, her face slackening before becoming impassive.

Eight officers spill around the corner. From the ruckus, they know I have escaped and assumed they would catch up. They have.

Catori squats down low, blades dragging on the stone behind her.

"Dammit," Callian breathes.

"What? What's happening?" What is she doing? They will be on top of her in seconds.

Callian's face pales before turning to stone. He shakes his head, knuckles gripping his swords that hang at his sides.

The officers surround Catori—just as she wanted them to. Their faces are adorned with smirks; they think they have her. One lets out a huff of laughter. But the blur of Catori's blades as she rises finds its mark on every man. In a matter of minutes, all eight lie lifeless on the stone floor, blood pooling and mixing. Catori steps over a body, reaching us just as another four men file around the corner. No sign of Fletcher, just his men. Catori spins on her heel, striding back to them.

"Catori, no, let's just leave," Callian hisses.

She doesn't respond.

It is over even quicker than the last round. Altogether, she has killed twenty men. Twenty in exchange for one. The reality of that sinks in, and nausea rises in my throat. Callian tugs my arm, nodding toward the exit door. Catori files past us, taking the lead. Callian falls in behind me, still swearing under his breath.

Within seconds, we make it to the door. Daylight washes through as the door cracks open. Catori takes off, running with the raging winds that seem to be guiding us home. Callian's heavier footsteps follow close behind me. The whine of him sheathing his blades is dulled by the dense forest life.

With every step, my legs burn. I can't take my eyes off Catori, can't shake from my mind what she just did, the price she just paid for my life—was *willing* to pay for my life. The pain that filled her eyes when she looked at my battered face... I swallow the lump in my throat, trying to push back the burning in my chest. The broken chains whip around my ankles, but the sting of it hardly registers with the turbulence in my mind and the ache in my chest as I watch her run.

She is taking me home.

CHAPTER 12
IMANI

It takes a whole three minutes to lower myself onto the short soft grass of the training area. My broken leg sends out a mixture of sharp pains and dull aches in protest. I guess I will stay here a while. I lie back on the grass, resting my hands on my stomach, watching the clouds skiff along the blue sky, processing.

I have a little brother. My mother is not a broken fool, not a weak, depressed shell of a woman. I left when she was first pregnant. Was it the morning sickness that made her weak and tired then? I didn't see it for what it was, only what I thought it was. I never bothered to even ask. Ugh. I let a moan rumble out of me. How could I be so stupid? But I suppose at age twelve, I didn't know about those things, so I wouldn't have realized what was happening. I shouldn't have snapped at Harm. I shouldn't have left Mason. I should have gone home to see my mother after I left.

I never do the right thing.

Soft footsteps interrupt my self-loathing. Harm stands beside where I lie, his face twisted with worry. I close my eyes; I can't look at him. Everything I have done over the past few months—the past five years—I have screwed up.

"I don't want to talk," I snap.

"Alright." The word is soft. Moments later, his steps fade back toward the village.

Hours later, I loose a long breath, rubbing my hands over my face. I sit up, ripping the grass from the soft ground, as if inflicting pain on the beautiful place that feeds me, shelters me, and allows me to be free will make me feel better. It doesn't. I watch the tree line for a while, hoping to see three figures emerge. But it's still. Nothing stirs.

I wait for an hour. Nothing. The sun hovers at its apex, and my stomach grumbles. Rolling onto my hands and knees, I grip my stick and push my way to standing. The ache in my leg cascades into shooting pains, and I teeter over the stick for a moment, trying to control my breathing, waiting for the pain to ease. Finally, it ebbs, and I stand tall, heading for home. Each wobbly step reminds me that I need to rest, and to make another visit to the healer for whatever she gave me to kill the pain.

A rustling in the undergrowth from the other side of the training area stops me in my tracks. I stand frozen. It's getting louder. I wobble through the turn back, leaning hard on my stick.

Catori bursts from the tree line, slowing her pace to a walk, hands digging into her sides. She circles tightly at the edge of the training area, looking back into the forest.

Where are the boys?

I hobble over as quickly as I can, readjusting my robe, pulling it tighter around my body. Someone from the village center calls out a warning behind me. Every step toward Catori feels like a mile. Another minute—nothing. I am halfway across the training area. I hobble faster, falling into a rhythm that sparks more twangs up my thigh. I ignore it.

Another minute. Nothing.

Catori's heavy breathing is ragged. She must have been flying. I almost reach her, and she turns to look at me. Her face is red, blotchy, her brows pulled down. She stops pacing and leans over, planting her hands on her knees.

"Where are they?"

She stays bent over, sucking in long breaths.

"Catori, please, where are they?" My voice cracks on the last word.

She rises, arms hanging at her sides, her eyes searching mine. "Behind me," she finally whispers through ragged breaths.

My whole body sags. I place a hand over my racing heart, pushing up on the stick with the other.

She looks me up and down. "Shouldn't you be in the healer's shelter?"

"I'm fine." I look to the trees again. "Mason, is he..." I choke up.

Catori blows out a breath, the rustle of the undergrowth catching her attention. "See for yourself," she says gravely and turns to wait for him.

Callian strides past the tree line, his face drawn and blotchy like his sister's, sucking in long, ragged breaths. "He insisted on walking the last mile."

"You had to carry him?" I breathe.

"Only for a little while. He ran out of steam, and we were in no position to slow down," he rasps, whipping a hot glance Catori's way.

Finally, Mason limps past the tree line into sight. A whimper leaves my lips. His face is swollen, blood coating his neck and chest, arms bruised and cut up. His wrists and ankles are manacled, short chains hanging from each limb. Tears sting my eyes as he tries to force a smile. I slap my hand to my mouth to cover the gasp that leaves my chest.

"You made it home," he chokes.

I drop my stick, hobbling across the distance between us. I throw my arms around him, and he lets out a low chuckle before wrapping his arms around me.

"I'm glad you're okay, Imani." His body shakes, still wrapped around mine. "I really thought I was going to watch you die."

I choke sobs into his chest. A heartbeat later, I pull back and examine his face, touching it gently with trembling fingertips. "What did they do to you? I'm so sorry I left you there. Can you ever forgive me?"

He breathes out a small huff. "If you remember, I told you to go."

I wipe the tears from my face, wavering on the spot. My stick appears at my side. I turn, and Harm is standing next to me, eyes lined with silver, face hard, jaw clenching.

Catori stands, staring between Mason and me. Her eyes lift to the sky, and she shakes her head, lips a thin line, before she sprints for the forest.

"What happened at the tower?" I ask Callian.

He stares at me with a hard look, before clearing his throat, dismissing whatever thought he was having.

"Is Catori okay?" I ask.

Mason drops his gaze to the ground and limps past me, heading for the village.

"Callian, what happened?"

"Catori, she..." He looks to the tree line where she disappeared. "I've never seen her like that before. She was fine, focused. Then she saw Mason. He was chained up, battered, half out of it. She lost it, Imani. Twenty Guardians are dead."

Wide-eyed, I drag my gaze to the forest. A raw scream rips through the dense foliage, and birds scatter skywards.

"What got into her?" Harm asks, his voice sending a pang through my chest.

"I think I know," I say, hobbling toward the tree line and leaving the boys behind.

Harm and Callian make for the village, no doubt to talk to Mason. But Catori is the only one who knows what we were doing in that tower.

She is sitting motionless on a fallen tree, vacantly staring into the forest. I hobble over to her spot and teeter my way down, sitting next to her. "You alright?" I whisper.

She doesn't respond. I lean my stick against the fallen tree. The undergrowth teems with tiny life, and I watch it, just sitting with her.

She cycles through a few deep breaths. "I lost it, Imani. I saw him chained up. I saw his face..." She exhales, bearing down. "... and I just *lost* it."

As I adjust my seat on the tree, memories of Harm at the gallows, when I was roped and held by Mason, edge into my mind. I shut my eyes, forcing the memory away. I recognize that face—the one Catori wears now. The fear of losing someone you love is worse than the fear of dying—much worse. Her shaking hands press onto her thighs. She bends forward and retches, losing her stomach on the grass at her feet. I rub her back. She breathes through the nausea, sitting back up, and stares at me for a moment.

"You'll be okay. You will both be okay, Catori."

She opens her mouth, but closes it again. "How did you know Harm was your person?" she whispers finally.

I sit scanning her face for a heartbeat, trying to find the words to describe the best thing in my life.

"He overwhelms me, in the best way possible. When we're apart, I only feel half alive, like a huge part of me is missing."

Her eyes widen, and she runs her palms down her legs, like the nausea is returning. I rub her back, and she forces a smile. "That's what I thought." She turns to look at me. "I'm in a whole lot of trouble, aren't I?" Her face crumples with a sob.

"That depends on whether you act on it or not. You can either choose to be happy, or choose to ignore it."

"What if he doesn't feel the same about me?"

I tilt my head to the side, trying to suppress the smile of happiness that threatens to split my face, and wrap my arm around her shoulders. "Being apart from him..." I draw in a long breath, remembering every tortured night without Harm over the past two weeks. "... is more misery than it's worth."

She turns to face me, and I drop my arm. "What is it?"

"You can't tell Hanola what I did. Please. She cannot find out."

"Your secret is safe with me." Standing, I grab my stick, and she stands tall beside me. I hobble through the forest toward the village, Catori wandering behind.

I find the boys at Callian's house. Mason is not there. I step over the threshold. Tension hovers between Harm and me, and Callian notes every move we make. He has changed, the bloody and dirty clothes he returned in thrown over a chair. His narrowed eyes stay fixed on me.

"Maybe I should go," I say, turning to the door.

"How could you do this to us?" he hisses, stepping forward.

I turn back. Harm has moved closer, eyes tracking from me to Callian, whose eyes are lit up with anger and hurt.

"Callian..." Harm warns.

"No. It's okay, get it out." I keep my focus on my friend, whom, as far as he knows, I have betrayed.

"How could you do that to Harm? To us? Then you just come home, like nothing happened?!"

"You boys carried us here. Last I checked, *you* brought us home —the three of us."

"I already regret that decision. Nirri was the only one worth saving."

My breath stops, hurt flooding my chest.

"I did what I had to do, Callian. I was *sent* there! I didn't *leave*!"

He stands frozen, letting the words sink in, the fire in his eyes changing to hurt. "Did Catori know about this?"

Harm flinches, and his gaze hits the floor. "No. Only me, and only because Hanola thought I was going to do something stupid, believing Imani had left." His throat bobs. "When I thought she had betrayed me."

I whip my gaze to him. What does he mean, "do something stupid"? What the hell happened while I was gone?

Callian spins, pacing the floor. "So, you and Mason were both *sent* there?" He turns back for the answer.

"Yes. And it broke my heart, leaving you all like that—leaving Harm." I push up on my stick. "But it had to be real. Our Blending had to be believed by the Guardians and the Chancellor... and by my father."

"But you got caught?" Callian presses.

"Yes, at the last door. Nirri helped me escape. You know the rest."

Harm brushes past me, his body tense. Pained, Callian watches him go.

"I did what Hanola asked me to do, Callian, to help Harm. That's all." I hobble out the door as fast as I can before I lose it on him.

I wander toward Hanola's home, hoping to find Harm or Mason. Voices banter back and forth inside: Catori, Hanola, and Mason. They stop talking, and I hear someone moving toward the door. Catori opens it. Mason is behind her.

"I'll see you guys later. I have to eat before I topple over,"

Catori says, heading toward the eating area. Mason should try to get something down too.

"You need to eat and get to the healer's shelter," I say to him.

"In a minute." He steps toward me.

"Callian knows everything. I filled him in. So, you should be alright to sleep there."

He nods, staring at the ground.

"You know, if you want to talk about it..." I offer.

He shakes his head, forcing a small smile. "I just didn't think I would..."

I drop my stick and pull him in close. He rests his head on my shoulder, wrapping his arms around me. "Thank you," he breathes, his chest heaving against mine. I push away from him, leaning back to find his face.

"You're safe, Mason. You're home." I rub my thumb over his cheek, wiping away the tears from his face.

A throat clears behind me. I turn my head, still holding Mason's arms.

Harm raises his head. Blowing out a breath, he turns and stalks toward home.

"Harm!"

He doesn't stop, doesn't turn back.

I drop my head, resting it in one hand. I never stop ruining things. I try to fix one thing, only for something else to fall apart. What is wrong with me?

CHAPTER 13
MASON

The bunk under my weary body digs into every rib. Soft voices banter back and forth—mostly healer talk. I hear Hanola's name. The voices become strained.

"She's getting worse," one woman says.

"The tonic for her lungs isn't working anymore. I'm not sure what else we can do for Hanola. She's not getting any younger, but refuses to slow down."

Wait... Hanola is sick?

They stop talking, and footsteps drift toward me. I close my eyes. A throat clears, and I open them to see the old healer leaning over me. I sit up. Imani is asleep two bunks over, her stick on the floor beside her.

"How's the pain today?" the healer asks.

"It's okay." I don't want to be a bother when Nirri is lying in the bunk beside me in much worse condition.

The healer's gentle hands wander across my swollen face, assessing every bruise, cut, and scrape Fletcher gave me. She prods my cheekbones, a thumb on each one. I wince, and she drops her hands.

"Swollen, but not broken. You are a lucky young man." The small wooden cart next to her rattles as she fingers through the small vials, jars, and tins, hunting for what she needs—what I need.

"This salve..." She plucks a small tin from the center of the top tier of the cart. "It will help your face recover much quicker." She hands it to me. The small tin fits easily in the palm of my hand.

"Thank you."

"You can use it on your face, wrists, and ankles. Come back in three days to let me check for infection. Otherwise, you should be fine." She offers a smile before pushing her cart over to the next bunk—Nirri's bunk. I turn and watch as she checks Nirri over, turning her head from side to side. Callian watches everything the old healer does, his hands holding Nirri's.

"Sit up for me," the healer says.

Nirri pushes up, and Callian places a hand under her back to help her rise. She is pale; the usual color of her happy face is nowhere to be seen. Her hands shake in Callian's.

The healer presses an ear to her chest, listening. "Nirri, cough for me, please."

Nirri coughs. Callian waits, brows pulled down, eyes fixed on the healer's face, watching for any clue as to how things are progressing. The woman sits on the bed next to Nirri and pats Callian's hands. He doesn't remove them. She smiles at him before turning to Nirri.

"You lost a lot of blood, and we had you asleep for quite a few days. Everything sounds fine, but you're still weak. You're free to go home, or you can find a home in the village to stay in, I guess. One of the other healers will attend to you once a day to make sure your strength is returning, and the wounds stay clean."

"Thank you," Callian says, releasing Nirri's hands.

"You're most welcome." Rising, she leaves with her cart.

"You can stay with Catori," Callian tells Nirri. "I'll have her get

Imani's old space ready. And I'll find you a proper bed." He stands, and Nirri smiles and nods, not looking at him.

Callian walks out, running straight into Catori.

"You're going to visit Mason?" he says flatly.

"I'm here for all three of our friends, Callian."

He strides off toward the village center. Catori slows over the threshold, taking in Nirri sitting up and me standing.

"Looks like everyone is up." She smiles, sitting on Nirri's bed. "How are you feeling?"

"Better. Sore, but better," Nirri says.

"I'm glad to hear it."

"I'm allowed to leave now, but I need somewhere to stay." Nirri's eyes search Catori's.

"You can have Imani's old bunk. Stay as long as you need."

Nirri just stares at her. Catori doesn't understand that Nirri can never go home. "I..." she starts.

"What is it?" Catori asks.

I move around the bunk, and Catori looks up at me, wincing slightly when her gaze meets my face. I must look hideous to her. "She can't go home, Catori."

Nirri forces back a sob.

"Oh..." Catori's gaze returns to Nirri. "Of course you can't. Sorry, I should have realized."

"I'm sorry to be a burden on you all," Nirri whispers.

Catori takes her hands and rubs the backs of them with her thumbs. "Hey, you are not a burden. You saved two lives—two lives that are very important to me, and to all the people in the forest and desert villages."

Nirri nods, a tear plopping into her lap. "I'm sorry. I'm just so tired, and—"

"Come on, let's get you out of this depressing place," Catori says, tilting her head, gesturing for me to help her. I move around the bunk and hold out a hand to Nirri. She swings her legs over the bed and grabs my hand. Catori slides an arm under her shoulder. She stands, wobbly, but easily. We wait a moment to let her settle, and I wrap my arm through hers.

"Ready?" I ask.

She nods, and we walk out of the healer's shelter, slowly making our way to Catori's house. Once we are inside, Catori removes her arm and busies herself making room for her new guest. I stand holding Nirri, in case she feels faint.

"I think I'm okay now," she says, and I let go of her arm.

Catori pulls a chair next to the hearth, and Nirri wobbles her way over to it. With one fluid motion, Catori has her in the chair. I grab a blanket from Catori's bed, permeated with her scent. I hold onto it for a moment, then walk back to the hearth. Laying the blanket over Nirri's lap, I excuse myself. Catori is stoking the fire when I walk out the door.

The door thuds and metal clinks, and a moment later, her hand grabs my arm. I turn back, and she is inches from my face, her green eyes burning into mine.

"I came to see you too," she breathes.

I shove my hands into my pockets and swallow.

Her hand reaches for my face, but she drops it, staring at me. I stand there and let her.

"Are you alright?" she says finally.

"I am now."

"Good."

I turn to make my way to breakfast.

"Mason, wait."

I turn back to her again. "What is it?"

"I..."

Callian walks around the corner with a bundle of blankets and pillows.

"Never mind," she says. "Can I walk with you to breakfast?"

"I would like that."

A small smile breaks across her face. "You know, I'm still responsible for you," she says as we walk through the homes toward the village center.

"You're still keeping an eye on me?"

"It sounds bad when you say it like that." She looks at the ground as we walk.

"It's alright, Catori. I don't mind *your* company."

Heat flushes through her face, and she clears her throat. "That's settled, then. Let's eat."

We find a seat near Harm. Imani walks over with her stick, coming from the healer's shelter. She sits next to Harm. He doesn't look at her. Catori throws a glance between them. Miya and Jeselle sit down beside me, Miya offering a brief smile.

"Hey, Mason, are you feeling okay?" Jeselle asks.

"Fine, just a bit swollen." I select food from the center of the table, dropping it onto my plate. Jeselle grabs her own and starts eating.

"How are you today, Imani? How's the leg?" I ask.

Harm's eyes shoot to mine, laced with fire.

"Stiff, achy, but still there," Imani says.

Harm ignores her. Imani takes a bite of her bread. A second later, forcing down a cough, she points to the mugs and water. Coughing, she thumps her chest, looking at Harm. He ignores her again. I pick up a mug and fill it half full, handing it to her. She downs the mug and thumps her chest again, recovering from the cough.

Harm's gaze sits on my face, his hands still, palms down on the table.

"What the hell's wrong with you, Travesci?" I snap.

"Mind your own business, Rayner." He pushes back from the table and stalks off.

The three girls at the table sit with gaping mouths, eyes full of disbelief, watching Harm stride home. Imani is quiet as she finishes her food. Miya and Jeselle finish and leave for the training area. Catori stands and offers a hand to Imani. She takes it, picking up her stick. I take her plate and mug and return our dishes to the ladies in the kitchen. Only one offers a forced smile. I guess I should expect that.

"I'm going to train with Miya," Catori says. "You can come and watch, or stay with Hanola, if you have no other chores to attend to."

"I'll grab you some more water for your house."

"Then come to training. Your arms still work, don't they?" Her mouth pulls into a soft smile.

I wander across the village center to the tanks behind the kitchen. A handful of large urns sit cleaned and empty. Grabbing the first one, I round the bench to the tanks. Imani is leaning against the tank, water running into her urn. Her hands cover her face, her shoulders shaking. A sob escapes her chest.

I walk over to Imani. "Hey."

She looks up, wiping away the tears on her cheeks. "Hey," she returns weakly, turning the tap off. Her urn is half full; that's all she can manage, walking with a stick.

"Imani, Travesci was being a prick. I have no idea what's gotten into him."

"He's never going to forgive me, is he?" Her face twists, ragged breaths shuddering her shoulders.

I drop the urn under the tap and turn it on, watching the water fill the round vessel for a heartbeat before looking up at her. "You didn't do anything wrong. You were following Hanola's orders."

"I don't think that matters." She hobbles off, carrying her half-full urn in one arm.

The water sloshes over the rim of my own urn, soaking the ground. I turn off the tap and haul the urn onto my shoulders. The caked wounds of my wrists sting. I walk the urn to Catori's, setting it down just inside the front door, fuming. Harm has some nerve treating Imani like that, after everything she's risked for him, and for these people. I stalk my way toward their house, blood thundering in my veins with every step.

Wood slamming against wood echoes through his front door. I plant my feet on the threshold, waiting for him to turn around. His frame is alive with the effort of shifting wood. Taking it to the hearth, he stacks it in a wooden rack he no doubt built himself. His axe sits nearby, leaning against the stone.

He stops, not moving for a moment. "What do you want, Rayner?"

"Why are you punishing her for this?"

No movement, only the steady rise and fall of his shoulders. "Get out," he snarls, staring at the wood pile in front of him.

"Imani did this for *you*—for all of us—and risked her life in the process." I take a step into their house, hands balling into fists.

He still doesn't move. "I said get out, Rayner!"

I stand staring at his back for a heartbeat. Bloody mongrel.

I stalk out of their home, slamming the door behind me. With fury coursing through my veins, I make my way to the training area. Maybe I can blow off some steam training with Catori and Miya.

Catori is dancing around Miya, weapons at the ready, a grin on her pretty face. I sink onto the grass and watch her move. She spins, ducks, and lunges like she has done this a million times before. The memory of her in the tower comes back to me—the way she spun and twisted, her long blades unfailingly finding their mark, spilling the blood of any Guardian they intercepted.

Twenty. Twenty Guardians: that was the price for my life. The price she was willing to pay to bring me home. My chest aches as I watch her.

Miya finally concedes, lowering her weapons. Catori sheathes hers, wiping sweat from her neck with a rag tucked into her weapons belt. She pads across the training area and stands in front of me.

"You want to go a round with me?" she asks.

"Aren't you tired from fighting Miya?"

"Nope." She tucks her rag back into her weapons belt.

I stand, pulling two knives from the rack, stepping into the sparring ring. Every part of me vibrates. I'm alive. I'm home.

Miya sits on the grass, and Jeselle makes her way over, plopping into her lap, receiving a peck on the cheek.

"I'll go easy on you, since you might not see me coming," Catori says. Half a grin briefly whips over her face, lighting up her green eyes.

"Ha ha. Let's do this." I take my stance a few feet away from her.

I lunge first, not letting her take the offense, showing her I remember what she taught me. She intercepts my blades with hers, stepping into my space. I throw her off, our four blades whining with the movement. She lunges, this time to my side, one knife aiming for my ribs, the other for my throat. I spin out of range, and she lunges again, not letting me retreat too far. This time our knives connect, and she tangles her arms through mine. A second later, she topples me to the ground sideways, knocking the wind out of my chest slightly. I scramble backward and jump up. She has already advanced, her face so close to mine, but her hands are at her sides.

"I'm glad you came home." Her chest heaves as she inches closer to me. Every part of me wants to pull her into me.

I slide a sideways glance at Miya and Jeselle, whose eyebrows have risen over their widened eyes. I step back, hoping Catori doesn't take it the wrong way. I don't want her to feel like this has to happen. I want it to, but not with an audience.

"Me too." I hesitate before I walk back to the rack, putting my knives away. She stares at me.

"Catori," Callian calls from the last row of houses.

She looks over to her brother, sheathing her knives.

"Hanola wants us all to come for a meeting."

She nods and waves. The three girls wander from the training area toward Hanola's. I follow a step behind. The information we brought from the tower must have been useful. What happens next, now that we have it?

Hanola will have a plan, for all of us.

She always has a plan.

CHAPTER 14
HARM

Hanola's house has never been so crowded. We stand around the strategy table, Hanola hovering over her stick. Imani is standing with Catori and Nirri. She hasn't spoken to me or even looked at me since breakfast. I don't blame her; the look on her face at breakfast almost gutted me. It was the same look my mother wore when my father shut her out, when I was caught and punished by the Guardians. Thirty lashes and a rift between my parents was the result of me trying to interfere with the way things are, to keep our boys safe. Remnants of that look still haunt Imani's face. I am no better than my father. The hurt on her face tears me apart. Then Mason talks to her quietly—like they're friends, like they're close—and every rational thought leaves my mind, replaced with anger.

Hanola taps her stick on the floor. "Harm, are you listening? This is important."

"Sorry, I am now."

"As I was saying, our infiltration was successful, thanks to the ruse Imani and Mason were able to uphold for as long as they did. These parchments and the maps and other information that were brought back are most valuable." She looks to Mason, then to Imani, nodding in thanks.

Callian shoots me a look, checking to see if I am okay. He stands at my side, as if I might pounce on his grandmother at any given moment. I release a slow breath.

"This information confirms that there is another section, a mountain sector. And our forest sits between the desert and the mountains. We know nothing of the people who inhabit this part. My only hope is that they will be up to joining us as well," Hanola says.

"That may not happen," Mason interrupts, and all eyes fall to him. "The mountain wilds, as the Chancellor calls them, is where ex-Guardians are sent, when deemed no longer useful or too old. They're not likely to rise against Arthur."

Every face in the room is gaping at him—all except Nirri's. She knew. She must know so much that we don't.

"He plans to conquer all three territories eventually, posi-tioning outposts and Guardians in all three sectors," Mason goes on. "The desert side is already in his control. He plans on sending Guardians to the forest next. Then he will cover the mountain wilds—the lands the ex-Guardians hold, and that of the original inhabitants, who are basically savages," he finishes, scanning every face in the room.

Nobody speaks. Hanola adjusts her hold on her stick.

"Why?" Catori asks.

"Because he can," Nirri mutters. We all look to her. "I grew up having to learn everything there is to know about the natural world around us, governments, and overseeing populations. I spent hours studying, so I could become the next Chancellor. He was..." She hesitates. "... disappointed that I was born a girl. But he decided to train me, nonetheless."

Callian's face is pulled tight, hands gripping the back of the chair he leans on.

"When I got to the dial, I couldn't change it. Can you?" I ask.

"No," Nirri says, her gaze finding an empty space in the room. "The gene I carry isn't strong enough."

"You've already tried, and it didn't work for you either?"

"Arthur locked me in that tower, in the dial room, for three weeks when I was thirteen. He told me I wasn't getting out until I got the dial to change. For three weeks, I ate rations and had to relieve myself in the corner of that tiny stone room. I was locked in, and guards were stationed outside."

Callian's face has blanched beside me.

Miya is studying the parchments and diagrams of the dial. She flips them over and back again. "Hold up... Maybe something was missing when you tried, Harm. On this parchment, there's a diagram that shows the base as open. Apparently, there's a power source. Maybe it just wasn't working?"

"There's something called an Atharex that the men in the mountain wilds protect. Maybe that's it?" Mason offers.

"So, the thing that powers the dial is hidden over another wall, in a place where none of us have ever been, guarded by who knows how many Guardians? Which is also teeming with savages, the original inhabitants of the mountains?" I say, the fire of my words landing on Mason.

"That about sums it up," he says, lifting his chin.

"No problem, then." Callian snorts, partially recovered from Nirri's story.

Catori turns her gaze to me. "You need that power source to change the dial. Without changing the dial, there's no point in us rebelling against the Chancellor, because the situation on your side of the wall, the desert, will stay the same."

"That is true, Catori," Hanola says. "Even with a united

people, if we are sharing resources across the three different territories, change will be incredibly difficult. One hint that we are all banding together as one united force, and Arthur will change the dial on the other two sectors. All three will end up like Harm's side, and our hope for survival diminishes significantly. Which brings us back to our original plan, and the reason Imani and Mason went into that tower. Harm must change the dial, evening out the weather across all three sectors, and Arthur needs to be removed from power." She leans hard on her stick.

Catori glides to her side, placing an arm around her grandmother. "She needs to rest."

"Meeting adjourned for today. We will come back tomorrow, same time, and go over everything we know and are planning from there," Miya says.

Within minutes, everyone has shuffled out Hanola's door. I hang back, watching Imani hobble along with her stick. She is right in front of me, but she may as well be miles away. The gutting rift between us feels enormous.

Mason falls back, walking with Imani. "Do you need to see the healer for your pain?" he asks.

She looks at him, a small smile on her face. "Later. I just want to go home for a bit and sit down."

"If you need anything, just ask," he says. She touches his shoulder with her free hand.

Catori jogs past me, catching up to Imani, she and Mason flanking her like they are protecting her. From me. A lump rises in my throat, and I shove my hands in my pockets. The ache in my chest turns to fire, and I pick up the pace, stalking past Mason, colliding with his shoulder on my way past. Mason bumps into Imani, and she topples sideways briefly. I turn and watch her falter, my gut twisting into a sharp knot.

"Imani?" Mason says, holding her arm.

My hands ball into fists in my pockets.

"I'm fine," she says, pushing back up on her stick. Her eyes burn into mine, hurt lacing every part of her face.

I did this. That look on her face—I put it there. I swallow past the growing tightness in my throat.

"Take your hand off her," I snarl at Mason.

He stands beside Imani, bracing his shoulders, but removes his hand from her arm.

Imani's face crumples. "Harm..."

"Don't be an ass, Travesci." Mason shakes his head.

"Butt out, Rayner," I growl, removing my hands from my pockets.

"No, I won't. We did what Hanola asked us of us, and now we're paying for it, apparently."

"*'We'?*" The fire in my body flares at the word. Imani and Mason. Nausea rips up my throat, and I swallow it back, letting out a long, low breath.

Mason stands there, curling and uncurling his fists by his sides. Good. Let him beat the crap out of me; I deserve it. Every word that comes out of my mouth seems to make everything worse.

"Like we didn't pay a price when you two left us?" I say, so quietly that I am not sure either of them hears it.

Imani's face changes, pain twisting her features. She heard me.

Mason takes two steps toward me. His face, still slightly swollen, is flushed as he shakes his head at me again. "You have no idea how leaving you broke her into a million pieces," he growls, the words seething out through his teeth.

"Oh, and I suppose you're the expert on Imani now?"

Imani's mouth falls open, wide eyes lining with tears.

Mason steps into my space, so close that his breath is on my face. "Go to hell, Travesci."

A tear spills down Imani's cheek.

Catori stands slightly in front of her, reading Mason's body language.

"You first, Rayner."

My fist connects with his face a heartbeat later. He falters slightly, shoving my chest with his hands. I stagger backward a step, and he moves in, fist hitting my nose. A shooting pain spreads through it, the blood rushing from my face.

"Harm!" Imani cries, hobbling forward on her stick, not afraid of Mason in the slightest.

I lunge at him, my fist connecting with his jaw. He grabs my shoulders, flinging me around, away from Imani. Shoving my feet into the ground, I pull him sideways. He topples, and I throw him to the ground. I plant my knees on either side of him and smash my fist into his jaw again. He grabs my arms and flips me over. Straddling my heaving chest, he grabs my collar and raises a fist.

"Stop it! Stop it, both of you!" Imani screams.

Mason hesitates, his pained, angry gaze fixed on me. His chest heaves, as does mine under his weight.

"Catori, please make them stop!" Imani pleads.

"Let them go, Imani. They need to get it out of their system." She walks away.

Mason lowers his hand to his side. Imani hobbles after Catori. Slowing her pace, she looks back at us, her face streaked with tears. A heartbeat later, she shakes her head and limps away.

I look back at Mason. His face has lost the redness, but his hand still grips my collar tightly.

"I listened to Imani cry herself to sleep every damn night. She was terrified that you would never forgive her," Mason rasps.

My heart pounds against my ribs, thrashing against the ache that has been strangling it ever since she left.

"She fell apart, Harm." Some of the fire ebbs from his gaze, leaving only sadness. "She's one of the strongest people we know, and she fell apart. Tortured herself over the possibility of losing you. And now, you're breaking her heart." His jaw clenches, and he runs a hand through his sandy hair. "Dammit, Travesci."

I go limp under his weight, and he releases my collar. I close my eyes and force back the stinging tears. Mason's weight leaves my chest. His footsteps fade, and I open my eyes, staring at the blue sky and green canopy scattered above.

Staring at nothing.

I walk through the door of our home. She is not here. It has been three days, and Imani still has not come home. She hasn't slept here, hasn't set foot in our house. Why would she want to? Her leaving for a mission with Mason is nothing compared to the stupid stuff I have done since she came home. I am the world's biggest idiot. Even Mason is behaving better than me. I really have lost my mind over this.

It stops now. I have almost lost her—twice. I won't make the mistake of losing her for good.

I flip through the memories of my parents, the days after I was lashed. What did my father do? How did he fix things?

My notebook sits open on a small table, the wind flipping the pages back and forth. The bed I designed for Imani covers the pages. Use my hands, clear my head—Hanola's words sink in, now more than ever. I grab the notebook and walk out the door.

Moments later, I knock on Petria's door. Excited steps hurry toward it. It is flung open, and the smiling face of Miles greets me.

"Harm! Come in, we were just having an early supper," he says, taking my hand and ushering me to the table.

"Hello, Harmen," Petria says, gesturing for me to sit. Just like the first time I met her—the first time I met Imani's mother, and her little brother. "What happened to you?" she asks, running a look down my filthy shirt.

I brush the dirt and grass off my clothes, apologizing.

"What do you have in your notebook?" Miles asks.

"The design for the bed I'm going to build," I say, turning my gaze to Petria. "I was hoping I could build it here, so it stays a surprise."

"Of course. Miles will be thrilled to watch you work."

"He can help me, if he likes?" I say to Miles.

"Really?!" he squeals.

"Sure. It's easier with an extra set of hands for a project this big. Plus, beds are a good piece to learn on." I ruffle his hair as he tucks into his meal.

"Can I come tomorrow and organize my tools and start cutting the wood?" I ask Petria.

"Of course. You can use the back room. This house is too big for just two people anyhow."

After a moment of silence, she adds, "Are things alright with Imani and you? I haven't seen you two together since she came home."

"I don't know," I admit. "Her time away has strained things a little, but most of it is my fault." My heart skitters across a beat.

She looks at me with kindness. "You and Imani remind me so much of how Daniel and I used to be."

My spoon freezes halfway to my mouth. "Fletcher?"

"Yes, everyone seems to call him that these days. But he was a teacher before he signed up for the regime. A good one." She chews thoughtfully before swallowing. "When Imani was born, the regime was just starting. It was new and exciting, a better position than teaching in the village, so he took it. But his work was never easy; it burdened him a great deal. The orders he had to carry out, training new officers, collecting taxes... And after a while, just after he signed up for his second round of service, they started executing people for not paying taxes, as you well know." She assesses my reaction, as if deciding whether to continue.

"Imani was always a strong-willed girl; she hated the work her father did," she goes on. "The day she ran away, he cried. It was the first time I had ever seen him break down. It broke him—the way she looked at him, the hate in her eyes, the running away. He changed after that day. I guess that was the day Daniel became Fletcher." Tears line her eyes.

I stay silent, not eating. Miles, already finished, plays in the corner with a small wooden toy.

"Do you think, if the regime falls, he will come home? To you both?" I ask.

"Maybe, maybe not. You can't make people do things. I learned that a long time ago. They must choose for themselves."

"Do you want him to come home?"

"Of course I do, Harm. Daniel is still my husband, despite what he is to everyone else."

I shove another mouthful in, mulling over her words, taking in the look of love and pain and loss and hope etched over her elegant face, which is so much like Imani's.

"I should get home," I say, pushing up from the chair. "Thank you for the meal. I'll see you tomorrow, Miles, for some building."

He smiles and waves, one hand still playing with his toy.

"Harm, she'll come around. Imani is stubborn, but she fights for the people she loves." She pulls me into a tight hug.

"I know." The words wobble from my mouth.

It takes only a few minutes to stride home. Every hurried step carries a prayer that Imani will be there.

A fire is going, the light flickering through the window. She's home. I hesitate at the door, willing the right words to leave my mouth, not the garbage it's been proffering lately. I open the door.

She is sitting in a chair by the hearth, a blanket over her legs. Her head is bent to one side, resting on the back of the chair. She doesn't move when I close the door behind me. I step around the chair, stopping in front of her. Her eyes are closed, her breathing steady.

"Imani," I whisper.

She opens her eyes slowly, adjusting them to the firelight. "Hey. I can go back to the healer's shelter if you want me to, I was just warming up for a bit." Her gaze tracks to the fire.

My heart quickens in my chest, and I pull in a breath.

No, I don't want you to leave. "Could you stay?"

Her eyes rise to meet mine. "If that is what you want, Harm."

Of course it's what I want. "Please."

She leans forward to push up on the chair, her hair falling around her shoulders. My breath stops. I offer her both hands to get up. She freezes, bent over, looking up at me, and swallows before slowly taking my hands. Hers fit inside mine, so soft and fine. It's the first time she has touched me since the day she left. My heart thunders in my chest, and my hands shake around hers. She pulls herself up, grabbing her stick once she finds her balance.

"Do you want me to sleep on the floor?" she asks flatly.

"Why would I want that?"

"I thought you might want your space, that's all." Turning away from the chair, she hobbles toward the door.

Please don't leave again! The strangled feeling around my chest tightens. "You can have the bed, if you don't want to sleep next to me," I murmur.

"Whatever you want." Making her way toward the bed, she doesn't meet my gaze.

I stand where I am, watching her sit on the bed and move her leg over the edge with her hands. Every part of me wants to lie down next to her and hold her, never letting go. But after my behavior recently, I'm not going to push it. It will be Imani's choice.

"This bed is big enough for two people, Harmen." Rolling over to face the wall, she doesn't look back.

I sway where I stand before padding over to the bed. I watch her lying on her side until her breathing slows again. She is asleep. I sit on the side of the bed and take off my boots and belt. Lying down next to her, I roll over, watching her sleep, watching the back of her head, the thick, dark waves that cover her pillow. Keeping a few inches between us, I close my eyes, breathing her in.

Home. She is home at last.

Now I just need to fix what I broke.

CHAPTER 15
IMANI

The sun finds me hours before I am ready to be awake. I roll over, and Harm is gone. I shuffle out of bed, push up with the help of my stick, and find my way to the dresser. My blue scarf is neatly rolled up in the top drawer. Someone has washed it and returned it to its place. Since no one else knows where my things belong, it must have been Harm. I pull it out, unrolling it. Twisting my hair up, I wrap the blue scarf around it.

I make my way to breakfast. Callian and Catori sit with Mason, Miya, and Jeselle, laughing and chatting. Harm is not here. I sit next to Callian, who gives me a brief smile, but goes back to his food.

"Morning," Miya says.

"Morning." They all nod at me. I grab food from the tray in the center and pour a mug of water.

"You're training with me today, Imani," Callian says, ripping some bread with his teeth. His weapons are already strapped to his chest and sides.

"Oh, I am?"

"You need to train, put some muscle back on. Plus, it will help your leg recover to go through some exercises. Also, Jeselle will help you with your archery after I'm done with you. Just in case."

Jeselle smiles, shoving some food into her mouth.

"Just in case what?" I look between Callian and Catori.

The huntress's gaze finds mine. "Hanola was worried that your leg may not make a full recovery. She was convinced that some other problems..." She clears her throat. "... may be impeding your recovery." Her eyes drop to her plate, and Mason shoves his food around with his fork.

"You all think my leg won't heal... because of Harm?" I search each of their faces.

"He hasn't exactly been easy on you since you came home," Miya says. Jeselle lays a hand over Miya's.

"Harm was in a bad place when you left. He's still processing it, what he went through when you disappeared, then you coming home and all," Callian says to me. The pain that lingers in his eyes tells me everything.

That look. I did this to him. Harm has never had a mean bone in his body. I did this.

I swallow the mouthful I am chewing and wash it down with a sip of water. Tears burn my eyes, and I struggle to stand. Callian stands, holding out a hand to help me up. I ignore him and hobble away from the table. I have no idea where I'm going—anywhere but here, with their sympathy and all-knowing comments. I drag in each breath, stabbing my stick into the ground with every painful step.

Moments later, I drop onto the grass next to the training grounds. I shove my head in my hands and let the course of sobs and ragged breaths consume me.

A hand rests on my shaking back, and Catori kneels beside me. "Imani, what my grandmother asked of you both was too much. Please know, we will all do everything we can to help both of you through this."

I ignore her, breathing through every scream that makes its way out of my chest. I knew what this would do to Harm, and I agreed to do it anyway. What the *hell* is wrong with me? I spent years protecting him, just to tear him apart when duty called.

I hate myself. In every way possible, I hate myself. I hate what I did. I hate that I hurt him. Dammit! My trembling hands tear at my shirt. I lie on my side, curling around my stick. I can't be useless. I want to run and climb and fight and love again, not be this mangled version of me, this helpless, pathetic, hobbling mess. Sobs chug out, one after the other, until I have no breath left. Ragged and trembling, I lie on the grass.

Two strong arms slide under my shaking body. I close my eyes to breathe him in. Sawdust filters in around his scent. Another sob chokes from my throat, and I tuck my head into his chest. Harm.

Tears hit my face. His. His arms shake with every step back to our home. His boot meets the door, and it slams open. The arms around me shift as we sit on the bed, his head resting on mine. Sobs vibrate through his chest, and I grip his shirt, breathing in deep and long. A salty stream runs down my face, soaking his shirt.

An hour later, I wake in our bed. I roll over, sliding a hand his way, but his side is empty, again. I push off the bed. There is a note on the table, just one word: *Hanola's.* Knowing I can't read, he just left a name to tell me where he went.

As I push through Hanola's door, everyone is standing around talking amongst themselves. Harm is standing near the table with Callian, his arms crossed over his chest. He looks up, offering a small smile as I walk closer. Everyone is here except Nirri.

Hanola pushes up from her chair and wanders to the table, coming to stand beside Catori. "Where did we leave off yesterday?" she mutters.

"We were discussing retrieving the power source for the dial," Catori offers.

"Right. Once we have that, we can change the dial."

"There is one problem," Harm interjects. "I couldn't understand any of the symbols on the dial—not one. And there's no translation on the diagrams to help," Harm says.

"There must be parchments or some sort of journal with that information in it. Perhaps we can retrieve those." Hanola looks to me, her face hardened.

"No, not happening. Absolutely not, Hanola," Harm says, releasing his arms from his chest, his face draining of color.

Callian's mouth opens, his eyes scanning Harm. A heartbeat later, Callian flies out the door. Hanola watches him go, her hard expression unchanging.

"Even if I wanted to," I say, looking at Hanola with an expression that matches her own, "I am in no shape to sneak in and out of that tower."

She stares at me, then at Harm, and her expression softens a little.

"There must be some other way of finding out what the symbols mean. Who created the dial in the first place?" Catori asks, her calm, rational voice diffusing the situation.

"Anyone who was around when the dial was created is either dead, or too old to be useful," Hanola says, meeting Catori's concerned gaze.

The door flings open. Callian stalks in with Nirri behind him.

"No one needs to go back into the tower," Nirri says, stopping next to Catori, Callian falling in beside her. "I know every symbol, every mark on that dial. I can teach you, Harm," Nirri says, paying Hanola no heed.

"That's settles it, then," Catori says.

"I can draw them from memory and teach you what they all mean, and I can teach you how to manipulate the dial when the time comes. I've been learning and doing mock runs on that stupid contraption for years," she adds, slightly breathless. Callian grabs the chair Hanola was using and pushes it up behind Nirri. She sits, throwing him a small smile.

"Can you start today?" Miya asks. "The less time we waste on this, the better."

"Yes, all I need is some paper and writing utensils," she says.

The color slowly returns to Harm's face. I release a breath, glad Hanola is not going to ask me to go into that tower again.

"We still need to get into the mountain sector and retrieve the power source," Catori says.

"I can help with that," Mason says. "There was always talk in the barracks of the mountain officers, and their purpose. I have a rough idea of where it is. And when we were in the tower..." He keeps his focus on Catori. Harm stiffens. "... we traced out maps of the mountain sector. The power source is hidden in the center, past the savages, in a fortified small building manned by a handful of Guardians."

"Only a handful to guard the one thing that operates the dial?" Callian says, incredulous.

"I guess the Chancellor figured if you got past dozens of half-mad ex-Guardians, you wouldn't be in any shape to retrieve the Atharex," Mason says.

"So, it's hard to get at, but not impossible?" Harm asks.

"Correct," Mason says—the first word he has said to Harm since he battered his face.

"Who's going over the wall this time?" Harm asks.

"We need the people who stand the best chance of getting in and getting out, and someone who knows what we're walking into," Catori says.

"Mason, Callian, Harm, Catori, Imani, and I will go," Miya volunteers.

"Imani can't go anywhere yet," Callian says.

My cheeks warm with everyone's gaze on me.

"Can you be ready in a month, Imani?" Catori asks.

I stare at her, then at Harm. "Yes."

"Good, that settles it. We have our plan and the team sorted out. Jeselle, Nirri, you stay here. Jeselle and her archers will protect the village. Nirri, you train. We'll need you in that tower eventually," Catori says, rolling up the parchments and maps and handing them back to Hanola.

"Well, now that that's settled and everyone is satisfied, we have something a little happier to plan," Hanola says.

We all turn, waiting for whatever she has in mind.

"My birthday is in three days. I will be eighty years old, and I would like to spend it with my family," she says, looking around the room at each of us. "You have given this old lady so much hope, and I want to celebrate."

Catori smiles and wraps her arm around her grandmother.

"Leave it to us. You will have the best party ever, G'ma," Callian says, rubbing his hands together, shooting a grin at the old lady, who beams back at him.

We file out of Hanola's one by one. I hang back, waiting for Harm. He stands unmoving as everyone else leaves.

"Are you coming?" I ask.

"In a bit," he says, hanging back with Hanola.

"I'll see you later, then," I say, deflated. He doesn't want to walk home with me. Or to training. Or anywhere, really.

I push through the door and out into the warm village center. My mother stands waiting by herself.

"Imani," she says, looking at my leg and stick before returning her gaze to my face, "how is your leg?"

"Fine." I walk past her.

"I was hoping we could talk?"

I stop, looking back. Her hands wring her skirt, her brows lowered and mouth tight.

"I have to get to training."

"Can I at least walk with you, then?"

"I can't stop you from walking around the village, Mother." I continue toward the training area, hoping either Callian or Jeselle will be there.

"How are you settling back in at home?"

So, she is here to vouch for Harm. Typical—it's always *me* that's the problem. "Just fine. Not that it's any of your concern." I quicken my pace.

"Miles would love it if you came to see him. Or perhaps he can visit you?"

"Whatever you want."

"Imani, please." Her hand rests on my arm.

I stop and turn to face her. "Please what?" I hiss.

"Please, just let us in. Let Harm in."

Heat rushes through my neck and into my face. "How is it that *I* am automatically the problem? Everything I have ever done has been the problem, according to you."

"Don't punish Harm for whatever lies between you and me, Imani." Her voice is firm.

"I am not punishing him, Mother. He is punishing *me*. For

doing my job, for taking risks, for being who I am!" I shake my head and stalk toward the training area, my stick hardly touching the ground as I go. Hurt constricts my chest as hot tears sting my cheeks, dripping from my chin.

Callian is cleaning weapons when I get there. Good. I drop my stick and rip a broadsword from the rack, walking to the center of the ring. "Let's train. Everyone wants the old Imani back. Let's get on with it, then!"

Callian's eyes widen, but he draws a sword from the rack and pads toward me in the ring.

I pace in circles, hands shaking, heart thundering in my chest. "Don't even think about taking it easy on me."

He nods, standing ready.

I lunge at him, wincing at the pain that rips through my leg. His eyes move straight to it, slowing his return. I hold his sword steady against mine.

He flings me off, and I spin sideways from the force. He lunges, and I intercept his blade, the impact sending shudders down my arms and spine. I stand my ground, teeth gritted, breathing through every fiery shooting pain in my leg. Pushing him off, I lean back on my good leg. He advances on me, and I spin on my heel, my back to his, rounding behind him. A second later, my sword is across his neck. He drops his and throws his hands in the air.

"Feel better?" he says softly.

"No," I rasp, removing my sword from his throat. I throw the sword back on the rack and from the training area, leaving my stick on the ground where I dropped it.

By the time I reach the village center, the pain is making me nauseous. I head for the healer's shelter. Her gaze widens when she notices me stalking across the shelter without the stick. "Imani?"

"I'm fine. I just need something for the pain."

"The stick is supposed to help you cope with the pain, as well you know."

"I'm not using that thing again," I spit. "I am *not* an invalid!"

She nods and smiles, rummaging through her cart before handing me a small vial. "One drop under your tongue twice a day will help keep the pain under control while you rehabilitate."

"Fine." I close my eyes, breathing out, reminding myself that she has helped me. "I mean, thank you."

"You're welcome, lass, but please don't push yourself too hard." She returns to her work.

I walk home, albeit awkwardly without the stick, hoping Harm will be there.

Voices drift from our house. Harm is home, with Nirri.

"How's it going?" I ask as I amble through the door.

"Fine," Harm says, not looking up from the drawings Nirri has done for him. She pats him on the arm, and he looks up at me. "Where's your stick?"

"I don't need it." I walk as upright and normally as I can manage over to the dresser and slide the top drawer out, placing the small vial in the center of my orange scarf. I turn back, and they are both staring at me.

"What?" I say defensively.

"It's just... your leg was so badly broken," Nirri says.

"It's healing, and I'm training with Callian. Broadswords today. Tomorrow, maybe fighting knives."

Harm's eyebrows raise with the tilt of his head. "Are you sure that's a good idea, so soon? Fighting knives require a lot more movement." His face tightens with concern.

"I'll decide what I can and can't do, Travesci." I stalk out the door, the limp in my leg barely noticeable.

The second I cross the threshold, I want to take the words back. *"Travesci."* Why on earth do I keep doing that—using his name like a weapon? I don't want to fight with Harm; that is the last thing I want to do. But the rift between us is almost impossible to get over with everyone around and everything that is going on. We can't even make it to meals together.

I miss him.

So much that it hurts.

CHAPTER 16
MASON

Every single lantern I hang sits crooked. Catori is going to kill me. This is the one thing she asked me to do today, and I can't get it right. The look on Callian's face when I went to talk to him about Catori has been haunting me all day. How can Hanola be so okay with it, but Callian can't even look at me, let alone imagine Catori and me together? I tug on the lantern, but it just tilts to the other side. Ugh... whatever. No one will notice with all the wine and dancing and piles of food anyway... hopefully.

"All done?" Catori says from behind me.

I step down the wooden ladder and turn to face her. She smiles and sweeps a hand over my hair. My heart leaps in my chest.

"You had leaves in your hair." She laughs, watching them fall from her fingertips to the ground. Her laugh replays in my mind. Pure happiness.

"Yes, all done."

Callian and Nirri are draping long garlands of flowers over tree branches, while Miya and Jeselle arrange the table decorations.

Candles, flowers, and leaves of all colors brighten the long wooden tables we use every day.

"It's going to be gorgeous when we light those lanterns," Catori says, and leans in to peck me on the cheek. Heat flushes my face, and I thank the heavens Callian didn't see it.

Harm is absent, as he has been for most of yesterday and today. No one seems interested in finding him. Whatever secret project he is working on, they all deem it necessary. So, Callian and I are the muscle today.

"Okay, the last long table needs to be shifted under the old fig tree, for Hanola and her special guests," Catori says, looking between Callian and me.

"Fine," Callian says, pushing a flower behind Nirri's ear. We make our way to the last table.

"I promised Imani I would help her train with the knives this afternoon. I'll see you guys later," Catori says, sprinting off to the training area.

I grab one end of the table, and Callian picks up his end. We shuffle our way under the oldest, widest, and most impressive tree in the village.

Callian drops his end, and the table jerks in my hands. His face is stone. "Just because the girls have forgiven you, Rayner, doesn't mean the rest of us have."

"By 'the rest of us,' you mean you and Harm?" I hold his burning stare.

"Something like that."

"Let it go, Callian," Nirri says, resting her hand on his arm. He looks at her for a moment before stalking off. She throws me an apologetic smile and follows him.

With no other pre-party chores, I head to the training area. Imani and Catori are circling each other in the sparring ring. A permanent grimace sits on Imani's face, her bad leg slightly slower than her good one. She is breathing through gritted teeth. Always the fighter. But this time, I suppose, she is fighting for herself.

They break apart, and Catori calls it.

"Enough for today. We'll do some more tomorrow. For now, Jeselle can help you out in the range." She tilts her head toward the long stretch of grass ending in six targets. Jeselle and Miya are both there, firing arrows. They are fast. Jeselle laughs as her arrows find their mark quicker than Miya's. Imani heads in their direction, and I grab a sword from the weapons rack, stepping into the ring with Catori. The corner of her mouth pulls up.

"What was that move you did in the tower? The one where you started off on the ground?" I ask.

Instantly, her smile falls. She sheaths her knives and walks over to the rack. Hands gripping it, her back to me, she doesn't speak. I walk over, standing behind her.

"I'm sorry, I didn't mean anything by it."

She turns slowly, eyes scanning my face. The arrows sailing through the air behind her are the only sound.

"I'm sorry," I breathe. Sorry for her having to be responsible for me. Sorry for getting caught. Sorry for making her do what she did.

"I'm not, Mason." Her chest heaves.

"I mean, I'm sorry you had to take that many men to save me. I put you in that position."

Her mouth tilts slightly, and her hands rest on my chest. "I'm not," she says again, this time barely a whisper. Her green eyes are lit up like I have never seen them before, her breathing rough and deep.

My throat tightens. "I thought I would never see you again." She closes her eyes, but I have to tell her this. "That was the hardest thing: not seeing you again, never having the chance to—"

"Catori," Callian calls from the edge of the village.

I step back, and she drops her hands from my chest.

"Duty calls," she says, rolling her eyes, a grin on her face.

"I don't think your brother is a fan of me being around you. Or anyone, actually."

"Is that so?" She searches my face briefly before stalking off in Callian's direction.

I head to Hanola's, hoping she is well enough to talk to me. Halfway there, Harm falls in beside me.

"Sorry about the other day, Mason."

"You mean when you punched me in the face, multiple times?"

"For that, and everything else that's gone on since you came back." He stops. "Since you came home."

I turn back to him. "She really did fall apart, Harm. It was the hardest thing I've ever watched. She wouldn't let anyone help her. Not me, not even Nirri."

"Nirri knew it was a ruse?"

"Imani told her after a few days. Nirri was so angry about Imani betraying you, and we needed her help. She had to."

"And that's why Nirri helped you?"

"Yeah, I guess so. But Imani also asked her to make sure the parchments and information would get delivered to Hanola—to you—if we failed."

He stares at me, the color draining from his stubbled face slightly as he swallows. "If you were both executed, you mean."

My throat bobs at the thought. "Yes."

He runs a hand through his hair, and sawdust falls from the tufts. I chuckle weakly, trying to lighten the mood, and nod at the sawdust on his shirt. "Been a while since you did that."

"A long time. It's for Imani. Please don't tell her."

"That's fine by me, Travesci. Getting between you two is not exactly a place I want to be. She's nearly as crazy as you." I grin and sidestep away from his punch to my arm. "She's one hell of a girl, Harm. Don't screw this up."

He forces a sad smile as I walk away, looking over my shoulder. Despite the rift between those two, I have a feeling they will be just fine.

Hanola is sitting on her cushions when Mandy lets me in. The elder woman waves a hand, ushering me in from behind her. I sit on a cushion opposite her and wait for her to open her eyes.

"What can I do for you, Mason?" Her eyes are still closed.

"I just wanted to talk to you about something." My stomach flips. Can I really do this? I rest my hands in my lap, my heart thundering in my head.

"You're here about my granddaughter?" she asks, eyes opening above the smile on her lined face.

I draw a long breath, trying to steady my racing heart. "Yes."

She picks up one of my hands in hers. "Young man, I have spent hours with the two of you, and I have known Catori her entire life."

"So, you know that I care about her?" The words are a vast understatement, but a man has to start somewhere.

"Of course I do, Mason. I saw you and who you are—who you *truly* are—long before you arrived in our village," she whispers, leaning toward me.

"Oh... I... I forgot."

"Catori is a different soul. She is one of the strongest people I have ever known—much like yourself. It is no easy feat to grow up in poverty and oppression, become ruined by a regime, lose your entire family, and then be able to rehabilitate the way you have. You two are kindred spirits, my boy." She tilts her head to one side. "And it makes my heart happy to see my granddaughter so happy. I am so glad that she found a way to bring you home."

She doesn't know what Catori did, doesn't know the price she paid to save my life. I nod, and she squeezes my hand.

"Is that all you wanted? My blessing? You have it, child."

"Thank you." Heart thundering in my chest, I try to dim the smile that is forcing its way onto my face. I fail. Hanola beams back at me and nods. With a light squeeze of her frail, soft hands, I stand and pad toward the door.

"Mason." Her classic move, a final piece of advice for you to ponder as you hover over the threshold.

"Yes?" I wait.

"Welcome home. And thank you for ensuring that Imani came home to Harm."

"I told you I would."

I walk out the door to find Callian.

"No way in hell are you and my sister going to be a thing," Callian hisses.

Well, this is going great.

"Catori can make up her own mind about who she's with, Callian," I grind out, forgetting that I came here with the intention of staying calm and asking him to hear my side of the story.

"I meant what I said earlier: you are not forgiven. Not by me. Harm was a *wreck*; it absolutely gutted him. Seeing you touching Imani, pretending you were her husband... I can't even look at you. Get out of my sight before I throw a knife in your chest!"

"Whatever!" I throw my hands in the air and march out of his house—the house I am supposed to be sleeping in. Now it's back to the healer's shelter, I suppose. The lanterns I hung earlier sway in the breeze, as if they too are mocking my intentions with Catori.

Imani is helping with the last of the flowers on Hanola's table under the old fig tree.

"Need a hand?" I ask.

Stepping back from the table to inspect the arrangements, she meets my gaze. "Nope, all done."

Footsteps approach from behind, and Callian takes in the adorned tables. "Nice work," he says to Imani.

"Thanks." She smiles up at him.

I fold my arms over my chest, watching as a group enters the village center. Three personal Guardians flank the few arriving guests. Nirri looks up from her decorating as soon as she hears her grandmother's voice. A grin stretches across her face, and she takes off toward them at a run. Voices excitedly banter back and forth from the village center, Nirri's audible over them all.

"Nirri! My girl, I was so worried about you!" Emmie says, holding her tight. Nirri pushes back from her grandmother, and they stand looking at each other for a moment.

"Elijah!" she cries, flinging herself at the Guardian, who is dressed in the white uniform of a personal guard. I guess Callian has some competition. Elijah wraps his arms around Nirri, holding her tight, running a hand over her hair.

"I've missed you, Miss Nirri," he says, holding her at arm's length, making sure that she is okay.

"I've missed you too," she says, closing the space between them and resting her head against his chest.

We didn't see that in the tower.

Emmie walks around Elijah, resting a hand on his shoulder as if in approval, leaving them with a smile as she heads toward Hanola's.

"Who's that?" Callian asks flatly.

"Elijah, Nirri's personal guard," Imani says.

"Looks like he's more than just her guard," I say, knowing full well that the statement will rub Callian the wrong way.

"Well, at least to Nirri, he is," Imani says, leaving to say hello to the new arrivals.

Callian stares at Nirri, unmoving, arms across his chest.

"Right-o. Fun's over," Miya says. "We have training this afternoon. Callian, you're with Mason."

Oh, great. Just great.

Without a word, Callian strides off to the training area. The rest of us follow. Imani and Catori drop onto the grass. Callian rips a sword from the rack, marching into the sparring ring. I choose a sword and follow, taking up my stance opposite him.

"This should be entertaining," Miya mutters. Jeselle slaps her arm, shaking her head. Harm sinks onto the grass next to Imani. She doesn't look at him.

Callian flips the hilt over and over in his hand, rocking from side to side.

I suck in a deep breath and lunge for him. He meets me halfway, blade raised. The metal clashes together, echoing through the forest. I push off his blade and step sideways. He lunges for me. I evade his blade again, and he spins, bringing it down just shy of my head. I intercept the blow. The force shudders through both of my hands around the hilt and all the way down to my bones as I hold his blade off my face. His chest is heaving, his face is twisted in anger. My arms shake beneath the force of his powerful muscles that have been training for years. I duck down, spinning away before my strength gives out.

Nirri and Elijah walk up to the sparring ring. "How's it going?" Nirri asks Miya.

Miya waves toward Callian. "See for yourself."

Elijah walks over to the weapons rack, running a hand over the blades and hilts.

Callian's focus follows Nirri's voice. He stands for a heartbeat, watching her, sword hanging beside him. That is all the time I need to step into his space and point my blade into his chest. He looks back at me, and his face has changed, softened. Where there was anger before, hurt and longing have taken its place.

"I think that means I win," I say flatly.

"Whatever, Rayner," he snaps, walking out of the training area to return his sword. He watches Elijah as he surveys the weapons, arms folded over his chest, taking a wide stance, just like the sparring stance Miya teaches.

"Right. Imani and Harm are next." Miya waves to them both.

It seems today is the day anyone with an issue has to get out their frustrations with a weapon in their hands. Imani throws Miya a hard look. But Harm rises and pads over to the rack.

"Let's go, Nirri," says Elijah, walking over to her.

"I want to stay and watch the sparring."

"I've seen enough. We're going." He grabs her hand.

Forcing a smile across her deflated face, she straightens her tunic. "Okay, I guess I'll see you all tonight!"

Every one of us goes still watching him lead her away. Callian's hands go white, now gripping the hilts of the daggers strapped to his hips. His face is stone. With a low growl, he finds a spot on the grass next to Catori.

Imani steps into the ring, armed with two fighting knives. Harm wields a sword, his face unreadable as he stares at her. She unwraps her hair, tucking her blue scarf into the weapons belt at her hip, and repositions herself across from him. She waits, staring at him. A handful of heartbeats later, she propels herself toward him, one knife aiming for his side, the other for his neck. He blocks her lower hand and steps out of range of the other. The air between them is thick with every unspoken word, every misread look, every day they were apart. Not a sound can be heard. Nobody speaks. Callian is holding his breath beside Catori. With every ricochet of their blades meeting, over and over, we watch them dance through the pain that tears at them both. Agony pulsing around the rift between them spills from each, simultaneously.

CHAPTER 17
HARM

Hanola's birthday party, with all the flowers, lanterns, and music, brings back every moment of our Blending ceremony. Every touch from Imani, every laugh, every smile, and the first time we let go together. It feels like a lifetime ago. The rift between us is only a small crossing now, but it still keeps her from me. Every day, I try to fix what I broke, praying that we get back to the place we were last time we stood under these lanterns.

Hundreds of people stand around, chatting, laughing, and drinking wine from the small mugs lined up on the kitchen counter, restocked continuously by the busy ladies in the kitchen. Callian and Catori's parents mingle, catching up with the friends they left behind when they moved to the next village over. Callian and Mason sit at our table, not speaking, both looking anywhere but at each other. The girls are not here yet. The crisp white shirt I borrowed from Callian is tucked neatly into the pants I have owned for years. My hair, freshly washed and brushed, is the neatest it has been since the last celebration here.

A small hand tugs on my pocket. Miles.

"Hey, Harm. This party is huge!" His eyes beam.

"Yeah, Hanola's parties are pretty great."

"Where's Imani?"

I chuckle and tousle his hair. "Still getting ready." At least, I guess that's what she's doing; she has been at Catori's for most of the afternoon. I haven't seen her for hours. It gave me time to organize her surprise, the bed I built for her, with a mattress Miya and Jeselle helped me cart home, and pillows and blankets that Petria somehow gathered for us. After all I have put her through, I pray she still wants to share it with me, to share our home. I hope she wasn't with Catori all afternoon just so she didn't have to be at home with me as she got ready, a reminder of the last time we dressed up. The air in my chest evaporates, and I shove my hands in my pockets. I need a drink.

"She'll be here soon. I'll tell her to come find you when she arrives," I offer, and he tears off to join the other children.

Petria pads over to me. With her hair down around her shoulders and wearing a dress most likely borrowed from one of the other women, she looks elegant, so many of her features the same as Imani's.

"Harmen," she says, giving me a brief hug.

"Petria."

"Where is Imani?"

"Getting ready with the girls." I hope she doesn't read into it.

"Really? Okay, have a good night, Harm." She laughs and winks, smiling as she trails after her son.

Apparently, if Imani and I don't arrive at a party together, everyone thinks something is wrong. I guess something still is.

I wander toward the kitchen, picking up a mug of wine. It burns its way down my throat, but I drain the whole cup.

"Drinking alone is unhealthy. You should really share," Callian says, standing behind me.

I pick up another two mugs and pass him one. He takes a sip and scrunches up his face. "This stuff doesn't really get any better," he says.

I laugh at him and take a sip from mine. Callian looks at Mason briefly, then back to me. "The girls are taking their time," he says.

"Well, you know, hair and all that."

He laughs and throws back the rest of his mug, shaking his head as he replaces it on the counter.

We wander back to our table, slumping onto the bench seat next to Mason. People are dancing already, the lively music sending them swaying around, some twirling their partners, some holding tight, ignoring the happy beat of the tune.

Nirri walks around the table, stopping in front of the three of us, Elijah beside her.

"Hey! Harm, Mason, Callian," she says, pointing to us in turn, "this is Elijah."

"Hi," I say, waving.

"We've met," Mason says with a half smile.

"Callian," Nirri says.

He looks up at her. "Hi," he says after a heartbeat. Standing, he holds out a hand to shake Elijah's. Nirri beams as Elijah takes Callian's hand. The slightest grimace registers on the Guardian's face before Callian pulls back, claiming to be thirsty.

"You want to dance?" Nirri asks Elijah, excitement blooming across her face.

"Sure," he says, leading her away, weaving his way through the dancers.

"Elijah: friend or foe?" I quiz Mason.

"I'll get back to you on that one," he says, watching him twirl Nirri around to the joyful music.

"You met him in the tower, didn't you?"

"I did, but he was…" Mason rubs the back of his neck, brows drawing down. "… different there."

We sit, watching Nirri dance around her guard, happiness all over her face. Callian leans against the wine counter, his focus on Nirri, his stance tense.

"Well, you two look happy to be here," Catori chirps, giving us an inquisitive look. Her blonde hair is up and dotted with flowers, two strings of beads wrapped around it, highlighting her green eyes.

Mason goes still beside me. Color flushes her face, but she holds out a hand to Mason, who briefly glances over the crowd at Callian.

"Maybe later," he says. "Can I get you a drink?"

Catori follows his glance, finding her brother. "Sure."

"Hey, stranger," Imani whispers, her body touching mine as she slides onto the seat next to me. My heart skips a beat. I turn to face her. Her hair is up, flowers and beads woven through her dark waves. Her blue eyes are lit with a fire I haven't seen for weeks. A lump rises in my throat, and I breathe through it. She puts a hand on my shoulder, fingers playing with my collar.

"You look nice," she says, her chin wobbling slightly.

Petria watches us from a nearby table.

"Imani," I breathe and stand up, offering her my hand. "Did you want to dance?" My heart thunders in my chest.

"I don't think my leg is up to it," she says quietly. But she manages training just fine; dancing should be easy.

No dancing, then.

Small steps.

A tap on my shoulder. I turn to find Petria.

"Care to dance?" she asks.

I look back at Imani. She is staring off into the distance, no doubt just to ignore her mother.

"Sure." I offer her my hand.

We find the edge of the dancing. Petria shows me where to place my hands, and heat rises in my neck and cheeks. She chuckles, and we start moving to the tune drifting around us. She looks over to Imani and then back to me. I spin her around my outstretched hand. I glance at Imani. She rolls her eyes, looking away.

"Did she just roll her eyes at us?" Petria laughs.

"Yep." A grin stretches my face.

"That girl will never change."

"I hope not."

She squeezes my hand. "Don't give up on her, Harm. She's stubborn, but she loves you. I can see that."

"I don't have any intention of giving up on her."

"Good. She needs you. You ground her."

I look away from Petria, my throat closing up with the tightness in my chest. It's me who needs Imani, not the other way around.

The song ends, and Petria releases my hands. She steps back, her gaze meeting mine. She forces a smile and cups my jaw with one hand, silver lining her eyes. "Thank you... for loving her."

I nod, not capable of words. Her smile widens before she removes her hand and wanders off into the crowd.

I breathe out a long breath and make for the water urns. I grab two mugs and fill them both. Turning back, I find Mason standing in front of me. Waiting for the water urns, he picks up a mug. Callian is only a few feet away.

Catori pushes through the crowd, tracking straight for Mason. Callian straightens up, watching his sister. Catori pulls the mug from Mason's hand and plonks it down on the bench next to the water urn. She grabs his hands. "You and I are dancing." Her face is lit up.

Mason hesitates with a wary expression, glancing at Callian.

"Catori," Callian utters.

"Callian, if I wanted your opinion, I would ask for it." A smirk pulls up on the corner of her mouth. Mason follows along, being led by the hand.

I pass Callian a mug of water. "Well, brother, I guess our girls make up their own minds." Judging by the number of drained wine mugs beside him, he needs it more than me.

He growls, watching his sister dance and spin, holding onto Mason. Happiness radiates from her face.

I return to the bench. Imani sits alone, watching her friends unwind, letting themselves sway and spin with the music. I hand her the mug, and she drinks half before setting it down. I settle down beside her, watching, noting the stark difference between the happy, free people in this forest village, and the darkness that covers the desert side. Despite the desert's bright sun and shimmering golden dunes, the forest is brighter, happier.

The music dies down, and people make for the tables. Food arrives on long platters, placed between the centerpieces on the tables. Mason and Catori sit opposite Imani and me, Miya and Jeselle next to them. Nirri and Elijah plonk down beside me, and Callian squeezes in beside Imani.

The rapid tinging of cutlery against the side of a mug echoes from Hanola's table, and every person in the village center stills. Hanola, flanked by Emmie and her guards, rises.

"Thank you, to all who have come to help me celebrate another decade of life in our wonderful forest. It is a privilege to grow old, but it is a blessing to do so with so many loving and special family and friends. Please enjoy every moment of tonight. I know I will." Holding her hands above her head and releasing a small chant, she claps her hands together, taking her seat.

"To Hanola!" Emmie calls, holding her mug in the air.

"To Hanola!" Every soul in this place echoes the words,

drinking before slamming their mugs onto the wooden tables in one thunderous move. The music bursts to life again, and we eat, the food disappearing from the platters in no time. After our bellies are full, I rise from my seat and extend my hand to Imani. This time I am not taking no for an answer.

"Harm..." she starts.

I hold out my other hand to her.

She stares at my hands. "I don't know if I'm up for dancing."

"I'll help. It'll be fine."

She looks at my hands before placing hers in mine. I walk her into the center of the dancing. A handful of people have wandered back in and are dancing around us, the beat a little slower now that everyone's bellies are full.

I take Imani's hands in mine and place them on my shoulders. I hold her waist and lift her onto my feet. She looks down at our feet, hers on top of mine, before looking up at me and letting out a small laugh. Her face twists, and her chin wobbles. I wrap my arms around her and start moving my feet, taking her with me in wide, goofy steps, just like I used to with Amaya. She rolls her head back, laughing. I slow the steps and make our movements smaller. She breathes out, her chest heaving against mine.

"You know," I say, resting my cheek against her hair, "Travesci is your last name too, if you want it."

She pulls back, looking at me, her eyes burning into mine for a moment, and my heart skips a solid beat. Silver lines her eyes as she grips my shoulders tighter. "I want it," she breathes.

I let go of her waist and wrap my hands behind her neck, and she nuzzles into my chest. I lower my head against hers. "Where you go, I go."

A sob rips from her chest, and I hold her tighter. We dance, her feet on mine for the rest of the song. When the last note plays,

Imani wipes her face and pushes back. She steps off my feet, taking my hand. "Walk with me?"

I nod and follow her through the crowd. She leads me to the grassy training area and lies down. I lie next to her. She stares up at the sky, at the constellations, eyes scanning until she lands on the Harmony stars.

Our stars.

"I looked at these stars every night while I was away." Her breathing is heavy now, and a tear slides down her temple, landing on the grass.

I find her hand with mine, lacing our fingers together. She pulls in a ragged breath as tears flood down the side of her face. "I left you, Harm. How will you ever forgive me for that?"

I meet her gaze, shaking my head while tears burn behind my eyes. "Already done." I prop myself up on my elbow and trace a finger over her cheekbones, over her lips, rubbing the back of my hand over her temple. She grabs my hand.

My breath catches. "What's wrong?"

"I..." Slamming her eyes closed, she sits up. I sit up too, searching her face. Part of me waits for the blow to come. She opens her eyes, and the tears course down her face again. I drop my eyes to the grass, waiting for her to tell something I don't want to hear.

"Harm." Her shaking hands meet mine. "Please look at me."

With air lodged in my throat, I look up at her.

Her chin wobbles, and she steadies herself. "Every minute we were apart hurt. Like there was a fire in my chest, through my whole body, and no matter how many tears I cried, I couldn't put it out. I can't breathe without you."

Her hands wrap around my face, fingers curled around my cheeks. I close my eyes, breathing her in through ragged breaths. I think back to the moment when I was on my knees in our home, struggling to breathe, thinking Imani was gone. Before Hanola told me the truth.

"Can you take me home?" she whispers.

I open my eyes and meet hers. All she needed was my forgiveness, and to know she hadn't lost me. There is nothing else. Guilt for doubting her twists like a blade in my chest. How can loving someone this much be so painful? I nod, my face still in her hands. Standing, I scoop her up in my arms and walk toward home. Imani rests her head against my chest, her hands around my neck.

I kick the front door open, and she huffs a laugh. I set her down in the center of our home, facing the hearth. She watches as I move behind her to rest a hand over her eyes.

"What are you doing?" she whispers.

"I built something for you. It's a surprise."

"Is it outside?"

"Nope." I spin her around to face the bed, my hand still securely over her eyes. Where our small bunk used to be sits a huge canopy bed, with a wide wooden headboard and footboard. White curtains are tied back to the four posts. The mattress, soft and filled with down, is adorned with pillows and cushions of white and blue. A grey blanket lies draped over the end of the mattress. White flowers are scattered over the entire bed. The head of the bed is carved with stars, for Imani.

For us.

I hold her steady, taking her two steps closer. Then I drop my hand. She stands there with her eyes closed. I move behind her and lace my fingers through hers, folding her into my chest. "Open your eyes."

My heart thunders. The roar of the crackling fire in our hearth is the only other sound. She opens her eyes, and her body slackens into mine. A whimper leaves her throat as she unfolds herself from my hold and steps toward the bed. She turns, searching my face, love and wonder plain on hers.

Imani sits on the side of our bed, running a hand over the blankets, touching the pillows. "Oh, Harm..." Her fingers find the carvings on the headboard. She traces each star etched into the dark wood. Her stars—our stars.

"Harmony," she breathes, fingers wandering over the etchings. "It's beautiful! You made this whole thing?" Eyes still fixed on the headboard, she studies the carvings that took me days to trace and etch into the hard wood.

"I needed to keep my hands busy when you were gone, and after you came back. The girls helped with the blankets and cushions." Tears sting my eyes.

Imani stands, stepping into my space. "Where you go, I go," she whispers, running her hands behind my neck, one reaching up through my hair. I pull her into me with one arm, cupping her face with my hand. She rests her head against my forehead. Her breathing becomes heavy.

"Imani," I utter.

"Harm."

"I love you so damn much," I whisper through a strangled sob.

A smile pulls up one corner of her mouth. "Harmen Travesci, I love you more than you will ever know. I always have." Her lips brush mine, and I hold back the moan that threatens to escape my chest. Her hand pulls me into her, her mouth on mine. Imani steps backward, taking me with her. Kicking off her shoes, she hops onto the bed, kneeling, her face level with mine. The fire in her eyes lights up my core. Every inch of me burns for her. She pulls the beads from her hair, and it cascades over her shoulders. I pluck the white flowers from it, throwing them on the bed. She tangles her fingers in my shirt, her soft touch on my chest sending a fire through it. Her fingers release the buttons on my shirt as I plant kisses all over her face. She pushes my shirt up over my shoulders, and it falls to the floor. I kiss her forehead, hands holding her cheeks, moving down to her mouth. She claims mine with ragged breaths. I trace my fingers down her throat and over her collarbone, running one along the binding that rests over her chest. Imani's breath shatters over my mouth, followed by a small moan that disintegrates the last of my control. I pluck at the ribbons of her corseted dress until it hangs loosely from her curves, only just covering her soft breasts. She fumbles with my belt buckle before flinging the belt to the floor with my shirt. Her hands dive into my trousers, and the groan that leaves my mouth rumbles through the both of us. She pulls back, ripping the dress from her shoulders, letting it fall to the bed. I breathe with fiery lungs, watching as she steps down from the bed, letting the dress hit the floor. Every inch of her trembles. With one hand, I push the rest of my clothes to the floor with hers.

"Harm." My name is somewhere between a sob and a plea as she runs a hand around my neck. I pull her hard against me. Running a hand down her back, her curves, I pull her up onto my hips, and she slams her mouth against mine. A breath later, I track kisses down her neck. She leans backward, throwing her head back, and I hold her up, my hands under her back, lips nipping the peaks of her breasts. Shudders echo through her, and the fire in my core threatens to give way.

I lift my head. "Shall we try out our new bed?"

She leans back into me. "Do you even need to ask?"

I kneel on the bed. Imani reaches behind me, tossing cushions to the floor. I lay her on the bed underneath me, and she pulls me down to her, claiming my mouth. I move my knees between hers, and she whimpers. With soft kisses to her neck and shoulders, I lift her hands above her head, lacing my fingers in hers. She breathes out, long and slow. I suck in a long breath, trying to slow down, trying to make every second last. My mouth finds her soft mounds, tracing my tongue around her peaks over and over until she is writhing beneath me, her hips lifting into mine, my name leaving her lips again and again.

I kiss her skin, tracking a path back to her forehead before leveling her gaze. "We will never be apart again," I breathe.

She closes her eyes, arching her back, her chest meeting mine. I rest my head beside her neck for a heartbeat. I have waited for so long for this moment, ever since Hanola told me that Imani had not truly left me, that her heart is still mine and will be forever.

Imani brings her gaze back to mine, tears running down her temples. "Never again. Where you go, I go. Always."

I nudge toward her, and she grabs the back of my neck with one hand, the other still laced with mine. Her hands run down my back, and she pulls me into her, a cry leaving her lips with every inch we join together. She puts both hands around my face as I find my rhythm inside her. With every motion, she arches closer to me. The fire in my core tips around the edge of release. I thrust deep into her, and she finds hers. Release barrels through me, her name ragged on each breath as her hands wander over my chest and face. Her chest heaves, her eyes burning into mine.

I lie beside her, tucking her in close to me. Her breaths slow, and she nuzzles into my side, kissing my neck. I pull the blanket around her and stroke her hair. Her scent winds around me, and I wrap my arms around her. Her breathing steadies as I close my eyes.

Finally, our two hearts have been put back together.

CHAPTER 18
IMANI

Blankets are tucked in around me. Harm is sitting up in bed, reading. I roll over toward him, pushing up off the bed. I lay kisses on his chest and up his neck, finding his mouth. He puts the book down.

"Good morning," he whispers.

"Good morning," I breathe back, my mouth still over his.

"How was the bed?"

"I slept..." I lower to kiss his neck. "... very well, thank you."

He chuckles, his throat bobbing under my lips. "We have to be at Hanola's straight after breakfast."

"I know." I move my legs to kneel over his lap, running kisses down his chest again, my hair falling around his torso.

"I didn't want to wake you earlier. You looked so peaceful, so happy." His voice is raw and low.

"You should have. I'm offended you picked that book over me." I make my way back up his neck before leaning back.

"It's a good book," he says, a grin across his face.

I nip his ear, and his hands run down my back. "We only have five minutes before breakfast."

"We should spend it wisely, then," he growls, pulling me over his hard length. As I sink onto his lap, a moan slips past my lips, and a heartbeat later, his mouth finds mine.

I pull my training clothes on, tugging the dresser open to find my blue scarf. With a well-executed twist and wrap, my hair is up and secured in minutes. Harm is waiting by the door for me. We wander through the homes, his arm around me. My leg is still slightly awkward, and my limp is a little deeper after yesterday from the sparring and dancing.

"You okay?" he asks.

"Yeah, it just niggles sometimes. Yesterday must have made it flare up a little."

His eyebrows lift slowly.

"The sparring, Harm, not last night!" I can't keep the smile from my face. He laughs, and it vibrates through me, his arm still around my shoulders. Heaven knows that is my favorite sound.

When we reach the tables, Callian, Catori, and Mason are already there. Miya and Jeselle sit next to Mason. We sink onto the bench seat across from them, and all eyes turn to us. It's the first time we have arrived at a meal together since I came home. A smile tugs at Callian's face.

"I see you two made up," Catori says, smiling.

"That must have been one hell of a bed you built, brother," Callian says, cheekiness lighting up his eyes.

Mason beams at me. I remember his words to me in the tower. *"Harm will forgive you, Imani. He won't even have a choice."*

I fix my gaze on Callian's, plucking a piece of fruit from the platter in the center of the table. "Oh, it is." I put the fruit between my teeth and rip it in half. Callian chokes on his mouthful. Miya snorts water trying to hold in her laugh. Harm throws his head back, laughing at the blush that fills Callian's face. Jeselle slaps Miya on the shoulder, trying to keep a straight face.

"You did open that door, little bro." Catori laughs at him. He chuckles, clearing his throat. I laugh with him, tossing a piece of fruit at his head. He plucks up a piece, tossing it back at me.

We quickly finish our meal, with random chuckles now and then as we enjoy the food and one another's company. When everyone is done, we make our way to Hanola's. Catori and Mason walk in front of us. Callian leads the way to his grandmother's, talking with Miya and Jeselle. Catori looks back at me, offering a smile that tells me she is happy for me. I smile back, and she beams. Turning back to the path ahead, she slips her hand into Mason's, lacing her fingers in his. He squeezes it tight, leaning over briefly to peck her cheek.

Harm looks at me, then at Catori and Mason. "You knew?" he whispers.

I nod at him.

"Since when?"

"Since the tower," I whisper, leaning on his arm, my hand in his.

"Oh."

"Yes, 'oh,' Harmen Travesci, you idiot." I dig him in the ribs with my free hand.

"Ouch, what's that for?"

"For thinking for a split second that I would ever leave you."

He stops dead in his tracks and turns to face me, hand still holding mine.

"What did you think went on in that tower?" I ask, the amusement gone from my voice.

He closes his eyes, letting loose a long breath.

"Why would you think that?"

He opens his eyes, gaze burning into mine. "I don't know, Imani. I guess all logic went out the window when Mason put his arm around you on that bridge," he whispers, holding my arms.

"Well, I sincerely hope you found it again. We're going to need it very soon." Pushing up on my toes, I kiss his mouth, his hands still wrapped around my arms.

"I did, hours later, when Hanola told me you had been sent there, that you didn't just leave—not by choice." His hand runs behind my neck and under my hair. "It was torture, you being there, us being apart." He leans into me and lays a kiss on my forehead. "Oh, and keeping it from Callian. Actually, that was the hardest part, come to think of it," he says, standing upright and backing away with a grin. I slam a fist into his chest, and he scoops me up, spinning me around, planting his mouth on mine. I wrap my arms around his neck. He stops spinning, his kisses so gentle and exquisite over my mouth. I bite his lip, plunging my tongue into his mouth. He groans quietly.

"If you two are quite done, we have a war to win," Catori throws our way.

I pull back from Harm's face, and he sets me down. Catori stands by her grandmother's door, a smile covering her face. She swings her arms toward the door, ushering us in. A small laugh leaves her mouth as Harm walks in behind me, his hands on my shoulders, planting a kiss in my hair. We make our way to the table. Every face around the table is lit up with happiness.

"No Nirri today?" Harm whispers to Callian, who stands crossing his arms and shifting on his feet.

"Nope. She's giving Elijah the grand tour."

Hanola clears her throat, and we all look to her as she checks that we are all paying attention.

"Have you been able to learn the symbols and translations for the dial with Nirri?" Hanola asks Harm.

"Yes, I can now understand most of the symbols. I've also been studying the diagrams and the information on the dial, and I've come up with a few different options to change it so that every sector has balanced weather."

"Excellent." She leans on her stick. "To get the most done in the least time, we need to ensure that every part of our plan unfolds at the same time. There will be two phases, which I will work through with you all. We will need to take out the wall, seize the prison near Etonia, take the tower, and change the dial, all within an hour of each other. We cannot afford to let the Chancellor have time to react, time to retaliate. If he does, many lives will be lost." Hanola grips her stick as she breathes out, scanning the unrolled parchments on the table.

"Do you think the mountain men would be of any use if we need numbers? I mean, they were sent to that place, shoved in with the savages, all against their will," Catori says.

Mason's gaze lingers on her face for a moment, as if thinking it over in his head, weighing the possibility.

"It's possible, but it's also possible that they just want to be left alone, or that their loyalties still lie with the Chancellor," Miya says.

"I guess there's only one way to find out." Every face turns to me. "We just have to ask them."

"We'll leave that to you, Imani," Jeselle jokes. I give her a coy look.

"For now, we will work on getting you all in shape to get over that wall and get back with the power source," Hanola says. "Then when we have everything we need, when every man and woman is ready, we will coordinate with the desert side and lay siege," Hanola says, raising a hand to let us know we are dismissed. We all wander to the doorway.

"Harm, Mason, could you stay, please? I have some small details to iron out with you," she says.

Harm rests his hands on my shoulders and kisses my forehead.

"Ready for an ass-whooping?" Callian jokes, wrapping a heavy arm around my shoulders.

Harm flicks me a brief semi-amused look, and Callian steers me out the door. He drops his arm when we cross the threshold, walking beside me.

"Imani," he starts.

I look up at him, and his usually jovial features are twisted, brows lowered. "What is it?" I ask, looking ahead, hoping I have the answer to whatever he is about to ask me.

"I'm sorry." He rests a hand on my shoulder.

I stop and turn to face him. "It's okay, Callian. I know you were just looking out for Harm."

He looks toward the training area and Catori.

"Harm is lucky to have you," I tell him. "I'm glad he had you..." I drag air into my lungs. "... when I wasn't here."

He turns back to me briefly. Walking toward the training area, he wraps an arm around me again, and I hold onto his hand.

"You know, I always wanted a brother," he says, a bounce now in his step beside me.

"I heard." I laugh.

"And now I've got one." He releases his arm from my shoulder and turns to face me squarely. "And I gained a sister too."

I step into his space and wrap my arms around his bulky shoulders. "Yes, you did." I squeeze him tight before releasing him.

One brow lifted, he says, "You do realize I'm still going to run you ragged with training today?"

I roll my eyes at him. "Do your worst, brother." I march toward the training area, my limp almost unnoticeable.

Three hours later, my limp has deepened again, and Callian shows no sign of letting up. The sky has turned dark, and we spin and lunge together in the rain. My hair and scarf are soaked, and my sweat mingles with the rain that slides down my body. The hilt of my broadsword slips in my hands with every motion. My chest heaves with every fiery breath, despite the cool rain that pelts down around us like a never-ending curtain.

I hang my blade at my side, waiting for Callian to take up his offense again. Harm walks over to the sparring ring, his hair tousled by the rain, his face wet with drops sliding over a day's worth of stubble. His wet clothes hang limply on his tall, muscular frame.

Callian strikes, and I refocus on the blade flying toward me. I hold his weapon off for a heartbeat before slipping out from under his downward force, spinning sideways. Three steps later, I am behind him, the point of my sword resting against the back of his neck. He slams his sword behind him, and I step out of range.

Harm watches, tracking every move I make, eyes lit with fire. I stand, waiting for Callian to lunge again. He sends a look to Harm, then a smile pulls up his face. He lunges for my left, and I sidestep away from him. My feet are swept out from under me, and I'm pressed against Harm's chest, strong arms holding me. Callian lets out a laugh before sheathing his sword.

"Like our new move?" Harm whispers, flicking his brows up briefly.

"Very funny, you two."

Callian winks as he walks out of the sparring ring. "I'm done for the day."

Harm doesn't put me down. Instead, he heads for the forest.

"Where are you taking me?" Rain pelts down all around us, running over his face. I place a hand on each side of his jaw and slam my mouth onto his, eyes closed. The soggy underbrush of the forest snaps beneath his steps. Minutes later, he sets me down on a fallen log, leaning me against the tree that grows behind it. His thumbs trace my cheekbones as he plants a kiss on my mouth. I run my hands through his hair. Water flies from my hands as I shove them inside his wet shirt. He steps closer, between my legs. He trails kisses down my wet neck, one hand behind my neck and one behind my back, drawing me closer.

Suddenly, yelling drifts through the rain and the thick tree line. I freeze.

Harm stops, raising his head to level his gaze with mine. "What is it?"

The yelling gets louder. My stomach plummets. "Something is wrong."

I look past his shoulders, and he turns to face the village. Through the curtain of mist and rain, through the trees, a group is gathering between the training area and the northern edge of the forest. I jump down from the log and grab his hand, weaving through the trees at a run, toward the yelling that has now turned to screaming.

Nirri.

Nirri is screaming.

CHAPTER 19
MASON

Six Guardians stand beside Elijah. His face is pained, but his body is still. Callian stands rigid, hands on the weapons at his hips. With a fire lit in his eyes, every muscle alive, he waits. Nirri is pleading with the Guardians, one of whom holds her by the hair. The others form a tight half circle around the officer holding her. Each man in uniform has a small weapon at their side, incomparable to the ones Callian carries. This is not going to end well for them.

Callian is silent, still waiting.

Catori runs up, halting beside me. She swears under her breath before stepping forward, her hands extended in front of her, like she is approaching a crazed animal. She is so calm. "Let her go."

"I don't think so, tree girl. We have orders to retrieve three persons from this village: Nirri, Imani Fletcher, and the traitor standing behind you." He nods to me.

Instantly, Catori steps between us. "They will not be going with you."

"Catori, be reasonable. Let them go, and nobody needs to get hurt," Elijah says. The distaste in his voice prompts Callian to step forward.

"I said, no one is leaving," Catori growls.

Nirri cries out as the officer holding her hair moves, trying to drag her backward.

Catori steps back with a look at her brother before meeting Elijah's gaze. "Very well. You've made your choice."

Imani and Harm arrive at a run. Out of breath, they stop one on either side of me. Imani takes a wide stance, reading Catori's position, and pulls her fighting knives out, flipping them over in her hands.

"Elijah, please tell them we're not going back with them," Nirri begs.

He stares at her before walking behind the other officers.

Nirri's eyes widen, her mouth gaping. "Elijah, no! What are you doing?"

Two officers make to retrieve me. Catori pulls her weapons from her chest, poised to throw both into any man who dares move in my direction.

Thundering of heavy hooves closes in on us. Every head turns to see Emmie astride her horse. The old lady's face is full of fear, and she dismounts in a hurry. Running through the mud, holding her dress up, she stops directly in front of the officer holding her granddaughter. "Let her go this instant!"

The officer doesn't move.

"Are you deaf?! Unhand her, now!"

"We have orders from the Chancellor. You have no authority here," the officer holding Nirri seethes.

Emmie grabs his hand, pulling his fingers from Nirri's hair. Nirri cries out in pain and whips around, shoving a knee into his groin. He doubles over instantly, and the next officer steps in to take Nirri. Emmie rushes at him, putting herself between the officer and her granddaughter.

"Don't take another step," she breathes, half bent over, gripping her side. He scowls at her, grabbing her by the arm.

Nirri's eyes widen. "No, stop it, you'll hurt her!"

"Let go of me, or your career will be short-lived, young man," Emmie breathes, pointing at his chest. On the inside of her wrist, a black mark sits on the fine, wrinkled skin—a bird in flight.

Oh, hell. Emmie bears the mark of the rebellion, just like Harm's birthmark, in broad daylight, for Arthur to see every day. She has been hiding in plain sight. Knowing the way his chauvinistic mind works, he probably thinks it just some silly female token.

Oh, this is just perfect.

The officer releases his grip on Emmie. Nirri steps between them, and he raises his hand to slam it into Nirri's face. Emmie drags her back, pulling Nirri out of his path, and his fist collides with Emmie's temple.

She drops to the ground.

Nirri spins. "No!" Dropping to her knees, she shakes her grandmother with frantic hands. Then she rolls her onto her back. Emmie's eyes are wide, the pupils just tiny points of black, her breathing ragged. Harm sinks down beside Emmie on the other side. He rests his ear on her chest. The rise and fall stops. He looks up at Nirri and shakes his head.

Nirri slumps to the ground, screams ripping from her throat. Callian looks at her, pain tightening his eyes, breaths ragged, hands white around each of his blades.

Nirri stands slowly and stalks toward the officer. He pulls his shoulder back, his hateful eyes burning into her. "Will you be coming freely now?" he spits.

Tears stream down her face. "Go to hell!" She turns from him to walk back over to her grandmother, and the officer steps in behind her, grabbing her arm. She spins around and slaps his face, hard, the crack resonating through the forest. In unison, the Guardians' eyes turn vacant, hands drawing their daggers.

Callian stills.

I almost feel sorry for the mindless officers. Catori grabs Nirri, pulling her out of Callian's range. Imani stands next to Nirri, wrapping an arm around her. Harm looks at me, I move to Emmie, and we lift her, carrying her away. I stare at her face. She was protecting her granddaughter. One moment, she was full of fire and life, and the next, she is staring blankly at the rain that falls on her unmoving face.

"Hand over the three traitors now," the officer snaps.

Callian flies at them, brandishing his blades in all four directions. The first man down is the officer who held Nirri by the hair. His blood mixes and fades into the growing puddles. Two other officers rush the warrior, and he meets both with the edges of his fighting knives across their wet throats. The remaining three circle him. He sheathes his knives and draws out his sword, the whine of the blade dulled by the pouring rain. He doesn't wait for their advance, lunging at the middle officer, impaling him instantly. The man drops into the mud before toppling face-first into a puddle at his feet. The other two flank Callian, thinking one can be bait and one can attack. But he simply spins on the spot, running the blade through each when they take a fatal step toward him.

Elijah stands frozen in the rain. Callian stalks toward him, rain dripping off his shaggy blond hair and coursing down his arms, alive with the thrill of the fight. His chest heaves with every labored breath. Elijah backs up a step, holding a hand up in protest. Callian stalks closer, not stopping.

"Callian, no!" Nirri chokes.

Callian raises his sword over Elijah. Catori adjusts her grip on Nirri.

"No! Callian, *stop*!" Nirri screams.

Elijah looks at Nirri briefly before turning his gaze back on Callian.

"Please, don't," Nirri sobs.

Callian grabs Elijah by the arm, sword still raised. He spins him around, tossing the blade in his hand to adjust his grip on the hilt, then slams it into the back of Elijah's head. Elijah falls to the ground, unconscious, but alive.

Callian stalks toward Nirri, eyes blazing. He brushes past her before marching for Hanola's. Catori releases Nirri, and she sinks to the ground, lying over Emmie, arms wrapped around her grandmother's body.

Hanola's cries echo through the village moments later. We stand and watch her hobble frantically toward her friend, face scrunched up in agony, hands trembling. Catori helps her down to the muddy ground on the other side of Nirri. Hanola looses a cry that sends shivers up my spine, raising a lump in my throat. Tears stream down Catori's face, her gaze fixed on her own grandmother.

We all stand there in the pouring rain, watching Nirri and Hanola mourn the only person who stood between the forest people and the Chancellor.

"Since when do Guardians carry weapons?" Harm asks.

Catori's eyes hit the floor. Her grandmother looks between me and Catori.

She knows.

Hanola holds Catori's gaze now. "Every action has a consequence."

"What happened to Elijah?" Nirri asks, almost in a whisper.

Callian slides a heated look her way. "He's in the cells, for now."

Nirri rushes out. Callian follows her. We watch from the living room of Hanola's home, the door wide open. They only make it past the threshold before Callian starts in on her. "Why are you defending him?"

"He's my friend." She raises her chin, stepping closer to Callian.

He grabs her arms, looking down at her face, upturned to his. "He would have *killed* you, Nirri."

"Elijah is my friend. He wouldn't have let them hurt me."

"They were already hurting you, and he let them!"

She rips her arms from his grip. "He protects me."

"He sure as hell wasn't protecting you just now!"

"He was outnumbered," she protests, walking in circles.

Callian steps up to her and grabs her arms again, turning her to face him. "That blow was meant for *you*, Nirri! You would have been the one who wound up dead."

Nirri slackens in his grip.

Catori flies to the door, hesitating.

"Shut up, Callian! Shut up!" Nirri screams at him.

"No. Open your eyes!" he hisses at her.

She scrunches her face up at him, sobbing through labored breaths.

"Callian," Catori warns.

"Nirri, you have to see what he is!" Callian's rough tone turns pleading.

Harm walks over to stand beside Catori.

"Please, before it's too late," Callian says, releasing Nirri, stepping back. His chest is rising and falling in deep cycles, hands shaking by his sides.

Harm walks over and puts a hand on his shoulder. "Brother."

Callian turns to him, eyes burning in agony.

Catori leads Nirri home, cuddling her sobbing shoulders with every step through the rain. Callian stalks off, hands running through his wet hair.

"Callian!" Harm calls, worry in his voice. Then he comes back inside, sinking onto a cushion next to Imani. Catori returns moments later. Callian doesn't return, nor does Nirri.

"What do we do now?" Catori asks her grandmother.

"We bury our friend and carry on with everything else. Things may need to happen faster, now that Emmie is no longer here to serve as the buffer between the forest villages and the Chancellor." Grief laces her words, her face carrying the sadness of one who has lost something very dear to them.

"How was it that she kept the Chancellor from infiltrating this forest in the first place?" I ask.

Catori slides closer to me. Hanola's mouth pulls up on one side, noticing the not-so-subtle move of her granddaughter.

"It was a promise made on their daughter's deathbed, a long time ago," Hanola explains. "When Nirri was born, her mother was dying. Emmie begged Arthur to send for a healer from the desert side. Ours had tried to help her and failed. Enid was the only healer left who would have been able to save Nirri's mother. The damage from the birth was substantial. But Arthur refused to let anyone from the desert side over the wall, knowing that if he did, the people would realize they were being controlled, oppressed. Emmie tried to reason with him, begging him to put their daughter's life before his own schemes. He did not relent. Ultimately, the forest healer could not save Nirri's mother. She died, leaving Nirri with Emmie. She was Emmie's only grandchild, her life's joy." Hanola sucks in a breath, resting a hand over her wobbling chin. "Emmie was heartbroken. Arthur eventually tried to fix things with her, and she promised that if he left the forest people alone and didn't do to them what he does to the desert dwellers, she would forgive him."

"And?" Imani asks.

"He agreed—but had the forest healer executed for her inability to save his daughter. Emmie was my friend, and for decades, we have helped each other. Enid is also my friend, and the only person who could have saved Nirri's mother." Hanola looks to Harm and Imani.

"She saved my mother and me during childbirth as well," Imani says. Harm turns his head to look at her. "That blue glass bottle she was given by the woman's husband for saving her life in childbirth —that was Fletcher. The bottle was my mother's, and I was the baby she saved. She saved both of us," Imani finishes.

Realization registers on Harm's face. Then he huffs out a laugh of awe at the memory it must have triggered.

"Three old ladies plotting and scheming against the one man in power," Hanola muses, fire in her eyes. "But the time has come for your generation to carry on our work, now that Harm and Catori are almost ready." She smiles at Catori, who shifts on her cushion beside me.

Hanola's face turns grim. "Just this morning, my scouts returned with some disturbing news. A small group of Guardians has been seen in the forest, between this village and the next. Close to where the boys found Imani and Nirri."

Catori stiffens, her brows lowering.

"So, it has started already—the scouting for the outposts," I say.

"It appears that way." Hanola nods.

"What do you want us to do?" Catori asks.

Her face is stone. "Pay them a visit. But please remember, our cells are almost full."

This is something we have never seen from Hanola: the willingness to end a life. Things have definitely changed. A pit in my stomach grows with every minute that she is quiet.

"Imani and Catori, you can go, and bring back as much information as you can. But I don't want another Guardian in my villages," she finishes and pushes off the floor. Catori jumps up, offering her a hand.

"We will leave tonight," Catori says to Imani.

"Make sure you both return unharmed," Hanola says, wandering toward her daybed, exhausted from the events of the day.

I stand with Catori and walk toward the door, and Imani and Harm follow us out.

"You'd best go pack some things. Meet you back here in an hour," Catori says to Imani.

Imani nods and laces her fingers through Harm's as they wander through the homes toward their own. I walk with Catori to her house. She doesn't say a word.

We push through the door, and Nirri is sitting on the chair facing the fire, staring at the flickering flames that threaten to die out at any second. I walk over to the metal wood rack and grab two logs. Squatting in front of the fire, I toss them on. Embers shoot skyward, flames engulfing the logs instantly.

"I need to check on my brother," Catori says, unwrapping her hair. "Come for a walk?"

"Sure."

We amble through the village slowly.

"Do you want me to come with you tonight?" I ask.

"Imani and I will be fine. Besides, it's safer for you to stay here. Miya, Callian, and Jeselle will make sure no other Guardians get past our tree line from now on."

I stop, and she turns back to face me, eyes weary, worry lining her face. I step up to her, placing a hand on either side of her face.

Her fingers curl around my wrists. She smiles weakly, her lips trembling as silver lines her eyes.

"Everything will be alright, Catori," I whisper, pressing my forehead to hers.

Her fingers grip my wrists harder, and she lets out a long breath. "I know. I just have a feeling it's going to get a lot harder before it gets better."

"If that happens, we will get through it, together."

"Together," she whispers back. Those were the exact words she spoke to me when I was working through my transition from ruined Guardian to someone who is almost whole again. She did that for me. Now, I can at the very least help her, if she wants me to.

"I should check on Callian. Something has got him all over the place. He's not usually this upset about things, even when they hit close to home like this." She pulls away from my hands.

I let her go, and she smiles back at me before walking into Callian's home.

CHAPTER 20
HARM

Imani's side of the bed is cold. I remind myself that she is only gone for two nights, with Catori. They will be fine. They will come back.

I dress and wander to breakfast. Mason, Nirri, Miya, and Jeselle are already eating theirs, and I sit opposite Mason. "Morning," I say.

They acknowledge me through the chewing and chatter. Nirri is pushing her food around her plate with her fork. Mason stares off into the distance, chewing slowly.

"Morning," Callian says, dropping down beside me, but his gaze tracks to Nirri. She drops her fork and pushes off the bench.

"Nirri, wait—" Callian starts.

She stalks away from the table. Callian rises and follows her. "Nirri," he says, and she whirls to face him, arms folded across her chest, eyes burning with grief and anger. Callian's hands hang at his sides. He starts and stops speaking a few times. She shakes her head.

"I'm sorry," he says, stepping toward her. "I'm sorry about

yelling at you, and I'm so sorry about your grandmother. Truly I am."

We have all stopped eating, watching Callian and Nirri. Her face is twisted into a look of hurt, sadness, and anger. Callian is motionless while she seethes at him, shoulders shaking.

Without a word, she storms off toward Catori's. Callian hangs his head for a moment before returning to our table. He sinks down beside me and throws a few pieces of food onto his plate. He stares at it, not touching it. I pour him a mug of water, and he takes it.

"Yesterday was a hard day for her. But things will get better," I say.

He looks at me for a handful of heartbeats before putting his mug down and shoving his plate away from him. "I'll see you at training." He leaves the table and walks toward home.

I pile my plate with food and eat, knowing how much energy I will burn in training.

Mason turns to me, fruit in his hands, and takes a bite. "We should get as much information out of Elijah as we can before our next meeting with Hanola," he says, dropping the piece of fruit back on his plate.

"Probably. But I don't think bringing Callian would be such a great idea."

"Nor do I. Later this afternoon, then?"

"Yep, after training. We'll see how the day shapes up." I finish the last of my food and wash it down with a mug of water. I jog through the village to the training area, hoping Callian is already there.

He is. Throwing the sandbags we use to run with into a pile, his frame is alive with exertion. He doesn't look up. I pick up one of the heavy bags and help.

Miya and the others arrive moments later, Nirri included.

Jeselle is talking with her, arm over her shoulders. Miya stops beside the weapons rack, waiting for everyone to focus. We all move closer. Callian picks up another bag and throws it on the pile.

"You too, Callian," she says, crossing her arms.

He blows out a breath and wanders over, not looking at anyone but Miya.

"Right. This morning, we're going to team up. Mason and Harm, you're on fighting knives in the sparring ring. Jeselle and I will take the broadswords, and Callian and Nirri, you can take turns on the climbing pole. I want to see agility and speed from both of you."

We all stare at her.

"Miya…" Jeselle protests.

"You have your orders. Off you go," she barks at Nirri and Callian.

He walks toward the climbing pole and stands beside it, waiting for Nirri.

"That's just cruel." Jeselle shakes her head at Miya.

"Callian's a big boy. He can handle it. Besides, they need to get their stuff sorted out. We have less time now than we did before." She waves the rest of us off.

Mason picks two knives from the rack, tossing them in his hands as if weighing them. I select two for myself and make my way to the ring. I stand facing Callian, not wanting to let him out of my sight.

Mason walks into the sparring ring, but comes to stand beside me instead of opposite me. "What do you think is going to happen there?" he asks.

I sigh. "I'm not sure. But Nirri is hurt and angry, and Callian is paying the price for it."

"From what Imani told me when we were at the tower, Elijah has been Nirri's only friend for around three years. A betrayal like that is harsh. I'd be more worried about her than Callian." Mason's gaze meets mine.

"Maybe," I utter, not wanting to hint at Callian's feelings for Nirri. If Mason hasn't picked up on them, I'm not going to be the one to tell him.

"Ready, Travesci?" Mason grins.

"When you are, Rayner." I lunge before he can raise a knife. He meets mine with his crossed over his head. Head shots are too easy for him. I shove him off and lunge for his side and throat, and his arms swing open, blocking both. He spins from the force of my blows and turns away, buying only a second before I advance on him again. But he is fast and drives his knife toward my chest and neck before I can retreat. I sidestep him and adjust my grip on the knives.

Nirri's cry splits the air. Callian stands under her, yelling instructions as she hangs from the top of the swaying climbing pole. We drop our knives and run for the pole, Miya and Jeselle falling in behind us.

"What happened?" I ask.

"She made it to the top in no time, but froze. I've been trying to get her to release her grip and start climbing down. She can't," Callian says, his focus locked on Nirri.

Nirri clings to the top of the pole, fear frozen on her face. "Please, I can't hold on any longer!"

"Her hands must be cramping up," I say.

Callian grabs a metal rung above his head and pulls himself up the pole faster than I have ever seen him go. Nirri stares at him, shaking. The pole sways with his weight under hers.

"What are you doing?! The pole will fall!" Nirri cries, her knuckles now white on the metal rungs.

"It won't. I've had to do this before," he says calmly. "I'll take you down."

She shakes her head violently at him.

"Nirri, if you fall—"

"No, don't touch me!" She moves away from him. "You can't carry me *and* climb down."

"Yes, I can. Please let me hold onto you."

She shakes her head, terrified eyes burning into his. Callian moves in beside her. The pole sways with his weight at the top. He wraps an arm around her waist, but she clings desperately to the post. "No, please don't, you'll drop me!"

"Nirri, I am not going to let you fall," Callian says softly. She whimpers and tries to let go with one hand, but grabs the metal rung again.

"Just put your arms around my neck, and I'll sit you on my hip and climb down," he says.

She stares at him for a heartbeat. The wind picks up, and the pole sways again as her eyes widen further.

"Okay, but just until I can reach the lower rungs."

"Whatever you want. We just need to get safely down from this height."

She nods and shoots a hand to his shoulder, legs still wrapped around the pole.

"Now your other hand," he says.

She sucks in a breath and grabs his other shoulder. He pulls her from the pole, and her legs wrap around his waist. Her eyes widen, then she slams them shut.

Callian climbs down the pole with one arm. He reaches the ground before Nirri opens her eyes and looks up. He lets her down, one arm still wrapped around her waist.

"You're safe," he breathes.

Her face changes in an instant. "Get your hands off me!"

His mouth falls open, and hurt lances through his eyes. "Nirri, I was just trying to help."

"Elijah would never manhandle me like that! Get away from me!" She backs away from him.

Dammit.

"How about I take you back to Catori's?" I offer, and she nods, wrapping her arms around her chest.

I walk beside Nirri, wanting to say a million things to her about Callian, but I keep my mouth shut. Now is not the time. We walk past the eating area, which is empty, save for the three ladies who work in the kitchen.

"Can you take me to see Elijah?" she asks, chin tilting upward, stopping to turn and look at me.

"Nirri..." I hesitate. "I don't think that is a good idea."

"Why?"

"Because he's our prisoner now. He betrayed you. Why do you want to see him?"

Fire fills her eyes. "None of you know him like I do. There must be a reason he did what he did."

She is right. I am sure there is a reason why he was her friend, why he made her think they had something special. But I don't think it's the reason Nirri thinks it is. Maybe it would be better if Callian were there to interrogate him; I doubt he would respond to anything, barring fear. For Nirri's sake, I am going to find out just what he is playing at.

"I'm fine from here," she says.

I stop and watch as she walks home to Catori's before I make my way back to the training area. Callian is sparring with Miya. She is the only person that can intercept his blows at the moment. The smashing metal of their swords is deafening. Callian's face is rigid, creased with hurt and frustration. Miya concedes, and Callian drops his sword onto the rack. He stalks past me.

I turn and follow, catching up to his fast gait. "You want to talk about it?"

"Nope," he growls.

"How about we run it off, then?"

He looks at me briefly, then takes off for the forest. A few strides later, I am sprinting alongside him. We crash through the tree line, and he plows through the undergrowth. I fall in behind him, letting him work through every word she said to him, every fiery look she gave him.

We reach a clearing, and he stalks in a circle, hands on his head, each heavy breath sucking in air. I bend over, drawing in deep breaths. "You okay?" I rasp.

"I'll live, I guess." He lowers his hands to his sides before pulling each one across his chest to stretch them in turn.

"Good, because I have a meeting with Hanola, and then Mason wants to question Elijah. You up for that?"

"Yep," he replies flatly.

I almost feel sorry for Elijah.

The meeting with Hanola only takes ten minutes. She wants me to think about what happens after the dial is changed, where I want to be, what my role will be. I am to have an answer for her in three days—like that's so easy to figure out, like I haven't been thinking about it since the day I left Amondo. I still don't know. I know things have to change. How do I make that happen, with no idea about governing a people or making a viable community of prosperous families? Nirri, at least, has had training. Catori has grown up knowing her entire life that she will take her grandmother's place.

The thoughts leave me as soon as I round the last house before the cells, and Callian and Mason stand waiting for me, arms crossed over their chests.

"It would probably be best if Mason asks the questions," I say to Callian.

Callian glances at Mason. "Fine by me. I'm just here to make sure he answers."

We walk through the cell door, one after the other. Every set of eyes within the small forest prison tracks our steps. Elijah sits on the floor of the cell Mason occupied months ago.

"Ah, this looks familiar," Mason says, shoving his hands in his pockets. I roll my eyes at him, a move I learned from my wife. He stifles a chuckle and composes his face. Callian comes to a halt beside Mason, arms still across his chest, head back, face unreadable. I stand beside him, watching Elijah scan the three of us. A sliver of fear whips through his gaze.

"We have a few questions for you, Elijah," Mason starts.

Callian shifts beside me.

"Catori found this written order in one of the officer's shirt pockets. Shall I read it to you?" Mason continues.

Elijah swallows, his gaze fixed on the paper in Mason's hands.

"'By order of the Chancellor, via the Guardian regime, the following persons are to be retrieved for execution: Harmen Travesci...' " He pauses, looking at me. I keep my face neutral, despite the fact that this is the first I have heard of this written order. "'... Imani Fletcher, Mason Rayner, and Nirri Westly.' " He folds up the paper. "How long have you known Nirri was to be executed for helping Imani and me?" Mason growls.

"I'm not telling you anything," he spits.

Callian turns and walks back to the guard. Keys clink as they exchange hands, and Callian stalks to the cell door. Within seconds, the door is open, and Callian has Elijah hard against the stone wall by the throat with one hand.

"Answer his question, and I'll let you breathe," Callian seethes.

"Ever since she left," he chokes out. Callian releases one finger.

"Was killing Emmie part of the plan?" Mason asks.

Elijah doesn't speak. Callian shoves him higher up the wall. He gasps for breath.

"Okay," he chokes, hands frantically prying at the warrior's hold.

Callian lowers him back to his feet and loosens his grip. Mason shoots him a look, and he lets Elijah go.

"That wasn't a written order," Elijah rasps. "But the Chancellor has long suspected that Emmie was helping the rebels, and he said if she was collateral damage, no officer would be punished for her death." He bends over, looking up at us as he rubs his throat.

"Why did you use Nirri to gain access to the forest people? What changed since we left the tower?" Mason asks, more curious than he was with the last few questions. Rayner is actually pretty good at this. That shouldn't come as a surprise, with him being an ex-Guardian, but it does.

"They didn't fully believe the cover story Nirri told me to tell them. They were going to execute me. But they said if I helped them capture the four of you, I could be absorbed by the general Guardian ranks and keep my miserable existence. Fletcher's words." He's looking at me now.

"So, you sold us out to save your own hide." Callian steps toward him. "You sold out Nirri, who trusted you. You were her *friend*."

Elijah just stares at Callian. "Some friend. 'Personal slave,' more like. It was all I could do, since she screwed everything up to save your sorry ass." He turns to Mason. "She could have just stuck to the plan and taken her grandfather's place, and I would have been able to rule alongside her. Stupid girl."

Callian slams a fist into his face, and blood pours from his mouth. "You're a dead man, Elijah."

I rest a hand on Callian's arm, which is drawn back with a

reloaded fist. "Callian, we might need him later. He has a few more days in him yet." My brother's body shudders with heavy breaths.

"We'll be back tomorrow for more information," Mason says. "I suggest you cooperate, since your life is literally in his hands." He nods to Callian seething inches from Elijah's face.

We turn and walk away from the cell. Mason plucks the keys from Callian's hand and turns the lock on the door before following us.

"You're all dead anyway! If you think you have any chance against the Chancellor, you're as dumb as she is," Elijah sneers.

Callian pauses, curling his fingers back into fists before walking out the door.

"Charming lad," Mason mutters as we walk out into the dappled sunlight.

"We should have just killed him on the spot. What else do we need from him?" Callian snaps.

"I don't know. I'll relay this to Hanola and let her decide," Mason says, heading for her home.

"Let's grab some food. It's been a long day," I say.

Callian nods and walks beside me for a while.

"You know what? I'm just going to go home and take a bath," he finally says.

"Alright, I'll see you tomorrow, brother. Don't dwell on that lowlife's words. You know where to find me if you want to talk about it."

I make my way to the eating area, making quick work of my meal, then trudge home. I could use a bath too.

Our home feels empty with Imani not here, despite her being away for weeks not so long ago. I sit on the bed and pull my boots off before undoing the buttons on my shirt and throwing it over the chair near the hearth. Walking behind the changing screen, I drop my pants and pour the last of our water into the bath. With the fire iron, I transport the kettle full of steaming water to the bath, then set it back on its hook and step into the bath. The steaming water burns for a second as I lower myself into the half-full bath.

Imani's soap sits on the side of the wooden bath. I pluck it from its sticky platform and rub it over my tired muscles. The lavender scent fills the air as soon as the soap touches the hot water. I lay my head back on the edge of the tub and relax into the suds, closing my eyes. My mind wanders to where Imani is tonight with Catori, sleeping under the stars—our stars. Tomorrow afternoon, they should return. I count down the hours until I will see her elegant face again.

CHAPTER 21
MASON

I jerk upright in my bunk. Everything is quiet.

Too quiet.

Callian's chest rises and falls with a soft rattle through every long, slow breath on his bunk across from mine, arm dangling over the side.

Something is not right.

I swing my legs from my bunk and slide my shoes on. Rising from the bed slowly, I creep toward the door. With a gentle move, I open it. Grey light filters through the village, the moon a crescent above the trees. Its light filters through the canopies of the old figs dotted around the village. Nothing moves in the village center. The door clicks shut behind me, and I pad toward the eating area.

A shadow moves in my peripheral vision to the right. I stop. Not daring to move a muscle, I scan for movement again.

Nothing.

Something tugs in my chest, and fear prickles down my spine. I pick up my pace, making my way through the village center. Not another soul stirs.

Another shadow moves, up ahead toward Hanola's. I break

into a jog, trying to keep my footfalls light. Slipping past each house, I stay out of sight of whatever or whoever is tracking through the shadows, and I weave past the homes of the sleeping people.

A door creaks up ahead.

A scream rips through the village center, coming straight from Hanola's.

Mandy.

Her terrified screams ripple through the giant canopy over Hanola's home. I sprint for her house, rounding the last house before it.

The door is open.

Muffled sounds come from inside, and I slam through the doorway. Two Guardians are there, dressed in grey, one standing over Hanola's bed, the other holding Mandy against the wall. Her body trembles, sending waves through her thin nightgown, her arms crossed over her chest to protect herself. Soft whimpers from Hanola are the only sound.

"Hey!" I charge the closest one. He releases Mandy and lunges for me, knife in hand. He slashes at me, and I sidestep him, but the blade runs a slice through my upper arm. Heat and pain run down my arm, and I slam into him again. He topples backward, landing on his back on the floor. I slam my knees hard into his chest, and the dagger falls from his grip. I toss it away from him. Hands curled into fists, I hit him with everything I have. His head lolls to the side.

I jump up from his limp body and lunge for the officer over Hanola. He stands unmoving, as if waiting, a blade in his hands.

Gurgling noises spill from her throat.

He looks back at me, then at his fallen comrade. Without a second look at the man lying on the floor, he sprints for the door.

I drop down beside Hanola. Her throat has been cut, sliced

right across her windpipe. Blood gushes from her throat with every heartbeat, her trembling hands trying in vain to staunch it. I place my hands over her throat, and she lets hers fall to her sides.

"Hanola, just breathe. Slow breaths."

I have no idea what to do.

She looks at me, forcing a loving smile. I let out a ragged groan. *Hell. Please, no—please not her!*

"Mason," she rasps.

"Don't try to talk," I choke.

She closes her eyes and then opens them again. My heart almost stops with her blink.

"Help! Somebody, help!"

Mandy stares, her face white and twisted with fear and grief. My bloodied hands shake over Hanola's throat. I press down as much as I can to stop the bleeding, still trying to let her breathe. She gurgles and chokes through a breath, but I don't dare take my hands from her throat.

Callian flies through the door. "What did you do?" he growls.

"How is that your reaction?!" I seethe, checking the placement of my hands as Hanola struggles for another breath. "Please, help her!"

Callian rushes to his grandmother, falling to his knees beside her. He takes in every part of her, the blood soaking her nightgown, now covering my hands. His face slackens, and he goes still, as if he knows it's too late. Sucking in a long breath, he strokes her forehead, his eyes scanning her neck. I lift my hands briefly, and blood gushes from the slit. His eyes burn into mine before moving to my arm. Blood now saturates my sleeve.

"What happened?" he utters, eyes wandering erratically between me and his grandmother.

"I woke up, and something was wrong. I could feel it. I saw someone in the shadows and followed them. Two Guardians attacked her. One was..." I look back to the floor where he had been, but there is nothing but the rug, the dagger still lying on the floor where I flung it. "One had Mandy. I knocked him to the floor. The other was standing over Hanola. I was too late." Callian's face twists, and I steady myself. "And then he fled."

"Callian," Hanola gasps, her frail, trembling hand finding his.

"I'm here, G'ma," he whispers, chin trembling.

She forces a smile, gasping for air. Her hand goes limp in his. Her chest falls, but does not rise. The blood pulsing against my hand stops.

"No," he utters, gripping her hand and shaking it. "G'ma, wake up, I'm here!"

Scuffling at the door catches our attention. Mandy lets out a terrified wail. Harm marches in, holding a Guardian by the arm, the bloodied knife in Harm's hand. His face drops as he takes in Hanola lying between Callian and me.

"No..." His gaze tracks from Hanola's lifeless body to Callian's distraught face. "Callian," Harm whispers, holding the Guardian in his unwavering grip.

"Kill him, Harm."

Harm spins the man around, whipping the blade across his throat before words of protest have a chance to form. He slumps to the floor, blood spreading over the mat in the entrance to Hanola's home.

I lift my shaking hands from Hanola's throat. Callian bows his head to her chest. Harm walks over and kneels next to him. He places his hand on Callian's shoulder. Callian roars into Hanola's chest. Tears slide down Harm's face.

Miya flies through the door, followed by Jeselle, robes wrapped around their nightclothes. Their hands press to their mouths seconds after they see Hanola. Gasps and cries ring through the home again. Miya pulls Jeselle into her side, holding her there.

Callian cradles Hanola's head in his hands, thumbs rubbing her cheeks, sobbing through ragged breaths. I watch him as he talks to her in soft whispers, my hands hanging by my sides.

Hanola is gone.

Her wonderful light. The spirit that saw us all, long before we knew who we were.

Catori.

Hell... Catori.

The knot in my gut twists, forcing a lump into my throat. I stand and wipe the blood from my hands onto my pants. Harm looks up at me.

"Catori," I breathe, almost unable to get her name out.

Harm shoves his hands through his hair, leaning his head back, letting out a groan. Callian sobs. His entire frame shudders with every breath as he pushes up from the floor.

"They're all dead. The minute Catori finds out, they're all dead," Callian mutters.

I walk out the door, unseeing, unfeeling, the cool night air not registering on my skin anymore. The grey light now feels too bright. I track back to Callian's and rip my shirt off, pull another over my head, and grab the rucksack from under my bunk. I pick up my canteen and fill it from the water urn. Then I grip the side of the large urn and hang my head for a heartbeat.

What is happening?

They have killed two significant people in as many days. I cup water into my hands and splash it over my face. Rivers of cool water run down the searing skin on my neck. I pluck up some of Callian's food stash from the table and slam it into my bag.

Footsteps from outside track through the door. Callian and Harm stand stunned in the doorway, watching.

"Where are you going?" Harm asks, words quiet.

"To find Catori." I stuff an extra shirt in my rucksack.

"I'll send a messenger," Callian murmurs.

"You're still a wanted traitor, last time I checked," Harm says to me quietly.

"I will not let her find out that her grandmother has died from some random messenger boy." I push past them both.

"Take one of the men with you," Callian says vacantly, not looking at me.

"They'll just slow me down, and I doubt Catori wants an audience for this." I stare at Callian, shaking my head.

"It's too dangerous, Mason, especially now that they're all armed," Harm insists, stepping toward me. "One of them got away. He's probably waiting for someone to come after him."

I look back at them, standing in the doorway. I throw the rucksack over my shoulder. "I don't care." I take off at a run toward the forest.

Toward Catori.

CHAPTER 22
IMANI

Hidden within the canopy above the officers sitting on the forest floor, Catori and I are perched, predators waiting for the perfect moment to pounce on our prey. Her steady breathing and the chatter from the three men below are the only sounds out of place in the lively forest this morning. Catori startled awake last night, gripping her chest. I watched her with one eye open as she sat waiting for her breaths to slow before lying back down and rolling over, going back to sleep. She said it was probably nothing when I asked about it this morning. But the pit in my stomach disagrees.

She holds three fingers up, and I get ready to drop from the canopy onto the ground beside the men. *Please let my leg hold up for the jump!*

Three... She folds a finger down.

Two...

Her hand makes a fist. One!

I release my grip around the curved, gnarled branch and drop to the ground in a crouch, weapons drawn. The three men jolt to their feet, ripping their small daggers from their belts. I almost feel sorry for them.

Catori stands on the opposite side, absolutely feline, eyes scanning each of them. "You have three seconds to tell me what you're doing in our forest before I slit your throats."

The officer closest to me huffs out a laugh and steps toward me. I remain in position. Catori flips her knife in her hand, once, twice. He takes another step toward me, his comrade more cautiously shuffling toward Catori.

A smirk tugs at her lips.

Thrice.

Her blade lands in his neck a second later. I lunge for the officer in front of me, who sidesteps. That was a mistake. I meet his movement and plunge my knife into his chest up to the hilt. He drops to his knees, eyes wide, hands grappling with the knife sunk deep. The third officer's face blanches, and a weak cry spills from his lips before he turns and flees, flinging his arms around as he barrels through the forest undergrowth.

Catori steps over the body closest and pulls her knife free. She searches his pockets and small grey satchel. Finding a small black notebook containing tallies, she flips through it.

With a start, I recognize the handwriting. "What is that? That's Harm's handwriting."

She looks at me, then flips through a few more pages. "The numbers of our forest rebels. The boys were gathering numbers before you came back."

"Their other belongings must still be out here too, then."

"Probably not too far. Spread out; look for the clearing they said they were in before they found you and Nirri." She tracks back through the trees.

I walk in the opposite direction, circling around a few times.

"Over here!" she yells.

I jog back toward the sound of her voice, breaking through the brush moments later. Two rucksacks and their weapons lie there, covered in fallen leaves and dirt near the remnants of an old fire. I pick up the rucksacks. Catori gathers up the weapons.

"They'll be happy to get these back," she says, pulling each blade out, checking for signs of damage. I open Harm's rucksack; his compass and notebook are still in the bottom, slightly damp from being out in the forest for weeks.

We sit down in the clearing. Catori rummages through the Guardian's satchel before tipping it up by the bottom. A small pen and a few small pieces of paper fall to the ground—the same type of paper that had our retrieval orders on it. Catori reads the order on the paper. "They were scouting for outpost positions in the forest."

"So, they started that then. I was hoping they would forget that plan once Mason and I went missing. Apparently not."

"Apparently not," she echoes dryly.

"It's not going to happen, Catori. We will not let the same thing happen to the forest dwellers."

She shoots me a weak smile and continues reading.

"You hungry?" I ask.

She nods.

I wander into the forest and gather the berries and the sweet bark we always eat out here. With my hands full, I wander back to the clearing. Catori is leaning back on her elbows, chewing on something from her rucksack. I drop down opposite the unlit fire and divide the food into two piles. I lean over the old coals and hand her the food. She takes it, popping a berry into her mouth. "Thanks."

"I guess we can go home now that they're dead and we know why they're here?"

"Yep, guess so."

"Do you think the third one will go back, or hang around?"

"No idea. If he's smart, he'll run home."

I chuckle and rip a small piece of sweet bark from the slab in my hand. The man's wide eyes as he fell to the ground replays in my mind. I shake my head and pluck a berry from the small pile of food in front of me and toss it in the air, trying to catch it in my mouth. Catori laughs and tries her luck with her own berries. The third one successfully lands in my mouth, and as I bite down, the sweet juice bursts over my tongue. Catori catches her fourth, groaning with pleasure.

"These sweet little things never get old," she moans, lying back on the grass. I swallow the last of my berries and lie back, hands under my head, watching the leaves dance and sway on the branches above us. Birds flit around, working on their small nests and foraging for any insects they can fill their bellies with. I close my eyes, noting every sound overhead and around me. The wind through the branches rattles the leaves that hold on with a thin green grasp.

A crunch and rustle sound from just beyond our clearing. I open my eyes, waiting for another sound. Footsteps pad through the undergrowth, steadily closing in on us. I sit up.

Catori's eyes are open, but she hasn't heard them yet—or she is lying in wait if she has. My hands automatically rest on the knives at my hips. A figure moves through the trees, tracking right for us. Not in a grey uniform, but my hands remain where they are. Catori watches my face now, not bothering to sit up. I realize right then that she trusts me, and warmth floods my chest.

I squint, focusing on the advancing person. Male—the figure is male. I recognize the sandy tousled hair first, then his gait. I stand and loose the hold on my weapons. Catori watches me, and realizing it must be someone we know, she closes her eyes and slides her hands under her head.

Mason clears the tree line. His pants have dark stains on them —dried blood. His eyes meet mine, then instantly track to where Catori lies. A smile tugs at her face. He stares at her, then back at me, not returning the smile.

Something is wrong. His face is drawn, brows down, and he grips the strap of his rucksack with one hand, the other hanging by his side.

"Catori," I whisper.

She cracks one eye open.

"I know. Mason is here," she says, still smiling.

"Catori," I say louder.

She looks at me, sitting up, then tracks to Mason's gaunt face. Instantly, she gets to her feet, scanning him from head to toe.

"Callian?" she breathes.

Mason steadies himself with a breath. "He's okay." But his chin wobbles, and he dumps the rucksack on the ground, stepping toward Catori.

Her eyes widen, hands overlapping as they press into her chest. "No," she whimpers and backs up a step.

"Who, Mason?" I ask, eyes alternating between him and Catori.

He takes a breath. "Hanola."

"No!" Catori screams, "No, no, no! *G'ma!*"

Mason stands wavering sideways slightly, chest heaving as he watches her heart break. He steps over and folds her into his chest. He strokes her hair, pain etched all over his face.

Catori pushes out of his grip and stalks off, disappearing into the trees.

Mason turns to face me, swallowing.

"What happened?"

"Guardians, last night. She died minutes after we found her."

"Oh, dammit..." I rub my hands over my forehead into my hair. "Is everyone else okay?"

Mason nods, not taking his eyes off the trees where Catori disappeared. Fresh blood runs down his arm, soaking his sleeve.

"You're bleeding."

He turns to me, then blinks and looks down at his sleeve. "I'm fine."

Catori's scream tears through the forest a couple hundred feet away, the rattle of her painful cry sending birds and small animals scurrying.

Another scream.

Another.

Another...

Mason's face tightens, and his hands grip the back of his neck as he starts tracking in a small circle. His frame tenses further with every sound Catori makes.

"You should go and find her," I say softly.

He stops, swaying on the spot. Another scream. His eyes close, and he draws in a raw breath.

"Go, Mason. I'll wait here. She needs you."

He tracks toward the trees before disappearing through the same spot Catori did.

Another scream, this time hoarse and long. A last cry.

I pick up the rucksacks and throw the boys' weapons in, strapping Callian's broadsword over my back. No more movement from the trees. I sit on the grass and shove my head in my hands, letting out the sobs for Hanola's precious life in waves. She has done so much for us—for all her people. She did not deserve to die. Callian must be a wreck; he loved her so much. I remember the day I met her, and the way his face beamed. Oh, heavens. Catori... This must be tearing her apart. I rock back and forth, cradling the rucksack in my hands. How could they do this?!

Moments later, Mason steps from the tree line, half holding up Catori. Her face is blank, her eyes vacant. Shock—she is in shock. I rush to her side, wrapping an arm around her. She chokes out another sob.

"I need to take her home," Mason says, his voice raw.

"We can make it to the halfway clearing before nightfall."

He nods, and we move out. He picks up his rucksack on the way.

I wrap the last of the strips of cloth from my rucksack around Mason's arm. The bleeding stopped a while ago; this will stop it from opening again. I return to my side of the fire. "That will keep it in check for now."

He shoots me a small smile, lowering his gaze to the fire. Flames flicker in the night breeze. Catori stares at them. Her face is blank. Mason sits next to her, his hand holding hers. He pushes her wet, matted hair back behind her ear. She has been crying on and off. He rubs a thumb over her cheek, wiping away the tear stains from earlier. She turns and looks at him, and her chin wobbles. She squeezes his hand.

"You two should get some sleep." I rub my bad leg, aching from jumping from the tree and walking miles today. "I'll keep watch."

"Thanks, Imani," Mason says. He rolls out two sleeping mats, helping Catori to the one closest to the fire, warming her back. He lies on his side, a foot away from Catori, keeping his eyes on her as she curls up, crossing her arms over her chest.

I lean against the fallen tree behind me and pull out a knife, cleaning the sharp edges with the cloth of my tunic. Catori stares at Mason's chest for a while, unblinking. The flames flicker and ebb, the colors climbing to yellow, then orange, before dying off to red. Embers pulse under the licks of flame. Night birds send calls through the leaves above us.

Catori rises from her sleeping mat on shaking legs and steps onto Mason's. He looks up at her, the light from the fire reflecting in his eyes. He holds his arm out, offering her a space near him. She sinks down beside him, lying with her face nuzzled into his chest. He wraps his arm around her and rubs her back slowly before closing his eyes. Her hands run up his shirt and grip his collar before her breathing slows.

The moon tracks across the sky overhead, poking its shimmering rays through the gaps in the canopy every so often. Mason and Catori sleep on the mat, her clinging to his shirt, him holding her through every hour, his chest rising and falling against her hands. I yawn and stretch my arms over my head. My gorgeous bed and my gorgeous husband would be nice right about now. Only hours until I am back in his embrace.

I close my eyes, sighing through my nose. Just for a few minutes. Then I will open them again to keep watch.

The trek back to our village feels like it is taking twice as long. My thoughts keep darting from Catori to Callian to Hanola. Each of them hurts. Mason has not left Catori's side since they came out of the trees yesterday. This morning, she was still huddled into him, his arm over her. He walks beside her in front of me. The path is an easy one that we have traveled many times. Today, it feels hard. I want to get home, but at the same time, going home is going to be agony for Catori and Callian. A lump pushes into my throat.

Catori's fist jolts up, and we halt instantly. I swallow past the lump and blow out a breath to reorient my focus. We stand scanning between the trees. I turn, facing our rear.

Movement.

Someone is following us.

A stick snaps. Catori spins, eyes homing in on the sound.

Grey rushes past the bushes mere feet from us.

Catori stalks toward the haze of movement. Mason and I watch her close in. We hear a grunt, followed by the sound of a body thudding to the ground. Catori storms out of the undergrowth, sheathing her bloody knife. Mason's face is set in stone as he watches Catori stalk toward us.

"Was it the third one from yesterday?" I ask.

"Yes" is all she says before stalking toward home.

Mason follows behind her, carrying her rucksack and the weapons we found. I take up the rear, Callian's sword on my back. Our procession of three feels like a mourning in itself. Hanola's death coming only days after Emmie's is not a coincidence. A heavy feeling settles in my chest. I readjust the sword on my back and scan the trees around me. How many more Guardians are wandering through the forest? With Emmie gone, there is nothing stopping them from infiltrating this side of the wall now. I just hope we can hold them off long enough for Harm to change the dial and put down the Chancellor.

CHAPTER 23
IMANI

The door to Hanola's is open, as always. But this time, she isn't waiting inside for us with her warm smile and wise words. Catori walks in first, greeted by Callian, arms wide open. He wraps her in a hug, sinking his drawn face, reddened eyes, and shaking hands into her hair. She holds her brother tight through every sob and every murmur. I stand there watching her be strong for Callian—strong for every person in Hanola's home.

Warm arms find me. I turn and huddle into Harm's chest. He envelops me, and I disintegrate in his hold. Tears soak through his shirt, and he tightens around me. It feels like we have all lost so much, Catori and Callian the most. I loose a long breath to steady myself and pull back. Harm's face is much the same as Callian's. He would have been up with Callian through every hour. He loves him like a brother. His chin wobbles as he wipes away a tear from my cheek, and I cup his face with my hands. Harm's forehead rests on mine. He breathes deep, working through the pain, for Hanola, for Callian, for all of it.

Mason hangs beside Harm, letting Callian and Catori comfort each other. Their parents stand with Mandy. They are just as Harm described them, and I see both Catori and Callian in each of them. Catori's mother pads over and pulls her into a hug, their father wrapping his arms around both his wife and his daughter. Callian watches his sister, the pained look on his face never fading.

He turns to face us. "I need help to build the timber pile for her," he says, almost in a whisper.

"Whatever you need," Mason says.

Callian just stares at him.

Harm releases me and moves toward Callian. "We will all help you, brother."

Callian nods, and Harm leads him outside. Mason follows, with a look at Catori, as if making sure she will be taken care of while he is gone.

Catori breaks away from her parents' hold and turns to find me, wiping a stream of tears from her face. "Imani, these are my parents. Anya..." She gestures to her mother. "... and Enzo," she says, gesturing to her father. They offer sad smiles.

A knot twists in my stomach. If they knew I am the daughter of the commander who was responsible for this, the smile on their faces would disappear in an instant. "It's nice to meet you. I am so sorry for your loss."

"We will need to prepare Mother for her cremation and ascension," Anya says, lifting her chin to give her mother the dignity she deserves.

Catori wanders to Hanola's side. She drops down beside her, taking in the white gown and hands resting across her chest. She touches a hand to her grandmother's. "Oh, G'ma..."

Mandy comes to stand next to Catori, resting a hand on her shoulder. "I have the cloth ready for wrapping. Miya and Jeselle are on their way," she says softly. Catori nods.

Anya moves to the opposite side of Hanola and beckons for me to kneel beside Catori. I take my place next to her, and she looks at me, offering a weak smile.

"I'm glad you're here, Imani. I forgot to tell you that when you came home," she whispers, linking her arm in mine. I slip my arm free and pull her into a tight hug. She coughs a small laugh and sniffs back the tears that have started again. Footsteps pad past us, and Miya and Jeselle take their place on either side of Anya. Catori turns to her mother, drying her face with the backs of her hands.

Mandy sinks to the floor at Hanola's feet and unravels the long cream cotton cloth, six inches wide. She gently lifts Hanola's feet and winds the cloth between them. Tying a small knot, she covers her feet and starts wrapping her legs upward. She nods for me to continue the process. I take the carefully wound cloth, wrapping it around Hanola's legs until it reaches where Catori kneels, at Hanola's hips. Her trembling hands take the cloth from mine. Her fingers are cool, and she sucks in deep breaths as she rolls the cloth over Hanola's hip to where her mother kneels, waiting for the cloth. Miya and Jeselle roll Hanola to one side, and Anya rolls the cloth to Catori. Gently settling Hanola back down, we repeat the process until her shoulders are covered. Catori wraps the cloth around her grandmother's neck, her breathing turning ragged as she scans the now cleaned wound that cost Hanola her life.

Anya rests a gentle hand over Catori's. "Breathe, my girl. Your grandmother had no fear of death, and she would not want you to be grieving for her. She is at peace now."

Catori nods, but a tear lands on the cloth in her hands. A heartbeat later, she continues wrapping toward Hanola's face. Jeselle moves to Hanola's head and lifts it tenderly. Catori sobs with every breath, the last of the cloth covering Hanola's kind face, the lines framing her eyes, the last of her silver hair, now plaited and already tucked away into her binds.

And then I see it. Under her plait, at the base of her skull, tucked beneath her grey hairline—it's the marking Enid carries, the bird in flight. My breath stops, and I stare at it. A second later, Jeselle moves her hands, and I lose track of it.

Jeselle takes the short piece of cloth from Catori's shaking fingers and ties it off behind Hanola's head. Anya chants, low and slow, her hands lifting a small pot of oil and resting it on Hanola's chest. Each woman dips the tips of their fingers into it. I do the same. They touch it briefly to their foreheads before rubbing the oils over the cloth. A peppery tang fills the air. Over and over, we dip our hands into the pot, rubbing the oils across every part of Hanola's wrapped body, chanting. The low hum of three words from a language I don't recognize oscillates, reverberating through my chest.

The tears on Catori's face have long since dried by the time we have finished with the oil. She rises on wobbly legs, and I lean over to catch her.

"Take my daughter home, Imani. She will need to rest before the ceremony tomorrow at noon," Anya says softly.

I wrap an arm around her waist and lead her home. She leans her head on my shoulder. Through the village center we amble. Between the gap in the houses, I see Callian, Harm, and Mason carrying logs, stacking them in a square, like the start of a small home, but one made from ribs and not walls. The top is a neat row of timber—a platform. Mason looks up from the log he is setting into place. He watches us as we walk past the next house and out of his line of sight.

I push Catori's door open, and she strays from my shoulder, dropping onto her bed. I pluck three logs from her wood rack and stoke the hearth. Fanning it to liven up the embers, I wait for the timber to catch. It flickers to life, and I note the irony of such a small part of life continuing when such a significant part of our lives has been snuffed out. Taken from us. Taken from Catori.

She lies there, green eyes vacant, watching me, and I pad over to her bed. Her legs hang off the side, shoes on, hands gripping the pillow under her short blonde hair. I tug her boots off and lift her legs onto the bed. She wriggles over. I sit next to her, my heart tearing to pieces. Stroking her hair, I lean back against the wall behind her bed. Catori closes her eyes. Normal village life continues outside, albeit subdued, their pace at half speed, like the life has been sapped out of them today.

At a soft rap on the doorframe, I open my eyes. Mason stands in the doorway, eyes on Catori. I move off the bed slowly, not wanting to wake her, and pad to the door. He stares at me, his jaw clenched. I can almost see his heart breaking for her, and I sigh, placing a hand on his chest. He swallows, letting out a low deep breath.

"I'll find her some food. You should stay with her," I say, and he nods.

I drop my hand, and he walks over to the bed. He sits on the edge for a while, watching her breathe. Then he slips his boots off and lies behind her, wrapping his arms around her like he did last night.

Without a word, I head to the kitchen to find some food.

Hundreds of forest dwellers stand surrounding the square ceremonial platform the boys built yesterday, steps roped onto the eastern side.

I wait with Catori in Hanola's home. She is wearing a long white dress with beads of all colors hanging over her chest. The women will carry Hanola to her ceremony at noon. Dressed in white, we all hang around in front of Hanola's.

Anya arrives, followed by Miya and Jeselle as the sun reaches its apex, light filtering through the trees.

"It is time, my girl," Anya says, walking inside. We follow and file in around Hanola's wrapped body. Catori stands at her head.

"On the count of three," Catori whispers.

We all place our hands under Hanola's small frame.

"One." Our huntress sucks in a breath.

"Two." She looks at each one of us.

"Three." We lift Hanola from her bunk, moving our shoulders under her wrapped and oiled body.

Catori stands motionless for a moment. "Let's take her home," she whispers.

Moving as one, we carry her light weight on our shoulders. As we reach the door, the men and women of the forest have made a walkway for us, people lining a path from Hanola's front door to the platform. Sad faces and tears greet us every step of the way. Every head lowers as we pass by them.

We reach the stairs, and Catori climbs each one with great strength, her focus on Hanola one last time. With one gentle, fluid motion, we set her down on the platform and walk back down the stairs. Heads rise when Catori reaches the bottom step, the last of us to descend.

We file in around the platform. A lit torch leans in a rack nearby, the flames licking around the oil-drenched cloth at its tip. Hanola's family stands at the front, Callian and his parents behind Catori. The healer, the forest leaders, Miya, Jeselle, and the guards flank us as we stand next to Callian. Nirri stands beside me, tears already streaming down her face. Her broken heart is written all over it, as she lost her own grandmother only a week ago. She holds her arms over her chest. Callian stares at Catori, not once looking at Nirri.

The village healer steps forward, holding a chalice of wine.

"From the heavens to the earth and back again, we deliver our beloved Hanola to the afterlife. May she rest in peace." Her chin trembles, the cup gripped tightly in her shaking hand.

"From the heavens to the earth and back again," the crowd chants.

Catori steps forward, lifting the torch from the rack. Every head lowers once more as she raises it toward the platform. She stands with her arm raised, flame inches from the stacked wooden mound holding Hanola. Callian steps up and offers her a sad smile. Her face twists a little, and he rests his hand over hers around the torch. They lower the flame to the platform. The oil on Hanola's wrappings flare up. Catori returns the torch to the rack and steps back from the heat of the flames.

An energetic chant begins deep in the crowd, spreading to every person—a final farewell to the woman who has taken care of every person on this side of the wall for decades. Callian stands next to Catori, his broken face split by rivulets of tears sliding their way down his jaw.

Nirri watches him, her chest heaving, face crumpled with sadness. "I can't be here." She turns, weaving her way out of the crowd. I squeeze Harm's hand and nod to Nirri, before letting his hand drop. He nods and turns back to face the fire.

Nirri drifts toward the last house on the eastern side of the village. I walk a few steps behind her. She rounds the house and leans against it, hanging her head in her hands.

I stop beside her. "Nirri?"

She goes limp against the house, head hitting the wood, choking through sobs.

"Hey." I pull her into a hug, and she leans against me.

"This is all my fault."

"No, that's not true, Nirri."

She pulls back, her tortured eyes searching my face, her hands wringing the cloth of her tunic. "Yes, it is. I trusted Elijah," she sobs, dropping her gaze to the ground. "I was stupid enough to think there was something between us." She groans and runs her hands through her hair, pulling at it.

"Hey, no. Look at me." I put both hands on her shoulders. "This is *not* your fault."

She looks back up at me, terrified. "I've only been out of that tower for five minutes, and look what's happened, Imani! My grandmother, Hanola... It's all my fault."

"No, it's not. Every bad thing that happens here or on the other side of the wall is because of the Chancellor."

Her eyes close and reopen, distant, pain filtering through them. "Tell that to Callian." She pushes past me, walking away from the village.

"Nirri!"

She doesn't respond, heading for the forest, alone.

Catori rests her head on Mason's shoulder. I huddle into Harm's side, exhausted from the past two days. The four of us vacantly stare into the flickering flames of Hanola's heart. The cushions under us, arranged by Mandy in front of the hearth, mark one of the many changes that have happened and will happen, now that Hanola is gone. No one speaks. None of us really knows what to say. Catori hasn't cried since just before midday, but her face still carries every line of grief. Her parents went to bed just after the sun went down, their faces reflecting their daughter's.

"I thought you all might like a drink," Mandy offers, holding out a tray with four mugs of something steaming. Mason picks up two, handing one to Catori. She takes it, her focus not faltering from the flames in the hearth. I pick up the last two and hand one to Harm. He takes it, planting a kiss on my forehead. I sit up and sip the hot tea. Fragrant mouthfuls warm my insides.

Heavy footsteps pass over the threshold, and Callian slumps down beside Harm. He hands Callian a mug, and he takes a sip, cradling it in his hands. Callian takes a sideways look at Mason and Catori before lying on the floor, head on a cushion, hands behind his head, closing his eyes.

"Where's Nirri? She's missing all the fun," Callian says dryly.

"I haven't seen her," I say. "She took off into the forest at the end of the funeral. You haven't seen her since?" I ask.

Callian, Mason, Harm, and Catori all turn and look at me. Surely one of them has seen her since the funeral. It was hours ago.

"I haven't seen her since just before midday," Catori says.

"Me either," Mason echoes.

"That makes three of us," Harm says, looking at me, his brows drawn down.

"What do you mean, she took off during the funeral?" Callian says, sitting up.

"She was upset. She blames herself for Emmie and Hanola. She wanted some space," I say, and my stomach twists into a knot. I shouldn't have let her go alone. "I assumed she would come back when she calmed down."

Harm jumps up from his cushion. He swings his hand toward Callian, who grips it and flies to his feet.

"Which way did she go?" Harm asks.

"She headed towards the wall, northeast," I say, putting the mug down and rising to my feet.

"I'll check the village. Maybe she's just at Catori's by herself," Mason says.

"I'll check the training and eating areas," I say.

Catori pushes to her feet. "I'll take the perimeter." Pulling off the beads, she dumps them on the cushion she was sitting on.

"Callian and I will head into the forest, in the direction you saw her leave. Maybe she didn't go too far," Harm says.

Soft knocking on the door draws every gaze.

"Sorry to interrupt," the guard says, standing just over the threshold, "but I thought you would want to know straight away. Elijah has escaped. From the looks of it, it was a couple of hours ago, just after the last shift change and rounds."

Harm looks at Callian, letting out a low growl. They both fly out the door without a word. I spin and look at Mason. Worry lines his face.

CHAPTER 24
HARM

Mason would have been able to track Nirri better. It feels like we are going around in circles. The dark night under the forest canopy is not helping. Callian has barely said more than a word for hours, stalking through the undergrowth like he's possessed. So far, all we have found is a small torn piece of white cloth—maybe from the white dress she was wearing at the funeral. Nothing but the sounds of night wildlife and the patter of the rain makes it through the thick branches overhead.

Callian stops abruptly. He tilts his head to one side, like he has about a hundred times in the last couple of hours. He straightens and takes a step.

A guttural scream floods through the trees toward us. We take off toward it.

Undergrowth thrashes aside under our quick strides. I reach the spot first and pull Callian down beside me, keeping him from barreling into Nirri's space. Her back is pressed against a tree, and Elijah stands only inches from her. Her hands tremble in front of her chest. "Please, just leave me be, Elijah."

He huffs a cold laugh, leaning into her. She flattens herself against the tree, hands dropping to her sides, sliding over the rough bark.

"This is all your fault! You should have just stayed in that tower, and everything would have been fine. You just couldn't let those forest rebel scum take the fall, could you? Typical, Nirri. Now neither of us has anything left."

Callian shifts, his body racked with tension. I grab his arm in warning.

She raises her chin. "Speak for yourself. I have plenty left."

Elijah backs away, walking in a circle, running a hand over his jaw.

"Go back to the tower and join the Guardians or something," Nirri spits.

He stops, staring at her. "I can't." He stalks into her space. "Not now. If I go back, it's to a cell."

"Why?" She takes a step toward him.

"I was only allowed to return if I brought the traitors back, which is impossible for one person to do."

"Then I guess you'll just have to hang around in the forest until the wolves find you."

He stalks over to where she stands and grabs her arm, slamming her into the tree. A small groan leaves her lips.

Callian stiffens.

"Not yet. Let her defend herself," I whisper.

"Get your hands off me!" she cries.

Elijah laughs at her, grabbing her other arm, pinning her to the tree with his body. She slams her knee into his groin, and he folds over. Nirri stands frozen, her face pulled tight, eyes wide. Elijah straightens, then connects his fist with the side of her face. She crumples forward with a cry, hands pressing into her now reddened cheek.

"Please, leave me be," she whimpers.

He takes another step. "I'll get something out of you," he snarls. He rips her dress down her chest with one hand.

Nirri's cry twists in my stomach. Callian crouches frozen, not moving as Nirri tries and fails to cover herself. Horror contorts his face. He's not even breathing.

I lunge from the undergrowth and slam into Elijah. He topples sideways, and I stand in front of Nirri.

"Get out of my way, rebel filth," he sneers.

"Or what? You'll assault me too?"

"I'll cut you from head to toe." He snatches a small dagger from his boot. He must have stolen it on his way out of the cells.

I stand my ground. "Do your worst, Elijah. It will be the last thing you ever do." Nirri's ragged breathing behind me tells me she's still here.

Elijah lunges with his small blade. I grab his arm, twisting it behind his back. My grip around his wrist tightens, and the blade falls to the ground.

"Let go of me!" he snarls.

"You know, if that's the way you treat the girls, none of them will ever like you," I whisper in his ear.

He pulls his head away from me. I spin him around to face Nirri. "Apologize."

He spits at her feet. Her face twists with hurt. Of all the rotten things he has done since he arrived in our forest, this appears to hurt Nirri the most.

A branch behind me cracks. Callian.

"Well, I guess if you won't apologize, you'll have to deal with my brother." I fling him back around and into Callian's grip.

Nirri's gaze shoots to Callian. His face is stone, and Nirri's expression changes to sorrow. Elijah recoils in Callian's grip, but the warrior holds him on his feet.

"Apologize," Callian growls. His voice is too quiet, fury bubbling underneath, barely restrained. Elijah's hateful eyes burn into Nirri. She swallows, still looking at Callian.

"Sorry, whatever," Elijah utters.

Callian slams him upside the head, knocking him out, letting him slump to the ground at his feet.

"Nirri," Callian starts.

She adjusts the top of her dress over her chest.

"I'll leave you two alone," I say, walking away a few yards to sit against an old tree, leaning my head onto the rough bark. The undergrowth below me sends up the damp scent of pine.

"Are you alright?" Callian rasps.

Nirri sniffs. "I'm fine."

Callian shifts on his feet, his tense body sagging as the fire drains from his face. "Did he hurt you?"

"Not really."

I watch as Callian steps toward her, hesitates, then closes the space between them. "Please, come home."

Stifling a sob, she grips her arms and stares into the forest, silver lining her eyes. "I can't."

"Yes, you can."

"No, I can't. You don't understand."

"Then help me understand, Nirri."

She looks up at him, and a tear spills down her cheek. Callian's jaw clenches, and he draws in a deep breath.

"I'm just a burden to you all," she mutters.

"How do you figure that?"

"Look what happened after I arrived!" she says, walking away and stifling a sob.

Callian's hands hang at his sides. "No one blames you for anything. Please, just come home."

"Then how come every time you look at me, you have that

stony expression on your face?" She spins to face him, arms still wrapped around her chest. Then she straightens up. "I'm not going back to your village, Callian." Fiddling with her dress, she tucks the top into her supports, covering herself up. She takes a breath, hanging her hands at her sides to match his. He stands unmoving.

"I don't blame you for anything, Nirri. None of this is your fault. Please come home," Callian breathes.

She shakes her head. "I don't want anyone else getting hurt. Not because of me."

"They won't. I'll make sure of it."

"You can't guarantee that. It's just better for everyone if I leave. I'll go over the wall to the desert side. You all did it."

Callian's mouth drops open, and he shoves his hands behind his neck. He turns on the spot, pacing back and forth. I push up from the ground and walk over to Nirri. Her reddened eyes find mine.

"Nirri, traipsing off into the forest at night alone is bad for a whole lot of reasons." I cast a glance at Elijah. He stirs, but Callian ignores him, now pacing in a tight circle. "Bears and wolves being a couple of the most immediate ones."

"Well, can you take me, and then I won't be by myself?"

Callian stops pacing.

"How about we go home tonight, the three of us? And if you still want to leave in a day or so, I'll take you to the wall myself."

Callian stares at me, brows lowered and jaw set. Nirri alternates her gaze between Callian and me.

"Fine," she sighs.

Elijah moans and staggers to his feet. Callian stands watching him, moving between him and Nirri.

He looks at the three of us before sidestepping toward the trees.

Nirri finds Callian's gaze. "Let him go."

"Fine. The wolves can finish him off." Callian's voice is no more than a growl.

Nirri turns to me. "You don't happen to have another shirt in your pocket or something, do you?" She looks sideways at the ground, readjusting the top of her dress.

Callian pulls his shirt over his head and hands it to her.

"I..." she starts, staring at his shirt draped over his outstretched hand.

"Let's go," I say.

Nirri pulls the shirt over her head, murmuring her thanks to Callian as she falls in behind me. Callian follows her, taking the rear protective position. I set off at a run. Both sets of footfalls track from behind as we run into the darkness of the forest for home.

Hours later, we break through the tree line, the smoldering fires of the half-lit hearths of our homes guiding us in. Nirri walks silently beside me as we make for Catori's house. Callian hangs back while she says her good nights. She glances at him briefly before pushing through the door. It clicks shut behind her.

"Want me to walk with you?" I ask Callian. He looks like he is barely holding it together. He nods, and we pad through the village center. I throw an arm around his shoulder as we pass through the eating area. "You okay?"

He doesn't respond.

"You should get some sleep."

He stops and turns to face me. "Are you really going to take her over the wall if she wants to go?"

"If she asks me to."

He swallows, looking past me into the village. "That bastard was going to—"

"I know. She knew it too, Callian."

"How am I supposed to keep her safe if she's not here?"

"I don't know, brother, but you can't make her stay if she doesn't want to be here. She'll end up hating you for it, and then any chance you have of making things work will be lost." Petria's words replay in my mind: *"You can't make people do things, Harm. They must decide for themselves."*

He slumps onto a bench seat. "How is this so hard?"

I sit next to him. Moonlight filters through the canopy, small shadows playing over the tabletops and the ground around us. "I don't know."

He shoves his head into his hands. I slap a hand on his shoulder. "Maybe because the hard things are the only ones worth fighting for."

He grunts into his hands, letting out a pained chuckle.

My brother and his big heart. Where would we be without him?

The bed creaks softly as I sit down to take off my boots. Imani's dark hair is sprawled over her pillow, her chest rising and falling in the dim light. I pull off my shirt and crawl into my side of the bed. I huddle in behind Imani, wrapping my arms around her. She murmurs something about the time, and I close my eyes, my whole body exhausted, breathing her in.

Something soft traces its way around my face, across my forehead, down my jaw, and over my lips. I crack one eye open to see the brilliant blue eyes of my wife hovering over my face.

"Hey," she whispers. Her hair is draped over her shoulders, the tips of it touching my bare chest.

"Hey, yourself."

She traces her fingers down my neck and over my chest. My body responds to her, sparking a burn in my core.

She sits back on her heels, brows lowered, mouth tight. "Did you find her?"

"Yep."

"But...?" she says, reading my tone.

"She wants to leave—for good."

"Where would she go?"

I stare at her for a handful of heartbeats. "She wants to go over the wall, into the desert."

Imani slumps, her mouth agape. "What? Why?"

"She's afraid that her being here is putting us all in danger."

"And her being over that wall puts *her* in danger! Especially if the desert dwellers figure out who she is." She gets out of bed. I let out a groan in protest and watch as she does up her tunic around her perfect curves and pulls on her pants. I sit up, and she grabs a scarf from her drawer, throwing it over the back of her neck. She twists her hair up, grabbing the scarf in one hand and twisting it around her bundled hair. A minute later, she is dressed, and her hair is wrapped up. Shoving her feet into her boots, she leans down and ties the laces.

"Where are you going?" I know full well she is going to see Nirri.

"To talk some sense into her." Grabbing her weapons belt, she stalks out the door.

I lie back in the bed, eyes burning from too little sleep. Loosing a breath, I roll over and groan into the pillow, trying to extinguish the fire in my core that Imani lit, just by being next to me.

I pull myself out of bed, if only because of the growling in my stomach. My body still feels weary, and every movement feels like an effort. I throw on my clothes and weapons and trudge to breakfast. Callian sits at the table alone, also late.

"Morning," he murmurs, plucking a piece of fruit from his plate.

"The girls up yet?"

"Everyone is at the training area already." He stares at his plate while he chews.

"Right." Imani must have gone there after seeing Nirri. "Have you seen Nirri yet?"

He looks from under his brow. "Yep."

"She okay?"

"Looked to be."

"You training this morning?"

"Yep, once I'm not feeling like a starving, rabid animal," he says, a smile cracking over his tired face briefly.

We finish our food and chug down water from our mugs. As we amble toward the training area, the sound of ricocheting metal reaches us before we set eyes on who is wielding the weapons. We round Petria's house to see Nirri and Imani in the sparring ring, broadswords clashing together again. Imani lunges, and Nirri sidesteps her. Imani spins and stabs toward Nirri's undefended side. We sit on the grass beside Miya and Catori, not taking our eyes off the sparring ring.

"Nirri, you have to intercept her before she's inside your zone," Miya calls. Nirri glances at Miya, noting our arrival.

"Imani, let Nirri take the offensive," she calls. Jeselle jumps to her feet and waves as she wanders over to the archery range. Imani nods and backs up a pace. Adjusting her stance, she waits for Nirri to attack.

Nirri stands turning the hilt over in her hand, looking at Imani and back at Miya.

"When you're ready, Nirri," Miya calls.

Nirri raises her blade and lunges for Imani head-on. I hold my breath as her blade intercepts Nirri's, the ringing metal echoing off the tree line. Nirri lunges again, and this time Imani spins. Nirri swipes, running the blade across Imani's stomach. Red soaks her tunic instantly, and I leap to my feet, wide-eyed. Imani touches a hand to her stomach before lifting her shirt. The cut isn't deep, but it's bleeding freely.

Nirri drops her blade, hands flying to her face. "Imani, I'm so sorry!"

"Don't be. I was too slow. You did good." Imani holds her hand over the shallow slice along her belly.

"You're bleeding! How is that good?"

"The part where you won the duel—that's good," Imani says, stepping toward Nirri.

"I can't do this," Nirri says, looking at me and then at Callian. She sprints toward the village, disappearing around the first home she comes to.

Imani pulls her scarf from her hair, wrapping it around her stomach, tying the knot off tight.

"She did good, and she's going to need skills if you're taking her over the wall, Harm." She marches past me, eyes full of fire.

CHAPTER 25
IMANI

The sun marks the half-day mark. Every person from every village in the forest stands gathered for Catori. Rows of branches have been set down, laying a path for Catori's bare feet to walk from her current home to her new home: Hanola's. Fires are lit along the path, marking every year of her life. Twenty flames burn. She stands between Miya and Callian, waiting for the signal from the village healer to start walking. She wears her white dress again, but this time it is adorned with green necklaces, her wrists and ankles wrapped in green strips of dyed cloth. Everyone is wearing green to honor the spirit that continues through the new leader of the forest tribes.

The old healer tilts her face to the sun, her leathered face absorbing the rays as her face softens and her arms slacken by her sides. Her arms rise, and every voice goes silent. Catori watches her with deep breaths. Miya holds her hand, and Callian takes the other. It is a reminder that nothing on this side of the wall is ever done alone; every burden is shared. Callian's face beams as Catori closes her eyes and the chanting begins. Still holding her hands, Miya and Callian take a step sideways to flank the leafy green path.

The chanting rises, louder and faster, and the clap of the old healer snaps throughout the village.

Catori takes her first step, eyes still closed. Slowly and purposefully, she walks along the green path, hands in Miya's and Callian's. The healer follows the green path, a few steps behind, coaxing the chant from every person here, a small bowl hanging around her neck.

Catori passes every year marker, not slowing. The chanting grows faster and louder still the nearer she gets to the leader's home, until Callian squeezes her hand, telling her to stop. The old healer stops as well and waits as Catori opens her eyes and turns to face her, dropping the hands that guided her.

The healer's hands rise once again, and the chanting stops. "To be a great leader is to trust your people, learn from your mistakes, and always have the courage to carry out the tasks you would not burden others with." She steps forward and takes Catori's hands, crossing them over our sister's chest. She dips two fingers into her bowl, and they come out dripping with yellow ochre paint. With slow, steady movements, she wipes the paint across Catori's forehead, marking two lines. "One for the life you live amongst the trees, the other for your predecessor's spirit, who watches over you from the heavens."

Catori closes her eyes.

The healer traces a short mark of yellow over each eyelid. "From your grandmother's spirit to yours. You now have the gift of foresight, as she did."

Thrusting both hands in the air over Catori's head, she takes up the chant once more. This time, the crowd drowns her out. Their love, admiration, and excitement for Catori radiates from their smiling faces. The tears that run down Anya's face and the grin on Callian's are reflected in every forest villager. Harm stands beside me, Nirri and Mason on the other side. Mason's face beams with pride and love, his jaw set as he pushes through long breaths.

The healer's waving hands drop, and silence descends all around. "People of the forest, I give you your new leader, Catori. May she serve you as well as your last."

Every last villager and forest dweller from other parts starts lining up at the far end of the green path by Catori's house, each waiting for a turn to speak to and hold the hands of their new leader. I stand in line with Harm, Mason, and Nirri, just before the first family to be seen.

Catori looks down the path. With an inviting smile, she nods for the line to come forward. Every person she greets, and every set of hands she holds, touching her forehead to theirs, man, woman, and child. The leaves are soft underfoot, and a piney fragrance filters through the air as the leaves covering the ground are trodden on the path to our friend. As I reach Catori, silver lines her eyes, and she takes my hands.

"Hey," I whisper, not sure if she is supposed to talk with me yet. She sucks in a breath, gripping my hands, and touches her forehead to mine.

"You did so good," I say to her, and she pulls me into a hug.

"Look what I got this morning," she whispers, tilting her head so that her hair falls away from her neck. A small mark, a bird in flight, sits under her hairline. The rebel mark. Harm's mark. The same one Hanola had, and from what Mason told us, Emmie too. All this time, the women of both sides have been playing the long game. It hits me, right then, just how big this rebellion really is—just how big my family truly is.

"Save me some food for later, hey?" she whispers, a tear spilling down her cheek.

"I sure will." Releasing her, I step off the path.

Catori takes Harm's hands next, touching her forehead to his.

He beams at her, and she huffs a small laugh before letting him go. Mason steps up to her, and she goes still for a moment, as if not sure whether being his leader is going to work. He takes her hands and sets his jaw. She blows out a long breath and touches her forehead to his. His hands tighten around hers slightly. Catori closes her eyes, murmuring something to him. He closes his eyes too. She lets him go, and he stands taking her in for a heartbeat before stepping off the path.

The sun has well and truly set beyond the horizon by the time Catori has greeted each forest dweller, with Callian and Miya the last to see her. They are her council leaders. She takes Miya's hands and touches her forehead to hers. Miya breathes a word, and Catori's chin wobbles. Miya raises her head and steps off the mat, leaving Catori breathless. Callian steps up to his sister, scanning her over as she wobbles where she stands. Hours of standing and bowing to every last person are now taking a toll on her. She grabs his hands in hers and touches her forehead to his, and he stands there, breathing for a moment, then he wraps her in a tight hug. They stay huddled for minutes, as if Callian can't let go, afraid she will crumple to the green piney bed beneath her.

Catori breaks from the hug and stands tall, swaying slightly. Callian moves to help, and she holds up a hand. He stands beside her, taking a spot beside Miya. The healer walks over to the three of them, pulling a small blade from the depths of her white dress. All three hold out their wrists. She slices a small line in each one and binds the three wrists together with her hands, holding them at eye level.

"The bond is made. The leader has chosen," she calls.

Cheers and whoops rise up all around us. Mason stands near Harm, still wearing the smile he had earlier as he waits for her. The villagers make their way to the tables, filing in for food and drink and what feels like another party. Catori, Miya, and Callian walk over to the table where Hanola always sat. But they space them-selves out, looking around the crowd, searching. Catori finds Mason first, beckoning him with one finger and a lopsided smile. He walks up to the table. She leans over and whispers in his ear. He straightens, hesitating before walking around the table to stand next to her. Jeselle wanders over to the table, following Miya's gesture. Catori points to Harm and me before pointing to the two seats beside Mason. Callian is still searching the crowd. I realize he is looking for Nirri, and my heart thunders in my chest. A knot twists in my stomach when I see she has met his gaze, but hasn't moved.

I drag Harm over to the table by the hand and stand next to Mason, leaving the spot next to Callian vacant. Nirri rocks from side to side, looking around the crowd, chewing on her lip, as if not sure what she wants. Callian's face still holds a welcoming smile. She looks to the ground for a heartbeat before slowly walking toward Callian. Passing the last table before ours, she hangs her hands by her sides, looking directly at Callian. A heartbeat later, she rounds the table and stands next to him.

Catori picks up Mason's and Miya's hands, and we hold the hands next to us in succession. When we are linked, all eight of us, Catori bows her head to the waiting seated people—her people. We bow ours.

Cheers and mugs clinking transform the silent spectacle into a party in a heartbeat.

"Let's eat!" Catori announces.

Music starts, and food comes filing out on platters carried by the women in the kitchen. Every plate is full in seconds. I pluck fruits and some smoked meat from the platter, letting one of the older boys fill my mug with wine.

"Is this our new table now?" I call to Catori.

"It is." She grins, clinking her mug with Miya. Throwing back the wine, she turns to me. "This table is for the leaders of the forest, Imani, and that's all of us."

"What do you mean?" I hold my mug halfway to my mouth.

"I'll tell you the details later, at home." She nods at Hanola's—her home now.

The eight of us sit in Catori's new home, on the cushions we have always sat on with Hanola. Everything feels different, less predictable, scarier than when Hanola, Enid, and Emmie were here to make the hard choices and comfort us when things went wrong. The realization that *we* are now that for so many people tangles in my stomach. Nirri sits next to me, fingers wrapped around a mug of tea, staring off into space. Callian sits beside her, not touching, not talking, as if he used up every scrap of goodwill getting her to sit next to him at dinner. Mason lies back on his cushion, hands under his head, eyes closed.

"There are two things I wanted to talk to you all about," Catori says, breaking the silence.

Mason cracks an eye open. The moon overhead is past its apex, and everyone is weary.

"I had to make a choice earlier today—one I hope you're all on board with. In hindsight, I should have asked each one of you, but with the events of the last couple of days, it slipped my mind."

We are all sitting up looking at her now, and she scans the circle of tired bodies around her.

"I had to appoint leaders, a handful of them, to keep the forest people satisfied that our home, our side of the wall is run fairly and not just a dictatorship. So..." She grips her mug. "I appointed Callian as my lead warrior, taking Miya's place. Miya is now my second-in-command. Should anything happen to me, Miya will succeed me." Catori watches every face, hesitating.

"Hanola had councilors?" Mason asks, breaking his silent stare in Catori's direction.

"Yes, but all but one has passed on now. The other relinquished their role, claiming to be too old, so Miya and I have unofficially filled that role for the past two years.

"And there's something else." She grips the mug in her hands a little tighter. Every set of weary, proud, and loving eyes falls on her. "I want you all on my council—all seven of you."

"But we're not forest dwellers, technically. Is that even allowed?" Harm asks.

"We only have minimal rules compared to the desert side, which allows for us to change things when the need arises. If I want you as part of my council, then there is no rule against a person who was not born on our side of the wall being a part of it." She breathes out, setting down the mug on the rug. "I do, however, understand if you don't want to take up the role. It doesn't mean you're bound to me in any way, just that we work as a team, when the need arises. You would still be free to live on your side of the wall, when the time comes."

Mason stares at his lap and clears his throat. "This side of the wall is my home now, Catori. I have no reason to return to the desert—or whatever it ends up being once Harm changes the dial. My home is here."

Catori sucks in a wobbly breath and smiles at him. He takes her hand, rubbing the back of it with his thumb, as if pondering the future.

"I would be honored to be considered part of your council, on one condition," Harm says.

Catori looks up at him, raising an eyebrow. Mason gives him an incredulous stare.

Harm flattens a smile. "That you are also part of ours."

Catori laughs and nods, taking Harm's hand with her free one.

"Well, I'm definitely in," I say, taking Mason's hand in mine and holding Harm's and Catori's still-joined hands in my other. Callian takes in the four of us, mouth tight and head cocked to one side. He glances quickly at Nirri before landing a hand over mine, atop Harm's and Catori's. "Count me in."

Catori looses a rough sigh, a shaky smile pulling up on one side of her face. "Like you had a choice, little brother."

He winks at her, and Mason huffs a laugh.

Nirri sits motionless.

Miya and Jeselle rest their hands over Callian's, joining the bond. The weight of hands over mine presses down. "Nirri...?"

She leans back slightly before shaking her head. Callian's face falls. So does Catori's.

"You can make the choice you feel is best for you, whenever you're ready—not a moment before." Catori's tone is gentle, Hanola's essence slipping through, the kindness and wisdom she held so evident in our new leader. Our friend, our sister.

Nirri places her mug on the floor and pushes to her feet. Her face twists, and she walks out the door. I watch the place where she sat for a heartbeat, trying to understand what is going on in her head. Our hands disperse, and Callian rises and walks out after her. I pick up my mug and sip, trying to fathom what he could possibly say to her now.

"Nirri, wait." Callian's voice drifts in from just beyond the door. Their feet shuffle to a halt.

"What?"

"If you're hesitant because of me, please don't be. There are no strings attached here. The offer from Catori is genuine, regardless of what is or isn't between us."

Mason's brows raise. Harm throws a cushion at him for failing to see what was in front of him this whole time. Catori tilts her head at Mason with a grin. Mason raises his hands, palms up. "What? I've been a little busy with my own life."

Callian's feet shift on the ground outside.

"It's not that," Nirri says.

"Then what?"

"You really want to know?"

"... No?" His word is more of a question than an answer. Collectively, we hold our breath.

"I have spent my entire life in that tower, preparing for the day I would become Chancellor. And in the last few weeks, the life I thought I was going to lead, the person I thought I was expected to be—it's all gone. For the first time, I have absolutely no idea who I am. No idea *what* I am, or who I want to be." Nirri's words are pained.

As if we've all just realized how much our friend has lost in the short time since she left the tower, our faces sag as one with devastation for her. Catori looks at the floor, as if searching for something no one else can see.

"I know how you feel about me, Callian," Nirri says.

Callian mutters something we can't make out.

Nirri continues, "And I really want you to get what you want —I truly do. I want you to be happy. Like, Harm-and-Imani happy. But how can I give you that when I don't even know who I am anymore? I want to go over that wall to see what else there is, what else I can be, where there are no expectations, no rules that I need to obey."

"I thought you had feelings for Elijah?" Callian asks quietly.

"So did I." She releases a long breath. "I realize now that was more out of loneliness than anything else. When he touched me yesterday, I was terrified. You don't feel that way about someone you love. And..."

"And what?"

"And when you held me, on the way down from that climbing pole..." She sucks in a breath. "I couldn't breathe, just touching you."

"But you screamed at me." Callian huffs a nervous laugh.

"I know. It took me by surprise, and so did the way I felt about you. I guess I went on the defensive."

"So, there's hope for us yet?"

"I don't know, Callian. If you're not all Blended by the time I figure out who I am, then maybe. I can't promise you anything. I need to do this for myself first. Please, understand that I am not trying to hurt you."

"I understand, Nirri."

"We can go back inside if you want. That's all I needed to get off my chest." She forces a chuckle.

We all make ourselves busy with the mugs in our hands. Harm runs a hand through my hair and over my shoulders. Catori leans back, reaching for something behind her cushion. Mason straightens, moving away slightly from Catori as Callian plops back onto his cushion. Nirri falls in beside him, still a foot away.

"What'd I miss?" Callian asks.

Harm clears his throat.

"Nothing, we were just about to read this letter from Hanola," Catori says.

"Let's hear it, then," Mason says, lying back on his cushion, head next to Catori's lap, hands under his head.

Catori opens the side of the letter, and tiny scraps drift to the woven mat as she breaks the wax seal. She unfolds the last half, holding the paper open. A heartbeat passes, and she lets out a wobbly breath, eyes scanning the words written in her grandmother's hand.

"My dearest granddaughter," she starts, then blows out a

breath and slams her eyes shut. Mason sits up and leans into her shoulder. She opens her eyes, holding his gaze for a moment. Then she straightens, folding the paper out again.

My dearest granddaughter,
For many years, I have watched and waited—watched you grow into a courageous and selfless leader.

Tears slide down Catori's face. Mason takes her free hand, and she laces her fingers through his.

And I have been waiting for our friend from the sands, Harmen.

Catori looks up from the paper. Harm's Adam's apple bobs, and he gives her a kind smile.

It is my intention to help you both through this inevitable time. However, if I am called to the other side before that time comes, these shall be your guiding words, for the both of you—the leader of the forest people, and the leader of the sands people.

You, Catori, are a leader by birth, and by virtue of the forest people. Harmen is the leader of the people of the sands, by birth and courage. I am grateful to have been able to be with the both of you before this time of transition.

That time has given me the opportunity to witness the two of you evolve into leaders whom your people will follow. Keep your circle close. Your success and Harm's lie in the hearts of you both, but also in the hearts of Imani, Callian, Miya, Jeselle, and finally, Mason and Nirri.

Catori pauses, wiping away the stream of tears with a shaking hand. Every one of us has a tear-streaked face. She blows out a breath and turns the page over.

I saw you all linked to each other, long before our first desert friend crossed the wall.

Every set of eyes is on me now. Catori grabs my hands and squeezes it briefly, releasing me to return her focus to the paper again.

With my passing, the gift of foresight is now yours. Use it, my girl. You have seen firsthand how my visions have added to your life and benefited you and those around you. Always lead from a place of kindness and love. A great leader knows that everyone and everything is connected, and love and kindness trump anything else in this world. It is the one thing always worth fighting for. Please remember, you are stronger than you realize. Believe in yourself and those around you. Fight well. Protect your people. Enjoy the little things.

Forever yours, Hanola.

Harm's chest works through deep cycles against my shoulder. It takes me a minute to realize he has tucked me into his hold. Nirri has moved against Callian, who now has one arm wrapped around her. Her head rests on his shoulder, her tears wetting his shirt. Mason sits with a stunned face beside Catori, his face dry but wrecked. I wipe away the river of tears that flow down my face, rubbing my wet palms on my pants.

Catori folds the letter up slowly, pressing on what is left of the seal.

"You two ready for this?" Callian asks, his voice raw.

Nirri sits up, creating distance between them.

"I guess we have to be," Harm utters.

Catori meets his gaze, a fire lit in her eyes. "We are ready, Harm." A smile grows across her warm face.

Mason stands and extends a hand to Catori. She looks up at him, pausing for a moment to search his face before taking his hand. She pulls herself up, swaying sideways as she tries to balance on her feet. He wraps an arm around her waist to steady her. Callian grunts, rising to his feet. Nirri is already halfway to the door. Harm pulls me to my feet, and I lean against his chest, exhaustion taking its toll. He runs a hand through my hair.

"Let's go to bed," he whispers, leading me home.

CHAPTER 26
MASON

Everyone is gone. Hanola's home—or Catori's, I suppose—is empty. Just the two of us stand here. Catori sways slightly on her feet. She pulls away from the arm I have around her. She only takes a few steps before slumping into a chair.

"I'm going to get you some food," I say, making my way to the door.

"I just need a minute."

I stand in the doorway, watching her push out of the chair she just sat in. She stands in the center of the woven rug—the same one Hanola sat on for decades. The same one I sat on for weeks, working through every damaged part of me, with Catori by my side. With every painful memory or thought that I relived, she was beside me. I watch as she teeters, staring into the distance. The moon is on its descent now; she has been up for hours. She turns to face me, her face wrecked from exhaustion.

Instantly, I move toward her, weaving my way through the scattered cushions. She drops to the floor, legs half tucked under her, shoulders slumped. Her shoulders shake, then the sobs heave from her chest in a never-ending cascade.

I pluck a blanket from the chair and wrap it around her shoulders. She shakes, rocking back and forth. I sit beside her on the rug, wishing I could take away the pain and whatever else is tearing her apart. I stroke her hair, and she lets out a long cry. Her breathing is erratic. Her trembling hands curl and uncurl. I move on the floor, sitting in front of her. With the backs of my hands, I brush her blonde hair from her hot, wet cheeks. She draws in long breaths, looking up from the floor into my eyes.

"She's really gone," she chokes through a sob.

Stroking her hair, I rub away her tears with my thumbs. My chin wobbles; the pain that twists her face is ripping me apart. I pull in a deep breath. "I'm so sorry."

She claws at my shirt with half-curled fingers. "I can't do this without her."

I swallow the lump in my throat that almost steals my breath. "Yes, you can. I know you can."

She lays a hand on her chest, steadying her breathing. "She was supposed to be here when I became the leader. How am I supposed to make the right choices without her here to help me?" Tears stream down her face, her green eyes burning into mine.

"We'll get through it together—the eight of us. You are *not* alone, Catori."

She nods, slapping a hand over her mouth, trying to hold in the sobs. I release her, and she looks up at me as I stand.

"I'll duck out and get you some food," I whisper and bend down to adjust the blanket around her shoulders tighter.

Out the door, I jog to the eating area for some leftovers. A row of platters of fruit sits on a bench. I grab a handful, dropping them into my folded-up shirt before making my way back to Catori. I walk back in, and she is standing in the center of the rug, watching the door. Her eyes follow me as I walk through the cushions back to her. She drops the blanket from her shoulders. Her face is red from crying, but dry now. Her breathing has steadied, and she stands with eyes locked on mine, while I hold the fruit in my shirt. I watch as her chest rises and falls. She takes off her beads and dumps them on a cushion at her feet, then drops her hands to her sides.

"Fruit?" I ask, holding a piece out to her.

She looks at the fruit and then back at my face. "I'm not hungry, Mason," she whispers.

She pulls the fruit from my shirt, dumping it on the cushion with the beads. She moves closer, her face only inches from mine.

"I should go, Catori."

Her beautiful green eyes search my face for... something. I know what she wants. Every fiber of my being wants her, and my heart thumps against my ribs as my hands drop to my sides.

"I really should go," I breathe as her lips brush mine.

Heavens knows I don't want to go anywhere.

I slide a hand around her waist. I don't want to leave. I want to touch every part of her; I want to love every part of Catori. I rest my forehead on hers.

"If we're going to do this," I say, swallowing hard, "then it will be when both of us are in a good place, so there are no regrets."

She blows out a small laugh and slides a hand behind my neck, the other combing through my hair. The fire in my core surges to life, and I let out a groan to ease it. Catori pulls back and looses a shuddering breath. "Please just stay."

"I want to—please, know that I do—but I can't. I don't want you waking up to regrets on top of everything else you have on your plate." I'm still holding her waist, not wanting to let her go. Ever.

Catori snuggles into my chest, and I sink my head into her hair.

"Stay a little while, then?"

"Until you're asleep," I whisper.

She pulls away, grabbing my hands, and leads me to the large bed in the small bedroom at the back. A small table by the wide bed with an empty glass and a jug full of water are the only other items in the room. The white covers and two pillows have been brought over from Catori's house. Mandy must have organized this for her. This is her home now.

She crawls onto the bed, making room for me to lie beside her. I sit on the side of the bed and remove my boots and belt. Lying on the bed, I roll onto my side to face her, the way we did in the forest. She huddles into me, hands curled around my shirt, fingers touching my chest. I wrap an arm around her and pull her tight against me, to keep her warm. One hand lets go of me briefly, and she reaches behind herself to pull a blanket over the both of us. She looks up at me with a small smile, her eyes full of tears. I kiss her forehead. She snuggles back in, and I run a hand over her hair.

"Night," I breathe.

"Night, Mason," she murmurs into my chest.

I lie with her, wrapped around her, until her breathing slows. It takes every ounce of self-control I have to let her out of my hold, slide off the bed, and pull up another blanket to lay over her. I stand by the bed for a heartbeat, watching her breathe. Her golden hair spills over the pillow, her pink lips slightly parted, her chest rising and falling. With a light touch, I sweep her hair from her face, tucking it behind her ear. Something in my chest snaps. My throat thickens, and the ache in my core shrouds my heart.

There is no going back now. She is my home.

I pick up my boots and belt and pad through Catori's home, tracking toward Callian's, praying he is sound asleep.

Three days later, we gather around the table that Hanola headed for our strategy meetings. Only now, Catori stands tall at the end of the table laden with maps, papers, and charts, her cheeks full of color. Every person in the room watches as she stares at the diagrams of the dial, then at the papers that hold the information on the power source. This is our last meeting before we go over the wall into the mountain sector. Every piece of information that Nirri and I can give her, she is asking for.

We stand for hours, racking our brains for anything big or small that will help us. Nirri has outlined the basic layout of the terrain and has made a haphazard guess at the number of ex-Guardians who live there. As for the "savages," as she calls them, she has limited knowledge. That is the part that worries me the most.

Callian folds his arms across his chest. "If we don't know what numbers the savages have, do we at least know if there are any allies amongst the ex-Guardians that share their side of the wall?"

"I'm not certain, but I highly doubt it. Guardians enter any territory claiming it as their own. I assume they've done the same in the mountain sector, which would not bode well for its original inhabitants," Nirri says.

"So, maybe the savages—the mountain men—would be interested in allying with us?" Catori ventures.

"It's possible, but it would be a risk to even enter their territory, Catori," Nirri warns.

"I guess we'll have to just get over there and see what we find, who is loyal to who, and what the numbers are. So, we go in with stealth, until we can assess what lies on that side of the wall," Miya says.

Catori hums, agreeing.

"When do we need to leave?" Harm asks, wrapping an arm

around Imani, as if the thought of leaving the safety of their home, even together, grates on him.

"In a week, I think. But I have a few more things to iron out. So, I'll let you know in a day or two," Catori says, looking around the room, checking where everyone sits with this plan, open to objections should we have any. I don't.

"Great. You're free to go." Catori smiles, and one by one, the faces that have become my family file out the door into the dappled sunlight piercing through the canopy. Nirri drops in beside Imani, Harm, and Callian, chatting about getting new blades from the smith. I watch them go, until only Catori and I are left standing in her home. She rounds the table and comes to a halt in front of me, leaning on the table, arms folded across her chest. Her bright-green eyes search mine, wanting to know if I have held anything back.

"What are you looking for?" I whisper, leaning my forehead against hers.

"Not looking, just thinking," she whispers back, and her hands drop to her sides.

"About?" I utter.

She lets out a small, loose laugh. "A few things, actually." Her hands rest on the collar of my shirt. I tilt my head to get a better look at her face. The dark circles under her eyes and the vacant stare have been replaced with her usual fire. Warmth radiates through my chest, and a smile stretches over my face. She responds, smiling back, her fingers tracing the curve of my smile, eyes following. My breathing becomes shallow. She closes her eyes.

"And what are they?" I finally rasp.

"What we'll find over the wall. Whether or not Harm and Imani are ready. What happens if we don't make it back..." She hesitates, her hand on my collar tugging it down, her fingers on my mouth dropping to grip the other side of my collar. "And..."

My heart thunders against my ribs. "And?"

"And the thought of putting you in danger, again. Putting everyone I care about in more danger than we have ever been in before. At least with the tower, we knew what to expect. This is worse. Being the one asking you all to do this is like a crushing weight I can't get rid of." Catori breathes through a shuddering breath, sinking her head into my chest.

I wrap both arms around her and hold on tight. I play the next words over in my head to make sure they sound okay, not wanting her to think I don't understand what she is telling me. I do, and all too well: sending officers to carry out abhorrent tasks, reporting on the ones who couldn't bring themselves to do their job, knowing full well they could end up trapped on the other side of the mountain wall, or worse.

"Every person that stood in this room today is willing to do whatever it takes. You may be the person who's sending us, but they're all ready to fight for what they believe in. We all know it's worth it, even knowing how hard it will be."

She breathes a long breath and stands tall, meeting my gaze. "If something happens to you, I..."

"We—you and me—will be fine, no matter what. I promise you that."

She closes her eyes, and I grab her face with both my hands. Her chin trembles.

"Catori," I utter.

A tear runs down her cheek. I move my hands around her neck and into her hair. She opens her eyes, silver lining them both.

Her hands tug on my shirt, pulling me closer. I lower my face to hers. She tilts her head up and brushes her lips on mine. My heart hammers in my chest, and every part of me comes alive.

This time, I kiss her back, and her hands wander up my neck to cup my face. Running both hands down her neck, I trace the lines of her collarbones before letting my hands fall to her waist. Her weapons belt stops my hands from moving any further. I place a hand under her arm and one around her waist, lifting her onto the table. She huffs a laugh and plunges deeper into the kiss. I move into her space, and she wraps her legs around my back, keeping me against her. I run a line of kisses down her neck. Her breath stops. My core burns with every inch I descend further down her neck...

A throat clears behind me, and Catori sits up instantly, hands checking her hair and tunic. Imani's light laughter drifts through the doorway. I relax a little, thanking my lucky stars it isn't Callian. I don't think either of us are ready for that conversation yet.

"I think you two are actually supposed to be training for something else?" Imani chuckles and steps into the room.

Catori's cheeks flush crimson, and I clear my throat this time, working through a few breaths while the burning in my core peters out. Turning to face Imani, Catori jumps down beside me, giving me a sheepish look before parading out the door, winking at Imani. Imani laughs, but gives me one last elated look. It's all over her face —happiness for me, for Catori. I follow Imani out the door.

Callian and Harm are hard at it in the sparring ring by the time we get there. Catori and Imani start running with the sacks, and Nirri and I have been assigned to the climbing pole.

"You want me to go first?" I ask, remembering the last time Nirri scaled this pole and froze at the top.

"Nope, I can go first," she says, shoving a foot onto the first rung. She makes it to the top in no time. For a heartbeat, she cradles the pole, letting it sway under her grip. The clash of metal from the sparring ring stops instantly. Callian stands, hands by his sides, waiting for any indication that Nirri is in trouble. She pokes her tongue out at him and flips him off, then lowers herself slowly, one foot after the other. Her face when she jumps down the remaining three pegs is lit up. Somehow, he gave her that—the courage—just by being her friend as she figures out what she wants. And who she is has rallied her spirits—and his.

"Right, Rayner. Let's see you do it quicker than me," Nirri says, gesturing to the pole with both hands, a grin wide on her face.

I push up on the first rung, finding a fast rhythm in no time. I reach the top quickly, as Nirri did. I pause for a moment, the massive canopy that lies in every direction reminding me of how small we are, how little we matter some days, how the big things truly outlast the little things. Swaying above the laughing and happy people below, I make a promise to myself that I will never let anything happen to any of them. We all get to be here for the good part at the end. We all get to live.

After everything each of us has lived through, that's the only fair outcome.

CHAPTER 27

IMANI

"'D-dry'..." I sound the word out, gripping the small tome Harm found for me to practice with. I say it over and over in my head, hoping it sticks, hoping that the next time I see this word, I will remember it.

"Good. Keep going," Harm whispers, running a hand through my hair. His bare chest is against my back, his legs flanking mine, and his face is bent down over my shoulder as he follows along with every word I painstakingly sound out like a small child. Heat rises to my cheeks, and he rubs my back with both hands. I lift my head back, stretching my neck, and start the next line in the paragraph.

"'He was on-only a sm-small boy.'"

A kiss lands on my neck.

Correct. I got it correct.

Honestly, at this rate, I should have bargained for a kiss for every word; we are going to be here all day. I groan and lie back on his chest, resting my head on his shoulder.

"Keep going. You're doing so well," Harm says, nipping my ear.

"I would rather do anything else in this bed right now than read," I groan impatiently.

"When you finish the paragraph, you can have whatever you like," he says, a smile pulling up his face. Prick. But heaven knows how much I love this man.

"'The boy lo-lov-loved his dog and his t-toy.'" I sigh. "Really, this is the most boring book you could have picked, Harm."

He laughs and turns the page for me. "One more line, and I am all yours," he rasps near my ear.

"'But one day, the boy's mot-moth… Ugh!" I blow out an exaggerated breath, "'… moth-er… mother sold the dog. The boy cr-cri-cri-ed. Cried,'" I finish.

Why would she do that? Horrible woman. I let out a grunt, tossing the book to the end of the bed.

"Stupid woman. All that, and she sold the boy's dog anyway. Why do you like reading this stuff anyhow?"

"Oh, I don't, it's completely boring." The grin that splits over his gorgeous face is absolutely obnoxious.

"Then why on earth are you making *me* read it?!"

"Because it's easy to learn. I still have no idea how you grew up a teacher's daughter and can't read," he jabs, whipping his eyebrows up, grin still plastered over his face. I elbow his chest, and he lets out a gruff laugh.

"I'm a rebel. I thought you knew that. Now," I say, turning around, putting my legs around his waist, "my turn to torture you."

Harm breathes out a laugh, sliding his hands behind my neck and pulling me to his mouth.

The rap on the door startles me some and annoys me more. I peel myself from the bed, tossing Harm his shirt before tidying my hair. I pass the small window to our house, pulling back the white cloth briefly on my way past. Callian is standing on the other side of the door. I run a hand over my clothes and look back at Harm sitting on the bed. I open the door, and Callian strides in, stopping in the center of our home, eyes alternating between Harm and me.

"What's up, brother?" Harm says, rising from the bed.

"Catori and Miya want to see you." He keeps his gaze fixed on Harm for a moment, then turns to me. "Imani, Jeselle says she needs you on the archery range for an hour or so, straight after breakfast."

"Okay, we were just getting ready for breakfast anyway," I say with a slight grin.

"Liar." He chuckles and wanders out the door.

I throw my hands up and feign a horrified look at Harm. He laughs, shoving his feet into his boots. I pull the dresser drawer open, snatching up my blue scarf and twisting it around my unruly hair. Most of it makes it into the wrap. Harm plants a kiss on my neck, his hands resting on my waist. I lean my head into his. He wanders toward the door, grabbing his weapons.

"See you at breakfast, or at training," he says, pausing with a hand on the doorframe.

"See you there." I grab my belt and buckle it. I sheathe every blade on my hips and slip on my boots.

My stomach grumbles most of the way to breakfast. How long have we been up reading for? Part of me wishes I could already read, so I could spend my mornings and evenings doing other things. But I know I need to learn, and Harm teaching me is as good as it gets.

Nirri and Mason sit at the table, eating, not talking. I sink onto the bench next to Nirri and grab a plate, loading it with one of everything in my reach. Mason pours me a mug of water.

"Morning," I say to them both.

"Morning," Nirri says. Mason smiles at me, mouth full of food.

"Where's Harm?" Nirri asks.

"With Catori and Miya. He'll be here soon."

"Are you on archery this morning too?" Nirri asks.

"Yep. Jeselle is expecting you too, then?"

She nods, shoving a hunk of bread into her mouth.

"The company will be good, then." I scrunch my nose up at her.

Mason watches the both of us, quietly eating his food.

"Well, it will be much better than my current archery skills, at least." Nirri laughs.

"Oh, heavens, mine too," I say picking a handful of fruit pieces from the plate.

"There was a little boy here looking for you earlier. You just missed him," Mason says, picking up his mug.

"Miles?"

"I guess so. The one Harm visits every other day."

I stop chewing. "Harm goes there every other day?" I'm not sure I want to know the answer.

Mason looks confused. "Was I not supposed to tell you?"

"No, it's... fine. Harm is free to go wherever he wants. It just surprised me, that's all." Truth is, I am surprised he still visits my mother and Miles so often. I shouldn't be; that is him all over: kindness personified. The heat of guilt creeps over me. If Harm has been there, I probably should have gone too, at least more than the one time, when I left angry and upset. Or does my mother just put it down to my problematic behavior, as usual? The thought of Miles knowing who I am to him and the fact that I never make an effort to visit or get to know my own brother winds a knot in my stomach. Instantly, I don't feel hungry anymore. Pushing the plate away, I chug down the water and stand. "I'll see you at archery," I say to Nirri.

She smiles and waves me off, food in hand. At least Nirri is happier, which is so good to see. Callian seems to be out of his dark mood that lasted weeks. That in itself is something.

I march my way to the archery range. Jeselle is already there, matching quivers and bows to participants. I fall in line behind the last girl. My gaze drifts to the home my mother and brother occupy on the edge of the village, bordering the training area. From here, I watch their figures move through the house. My mother ambles through her kitchen. Miles runs out the front door, playing ball with himself, hopping from side to side as if he is two people. He is quick and agile, like me —a trait we no doubt received from my mother. Her build is identical to mine.

Voices beside me get louder above the clatter of wooden bows being arranged on the table. A figure moves in front of me.

"Earth to Imani." Jeselle laughs, waving a hand in front of my face.

I tear my gaze away from Miles to Jeselle. "Imani to earth. Sorry."

"You alright?"

"Yeah, sorry, I was a million miles away."

"We noticed." Jeselle gestures to the row of archers ready to shoot, waiting on me, the last to be equipped and positioned.

"Sorry," I whisper.

She laughs, eyeing me over for size. She hands me a recurve bow, four feet long, and a quiver of what she warns me are sharp-tipped arrows. I throw the quiver over my shoulder and grip the bow in my left hand, stepping up to the row, in line with seven other archers.

Nirri is not here yet.

"Listen up. This morning, you're just getting used to the feel of your bow, the weight, and the angles you need to hold it at, and practicing nocking your arrows. We're not here to hit the bullseye; that is another lesson entirely. On my count, you will raise, nock, and fire. We'll have ten rounds; each of you has ten arrows. Then we'll have a five-minute break and go again. Any questions?" Jeselle asks.

Every head shakes a no.

So far, it all seems straightforward, and I have already had a couple of lessons with her when I was rehabilitating my leg, so I have a rough idea of what I am doing.

"Take your arrow," Jeselle calls.

Every person in line pulls an arrow from their quiver.

"Nock," Jeselle calls.

The clatter of eight arrows nocking echoes around us.

"Draw back," Jeselle calls.

Bowstrings groan, breaths are loosed, and a few arms shake under the weight of the force.

"Hold... Three, two, one, fire!" Jeselle calls.

Eight arrows whip past the wooden curves supporting them, sailing for the round targets twenty feet away. A few hit the boards, but most do not.

"Good! Again!" This time, she plucks her own arrow, settling the bow in her right hand, her fine fingers curling around the old wood. With her bow nocked, she calls the steps out as she does it herself. We draw back as a collective, with more groaning strings, but less shaking arms this time.

"Fire!"

Every arrow sails, some straight, some not. Jeselle's arrow sinks deep and true into the bullseye. She turns and smiles at her line of students.

"Next arrow," she calls. She works through her quiver of arrows along with us, until all ten are done and our arms ache.

I prop the bow against my leg and shake out my arms, which are aching from the weight of the string.

Nirri runs up to the range, apologizing for being late. Jeselle steps toward her, sizing her up for her equipment. A heartbeat later, Nirri has a quiver slung over her right shoulder and a bow, the same size as mine, in her right hand.

"You're left-handed?" I ask.

"Yep, much to my grandfather's disgust. Apparently, he dislikes anything that's not *his* normal." She rolls her eyes.

It is the first time I have ever heard her speak about the Chancellor as her grandfather. She has already lost her grandmother and has no parents or siblings. My stomach plummets, realizing that if we remove the Chancellor from power, if he gets put down, she will have *no one* left. No family left. I loose a breath, fighting the prickling in my eyes. It is the first time I have truly understood how much Nirri has lost and still stands to lose in all this, yet she participates anyway. She is here, helping us. The load she must carry far outweighs any that the rest of us do.

She readjusts the bow in her right hand, readying her left to draw back, practicing while we all recover from the first round. Her face is happy, and her eyes are bright.

And my heart aches for her.

Both Catori and Nirri feel more like sisters than friends. I want to wrap my arms around her and tell her she will not lose another person, that she will never lose anything else that she has held onto her whole life. But I can't; it would be a lie. All I can do for her now is add to her life, the way I wanted to for Harm.

"I'm certain you're going to be better at this than me. You have a feel for it already," I say.

She drops her arm, holding the bow horizontally by her side. "I've always wanted to have a go at archery, but there wasn't really room for flinging arrows in the tower."

"Well, only one way to see if you're going to like it," Jeselle says, gesturing for the nine of us to take our positions in the line.

Nirri stands next to me, her curly blonde hair blowing around her shoulders, her eyes drilling into the targets beyond us. Then she takes a stance, feet slightly apart, waiting for Jeselle's instructions.

"Bows ready," Jeselle calls, raising her own on the other side of Nirri.

"Nock your arrows," she calls, mostly for Nirri's sake this time. Jeselle watches as Nirri slides the arrow onto the string and rests it on her fingers wrapped around the bow. She nods in approval, and a wide smile grows over Nirri's pretty face.

"Draw back," Jeselle calls.

My arm burns, despite the brief respite.

"Hold... One, two, three, fire!" Jeselle calls.

I loose my arrow, not watching where it flies. Instead, I track Nirri's arrow to the target. It hits the edge of the board and flips to the ground. Only hers and Jeselle's made the board this round. Nirri's eyes stay fixed on the board, taking in the lack of arrows on everyone else's boards.

"Wow, that felt good," she breathes.

"Good work! Let's go again," Jeselle says, calling out her instructions.

Ten arrows later, Nirri has most of hers sinking into the target board somewhere. Mine, however, have mostly found homes in the grass to either side.

Our arms hang trembling. Jeselle sends us off to our other training and daily tasks. She asks Nirri to stay back. Nirri's excited face meets mine, and I wrap her in a hug.

"What's that for?" she whispers.

"For being much better at archery than I am. And because it's so good to see a smile on your face." I let her go.

"You did okay too." She bites her bottom lip.

"I think I'll stick to fighting knives," I say with a laugh. With a wave, I wander back to the village.

My focus returns to Miles and his ball. He is still playing, albeit a slightly different game: kicking the ball against the house. I let out a long breath and walk toward my mother's house. Miles's face lights up when he sees me coming. He charges toward me, ball in hand. I beam a smile, feeling the pang of guilt for not coming sooner. Better now than not at all, I convince myself.

"Hey, Imani, I saw you shooting arrows! That looked awesome!"

I crouch down, meeting his gaze. "I wasn't very good at it. It's harder than it looks, for me at least. What are you playing?"

"Nothing. It's kind of boring by myself." He rolls the ball across his stomach sideways, over and over.

"You don't play with the other kids?"

His face falls. "I did once. They didn't really want a desert dweller in their games."

My chest tightens. "Oh, well, you know, Harm and I are also desert dwellers, if you want some people in *your* game."

His face brightens, and he studies my face, as if not believing I will stay and play. I don't blame him; I have not come to see him, not even once. In this moment, I am so glad Harm did.

"Do you think Harm would play with us now?"

"Well, I have to go and find him, but if he's not busy, I'm sure he would love to."

"Yes!" he squeals, throwing his ball into the sky.

Footsteps track toward the front door. "Who are you talking to, Miles?" Mother appears, drying her hands on a tea towel. I straighten up and stand next to Miles. Her gaze finds mine, and her mouth opens slightly.

"Imani." For a heartbeat, she looks between Miles and me, as if it's the first time she has ever seen her two children standing together. Silver lines her eyes. She clears her throat.

"Did you want to come in for a bit? I was just making morning tea," she offers.

Miles looks at me, waiting with excited eyes.

"Sure."

He grabs my hand with his small fingers and drags me into their home. Across the threshold, everything looks familiar, as if my mother has simply picked up her home in Perendi and dropped it in the forest. The table, in the center of the front room, as it always was when I was growing up, is set with three places. Food is piled onto a plate in the center.

"I'll just get another chair and set another place," she says, puttering around her small kitchen. Instantly, I feel like a small girl, with my mother buzzing around while I wait for supper. Waiting for my father to come home in his grey uniform, weary and stressed. She drags another chair to the table; it looks new compared to the others. It's like the ones in our house, but with slightly different joints. I have seen them somewhere before.

"Someone else coming?" I ask, sitting next to Miles. He fidgets with his plate, swirling it around, and it clatters on the wooden table.

A throat clears behind me. "Yep—me," Harm says from the doorway.

I turn in my seat. Miles springs out of his and jumps into Harm's arms, wrapping his arms around his neck.

"Hey, buddy," Harm says softly and sets him down on the floor between us. I rise from my seat, gaze fixed on his eyes. My mother's puttering has gone silent. Today must be one of the days he visits, and my mother fixes him food. A stone lodges in my throat. I remind myself that I am here for Miles.

"Great, I'm starving," I say.

Harm raises an eyebrow and sits down beside me. Miles sits on the other side, leaving the seat across from me open for my mother.

"How was archery?" Harm asks.

"Not great, but Nirri was fantastic." It's the truth, and I am glad to make conversation to break up the awkwardness.

"I saw you, Imani. You didn't look that bad," Miles says.

"Thanks. Have you decided what game we're going to play with Harm yet?"

Harm turns to me and stares, letting out a small sound, as if he has waited for this day, and seeing it has him a little impressed. I pluck a morsel from the plate. Miles grabs a piece of fruit and sinks his teeth into it.

"To the desert dwellers," I say, holding my mug to Miles's. He picks it up, clinking it against mine. I wink at him, and my mother sinks into her chair, face twisted between overwhelming love and happiness.

A kiss lands on my cheek from the man to my left. My heart all but explodes.

CHAPTER 28
IMANI

"Miles, honey, can you take Harm out back and show him the broken door?" Mother asks.

The two of them leave the table and wander out the back door, Miles chattering away about some game he has invented.

"Imani, I need to ask you something—and please don't get angry at me for asking."

It must be something important, if neither Harm nor Miles is wanted here. I fold my arms across my chest in preparation for the onslaught. "Go ahead."

She sighs and plays with the last bite of food on her plate, eyes tracking its movements and every crumb that falls from it.

"Are you going to kill Fletcher?"

My breath stops.

Why would she ask that? Is that not what needs to happen?

"You think he deserves to live?" My voice is low and raw.

"I think he's a product of the regime—and like your friend Mason, he could change, if he wanted to."

I blow out a breath. "Hanola was responsible for Mason's rehabilitation, and she is no longer here." Trying to remain calm, I run my hands up and down my legs before gripping my knees.

"I realize that. But surely there's someone else who could help him," she says, looking through the door distantly before her gaze returns to me. "You two have never seen eye to eye about his work, but he adored you. It broke his heart when you left."

"So, again, this is my fault? Every atrocity he has carried out is *my* fault?"

Her face softens. "Of course it isn't." She reaches across the table, palm up. I leave my hands on my knees. "I just mean, he's your father. But he is also Miles's father. If you take his life, you take him from Miles and me, just as much as from yourself."

Miles. I stare at her, fighting back the burning tears that threaten to fill my eyes. I stand and lay a hand on the table.

"I don't know. That is the answer to your question."

It's the truth. Every part of me has longed to punish him, since the day he left me stranded in the desert, carting Harm off to prison. But when it came to it, in the tower, I couldn't do it. It was like my senses were dulled. My will to inflict as much harm on him as possible ebbed with just one tiny memory from my childhood. Instead, he went into some trance and was seconds away from killing me. When it matters, every morsel of empathy and humanity has been trained out of them; they can kill without a conscience. Mason turned that part off, but he was only in the regime for just over a year. Fletcher has been part of it for over fifteen. Could Fletcher do that too? Would he want to?

Would he even want his family back?

The thought of unraveling that scenario terrifies me.

"No! Absolutely not!" I yell, feeling less imposing than I sound sitting on our bed.

Harm's brows deepen, and he hangs his head, hands braced on the post of our canopy bed. "Come on, Imani. This isn't just for you."

I slide off the bed and pace the floor in front of the hearth, hands on my hips. My mother's words are in my mind. Miles's happy little face hovers in the front of every thought.

"And what happens when it goes wrong? What if you can't get in and out? Or what if you can, and he hurts one of them?" I cry, almost breathless.

"He won't. We will all be there," he says, voice softer now.

"You cannot be there. He'll kill you without a second thought."

"So, you're thinking about it, then?" He smiles.

"Maybe I'll save him the trouble," I growl, stalking over to Harm. He looks up at me, brown eyes burning into mine. I loose a breath. Heaven knows he could get whatever he wants with that look alone. "Have you talked to Callian or Catori about your ridiculous plan?"

"Not Callian, but Catori actually put it on the table yesterday, before breakfast. I assume it was Mason's idea originally. At least, it would be a smart strategic move, if it works."

"And if it doesn't, and you go to all that effort, and my father has no interest in swapping sides?" My voice is a low growl.

"Then at least we can say we tried. At least we gave him the option of coming home—to you and Petria," he says.

"Why just me and my mother?"

"He doesn't know about Miles, yet. Petria was only two months along when you left, and he started living at the barracks. She was not in a great place, and she never had the chance to tell him. Honestly, I don't think she had the heart to," Harm says flatly.

I stand, mouth agape, stunned. My heart flips in my chest. "He doesn't know he has a *son*?!"

Harm shakes his head. "No. But if he did, maybe he would want to come home." He cringes the moment the words leave his mouth.

"It's okay, I get it," I whisper. This is not new to me. The daughter whom he never got along with is not a very big draw. But a son—that's another chance for him. That may be big enough.

"You really think he's going to give everything up and live under you and Catori's rule to be with his son?"

"No. For his family, for his second chance," Harm says, a small smile pulling his lips up.

"I still don't like it. If he hurts you, this time, I really will kill him."

I need some air.

"I'll see you later. I need to process."

He watches me as I leave, shutting the door behind me. Breaking into a run, I make my way toward the forest, heading toward the first clearing.

Callian's larger figure moves ahead of us, the dark mostly covering us. After an hour of arguing with Harm, we have left him and Catori in the village. Mason, Callian, and I stand with our backs flat against the stone wall, waiting for the guard to change so we can slip through the stone door. The recurve bow I insisted on bringing digs into my spine. Cool, dark air floats around the three of us. We tug our head wraps tighter, pulling the last strip around our faces, with only our eyes visible.

Soon, chatting overhead signals that the men are swapping over. Callian hunts for the stone in the wall to press.

Mason stands behind me, as if guarding a precious asset. The groan of the heavy door makes me cringe, and I cast my glance upward, checking for any recognition on the faces of the Guardians standing above us. We slip into the narrow passage and wait for the door to slide shut behind us. I lean my bow and quiver against the wall near the door. Everything is pitch black.

Flint scratches behind me, and Mason's face illuminates above a small flame flickering in the almost nonexistent draft inside the wall. Callian stands beside me, hands on his weapons, his jaw set. Even in the dim light, his concern shows.

"This way," Mason says, leading us deeper into the wall.

Minutes pass as we pad through, moving toward the Guardian barracks. None of us speak. We have gone over this plan three times. Every part of it is risky. But if we can pull it off, there is a chance that we can gain a powerful ally.

"Just around the next bend, there's an interior door. The only problem is, we won't know if there's anyone on the other side of it until we crack it open. It isn't locked. Nobody ever wants to get into the home of the regime," Mason whispers.

Callian's brows drop again, but he nods for Mason to go ahead. Passing me the last of the flickering torch, Mason lays a hand on the door handle. The metal door rattles slightly with his movement. I strain to hear any footsteps on the other side. Mason presses his ear to the door, doing the same. With a small fluid movement, he presses the lever down and cracks the door open slightly. A sliver of light bursts through.

No movement. No noise.

He pushes the door open further, poking his head through, swiveling it left and right before opening the door completely to let us through.

"There won't be anyone on guard inside the barracks. But we'll need to get past the officers' living quarters to get to Fletcher's quarters. To do that, we're going to need to make a pit stop first." He tracks along the corridor as quickly as possible without making unnecessary noise, and we follow closely. We pass two doors on our left before slipping into the third one. Rows of small square shelves line the long room. Each one has a name and number on it. Some have the names scrubbed out with others written over top. Every single hole has uniforms in it. It's like a sort of laundry collection room.

"Here, Imani, this fellow is about your size," Mason says, passing me the uniform from Johnathan Bendel's spot. He wanders a little further and pulls out a shirt and pants, considerably larger, tossing them to Callian. Finally, he plucks out a set for himself. I slide the pants over my fitted forest clothes, slipping the shirt on as fast as I can, then the pants. The boys have theirs on before I am finished. Mason hands me a hat to hide my hair. I shove it on my head, and the mass of hair I have wrapped up beneath it makes it tight.

"Right. Now we stand a chance," Mason says.

Callian looks down at his uniformed body and frowns.

"You look fine," I say, noting the bulk that strains under his shirt. That is going to be obvious.

"Let's get this over and done with," Callian says in a low, strained voice.

We slip back out the door, heading toward the living quarters, passing the mess hall. Officers sit at rectangular tables, some eating, some talking. Every man seems to be comfortable. Nobody notices us passing by the door. We walk down the hallway to the last one.

It's closed. A white-and-silver label is affixed to the door: Daniel Fletcher – Commander. My throat tightens. It has been an age since I've seen my father's name written anywhere, and even before I learned to read, I have always been able to recognize it—on orders I plucked from officers' pockets in busy village squares, on the paper that sits between my parents Blending sands, on the books he used to carry home as a teacher.

Mason knocks. Callian stiffens beside me.

"Come," my father's voice drifts from inside the room.

Mason shoots us both a look, reminding us of what we need to do, and opens the door.

Fletcher sits in a lounge chair, a pile of papers on a small side table next to him. One is in his hand as he scans the lines of text. He doesn't look up. Mason shuts the door, flicking the lock.

"Whatever it is, can it wait until morning?" Fletcher asks.

Mason looks at me.

"Probably not," I say.

The paper hits his lap. His gaze finds mine. Eyes widening, he takes in the three people in his now locked room. The hatred in his eyes shifts to Mason.

"Catching up on some light reading, Commander?" Mason mocks, hands trailing over Fletcher's neat desk.

"How the hell did you three get in here?!" he spits, standing up, sending the chair backward a few inches.

I raise an eyebrow as a smirk grows across my face. "We walked."

"Imani," he growls.

Ah, at least he recognizes me in this ridiculous uniform. "We won't take up much of your time. Sit down."

"Or what? You'll throw a knife into me?" he snaps, stepping closer.

"I told you it would be the hard way," Callian mutters to Mason.

Mason rolls his eyes before dropping his head and closing them. "Fine," he breathes.

Callian stalks toward Fletcher. I slip a hand past the baggy grey trousers and into the pants pocket of my forest clothes, pulling out an oil-soaked rag.

"Your daughter told you to sit, old man," Callian warns, inches from his face, hands on his weapons.

"Just do it," I say, exasperated.

Fletcher drops back into his seat, eyes burning into mine. Callian walks around the chair. Mason snatches his hand up from the desk, pulling himself away from whatever caught his attention, and walks up to Fletcher, standing directly in front of him.

"I see you've been busy terrorizing village people over the wall," Mason says, distracting Fletcher from what is happening around him. Fletcher snarls at him, hands gripping the arms of the chair.

I reach the side of the chair, hands covertly unfolding the rag. Callian grips his shoulders. He opens his mouth to shout. I slam the oil-soaked rag over his mouth and nose. A few heartbeats later, he slumps over in his chair.

"Phase one complete. Now the most dangerous phase: exiting," Mason says.

Callian and Mason rip Fletcher from his chair, one under each arm. We make for the door. I flick the lock and turn back to them.

"You're going to have to make it seem like you care about him, especially if you're taking him to the healer's quarters," I say.

The boys readjust Fletcher between them, making it look like they are carrying him, not dragging him. I open the door and lead the way back toward the exit, three doors and one mess hall away. We approach the mess hall, and three officers come out, laughing and throwing the last of their food into their mouths, like their entire existence is one big game. I hold my breath, head down, and walk past them.

"Hey, you guys okay?" one says.

Mason is on the opposite side; I pray they don't recognize him.

"Yeah, he passed out in his room. We're taking him to the healer's quarters to sleep it off," Callian says calmly.

The blood in my head thunders. I shove my shaking hands into the pants pockets of my uniform.

"Night, then," another says, padding down the hall. His comrades follow. They don't seem too concerned about their commander. Figures.

We keep going. The exit door is only a couple of yards away. Fletcher makes a noise, and Mason picks up the pace. The oil fumes should have him out for hours; I mustn't have held it on long enough. I slip my hand back in my pocket for the rag.

It's not there. I must have left it on his desk. Dammit.

I shoot Callian a look, concern mixed with something like fear. He gets the message and pulls the door open. Mason and Callian shove Fletcher into the darkness, and I click the door shut behind me, leaning against it for good measure.

"What?" Mason whispers.

"I left the rag in his quarters."

"Guess we'll have to do it the old-fashioned way if he wakes up," Callian says dryly, a grin growing across his face.

"Let's just get out of here first," Mason says, scratching another flame alight.

We make our way back to the stone door. The guards above us will no doubt hear the door this time. But unlike last time, we only have to run to get away. I feel every inch of stone next to the door for the brick to press.

Fletcher stirs in Callian's and Mason's arms.

"Hurry, Imani," Callian whispers.

Fletcher lets out a guttural growl, and I whip my hands over the stony surface faster. My trailing fingers find the right stone a few heartbeats later. I push it in and stand jiggling on the spot, waiting for it to open far enough for us to slip through. I pluck my bow and quiver from against the wall.

Another growl from Fletcher, and he strains against the hold on him. Callian shoves him back into the darkness. Mason's flame reaches his fingertips, dying out instantly. Dammit, we are going to get caught!

A voice from above calls down. I press my back against the stone wall, forcing slow and steady breaths. Then Fletcher starts yelling.

Callian grinds out a curse.

Thud.

Mason steps out of the darkness. A second later, Callian steps out, Fletcher slung over his shoulder like one of the training sacks of sand.

"Run," Callian growls.

Mason takes off for the trees.

I see Callian go and then take off after him. I nock an arrow and let it fly toward the guard above us, who is now shouting for us to stop. It misses, but he ducks and stops yelling for a moment. I nock another, sliding to a halt. I aim for his head. Breathing in, I draw back the string. Breathing out, I release the tension. The arrow sails toward the stunned Guardian, hitting him in the leg. He folds to the floor beneath him.

Better than nothing. I spin around and charge after the boys toward the tree line.

CHAPTER 29
HARM

My gaze meets Petria's determined face. "If you've changed your mind about this, now is the time to tell me."

She only shakes her head. Her focus returns to the path in front of us. We are en route to the abandoned shack that Callian, Mason, and Imani are hopefully heading to as we traipse through the forest. Miles is keeping up, asking about every type of tree or shrub we pass by that he hasn't seen before.

"How old are these trees, Harm?"

"Not sure. That's a question for Catori. She could probably tell you."

"Oh, okay," he sighs.

I halt in my tracks, turning to face him as he pulls up behind me, his mother coming to stop by his side.

"You don't want to talk to Catori?"

"The forest people don't really like to talk to me." He kicks the grass at his feet, staring at the ground.

I squat in front of him, resting my hands on his thin arms. "Catori will talk to you. Any time you have a question, I'm sure she would love to answer it. And if she's busy, Callian is her brother; he grew up here too. He could help."

"Maybe," he says, shuffling his feet now. The vacancy in his eyes gives way to hurt. A sister who rarely visits him, a father he has never known, and a village full of kids who won't play with him. My chest aches, watching his brilliant blue eyes line with tears.

"What about your friends in the village?" I ask.

"I did have one friend. But his father, who works at the tower, hasn't been home for a few days, and he's not allowed to leave the house," Miles says.

"That's no good. I'm sure he'll be home soon. You want a piggyback ride?"

His eyes light up. Petria smiles at me, resting a hand on my shoulder. I squat down, and he climbs up. I jump up, shaking my head, neighing like the horses that Emmie used to ride. Miles's giggle bounces off the trees around us. Petria laughs from behind me. We keep moving, heading closer to Fletcher.

"You know, Callian is my best friend. He's like my brother, and..." I pause, looking back at Petria. She nods gently. "... and so are you, because I'm Blended with Imani."

"Really?!"

"Yep. I think the three of us—three brothers—should do more things together. Family is very important, after all."

Miles rests his head on my shoulder and looks at me with curious eyes. "What do you think we could do?"

"Well, camp out in the forest, for one. It's Callian's favorite thing to do. And maybe we can train together. You're never too young to learn how to defend yourself."

"You mean I could have a sword like you, or fighting knives like Imani?" he gushes.

"We'll see what Miya says. She's the boss of the warriors, so she decides what all the new trainees get to do. Would you like that?"

"Would I ever! That would be so much fun, and *really* awesome!"

Petria chuckles from behind.

"Excellent, it's all settled, then. I'll talk to Miya and Callian when we get home."

Miles wraps his arms around my shoulders a little further and squeezes them. "Thank you," he whispers.

"You're very welcome, buddy."

We pick up the pace, only a few miles from the rendezvous point now.

"You are not going in there," Imani warns. Her hands are on my face, eyes linked with mine, fire blazing behind hers.

"I have no intention of going in there, but if anything goes amiss, I will be in there in a heartbeat," I whisper, dropping my forehead to hers.

"It won't," Imani growls and releases my face.

Callian and Mason are busy ripping the pilfered uniforms from their livened frames. Callian gives me a serious look, alternating his gaze between Imani and her small family, who stand waiting for the go-ahead to enter the run-down shack. Through the gaps in the wall, the inside of the small building is visible. Fletcher sits bound and gagged on an old, rickety chair. His head is bent down, eyes closed. They have knocked him out.

Now, we wait.

"Are you sure Fletcher doesn't know?" I ask Petria, not using Miles's name—not when he is standing right next to her.

"I'm sure. He left before I had the chance to tell him. Jonah swore to not tell a soul. We decided it wasn't safe for..." She nods toward her son at her side, confirming what she told me earlier. I was allowed to tell Catori, on the off chance that it might help with getting her husband back or bringing him to our side, at least as some sort of semi-ally. It's worth a shot. There is more reason to try than not to. Miles huddles in close to Petria, fiddling with her skirt. Her face paled the moment she saw Fletcher through the gaps in the boards. I can't even begin to imagine what she is feeling right now.

"Why do we have to see this man, Mama?" Miles asks again.

"To meet him, just this once, just to say hello." She forces a smile, her eyes scrunched with remnants of fear. She lets out a long, wobbly breath and looks at me. I step over to where she stands and wrap an arm around her. She is shaking.

"If you could just let me see him first, alone? Then if everything works out, send Miles in?"

"We do this your way. If at any point you change your mind or it's too hard, just say the word, and Imani and Mason will have you out of there in seconds."

She nods and clears her throat.

A groan from the tied-up man inside pulls every gaze to the center of the small hut. Mason pushes his shoulders back, and Callian moves in closer, hands on his weapons. I release my hold on Petria and squat in front of Miles. His eyes track my movements.

"If you get scared or don't want to go in there, you let me know, okay, buddy?"

"Okay, Harm," he says, lifting his chin in defiance. I pull him into a tight hug, ruffling his hair on release. He smiles and leans back into his mother.

"Let's do this," Imani says, pushing off the wall of the shack she has been leaning on.

CHAPTER 30
IMANI

The look of disgust on my father's face has no effect on me. Not anymore—and *definitely* not now. Bound and gagged, he still manages to think he has the upper hand. Typical. I lean against the wall, cleaning my nails with my fighting knife. The sharp blade scrapes the underside of my nails, leaving perfect white crescents. Satisfying—almost as satisfying as watching him try to seethe at me through the gag. He grunts against the cloth. I can only imagine what is going to pour from his hateful mouth the second it's removed.

I push off the wall and saunter toward him. Sheathing my knife, I rip the gag from his mouth, standing a foot away from him. He looks up at me, his chest heaving, and the fire in his blue eyes matches mine exactly—the color, the hatred.

"Whatever you think you're doing, Imani, it won't work," he growls.

Releasing a cool laugh, I wander back to my wall and lean against it, ripping my knife from my hip, running the tip under the pointer finger of my other hand.

"If it's revenge you want, do your worst. It won't be long

before my men realize I'm missing. And very soon after that, you will face the reality of what you have done," he hisses at me. His wrists tug at the binds.

I let out a bored sigh. Looking up at him now, I see that he has stopped talking. "You done?" I ask flatly.

"Why am I here? What could you possibly think you're going to get away with now?" His hatred simmers to cool distaste.

"You're not here for my benefit, fortunately for you." My eyes linger on his weathered body bound to the chair, his usually perfect uniform crushed and sweaty. "You are here for *your* second chance." I flip him a smirk and wave a hand toward the door.

He turns as much as he can, waiting for whoever or whatever is about to come through the door.

My mother's face is almost white, and her hands tremble as she forces them away from the skirt that she had them tangled in a second ago. She halts just beyond the door, tilting her head down, and breathes out through her mouth, long and shaky breaths.

Eyes fixed on her, Fletcher's face drains of color, his gaze trailing up and down the woman standing in the doorway. She has let her dark hair down, which cascades in waves around her shaking shoulders. She wears one of her better button-up blouses and a long navy skirt. Fletcher's wide eyes stop scanning and rest on her face. He swallows, his throat working as he lets out a small huff. His once-fiddling hands have gone still. I watch every move he makes.

Mother's gaze pulls from his face, finding mine. "Does he need to be restrained?" she whispers.

"Yes," I say flatly.

Her eyes move back to Fletcher, and she steps toward him. Something like longing flickers through his eyes as he watches her move toward him.

"Daniel," she whispers, her mouth flickering from smile to

wobble and back again. She sets her shoulders back, silver lining her eyes, and forces a more permanent smile for him.

He stares up at her.

I hold my breath, double checking every point he is bound by.

"Petria," he says softly.

She takes the last step to stand in front of him. He tracks her movements again, shaking his head this time, as if her presence is something like a daydream.

Tears gush down her face. "I just needed to see you."

He stares at her for a heartbeat, his chest heaving as he swallows. He jerks, as if something has hit him, and he turns to me, face turning to stone. Then his eyes glaze over.

We've lost him.

"You kidnapped the commander of the Guardian legion because your mother wanted to see me?" he snaps.

Petria sucks in a breath, taking a step back.

"Yes," I say, meeting his gaze.

"That's ridiculous."

Mother's face twists with hurt, but she stands in front of him, not moving. She told Harm she knew it might be a long shot, and even if it worked, it would be painful. But the ache in my chest for her right now squeezes the breath out of me. Fire swirls, growing in my chest. "Is it?!"

"What do you want, Imani? You should have left your mother out of your rebellious games." Hate and annoyance lace each word.

"Daniel," she says again, this time with authority.

Here it comes. She grabs the half-rotted chair from the opposite corner of the room and places it in front of him.

She is too close. I push off the wall and step toward her. She looks back with a small smile, telling me she is okay. I rest my hands on my knives anyway. He looks at her, and the cold Fletcher we all know and loathe is back.

"What, Petria?" he says dryly, as if letting her know his defense against her pleas is already in place.

She lays her hands in her lap. "There is something you need to know."

"What's so important that you needed to have me kidnapped?" He sounds almost bored.

She sits back in the chair, lifting her chin and bracing her shoulders, not allowing him to bring her down. She is his equal, not his subordinate. "You have a son, Daniel."

His eyes narrow, and he looks around the room, like the boy could be hidden in the gaps in the walls.

"No, I don't. You might, but I don't." His tone is harsh.

"Yes, you do. When you moved into the barracks after Imani left, I was two months pregnant. *You...*" She places emphasis on the word. "... have a son. He is yours, and he is mine." She leaves her gaze connected to his, searching for a reaction—any reaction.

"And you chose to tell me this *now*? Where is he, then?"

"Imani," she says, tilting her head back to me.

I wave to Mason, standing just out of sight, on the other side of the door. He ushers Miles in. My little brother stands in the doorway, petrified. He must have overheard everything.

"It's okay Miles, you can come in," Mother says softly.

Fletcher looks at him with widened eyes, then back to Petria, before finally laying his gaze on me. The hair, the eyes, the skin—all the same. His mouth opens to speak, but he closes it again. After a handful of heartbeats, he blows out a long breath, then huffs a short, rough laugh. "If you think bringing some random child into this derelict shack you have tied me up in, after kidnapping me, is something I would fall for, then you are sorely mistaken."

Petria rises from the chair and makes for the door, sheltering Miles before shoving him outside.

I stalk across the floor, stopping inches from his face, mangled with hate. "You don't deserve a family."

A smirk curls one side of his mouth, mocking and sadistic. "I don't know what you think you're trying to prove, Imani, but your tricks won't work on me."

The heat builds in my veins, and blood screams through my head at a hundred miles an hour. In this moment, I hate this man in front of me more than I ever have before.

"No, you know what? You're right. We shouldn't have kidnapped you; we should have *buried* you." Shaking, I ball my hands into fists at my sides.

"You can't win this, Imani. You shouldn't have even bothered trying."

My hand connects with his face a heartbeat later. Fire spreads through my palm, and I stand over him, my mouth pulled into a snarl, breath fast and heavy. "Go to hell, Fletcher!"

I stalk out of the shack into the trees.

Miles rides on Harm's back behind me. I haven't said a word to any of them since we left Fletcher at the shack, still bound, re-gagged, and under the protection of two forest cell guards Callian sent for earlier. The look on my mother's face when he accused her of trying to trick him with the existence of his own son... If I've ever wanted to run a blade across his filthy, arrogant neck, it was in that very moment. How on earth could I ever have come from such a repulsive human being? How does my mother still believe he can be rehabilitated? Her Daniel—*my father*—is gone. He is not in there anymore. The regime has made sure of that. We should have just killed him. But Catori's orders are to keep him locked up for the time being. She says killing him outright would result in a retaliation that we are not yet prepared for.

"Imani." My mother's voice, again. Ignoring her for the past hour has worked, but after what she just tolerated from her so-called husband, I feel terrible for her.

"What, Mother?"

"Are you okay?"

I stop in my tracks, and she does too, turning to look at me. "Not really. Are you?"

Harm, carrying a half-asleep Miles on his back, walks past us, offering a small smile of reassurance.

"I'll be fine. I knew it was going to be hard."

"He was horrible. Worse than horrible. How can you not hate him with every fiber of your being?"

She tilts her head and places her hands on her hips. "Because that was not Daniel; that was Fletcher. Your father—my husband —is still in there somewhere. I saw him, felt him. We planted a seed today. Mark my words my love, one day that seed will mature. I have known that man for a long time. He may have been on the defense today, but he was in there. I saw him. And..." She swings an arm around my shoulders. "... he saw me."

"You sound just like Hanola," I grumble.

"If I could be half the woman that lady was, I would be happy. But for now, baby steps. The next time we see him, we will try again."

"There won't be a next time, Mother." My brows are drawn, my mouth tight.

"We'll see." She smiles and tugs me along beside her. I let out a long, pained groan, my feet stepping in time with hers. She is happy, despite the events of the past hour. And she is the strongest I have ever seen her. Part of me believes she is right. I hope she is, for her sake.

We catch up to Harm and Miles, who has fallen asleep on Harm's shoulder. "What makes you so certain he'll realize Miles really is his son?" Harm asks.

I let my gaze wander to the greenness between the trees.

"Apart from the fact that Miles has his eyes and my hair and complexion, just as Imani does? Miles was his father's name. We had it saved for the day we were lucky enough to have a son," she says, elbowing me. I roll my eyes at her. But her face falls into a serious expression. "He will know who he is once he puts those things together. When he remembers who he was, how we were, before he left," she says softly.

A wish, or a prayer. But it's something.

The light is fading fast by the time the six of us make it back to the village. Miles, who has been asleep for a couple of hours on Harm's shoulder, is full of conversation and a ton of questions. Most of them are answered. Some are redirected—the ones about the man in the shack, at least. Mother will have an eventful night with him, no doubt.

Harm swings an arm around me. We wander to the eating area, starving from a long day, Callian and Mason trailing slightly behind.

The eating area is buzzing with people. Nirri sits at our table, no plate or drink, wringing the ends of her scarf through her hands. Catori sits beside her, scanning the area every few seconds.

"Thank the heavens," Catori says, rising from the table. She jogs over to Mason, wrapping her arms around his neck. He chuckles and folds her into his chest.

Nirri stands slowly, eyes searching Callian as if checking for injury. She rounds the table, dropping the scarf from her hands, letting it hang around her neck. Draped over her chest, the scarf rides the shallow breaths she works through. As she comes to a halt in front of Callian, her face is slightly twisted, her hands shaking by her sides.

"Need a hug?" Callian asks softly.

She nods, and he pulls her in tight. A small whimper leaves her throat. A heartbeat later, she pushes back. Straightening, she lifts her gaze to his. Callian's eyes are set on her face, his mouth a half smile, his eyes narrowed under his lowered brows. "You okay?" he whispers, raising an eyebrow.

"You—the three of you—were gone for so long. I was worried." Swallowing, she folds her arms across her chest, and her gaze drops to the grassy ground beneath us.

"You don't need to worry about me, Nirri," Callian says after a moment, lifting his head a little.

She looks back up at him, her face slightly puckered. "I can't help it, Callian." She turns and walks back to the table.

A smile grows over his face. Harm slaps him on the back, giving him a wink. The three of us walk to the table where Nirri, Mason, and Catori already sit, loading their plates. I plonk down on our new bench. I am still not used to sitting at Hanola's old table.

"I don't think I'm cut out to be a warrior like you or Imani," Nirri says to Callian. He stops piling food on his plate and turns to face her. "I mean, I would be terrified if I had to do the things you do."

"I'm not always brave, Nirri. I get scared, just like anyone else."

"It doesn't seem that way."

Callian places his hand on the table next to hers, palm up. "All I know is that what's on the other side of whatever is in front of me in that moment is worth fighting for." The words are no more than a whisper, and he leans closer to her. She slides her hand into his, and he curls his fingers around her small hand. "That's what makes me move, makes me fight. Fear is still there, but it's not the only thing."

Her gaze lingers on their joined hands before she pulls her hand back and starts gathering food for her plate. He studies her face, and she tries to suppress a smile. Callian lets out a low chuckle and pops a berry into his mouth.

Harm grabs two plates and starts loading them up. I shove my head in my hands, releasing a long and exhausted breath.

"Here, eat. Then we can go to bed early," he says.

"To sleep?" A cheeky grin pops up on my face, lighting his up.

"Whatever finds us first, sleep or otherwise," he whispers in my ear.

I chuckle, popping a bite of food into my mouth. He brushes away a piece that sticks to my mouth and throws a piece of fruit in the air, trying to catch it in his mouth, face tilted to the sky. It lands on his chin and falls onto the table. Callian throws another piece for him, and he maneuvers to line up his mouth, snapping the fruit between his teeth. Callian and I laugh, and he chews with a smile that radiates happiness. Then his warm, lit-up brown eyes find mine.

Oh, we are not getting any sleep tonight.

I run my fingers over his lightly stubbled jaw and kiss his still-chewing lips. I stand and pick up both of our plates, nodding my head toward home. He stands and wishes everyone good night before following.

Imani's soft fingers tangle in mine, playing and tracing their way across my palm all the way to the fingertips. She lets out a long sigh against my side. I roll over on the bed slightly to face her, pushing her hair back from her face with my free hand.

"Do you honestly think Fletcher could be rehabilitated, the way Mason was?" she asks, staring at her fingers weaving in and out of mine.

"Hanola would have thought so. I hope so, for your mother's sake."

She closes her eyes and swallows. "I remember the last thing I said to him, at home, the day I left." Her voice is quiet and pained.

"What was that?"

"He had just come back from his day at some village he didn't name. Four boys were taken back to the barracks. He was in the kitchen, telling my mother. Her face was scrunched up, listening to words that made her skin crawl from the mouth of the man she adored. All I remember was feeling so angry—for her, for the boys they took. Then he told us he had signed up for another ten years of service."

"Most people would feel that way. It would be hard watching your father choose to stay on."

Memories of Arlo whip past, and I swallow, trying to dislodge the ache in my chest.

"He told me, and these were his exact words: 'I will have more influence over what happens now. Things can change.'" She breathes through a wobbly half laugh. "And do you know what I said to him, even after he told me that? I got in his face and told him he was a coward, that he should have left when he had the chance." She wipes a stream of tears from her face. I fold her into my chest, and she lets out years' worth of pain, guilt, and torment over the relationship she has had with her father, and for the mutually hateful one she now has with Fletcher, who in this moment feels like an entirely different person than the man Petria and Imani remember. Not the man who sacrificed another ten years of his life, hoping to change things for the better.

"Hanola was right, Harm. What they are, what was done to them, by the regime, by the Chancellor..." she whispers through faltering breaths.

"I know. At least, I do now. It took me a while to figure that out with Mason, that the way he was as a child was because of his father beating him daily. And then the regime... Hate is like a disease." I move back a little to take in her face. Her fingers find my jaw, and a crooked smile pulls up on her face. "But we have the cure. For any who make it through this war, at least."

Imani props up on one elbow, scanning my face. "You want to fix the Guardians when this is all over?" she asks, words soft, not judgmental.

"I've been thinking about it, ever since Hanola died. It would be her greatest legacy. Catori was with her and Mason for every session. She must know what Hanola did to help him."

"That would be a huge undertaking, Harm."

"Most things that are worth it are." I grab her under her arms and drag her on top of me. She lets out the sweetest, softest chuckle and plants her mouth on mine.

Catori's home is lit by sunlight streaming through the canopy, the day already unbearably humid. Each of us stands around the strategy table, eyeballing the maps of both sides of the wall, hunting for the perfect place to take our stand on each section. The desert side will be easier to pinpoint, with the village of Etonia making the perfect place to come up against the prison Guardians. Any officers out on patrol or in the outposts will straggle in, allowing for the tail end of our host to take them out easily. The brunt of the battle facing the prison wall is where we know they will outnumber us, but we have the weapons and skill, and the explosives. Christopher has been hoarding them for months. He plans to take out the wall. Jonah and Enid are still discussing whether that is a viable option, not knowing how the dial will alter things. I suggested we change the dial first and then see what effect taking down a small part of the wall has. But that fell on deaf ears as far as Christopher is concerned. I swear my uncle just wants to blow some stuff up.

"I say we take our stand at the servants' access door. There, they have limited range to get to us, but we can spread out to meet them, and worst-case scenario, we can retreat into the trees. Jeselle's archers can spot from the trees, releasing waves of arrows as we need them if the numbers become too great, or if we take on too many losses and need the cover," Miya says pointing to the clearing just shy of the tower on the map.

"Agreed," Callian says, his face tight.

"Well, that's settled. Now, we just need exact numbers and a few fallback plans, and then we're ready," Catori says.

"What if they have a lot more numbers and weapons than we anticipate?" Mason asks. Every set of eyes looks to him. "I mean, if Fletcher or Arthur got word of what's being planned, maybe from Elijah, then they're going to counter by amassing numbers. It's the only strategy they have left in this short a time span."

"True." Catori ponders the words as she scans the map, not seeing, just thinking. "If our plan with Fletcher had worked, that would have changed things in our favor more. But we need to plan multiple strategies regardless, I feel. To not do so would be naive, and a fast way to lose this war."

"What else can we do except meet the Guardians head-on?" Imani asks.

"Most of their food and supplies come from our outlying villages. Their other provisions—namely taxes—are collected from the desert side. If we stop feeding them, they will fade out pretty quickly," Callian says.

"They most likely have planned for something like that, and they have months' worth stored away—enough to buy them time to reinstate their order," Catori says, looking to Mason.

A small grimace washes across his face. "They do. Rooms full of the nonperishable stuff, at least."

"So, that tactic is out. Anything else?" Catori asks, eyes wandering to each one of us standing around the table.

"Take out their two most prominent leaders: the Chancellor and Fletcher?" Miya asks.

Every set of eyes falls on Imani and Nirri, who stand together.

I watch as the horror melts from Nirri's face, and she sighs. "I don't think that is an option we need to discuss at this point."

"I don't want to be crass here, but at some point, both of those men are going to be put down, or at least imprisoned indefinitely," Miya snaps.

Imani holds Miya's heated gaze, returning the fire that she forever embodies—the fire she keeps alive for her family. For her mother and little brother, if not for Fletcher.

"Right now, we need a way to win the war," Mason says softly. "Once all opposing parties are imprisoned, and the dial has been changed, we can decide the fate of whoever is left." His eyes are locked on Miya's, as if in warning.

"Fine, but if either of them meets me on the battlefield and doesn't stand down, they're good as dead," she says.

"Fair enough," Catori says.

Her words are final. An awkward silence weaves through the room before Callian clears his throat.

"So, numbers. We have the tallies from the forest recon run we did. The numbers are small, but skills and weapons are aplenty in every village. One could say they've been preparing for this for years," he says, a grin blooming across his face as his eyebrows rise slightly.

"Yes, Callian, they have. Hanola, Emmie, and Enid have been preparing for this for decades. Let's not screw it up now." Catori rolls her eyes at her little brother, and he mock salutes her. She flips him off, and we all laugh, the tension fading with the siblings' banter as quickly as it arose minutes ago.

A harsh rap rattles the wooden door of Catori's home. Mason pads over, opening it. "Can we help you?" He stiffens slightly as he takes in the robed figure in front of him.

"Is Harm here? I need to speak to him now," the voice of a teen boy pleads.

Mason opens the door farther, and the boy steps in, desert traveling gear still covering every inch of him. He shoves his hood back and searches the room.

My breath stops.

Marshall. The boy we saved from the Guardians months ago. What is he doing here? He's supposed to be hiding with Enid.

I round the table in seconds, moving to him. The worry and pain on his face have my heart thundering.

"Marshall, what's going on? Enid—is she alright?" I grab his arms with both my hands before hugging him briefly.

"She's fine. But..." He looks around the room, taking in the plush furnishings, the abundance of everything. "They took them all."

"They took who?" I tighten my grip, hoping he will focus on what he is telling me and not where he is.

"The children. They took them all, from tiny babes up to twenty-year-olds—every single one. In every village. They're all gone." He starts to shake.

I turn him, guiding him to a chair. "They took every child?" I breathe.

He nods.

"How are you here, then?" Mason asks.

"Enid always keeps me hidden. They didn't know I existed. But the others—they knew where every one of them lived. They fogged out every village. When we woke up, they were gone. The screaming... The women were screaming, so loud. It was so loud..." He shoves his hands over his ears as if he can still hear it.

"Harm," Imani utters from across the room.

I force myself to turn and look at her, force myself to breathe. I swallow past the thick lump in my throat. Tingling starts in my hands, and tightness takes over my chest.

Callian appears beside me, his hand on my arm. Imani has sunk to the floor with Nirri draped around her.

Catori appears at my side. "They're just trying to flush you out again, Harm. Both of you."

"Truly, they wouldn't execute every child from every village," Mason breathes. "They would have no people left in a few decades. It would be genocide."

"Fletcher can't be that far gone, surely," Callian breathes.

Nirri stands, now meeting Callian's stunned gaze. "But Arthur is," she says, her chin wobbling.

"What do you mean?" Mason asks.

"It's his way or no way. If he thinks we're getting too close, or we have him backed into a corner, he would do it—he will kill every last person, just so we can't win." Her voice trembles through the last few words, eyes widening.

Callian deposits me on the chair beside Marshall before reaching for Nirri and walking her outside. She loses her stomach on the grass outside. The rest of us have stilled, as if frozen in time, staring between one another, staring at nothing.

The door swings on its hinges again, and a forest guard limps in.

"Report," Mason snaps. His Guardian ways come through with his distress.

"He's gone. The two officers we were sent to relieve, dead," he rasps. He wavers on his feet, pale-faced and chest heaving, adding to the panic that has flooded the room.

"The bloody mongrel," Miya spits.

I grapple air into my lungs, eyes closed.

The next right thing to do. What is the next right thing to do?

"We're going over the wall to get those children back, or at least make as big a dent in their guard as possible," I say.

It is as if time has slowed down for every person in the room as they slowly turn their heads to where I sit.

"That's suicide, Harm. For you, and anyone who goes with you," Miya hisses.

I stand from the chair. "I realize the risks involved. But these are our *children*. Without them, in only a small amount of time, our very existence vanishes. I'm going."

Marshall stands beside me, crossing his arms over his chest, lifting his tear-stained chin a little. Miya slumps her shoulders, mouth pulled into a thin line. Imani moves across the floor to stand beside me. Nirri and Callian walk back in the door.

"I'm with you, Harm," Nirri says.

"Nirri..." Callian breathes.

"I lost who I was, Callian, and I was going over that wall regardless. At least now, I'll be going with a purpose." She forces a small smile. Callian thumbs a single tear from her cheek. He nods gently, returning a tortured smile for her.

Catori walks over, standing in front of me. She takes my shoulders in her hands. "This is your home for as long as you want it to be. But I understand that they are your people. I won't stop you. Your people, your choice. But Harm..." She pulls me into a tight hug. "I'd better see your sweet face again, you hear me?"

She steps back, taking Imani into an even tighter hug. "And I will most definitely see your beautiful face again, sister." Her face is wet from the tears she allows to fall.

Imani chuffs through a sob and pulls her back into her embrace. "You'll see me sooner than you think, sister," she whispers.

Mason stands staring at Imani and me before padding over to where we stand, his face set in stone. "Don't worry, I'm not going to hug you, Travesci." He grabs something from his pocket and shoves it into mine. A half smile tugs up on his face, and he hugs Imani tightly before stepping back to where he was standing.

"Look after my family while I'm gone," I say to him.

"You have my word, Harm," he rasps, his jaw clenching slightly as we walk past, Nirri behind Imani. Callian stands at the door—

the last warrior standing, the last waypoint before we leave the sanctuary of our forest family. "You don't have to do this, Harm."

I pull him into a hug. "Yes, I do, brother." He hugs me back. "I'll see you soon. Take care of your sister and Rayner."

He looses a long breath and breaks the hold. "I'd better see you again, or I'll find you in the afterlife and torment you to no end."

"I'll be back to whoop your ass in the sparring ring before too long." I slap my hand on his shoulder.

He chuckles a deep laugh and throws his head back. "See you, brother," he says as I walk past.

Imani steps into Callian's space. He wraps his arms around her, lifting her up as he hugs her. "Make sure you use that fire of yours, little sister."

"You too," Imani chokes.

He sets her down, and his gaze flickers over her shoulder to Nirri.

"I will protect her with my life," Imani whispers, clasping Callian's hands in hers.

"Thank you," he whispers, and Imani walks over the threshold and stands next to me.

Nirri walks up to Callian. Her fine features are twisted with pain. Callian rests his hand on her cheek, and she leans into his touch.

"I know you don't want me to leave. But I need to," she starts. He pulls her closer with a hand on her waist. "Callian..." she whispers.

He lowers his head, pressing his forehead to hers. "If I give you my heart, it will be all of it—not a lost, broken version of it. You deserve more than that. You deserve the whole thing. You deserve to be happy—like Harm-and-Imani happy."

She huffs a laugh and swallows, her fingers working around the edges of his collar. "Please know, I am not leaving to hurt you. I'm leaving to find myself. And if there's a chance for you and me, you'll get all of me—whoever that is—when I'm done."

Callian's shoulders shake, and she pulls him into her, resting her head on his chest. He rubs her back with his hand before pushing her back, sinking his mouth over hers. Nirri's hands hang by her sides. A heartbeat later, he breaks the kiss and whispers something before releasing her.

Nirri pads over the threshold as if in a trance. Imani takes her hand, and we walk home to pack. Nirri wanders to her house, Catori's old home. Imani trails behind me silently. We walk through the door, and Imani shuts it behind her.

"Harm," she whispers.

"I know. We will come back, I promise you that." I pull her into my arms. She rests her palms on my chest, and I run my fingers through her hair. In this very moment, I feel it, like I have everything to lose—and the possibility of losing it all is far greater than I care to admit.

CHAPTER 32
MASON

The food tastes bland. The people sitting beside me are oddly silent. Nobody is hungry.

It feels as if half of our hearts have been ripped out, half of our family already taken. Catori sits beside me, mindlessly shoving food around her plate. She has taken two bites the whole time we have been sitting here. Callian is lost in thought. Miya and Jeselle eat slowly, sitting closer together than they usually do, the pain of what we all feel we have just lost affecting them just as much as it does the three of us.

"I'm not hungry." Callian shoves his plate aside and storms away from the table. I make to rise, and Catori's hand lands on my thigh.

"Let him go. He lost more than we did, Mason."

I wrap an arm around her, and she leans her head on my shoulder.

Miya looks up from her plate. "They'll be okay. You have to believe that, Catori." Her fork rests in her hand, suspended over her plate.

"I want to, Miya, I really do. But this is not a coincidence—not after us kidnapping Fletcher. This is the consequence—a very real and very dangerous one for Harm and Imani. And Nirri, if they discover who she is…" Catori wiggles under my arm, and I drop it as she stands. "I'm going to bed. Maybe tomorrow, we will have a plan to help, or at least send some warriors to help. Right now, I can't even think straight about those three. Night," she says to Miya and Jeselle, then turns to me. "You coming?"

"Yeah, I guess I'll head home too." I stand and bid the girls left at the table good night.

"I'll walk with you," Catori says, lacing her fingers in mine. I smile at her, and she nods her head sideways, beckoning me to follow her. Callian's house is in the opposite direction, but I let her tug me along. I can stay for a little while, I guess.

Catori pushes through her front door. She releases my hand and closes the door behind us. I look at her as she leans against the door, palms flat against it behind her back. The devastation from moments ago has given way to a fire in her eyes. I pull in deep breaths.

"You want me to stay?"

Her soft pink lips pull into a smile, and her breathing shallows. "Do you want to be here, Mason?"

"Yes, very much."

She pushes off the door and pads toward me, hands hanging by her sides. Running a searching gaze over her face, I rest my hands on her waist and tug her into me. She lets out a huff through a small smile pulling up on one corner of her mouth and wraps her arms around my neck. Her hands tangle in my hair, and she pulls my mouth to hers. I kiss her with every piece of my heart, tender and full, soft and strong. Her hands trail down from my hair and press against my chest. Stepping forward, she pushes me backward.

We move together, me going backward, her body against mine until my back hits the wall near the door of her room. As I kiss her with everything I have, fire sparks to life in my center. I grab her hands and spin her around, pushing her back up against the wall, lifting her hands over her head. Her mouth devours mine. Her chest heaves, and I break away and dot kisses down her soft neck.

"If we don't get through the next few weeks..." she breathes, the last word sticking in her throat.

I lift my head to meet her gaze. "We will get through it. We'll be back here, safe and happy, together."

"I can't lose you, Mason." She loses her breath to sobs, her face twisting a little, and tears line her eyes.

"Hey," I say, releasing her hands to cup her face. "You are not going to lose me, ever. Okay?"

She nods, and the tears that have pooled in her eyes fly down her cheeks. "I can't stay away from you any longer. Every time I'm near you, all I can think about is being wrapped up in you." Soft fingers trace my jaw, then my lips. I swallow the lump that is closing off my throat and drag in a deep breath.

"That makes two of us, then," I rasp, nuzzling into her neck, nipping and kissing as I trail downward, reaching her collarbone. She sucks in a quick breath, and her hands squeeze mine as she lifts them back over her head against the wall. I rest my head on her chest for a heartbeat, breathing her in. The rise and fall of her breaths are studded with the hammering of her heart.

"Mason." My name is nothing more than a trace of a whisper.

I track my way back up her trembling body, my own breath short now. She pulls her hands from mine and undoes the buttons on my shirt. I stand, breathing deep, watching her face as she discovers my body. I am thankful now for every last torturous training session Miya and Callian put me through as she searches the lines on my toned chest. My shirt hits the floor. Her hands and fingers flutter over my collarbones, the way mine did hers. She runs one finger from the hollow of my throat down my chest, over my stomach, until she hits my belt. Her eyes flicker between fire and longing. I stop breathing.

She lifts my hand to her tunic, lowering her head slightly, huffing another small breath. "Can we do this now, before I lose my mind?" She lifts her hands, and I pull her shirt over her head, tossing it. Her fingers work the soft fabric around her chest loose, and it falls to the floor too. She bites her lower lip, eyes crinkled with intensity. Her hands wander to my belt, and a moment later, the metal buckle and leather clunks as it drops. She pulls me into her bedroom and undoes the laces on her pants, and they fall. She shoves her undergarment to the floor. Moving me beside the bed, she releases the buttons on my pants, and they join hers. Her eyes wander up and down my body. Her breathing is almost erratic now. My heart hammers against my ribs, arms aching to hold her, the fire in my core almost unbearable.

"Catori."

She steps into my space and covers my mouth with hers, hands trailing from my chest to my hips. She pulls me hard against her. I slide my hands underneath her bottom and pick her up, and she wraps her legs around me. I spin back and slam her into the wall next to her bedroom door. A little moan rips from her throat, her mouth pulling into a half smile against my lips. She liked that. I trail kisses down her neck and find her round peaks. Her breath stops, her hands tightening on my biceps. Her soft peaks harden in my mouth, and she moans, the vibrations from her chest shuddering under my lips. Her hands move from my arms, fingers curling around my jaw. She raises my head, her pupils fully dilated, her ragged breath telling me she is ready. I move my hands around underneath her and pull her close, taking a step backward toward the bed. She nuzzles my neck, kissing it, her mouth resting over my Adam's apple. Swallowing, I try to slow myself down.

"Mason." My name is torn between a plea and a whisper.

I lower her to the bed. She groans at me, as if too impatient to be handled nicely. I kiss her mouth, slowing the pace. This is going to last. I want to feel everything, every part of her, and for her to feel every part of me. I nuzzle my way back down her body. Her back arches when my mouth reaches her peaks again. I pay a visit to each briefly before dotting kisses down her stomach. A whimper leaves her mouth. My core waxes with heat, the fire burning deeper with every small movement her hips make toward me. I take my time trailing kisses over every inch of her.

"Mason," she utters.

My mouth finds the bundle of nerves at the apex of her thighs.

"Uh-uh," I murmur, and the vibration of the word has her body shaking beneath me. I grip her thighs with both hands.

"Get up here, now," she grinds out.

I chuckle, and her hands grip my shoulders, hard enough to make me wince.

"Alright, I'm coming back." A smile grows on my face, but fades as I meet Catori's silver-lined eyes.

"The things you do to me, Mason Rayner."

"I'm all yours."

She runs her hands over my back, pulling me into her. The throbbing hardness of me finds the warm, soft trembling part of her, and she meets my gaze, resting her hands on my chest. I push up on my hands, her hair splayed out on the pillow around her beautiful face, and watch her eyes roll back and close as I move into her slowly. She sucks in a deep breath as the last inch of me finds the very depths of her, and her fingers curl into my chest, nails digging in slightly. I close my eyes, willing my breathing to slow down again. Her hands move, weaving behind my neck, and she drags my mouth down to hers. Hovering over her for a heartbeat, I grapple for some sort of control. I open my eyes, and she is watching me, a small, loving smile tugging up on her soft pink lips.

Her hands trail to my chest and then back to my neck, then to my face.

"Mason."

"I know." I force the words out past the lump in my throat.

She pulls me down onto her mouth, and I take up a slow pace for the both of us. The sweetest moan curls through her lips onto mine. Every movement feels more intense than the last. Release threatens to take me on the tip of every thrust. I stop for a heartbeat, and she tugs me in close, her hand pushing my shoulder to the side. I slide an arm under her and roll with her wrapped in my hold. She readjusts, straddling me. A soft smile tugs on her face before fading into pure desire. Deeper still we are joined, and she lowers down, kissing my mouth, taking up the rhythm between us. Her hips move around me, and the fire burns so close. I grab her waist, slowing her down.

"Catori," I breathe, slamming my eyes shut.

"I know." Her waist moves backward in my hands, and I open my eyes. Her head is tilted back, and her back arches as her whimper turns into a long, heady cry. Her hands find mine, lacing through them with a fierce grip. Every last whimper drains from her body, and she sits over me, gaze meeting mine, her breaths quick. She bends down and pulls me up. "Your turn," she whispers into my ear, her breath still deep and fast.

I swing my legs over the bed and stand. She wraps her legs around my waist and pulls my mouth into hers. Her swollen softness throbs around me. With every step, I hold my breath, until her back hits the wall. She lets out a breathy laugh and grips my arms, waiting for me. My gaze tracks from her heaving, gorgeous chest up her neck to find her eyes.

"I'm all yours," she utters.

I let out a low, raw growl and slam into her over and over. Her breath quickens again. The fire that I suppressed while watching her find her climax rips through me, barreling toward a cliff, and I ache to tumble into that beautiful agony only Catori can give me.

Catori whimpers, loosing small cries as she finds release again. The sweet sound from her lips pulls me over the edge. Fire splutters, giving way to release, and every part of my body trembles as fine tendrils of pleasure course through every inch of my tensed frame. I move through the last waves of it slowly, drawing out each sound from her.

I nuzzle my face into Catori's neck, breathing her in. It feels like the first real breaths I have taken since I lost myself, just before the regime claimed me. Catori leans her cheek against my head, and her ragged breaths slow to deep, heavy ones. Her fingers travel up my neck, weaving through my hair. In this moment, I have never felt more loved than I do now with her tangled around me. A tear tracks down my cheek and lands on her shoulder. She sucks in a breath and holds me tighter.

"I love you, Mason. I have for a long time." Her chin wobbles.

"I love you too." I let go. Tears plummet from my already burning cheeks onto her trembling shoulders. I lift her from the wall and set her down on the bed. She tugs the blanket back and crawls between the sheets. She pats the bed, and I crawl in beside her. I tuck my legs under, and she moves closer, nuzzling against my chest. Her hands rest there, her fingers tracing shapes on my skin, and I lie breathing next to her, wishing this moment would last forever.

"If I died right now, every second of my life until now would be worth it," I breathe.

"You'd better not die on me, Mason Rayner. I plan on doing that with you every day for the rest of our lives." Pushing up, she plants her hands on either side of my face and kisses my lips, biting the bottom one briefly before tracking around my neck.

Moments later, my arm that is wrapped around her slackens,

and my breathing slows. She dots a handful of kisses on my chest and looses a sigh. Her fingers, still tracing patterns over my chest, slow.

The moonlight that illuminates Catori's room wanders over the blankets as if dancing through the swaying canopy above. I reach for Catori. Her side of the bed is empty, but not cold. I shove the blankets off, getting out of bed and walking into the living room. She is standing by the window, leaning against the frame, cup in her hands. She takes a sip. The moon lights up her face, high-lighting her cheekbones, her eyes, her lips that are pulled into a small smile as she is lost in thought. I pad to her side.

"Can't sleep?" I whisper, touching her cheek with my hands, rubbing a thumb across the elegant bones on either side of her sweet nose.

"No, just needed a drink. The moon is so pretty." She nods to the pale round orb hanging so close to the canopy that it looks like it is skimming the tops of the trees. Her green eyes are lit up in the soft silver light. Her skin is cold, still bare from earlier. I wrap my arms around her, and she rests the cup on the windowsill.

"You're so cold," I whisper.

"Well then, you'll have to warm me up." She covers my mouth with hers, hands on my waist, pulling me close to her.

"Anything you want, I will give it to you, Catori."

"I just want you," she breathes, dragging me backward to the strategy table. With one hand, she shoves the papers aside, releasing me briefly to sit on the table. Her gaze darkened under hooded brows, she beckons with one finger, her mouth pulled up on one side.

I step between her legs into her outstretched hands. "You

have me."

She wraps around me with her arms and legs and lays kisses over my neck, nipping my ear, then trails them to the base of my throat. Heat grows in my core again, and I pull her tighter against me. Her hand moves around the hardness of me before she wriggles her hips forward. She plunges her mouth over mine, her hands gripping my hips, pulling me into her. My breath catches, followed by a low groan reverberating through my chest. I take up the rhythm that makes her arch into me, savoring every second of her around me.

Greyness. Everything is grey—smoke or haze. An acidic smell, something like the ochre paint the Guardians use on the houses of people sentenced to execution, or dune buggy fuel, filters through the air around us. My body feels too heavy.

Catori is sound asleep beside me, but her steady rise and fall is so shallow. Something's not right.

I grab her arms and shake her. She stirs, but doesn't wake.

Smokey fumes drift in the window. I fly out of bed and jerk my pants on. Pushing my feet into my boots, I turn back to the bed.

"Catori, wake up!" I shake her arms again. She jerks, eyes opening. A heartbeat later, her eyes have adjusted. Horror fills her face, and her eyes widen. She scrambles out of bed. Pulling a robe around her slim body, she ties it off and looks around the house.

"No," she whispers.

Gas.

The children.

Hell.

I move through the door, Catori right behind me, but our stride is too slow. My head feels like it's stuffed with straw. We stand in the curling fog for a moment. There is no other movement. We both scan the village for any sign of life, expecting Guardians to appear at any second.

The first scream—the voice of a devastated woman—rips through the entire village, rattling through the trees that line our home. More follow, and women and men stagger out of their houses. Catori rushes to every home, her gait wobbly, checking quickly before going to the next. Miya and Jeselle reach the village center, still dressed in their nightgowns. Callian thunders in, swaying to a halt beside them, in pants and boots, no shirt. He looks me over before taking in his sister. His mouth pulls tight. "What's going on? Is it the children?"

"I think so."

Catori wanders back, her hands shaking, her breaths short. "They're all gone—every last one of them!"

From across the village center, someone is calling for Harm. Her screams penetrate the fog, arriving before her figure does. We watch her silhouette move toward us, erratic and desperate.

"Harm! Please, someone help! I need to find Harmen and Imani!" Petria screams.

Callian walks over to her. She looks up into his face, hers tortured and twisted, grabbing his arms to steady herself. "Please, they took Miles! They took my son!"

"Miya, select six warriors to go over the wall and help Harm," Catori commands. "The rest of your host is with us, to the tower."

Miya opens her mouth to object.

"Do it, now!" Catori snaps.

Callian looks back at me. The color has drained from all of our faces. This is all our fault.

Arthur. He has taken every last child, no doubt from every forest village as well as every desert one.

What have we done?

CHAPTER 33
HARM

The second the stone door slides shut behind us and our feet sink into the hot sands, a heavy feeling of unease drops into my gut. Imani and Nirri flank me, both dressed in desert traveling robes, their long hair twisted into scarves, hoods and wraps covering them up. Marshall trails behind, as if taking rear point. He has caught on quick in just a day of being around Callian and me. I adjust the wrap over my face and toss the ragged hood up, pulling it down low, concealing myself as much as possible.

"The sooner we get this sorted out and get back to this door, the better," Imani utters, stepping into the sands that she grew up in. Now, this side of the wall only serves to remind us of all we have run from—the oppression, living on scraps, and a people that would see her stuck in a kitchen, tending to a family she may or may not want. So many things need to change on this side of the wall.

"Agreed," I say, following her, Nirri falling in behind me.

We track straight for Etonia, avoiding any outposts or groups of people along the way, minimizing the risk of exposure. Three of the four of us are well known to the officers of the Guardian regime, for a host of different reasons.

The two hours we spend trudging through the sand feels like a day's worth of walking, as we are not used to the heat and heavy going anymore. Our bodies may be fitter, but they are also heavier. The light, bony frames we had growing up here have given way to healthy, nourished, toned bodies. Marshall takes the lead, and I fall back to the rear.

"How do we get into the prison to find the children? How do we get them out?" Nirri asks, her voice carrying on the hot winds that whip around my hood, flapping it against my cheeks.

"Getting in isn't a problem. I know a way in," I say. "Getting the kids and us out... That we will need help for." I run through my plan for Tobias and the diversion I have replaying in my mind, making sure every detail is solid, that it increases our chances of getting out and decreases our risk of being caught. Still, the anvil in my stomach presses down. And I can't shake the feeling of something akin to impending doom. Right now, I'm starting to doubt everything. With each step closer to Etonia and the miserable dark and stained walls of the prison, my mind grows murkier.

Pressed against the grey wall of the prison, we wait until the hustle of the lunchtime crowd filters in. I lead Imani, Nirri, and Marshall to the small door in the wall where we have hidden out many times before. The girls stay close, heads down, while Marshall scans our surroundings repeatedly. Guardians patrol the village in pairs, circling around the more popular stalls, ready for any sign of trouble. The heat has sweat dripping down my arms and running down my spine. My mouth is parched, and my hands shake, maybe from the desert conditions, maybe not.

We round the last house before the section of wall that surrounds the small access door. Every hot, deep step toward it feels as if time has slowed down. I pick up the pace, almost in time with my thundering heart. The girls adjust their pace too, coming up beside me. We reach the door, and I grab the handle, Marshall bringing up the rear as he watches for any sign of movement in our direction. The heat of the metal burns my hands. I press down. It doesn't budge.

A pair of Guardians round the house now, chatting as they scan the area around the village perimeter.

I push down again. It still doesn't budge.

Imani and Nirri move in closer, shielding me from sight, pretending to be whispering about something, and Marshall huddles in.

The door rattles from the other side. I jerk back.

"Everything alright, girls?" one of the officers calls from the edge of the village.

"Yes, fine, thank you," Nirri calls back, giving them a small wave. He nods, and the pair move on, walking down a side alley.

The door cracks open. An aged hand slips around the edge, the figure only just visible in the dim light. But it's enough to make out that they wear no uniform.

I remove my wrap, revealing my face to whoever is also hiding in this section of the wall. A long, thin arm reaches out, pulling me in. I stumble into the darkness and am instantly met by the aroma of herbs. Imani and Nirri follow close behind. The door shuts behind us with a soft thud under Marshall's hand.

I have barely removed my hood before the thin hand slaps my arm.

"You should not have come, my boy," Enid says.

I breathe out, scanning the small space for Jonah. A man's figure is slumped against the wall, arm over his chest.

"Enid, where's Jonah?" Imani asks.

Nirri stands beside her, eyes searching the dim space. Marshall steps up beside Nirri.

"Imani, you should not be here either," Enid scolds, but takes her hand, leading her toward what must be Jonah. I follow, gesturing for Nirri to do the same. She falls in beside me.

"What is this space, Harm?" Nirri asks.

"We're inside the wall. A hideout of sorts."

"Oh." Her eyes track to Jonah. His shallow breaths, his head bent to one side. Even in the dim light, I can tell he is in bad shape.

"What happened?" I ask Enid.

She releases Imani's hand and steps back to me. Imani sinks to the ground next to Jonah, and Marshall follows her.

"He was trying to get Indie's boy back. They flogged him until he lost consciousness. I think he has a few broken ribs, a lot of bruising, and his face is cut up, but he'll survive."

"Jonah, wake up, it's Imani." She rests her hand on the arm dangling by his side.

Enid lights a small lamp with a match, carrying it over to Imani so Jonah can see her face.

"Jonah," Imani whispers.

He groans, opening his eyes, taking a while to focus on her face.

She runs a hand over his cheek. "Hey."

The old man looks her over, a small smile splitting his lips. Then he coughs and moans, holding his chest with both arms wrapped around him.

"Dammit, what did they do to you?" she breathes.

"They'll do a lot worse to you and Harm, my girl, if you stay here. Go—and don't go where I think you're going. Please." One arm releases from his chest, and he grabs her arm.

"They have Indie's boy?"

He nods. "Please, Imani, just this once, listen to an old man. Please go back to the forest. I won't lose another child. Losing Luca to the regime was impossible. I cannot lose you too. Run." His voice is raw, breath hard and deep as he pleads with her.

She raises his big hand that is wrapped around hers and kisses it. Leaning forward, she gives him a long, tight hug. "I'm not going back, Jonah. If we run now, when will we stop? When will we stand and fight? When there are no children left? When there are no villages left?" Her voice matches his now.

A combination of pride and terror grips my core. Jonah closes his eyes, and a tear runs down his square jaw over the stubble on his face, dripping onto his shirt.

Imani rises and turns to face Enid and me. "How do we get in there?"

"There's a door that leads to the cells, behind Saraya's stall," I tell her. "Tobias is a friend; if we can get a message to him first before we go in, he can help. We'll need a diversion—a good one —and maybe backup. Are your rebels anywhere near?" I ask Enid.

She stares at me, seeing, but not hearing.

"Grandmother, did you hear me?"

She shakes her head and focuses on my face.

"Are your rebels anywhere close by to assist?"

She clears her throat. "A few are, but most likely not enough— not in time, at least."

"We can wait a day, or a day and a half, tops. The sooner we get in there, the better," Imani says. "If they've taken every child, including the newborn babes, they're all going to need to be fed. I seriously doubt the Guardians have the resources or the will to feed the infants."

"I didn't think of that," Nirri whispers, and the horror of the realization is plain on her face.

"You can't come with us, Nirri, they'll recognize you," Imani says.

"I am not staying here."

"The second one of those Guardians that lays eyes on you,

they'll know who you are. It's not safe. We will find you a passage out, to one of the outlying villages," I say.

"Indie," Imani says, pacing back and forth in the small space beside me. "Send her to Indie."

"Do we even know where the gypsy camps are?" I ask.

"They're camped just beyond the boarder, south of Amondo, actually," Enid says. "Nobody has been there since the poisoning. It's the quietest part of the sands at the moment. They moved there a day ago, after the children were taken." She looks at Jonah.

"Okay, Nirri, you go there with Enid and Jonah," I say.

Enid's face bunches up in protest.

"I'm not asking, Grandmother."

"Enid is the best healer on this side of the wall," Imani says to Nirri. "Go with her. You might be of some use to her."

"Second-best healer on this side of the wall now, actually." Enid smiles at me. "One of your childhood friends has recently surpassed my abilities. But unfortunately, she is now with the other young people in the prison. It would be a shame to lose her." She sighs.

"When we get them all out, we'll know where to find you then," I say. Her shoulders drop, and she glances at Jonah before nodding. I meet Imani's gaze. "Well, that's settled. All we need to do now is get the message to Tobias, get in and get out, transport dozens of children to Amondo undetected, and disperse them across the desert to their families." I shove my head in my hands, sinking onto the cool, damp floor. Imani flops down beside me.

"Leave the reuniting with their families to us," Enid says. "We have the means with the caravans to do that over a week or two."

A few moments later, I rise to my feet. "Right. Let's get to Saraya's. The sooner we get the message to Tobias, the better." I extend my hand to Imani, and she takes it, pulling herself up.

"I'm coming with you," Nirri says.

"Fine, but you and Marshall have to part ways with us before we go inside."

I crack the door open, and the sliver of sunlight burns my eyes. Nothing—the village is even quieter than before. We slip out the door and head toward Saraya's stall. The crowd, somewhat thinned out, is still alive with trading, despite the children of every village being held hostage for heaven knows what reason. I weave through the robed people, moving at a normal pace toward the last stall in the row along the prison wall. A flash of green and grey moves ahead of me, halfway to the prison entrance.

No. It can't be.

Another one, only just concealed under traveling robes. Six of them trudge through the sandy market center, en route to the prison entrance. Forest warriors. I stop and wait for Imani to come to a halt next to me.

"What is it?" she breathes.

"Forest warriors, heading for the entrance."

Her hand flies to her mouth. "Surely they're not going to try and get in through the front door?"

"I hope not. Maybe they're just scoping it out."

Imani grunts and makes her way to Saraya's, her pace quickening. Marshall meets my gaze with wide eyes. I let Nirri go past and then tail them to the stall, Marshall in tow.

Saraya stands behind her counter serving a customer, who is buying a pile of clothes. She looks up as we enter her space. With our veils and robes still down, her focus returns to her patron. A moment later, they walk out, bundle in hand, nodding a greeting. Imani gives a small wave in return. I walk up to the counter, removing my wrap, but keeping the hood in place.

Saraya's gaze meets mine, and she sighs, long and hard. "Again, Harmen. Did you not learn the last time something like this happened?" she warns, her voice low and deep.

"Apparently not." A half grin whips across my face briefly.

"What can I do for you and your friends today?"

"Just a note to our friend, a heads up. That's all."

She slides her hand under the counter, producing a small slip of paper and a pencil. I scribble out a note for Tobias and return both to her waiting palm.

"You are persistent, I'll give you that. Don't get yourself caught, please. We all need you to stay alive." She rounds her counter and pulls me into a hug.

"I'll do my best."

"I know you will."

A throat clears behind me. I turn to see the wide eyes on Imani. Only feet away, patrolling the stalls, two Guardians are closing in.

"You need to go, now. No, not out the front—here." Saraya rushes to the back of her stall, moving a large curtain to reveal the access door.

"We can't—not until Tobias gets our message," I say.

"I will get it to him now. You go, before it's too late for the four of you," she urges.

We stand hovering by the door.

"If some of our friends come by, you will recognize them by their clothes. Send them our way," I say.

Confusion whips across her face, but she nods and pulls the door toward us. Imani slips inside, pulling Nirri in with her. Marshall follows Nirri. I give Saraya one last look.

"I will send them, I promise. Now go," she hisses.

I slip through the door, and she quickly closes it, almost catching my robes in the crack. The voices of the two officers echo through the small door. We sit in the dark. I rummage through my rucksack, hunting for a match. Finally, I find one. A short scratch, and we have light. Both girls stare at me in fear. This was not the plan. But at least the forest warriors are here.

"Now what?" Imani asks.

"We could wait until she sends the forest warriors through the door to us, then go in together?"

"That would make us more likely to get caught," Imani says.

"Nirri, you're supposed to be with Enid. This was not the plan. Callian will have my head if they catch you," I murmur.

Her hand rests on mine. "I can take care of myself, Harm. I'll just wait until things simmer down, then make my way to the hideout."

"I can take her, Harm," Marshall offers.

"Fine, but don't for one second think you're going to help us. You need to get away from this village as soon as possible," Imani says, her eyes burning into Nirri's.

Nirri nods vaguely, giving Marshall a small smile of gratitude.

Movement on the other side of the door startles the three of us. Men's voices—none that I recognize. None of them are from the forest.

"We need to move." I grab the girls' hands, dragging them further into the dim tunnel. Marshall follows at the rear. The uneven floor makes moving fast difficult, but every step puts more distance between us and whoever is on the other side of that door.

We pick our way through the tunnel toward the inner parts of the prison. Around the first bend, we stop and lay back against the wall. The flame in my hand flickers out. As I hunt for another match, my rucksack presses against my pocket, and something hard digs into my leg. I almost forgot! Mason folded it into my hands days ago. I return my hand to the pocket, curling my fingers around the cool metal. I huff a breath and pull it out. The chain dangles in the dark.

"Here," I say to Imani.

"What?" she breathes.

"Your pendant," I whisper.

Her hands fumble in the almost pitch dark, finding my arms and trailing toward my hands. Her fingers flutter over the chain in my hands, and she breathes out a happy laugh. "How did you get it back?"

"You can thank Mason next time you see him. He must have plucked it from the commander's desk when you three snuck in."

"Oh." Her voice is thick as she fumbles with the clasp.

I fold my hands over hers. "Let me."

She steps toward me, her face almost touching mine. I fiddle with the chain until I find the clasp. Releasing it, I slide the pendant around her neck and fasten the clasp by feel. I run my hands down the chain to the pendant, letting it rest on her chest. Her hands grip my arms, then wander up along my neck, finding my jawline. She leans in, her lips finding mine in the dark. I wrap an arm around her waist and tug her against me, kissing her deep and fully, and she meets my desire with hers. Her hands trail around my neck and into my hair.

Shuffling beside us slows the fire in both of us.

"I think someone's coming," Nirri whispers. I had almost forgotten that she and Marshall are with us.

We freeze, straining to hear anything farther down the tunnel. The short sharp cries of an infant echo toward us from inside the prison. Nirri takes off toward the sound.

"Nirri, no, stop!" Imani whispers fiercely.

Nirri picks her way toward the sound as fast as the dark allows her. I shove my hand into my rucksack, ripping out another match. Flame flickers to life, and both girls are already farther down the tunnel than I would have thought. I take off after them, tripping over rocks and slipping in the slimy, moist patches.

"Nirri, stop, they'll catch you!" Imani calls after her.

I catch up to Imani, and she shoots me a look devoured by worry and fear.

"We go in together, then." I drop my rucksack and pull fighting knives from my weapons belt. The whine of Imani's blades echoes mine, and we run, slipping and stumbling down the tunnel, reaching Nirri only seconds before she reaches the door that opens to the cells.

"I would tell you to go back, but I'm guessing you won't listen to me," Imani growls at Nirri, her blades turning over in her palms.

"Do you think Saraya got your message to Tobias?" Nirri whispers.

"I hope so, because we weren't able to organize our distraction, unless Enid thinks of something when she realizes where we are," Imani hisses.

"If we go in, we go in as a team," I say, eyes burning into Imani's, who has lost all patience at this point.

The thunder of boots filing past the entrance door has the three of us slapping our backs to the wall behind us. More thunder, dozens of Guardians filing past at a run.

"I guess we have our distraction, then." Saraya must work fast. "As soon as the footsteps die off, we move out," I whisper.

Imani nods.

Nirri swallows, and blowing out a low breath, she nods too.

Moments later, the hallway is silent. I crack the door.

Nothing. Every Guardian that usually patrols the cells must be gone. I slip through the door, and the girls follow. Our footsteps pad softly through the corridor. The soft whimpers of scared children are our only compass. Imani drifts past me, hunting the sound like a predator, not wasting any time.

Nirri walks behind me, eyes scanning every inch of the inside of the prison. We reach the end of the hallway. The sounds come from our left, in the opposite direction from the cells. Imani stalks silently toward the door to the left. I reach her side. She gives me one last look before turning the lever and pushing the door wide open.

The stunned faces of the terrified children who huddle on the floor in the large room go still. Bars line the windows. The older children, some almost our age, are in a cell at the back. We walk in, and Nirri closes the door behind us, flanked by Marshall. Some of the children stand. Some cry, frightened that we are here to hurt them.

"It's okay, we're here to help," I say.

The room has dozens of children—more than I expected. I wander through the huddled groups.

"Harm?" A small voice drifts from the cell at the back.

I look up, and her eyes meet mine, her hands gripping the bars.

In seconds, I am in front of her. "Felicity?" I whisper. Flick. I haven't seen her since Amondo, on the day my family was executed. She was my betrothed.

She nods, tears running down her face. Her hazel eyes are drawn with fear. Her light-brown wavy hair is matted and dirty.

"Are you alright, Flick? Did they hurt you?"

"They haven't hurt any of us... yet. You have to get us out of here! I heard them saying they plan to execute every last one of us!" Her hands tremble around the bars.

"That's the plan. Is there a key for this door?"

"They took it with them," she whispers. Her gaze moves to Imani and Nirri as they wander through the room, grabbing small hands and helping the children up.

I pull the broadsword from my back and shove it through the lock holding the door closed. It gives way under one swift push down, and I tug the door open. Felicity and nine other older village children spill from the cell.

"Nirri, this is Felicity. Stay with her. She's a healer. Help anyone who needs assistance," I say.

Imani and I gather the remaining children into a group, ready to move out.

Suddenly, the door behind me clicks and swings open. Fear spirals through my core, snaking its way through every inch of flesh. Imani's eyes meet mine before we both track our focus to the five Guardians who have come to a halt just inside the door.

Instantly, the children start screaming. Nirri tries to calm them, shushing them and holding her hands out like she is fending off a pack of wolves. Felicity tries to soothe the three little girls under her arms. It is no use; they are terrified.

"And what have we here?" An officer steps forward, slapping the end of his cane in his palm, a smirk plastered across his face. His eyes drift from Imani to Nirri, where they stay.

Please don't recognize her. Please, no.

"Do I know you?" he croons to Nirri.

"I doubt it," she hisses, chin lifted, upper lip curled slightly.

Dammit.

He walks toward her. "Yes, I think I do."

I curl my hands into fists. Imani's hands rest on her fighting knives. She would have a clear shot at his neck from where she stands.

"Remove your hood," he snaps.

"No," Nirri growls.

The small children beside her back away, bumping into Felicity.

"Take off the hood, girl!"

Nirri rips both fighting knives from her hips. He huffs a laugh and stalks the last two steps toward her. She lunges with her knives, and he blocks both effortlessly with his cane, shoving her backward. She falters a step and takes a second to gain her balance.

The remaining Guardians stalk toward us, canes raised. We are outnumbered and surrounded by innocent children. Throwing knives and wielding broadswords is not a great option.

The officer grabs Nirri by the throat. She lets out a whimper, and her knives clatter to the floor.

Imani's face turns livid.

Suddenly, a silhouette fills the door behind the Guardians.

"Take your filthy hand off my friend," Miya growls from the door, where five forest warriors stand behind her.

Marshall moves, putting himself between the Guardians and Felicity, unarmed.

Imani's eyes widen. She rips both fighting knives from her hips. I pull the broadsword from my back, letting its whine echo through the room. The faces of the Guardians drain of color, the five of them now trapped between the ten of us.

Nirri gasps for breath as the Guardian drops his hand from her throat and turns to face Miya. She stands with her shoulders back, face stone, two long blades flipping over and over in her palms. Seconds later, one is lodged in the Guardian's throat, the other finding its mark in the officer closest to me. Imani sends hers toward the men who stand frozen between us. One sinks into the chest of the man to the left, and the other lodges in the neck of the man to the right. The remaining Guardian stands with his two comrades fallen beside him, eyes wide with terror.

Abruptly, curls of smoke waft between his feet. It doesn't register until the smell does, and I realize it's the acidic smell of fogging gas. I shove my hand over my mouth and nose, waving for Imani to do the same. Miya's eyes meet mine before she plummets to the stone floor, her five warriors dropping behind her. The small children drop first as the gas reaches the back wall, creeping along the floor, circling around us like a throng of desert vipers. I cough into the crook of my elbow.

Tobias rushes in, handkerchief over his face. He tugs at my arm.

"No, get those two out." I point to Nirri and Felicity. Marshall stands guarding them, a rag over his mouth and nose. Smart boy. I should do that. But my movements are too slow.

Tobias's eyes widen, and he stands hovering in front of me as I struggle to stay on my feet.

"Do it!" I yell at him.

He picks his way over to the two girls. Flick is still awake, but Nirri is out. Marshall scoops up Nirri and follows Tobias through the unconscious bodies lying in the clouds of fog. Imani makes a small noise before crumpling to the floor beside me, arms over her head, like she is sleeping.

I search for Miya. She is slumped near the two dead officers. The shallow rise and fall of her chest is the last thing I see before my eyelids drop and I hit the floor.

CHAPTER 34
MASON

The large, heavy boots of the Guardians make for easy tracking. Callian, Catori, and I are doing recon while the remaining warriors ready to infiltrate the prison in the tower. It has been hours, and the damp air that hangs around us makes the humidity another annoyance, adding to the bad feeling that is clawing through my gut. That has been there since the second I realized we were standing in the fogging gas. I saw it on Catori's face: this is it. We move now, praying that Harm and Imani are doing the same on their side of the wall.

Time is up. This was the last straw—the last cruel act we will tolerate from the Chancellor.

None of us have spoken a word since we left. All I can think about is how we are going to pull this off, with only three of us, and maybe backup if the remaining warriors are not too late. I lead, tracking the dozens of soggy boot prints as we head toward the tower. It's late in the afternoon now, the sun stewing us even beneath the canopy.

I break the tree line just before the tower and stop dead in my tracks. The smell hits me before the realization does. Hanging by ropes from every window of the tower and the bridge that spans between the barracks are the bodies of the forest people who work in the tower. Scavenger birds hop from head to head, feasting on anything that they can pull off the bloated, rigid bodies. A cry leaves Catori's lips, and her hand flies to her mouth and nose. Callian scrunches up his face, covering his mouth and nose with a rag.

The place is silent, as if too much death has struck every living thing around us mute.

"Damn the heavens," Catori breathes.

I search the distorted faces of the swaying bodies, hanging by their necks from rope nooses. The woman who served us in the tower, running Imani a bath—the blacksmith's wife—hangs from the window of what I imagine was our room.

Bile rises in my throat. I cough through retching and turn back to the forest. I pad into the trees, slumping against one. The rough bark scratches my back.

Catori returns to the thick forest, her hands trembling by her sides, her face twisted with pain and anger.

Callian appears at her side a heartbeat later. "They've taken the children into the tower at the servants' entrance. My guess is that they killed the servants first, so no one could help the children escape." His voice is raw.

"What kind of monster hangs dozens of people and then steals every last child?" Catori utters.

"Catori, we're going to need more than just three of us to pull this off," Callian warns.

"I know," she breathes. She drops into a crouch, resting her head in her hands. Her blonde hair splits through her fingers as she moves them backward.

"We go home and regroup, then come back in full force," I say.

She shakes her head. "We are not going home. We go to the next village, see what they need," she says, stalking off into the trees toward the closest village. Callian and I follow. Catori flies through the undergrowth, her pace faster than Callian and I can keep up with.

Hours later, we reach the nearest village, and she slows, pacing in a tight circle, hands digging into her waist to stem the cramps that are no doubt stabbing at her insides from holding that pace for so long. The last remnant of fog still twists along the wet ground of the village. The cries of distraught women bounce around the village. Catori embraces the first woman she comes to. They plead with her to bring their children home, gripping her hands and arms like she holds the very oxygen they breathe. The silver that lines her eyes gives way as she swallows, tumbling down her cheeks. Callian comes to stand beside her. I wander the village center, looking for anything helpful. Boot tracks, nothing else— screaming and boot tracks and the heavy dread that fills every inch of me.

"I will bring your children back, I promise you," Catori breathes to the women surrounding her.

They all nod solemnly, fear and doubt lining their eyes. She lingers for a moment, reaching out to any hand that needs comfort. After every single mother has been comforted, she pulls herself away.

"Next village," Catori snaps. The women release her, and Callian heads toward the outskirts of this village in the direction of the next.

We run, again. This time Catori's gait is slower, as if she is turning over everything she has seen and everything she is planning with every long stride.

Twilight is settling in as we reach the next village. This time, there is no screaming; it's quiet. Unnervingly so.

The same fog lies on the ground, as if it has had its fun and lost interest. Long lumps lie in the waves of fumes this time.

Catori freezes, her hands hanging by her side. Callian swears under his breath.

Then I see it: those long lumps are bodies. I step between the limp, still corpses of the people of this village. Their vacant eyes look toward the canopy overhead, not seeing. Catori is whimpering, more so with every person she recognizes. I pad closer to her.

She stops, lifting her head to scan the village center. They are all here. What happened such that they are all in the village center? Only adult bodies line the ground. The children of this village have been taken as well.

I fold Catori into a hug. She stands trembling, arms by her sides.

A grey figure moves near a home just beyond the village center, across the eating area. I let her go and track to where I saw them. The fog is slowly clearing, but not fast enough. Weaving between the rows of houses, the figure slips behind a house a few rows down. I break into a run until I reach the house.

Nothing. No one is inside.

I round the side, coming to the back. Nothing. I could swear I saw a person—a person in grey. A Guardian uniform. I rip a blade from my belt and track the barely visible boot marks that lie under thicker drifting fog, holding my hand over my mouth as I stalk the tracks. They wind back to the village center.

I freeze as a small figure stumbles from the door of the house in front of me. She buckles when she reaches me. "Help me, please..."

I grab her arms and lower her to the ground. She has stab wounds on her arms, and blood is seeping through her tunic near her waist. I sheathe my blade and slide both arms under her, taking her into the nearest house to find something to staunch the bleeding. She looks at me, her wide eyes scanning my face.

"You're Catori's match," she chokes.

I force a small smile, nodding briefly as I set her on the nearest chair. I search the room for cloth of some sort. I run over to the kitchen and grab the towel from the cooker, then make my way back to her and rip the cloth in two. I press it to her arm and tell her to hold it there.

"May I lift your shirt to see the wound?"

"Go ahead."

I lift the tunic. She has a neat but deep slash across her side. I fold the cloth into a rectangle and press it against the long incision. She whimpers and puts her hand over the cloth.

The whine of a blade reverberates through the foggy air.

No. Callian has the only broadsword. Something must have happened.

"I have to go," I say to her.

She nods and curls her shoulders, as if trying to disappear into the chair as I burst back through the door.

Metal connects with thuds. Grunts and shouts give way to taunts. Both Catori's and Callian's words echo through the fog toward me. I run as fast as my legs can take me. My heart hammers in my chest as fear spikes through my core.

Catori.

There are more male voices than before.

No.

Someone laughs—a taunting sound. I swallow the lump that fear created, giving way to the air that I suck down, the toxic gas filtering into my lungs. My steps slow a little. I fight the dizziness that is creeping in from the sides.

"Catori!"

Another sadistic laugh washes toward me. Callian's fierce growl meets their sickening taunts. I round the last home, and the center appears vacant. The long, immobile bodies of the slaughtered village people still lie prone on the slimy ground.

No Guardians are here. Where did they go?

Is this just a trap to draw me in?

"Catori, Callian, answer me!"

Nobody responds.

I stand, searching the ground for any sign of movement. My breath rips through my chest, erratic and burning. White points appear and fade at the edges of my vision.

Figures round the row of houses skirting the village center.

"Mason," Catori chokes.

I scramble toward the sound.

"Mason," she says a little louder, then "run!"

I swing my head from side to side, desperate to find her.

"Catori, where are you?"

"No, Mason, run!" Her voice is ragged, raw and broken.

She is right next to me. Where? I spin round, arms flying out from my sides, boots slipping on the muck beneath me.

A whimper. I move toward it.

Thud. A body falls to the ground.

No!

"Catori!"

At the edge of the village, two officers are dragging the limp body of Callian between them, his feet sliding through the mud, blond head lolling to the side, weapons gone.

Mere feet from where I stand, an officer moves, picking up Catori.

"No, stop! Please, I'm begging you!"

Her head bobs over his arm as he walks away. I make to move toward him. Something bulky covers his face. Soft footfalls come from behind, but I don't turn, not wanting to lose track of Catori.

Then a dull crack from behind me sends a sharp pain through

the base of my skull, skittering toward my eyes. The village turns sideways. Mud slaps my face. White points turn to grey.

Darkness.

A thundering throb splits my head in two. I touch the back of my head, and my fingers come away covered in blood.

My blood.

I push up from the ground, swaying to a stop on my knees, wiping my hands on my pants. The fog has almost cleared. I'm not home. We were in that village—the one where everyone was dead. All but one.

Catori.

No, no, no, no. Please, no!

I scramble to my feet, scanning the sea of bodies that surrounds me. Tiny wisps of fog play around the long lines of lifeless people. But the spot where Catori was lying is bare.

I shake my head. The boots. The uniform. Her cries for me to run. It all comes flooding back in. The sweeping arms of the officer. Catori's lifeless body. Her head bobbing over his arm.

No, no.

A guttural roar leaves my chest, my hands ripping at my hair. I sink back to my knees, rocking back and forth. Screams rip from my chest, the thundering of my blood turning to acid heat with the agony of every heartbeat.

Tears flood down my face, the heat from every drop burning my skin. No, this cannot be happening.

My hands tingle and curl up. I slump, palms hitting the ground, agony flooding through my fingers, a heavy, aching fire crushing my chest.

"Catori!"

Breaths and sobs become one, choking their way out, my hands balling into fists, curling up mud between my fingers. I slam them into the muddy ground, screaming her name over and over.

They took her. Callian too.

Three days. They will have three days. Three.

The air leaves my lungs and doesn't come back.

CHAPTER 35

IMANI

He sits on a small bench, his back to me. His hands are busy, working the tool back and forth, carving, shaving. Curls of wood fall. The golden light from the dunes outside filters into his small workspace. The grains of sand that have made it into the room dance over the floor like playful children. His forearms flex with every movement. I pad up to him, laying my arms around him, nuzzling my face into his neck. He looses a sweet chuckle, and his hands stop. The tool clatters to the bench, and he spins in my hold, legs swinging over it to land on either side of me. The deep brown of his eyes finds mine, his hands resting on my waist. He tugs me closer. I let out a laugh as he runs his hands up my spine, dropping his forehead to my chest. His hands reach my shoulders, then trace down my arms, and he wraps his hands around my wrists. He pulls me down onto his lap. He tugs my wrists again, his eyes glazed over. And again.

"Harm." I laugh in his ear. "What are you doing?"

He doesn't speak. His face turns vacant—like Fletcher's did seconds before he raised my own blade to run me through.

He tugs again. And again. My wrists burn in his tight hold. I lean back, searching his face for something I recognize.

He tugs again. This time, the burn lasts, and I draw in a deep breath.

"Harm, stop, you're hurting me."

His eyes slowly track over my face before meeting my gaze.

"Wake up, girlie." A gruff voice breaks into the golden space around me. My body wriggles, legs hanging like weights. My wrists burn, and the sting grows, my feet a mere six inches from the ground. A rough hand pats my face. A harsh glare burns my eyes, glinting from the blanket of crystalline whiteness that covers every inch of the ground. Sparse woody trees dot a village of log huts, smoke billowing from every chimney. My teeth chatter, like they did when I had a fever as a child. My skin is pricked all over with goose bumps. My entire body shakes as the breath leaves my lungs in puffs of steam.

Low, daggy clouds hang in the sky, skimming the tops of the pale grey trees, their branches lined with the same sparkling whiteness. A group of dirty-looking men leer at me, from my age to Jonah's, all clad in full clothing and furs. They wander around the pole I am strung up on as if inspecting a rare treasure, ogling every inch of me. One of the older ones runs a grotty finger down my arm, only to be pushed aside by another from behind. His gaze and mouth full of rotten teeth turn up to me. He holds out a shaking stumpy finger, prodding my stomach. I twist away from them, growling through my frozen throat, not able to escape their vile touch. Blood pulses through my veins, the cold reducing it to a sluggish thump, and my head burns from the sides inward.

A frigid wind carries the pine scent of the forest, but crisper, less earthy. My forest tunic and fitted pants offer no protection from the chill it brings, and my body shakes, climbing to a new level of tremor. The peaks of my breasts are clearly visible under the thin fabric of my tunic. My head wrap is gone, the freezing mass of my hair tumbling around my neck and shoulders. I can barely feel it, my body so cold now that I am partly numb.

A younger man walks through the crowd, pushing his way past the ogling faces. They let him pass, not concerned by his presence. He stands beneath me as I shake on the pole, arms strung up over my head, teeth chattering so hard that my jaw aches. The slow, dull ache of my heartbeat plods along in my chest. Every breath burns with the cold. I try to lower my eyes to his, neck stiff, triggering a shooting pain as I force my head lower to meet his stare. Clouds of breath shoot from my mouth toward him.

His light-brown hair pokes out from under the fur-lined hood that covers his head as his hazel eyes find mine. His hands, firmly shoved deep in the pockets of his roughly sewn coat, leave their sanctuary, hesitatingly moving toward me before folding across his chest.

"Get her down, Clancy, and inside, before she freezes to death." He turns and walks back through the hoard of salivating, filthy men.

Clancy—as in commander Clancy O'Neill. I see it now.

The ex-commander pulls a knife from his boot and trails it down my chest before placing the tip under my chin. I raise my head, sucking in a ragged, freezing breath. He grunts. "Here, hold her legs while I cut the rope," he says to one of the younger men, who grabs me around the waist. I watch him as he grins at me, his arms wrapped around my center. A small cry of horror melts from my stiff lips. The blade tugs at the ropes, then the pressure releases, and I slump into the young man holding me up. He holds my shaking body for a moment. In one swift move, he throws me over his shoulder. My arms, numb and tingling from being strung up for who knows how long, flop helplessly against his back. I suck in deep breaths, trying to regain my strength, so I can fight the minute my feet hit the frozen ground. My boots, at least, still cover my numb feet.

He strides toward the largest of the log huts, kicking his way through the front door. Wood scrapes on the stone floor, and the room spins as he pulls me back over his shoulder. I land on a chair and move my arms to my lap, trying to get them to wrap around my still-trembling body. Agonizingly slowly, I raise them and cling to my tunic, fingers stinging as the prickles of numbness ebb. The room has a hearth, twice the size of the one in my home, with two small windows, a wooden table, a large bed covered in furs and blankets, and a washbasin and chair with clothes piled on it, a coat draped over the back.

The door thuds shut. A handful of the older men stand inside, faces pulled into menacing smirks. Clancy removes his coat and saunters across the stone floor. He places his hand under my chin.

"Don't touch me," I hiss, staying motionless as his narrowed eyes look me over. I stare back at him, giving him nothing, my face blank. My heart races against my ribs, stomach plummeting as his touch moves down my neck. I lean away from him, tilting my head to put space between my face and his hand.

He steps behind me, muttering something I don't understand and don't want to know. Pulling my arms back, he ties my wrists behind the chair. With the last knot tied, he steps around me, coming to a stop at my knees.

"You know, the way I see it, girlie..." He leans over me. "... we saved you from freezing to death in those mountains. You owe us, I'd say." He towers over me, running an unwashed finger across my collarbone, skimming the top of my tunic.

"Don't, Clancy. Chief will string up the lot of you to that pole if you touch her," one of the men says, standing closest to the door.

"Shut it," Clancy spits, not bothering to turn and face his

comrade. But his hands ball into fists and release slowly. If the commander is not the leader here, what kind of man is? I shudder at the thought.

He circles my chair, running a hand around my shoulders as he goes. I close my eyes and will the bile in my throat to stay down. He pulls a long piece of cloth from his pocket and ties it around my mouth, knotting it behind my head. The gag is tight, and I breathe through my nose, trying not to choke on the filthy rag. I grunt against the gag, shooting a fiery look of hatred at him.

He grabs my shoulders. "What was that, lass?" He chuckles.

I struggle against his hard grip, pulling my shoulders back one at a time. Two of the men hanging back step up beside Clancy, a predatory look crossing their faces. I run my gaze over each one, hoping to find a glimmer of empathy.

Nothing.

Clancy grabs a handful of my tunic over my right breast and rips it down. The men beside him grunt out laughs, as if taunting me makes the game better.

"Chief will have your heads. Leave her be. I'm warning you," the young man growls from his position at the door.

Clancy paces over to the hearth. Picking up a tin mug, he dips it briefly into the large iron pot suspended over the fire and tosses it at him. Hot, lumpy brown liquid hits the wall behind him, spilling over the floor.

"I'm sorry, miss," he utters and jerks the door open, slipping outside before tugging it shut.

I pull at the rope on my wrists. If I can get my hands free, I can at least try to hold them off. Clancy leans back in, his tanned, lined face splitting into a menacing smirk, exposing his half-rotted teeth. A putrid stench hits my face with every breath he takes. I wriggle the chair closer to him. He looks me up and down, stopping at the rip in my tunic. His hand moves toward my breast. I slam my knee into his groin. He falters sideways, moaning through the pain, hands clutching himself. One of the men laughs. Another grabs some rope from hooks by the door. He crouches beside me, tying my ankles to the chair. When he stands back up, his menacing stare turns to one of neutrality.

Clancy rises, now recovered, and stalks over to me. His face is red, eyes lit with hate, teeth bared. He grabs my hair, ripping my head backward. I growl through the pain, forcing deep breaths. A rough hand slams into my throat, fingers closing over it, tighter and tighter until I choke out a whimper.

The door opens, then closes again. Two sets of footsteps.

How many more are going to try to molest me? When I get free from this chair, they are all dead. Every. Last. One.

"Make one more move, Clancy, and I will end your miserable existence," a deep voice growls from just inside the door.

Instantly, Clancy's hand releases my hair. I lower my head, swallowing past the lump in my throat, forcing back the sting of tears. The men back off in unison, heading toward the door. They slip outside behind the two young men who stand staring at me. They both wear furs, powdered with the same whiteness that covers the ground outside. They remove their hoods, dusting the white from their shoulders. One steps forward, pulling off his coat. His muscular frame is obvious even under his layers of clothing. Dark, tufty hair offsets his bright hazel eyes—so familiar. He rubs a hand through his neat beard, searching every inch of me—for what, I have no idea.

I straighten and roll my shoulders back, tilting my chin up slightly. He steps closer still. He is young, around my age, maybe five years older.

This is their chief?

The man by the door removes his coat too, his red hair the same length as his dark-haired companion's. His brown eyes, almost the same as Harm's, track to the hearth. He wanders over, hands extending to the warmth of the flame.

Oh, heavens... Harm!

Fog. That gas... It was everywhere.

Dammit.

The last thing I remember is him lying on the prison floor, hand holding mine, Tobias and Marshall leading Nirri and his friend Felicity over the limp bodies of the children and Miya.

Oh no! Miya and her warriors! My breath flings from my chest in rapid intervals. Harm... Tears prickle behind my eyes. No, dammit. What happened? Where am I? I need to get back.

The man's eyes narrow, a brow raising, before his gaze tracks over my chest, and he moves into my space. He raises a hand. I flinch backward, and he goes still before retracting his hand slightly. I relax slightly, and he pulls my tunic back over my exposed chest. The warmth of his hands feels like fire on my frigid skin. He pulls the gag from my mouth.

I strangle back a sob. "Thank you. Where am I?"

He turns and pads over to the hearth. Picking up a mug from the mantel, he ladles in the hot broth and walks back over to me. He cradles the mug between his hands, taking a tentative sip as he scans my shaking body from head to toe. "Oh, don't thank me just yet."

I still myself as best I can, trying to read him. He steps closer, the steam from his mug drifting past his face. He swallows another mouthful, lowering the mug slightly. Bending down, he places it on the floor. In one stride, he stands over me, lowering his hands to the back of the chair, one hand gripping the wood on either side of my neck. His head tilts to one side as the smirk grows across his face and his eyes light up.

I fiddle with the rope around my wrists with my stiff fingers. His face is so close to mine, and I hold my breath. Slightly warmer than before, my heart thumps, rattling against my ribs, sickness claiming my stomach, creeping upward with every shallow breath.

As he moves closer still, until his mouth is beside my ear, his grip on the chair behind me tightens. "Tell me, how did the daughter of my enemy end up on this side of the wall?"

CONTINUE THE STORY...
TAP THE IMAGE TO PRE-ORDER THE FINAL BOOK!

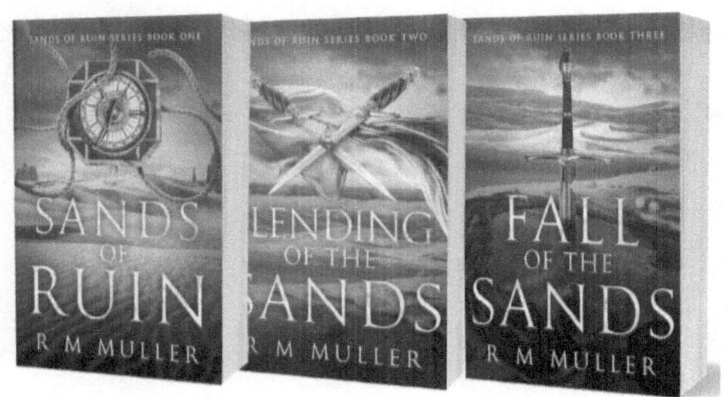

Book Four coming soon...

If you enjoyed this book, I would really appreciate it if you would leave a review. It would mean the world!!

ACKNOWLEDGMENTS

This far into the series, the people I want to thank are my readers!

Without you, this series would have just been a handful of daydreams and scribbles on random pieces of paper piled on my desk.

To my wonderful editors, Robyn and Lindsey. Thank you for everything you do to make Harm, Imani and Mason's world the best it can be.

To Christian Bentulan and his epic cover design skills... Love your work!

To every ARC reader who has waited for each instalment, patiently. I promise it is going to be so worth it. ;)

Thank you to every reader who has found themselves on this page (and perhaps in these pages), you are truly rockstars!!

About the Author

Perched on a thin limb in a tree that had stood for decades, was a skinny, little farm girl. Her focus was solely on the scrappy notebook and pencil in her hands. Oblivious to the swaying branches around her and the voice of her mother calling her down, she scratched out a story. For the first time her imagination made it to paper, and she was obsessed.

Rose-Marie is a mother to four vivacious daughters, wife to a grazier, sister, daughter, etc. Stories and her little bunch of humans keep her alive and give her purpose every day, and the reason she spends a disturbing amount of time with imaginary people, in imaginary worlds, most days.